**THUNDER FR(**

IS NOW AVAI
AMAZON K

CW01066511

MANUAL
FN
CY

_take
to desk).

**Please return this book on or before the due date below**

E

This edition published in Great Britain in 2012
by
Farthings Publishing
8 Christine House
1 Avenue Victoria
SCARBOROUGH
YO11 2QB
UK


http://www.Farthings-Publishing.com


ISBN 978-1- 291 – 20689 - 0


December 2012 (d)

# DEDICATION

In writing this book I would like to thank my wife, Norma, who has supported me throughout.

Also, David Fowler, of Farthings Publishing, who has gone to enormous lengths to assist and without whose dedicated help this book would never have made it into print.

I feel proud to say that this is a story, set in Scarborough, written by a Scarborough resident and published by a Scarborough publisher.

# CONTENTS

# CHAPTER 1

## November 17th 1914

Kapitanleutnant Johannes Feldkirchener, commander of U17, braced himself against the choppy swell of the North Sea as he swept his binoculars from left to right, the boat wallowing like a partly submerged whale.

A tall cadaverous looking man, some said too tall for the submarine service, his little goatee beard neatly trimmed. He turned to the seaman on watch, binoculars glued to the man's eyes.

'A very close watch now Weldman, to be seen now would be fatal.'

They were approaching the British coast near Flamborough Head, a notorious stretch of water for shipping. His attention needed to be absolute.

The 564 ton boat was low in the water, deliberately trimmed to show as little upper works as possible.

It made for uncomfortable conditions in the conning tower.

Water slopped over regularly, making him grateful for the heavy oilskins over his uniform. He was acutely conscious of the need for stealth.

He had opened his orders early that day, from Admiral Franz Hipper no less. They instructed him to make an assessment of the English coastal towns from just below Scarborough and all the way up to Hartlepool.

He was tasked with deciding if these towns were defended, and if so how heavily.

He ordered the boat submerged just before Scarborough, proceeding on the boat's two AEG electric motors to creep past the town unseen.

Using the periscope on high magnification he made close observations of the coast around Scarborough and the harbour and castle area.

He surfaced after slipping well past Scarborough unseen and then proceeded up the coast to Whitby, all the while watching for any passing shipping. Feldkirchener then did exactly the same at Whitby and likewise at Hartlepool before turning out to sea and proceeding back to port.

His written report to Admiral Hipper stated that there was little sign of shore defences. No mines within twelve miles of the shore, leaving a clear area of passage for coastal shipping, and lots of close shore shipping activity.

Both the British and German navies had set extensive mine-fields stretching some thirty miles off the coast of north east England.

Charts of these were issued by the Admiralty to British merchant shipping showing in particular the extensive field off Flamborough Head.

One of these charts had fallen into Feldkirchener's hands in October of that year when he sank the *SS Gitra* off the Norwegian coast. This, with his written report gave the German High command all the information they required.

The future was set.

# Scarborough, Monday 14th December 1914

Terry Sheader straightened his aching back and wiped his arm across his sweaty brow.

His left leg was aching like hell, the result of a Boer bullet in the 1900 relief of Mafeking. He'd been a young man of eighteen then.

He had a vivid memory of struggling to the front of the crowd outside Scarborough railway station in 1902 to see the return of the Boer War veterans.

The sight of them forming up outside the station in full dress uniforms and then marching around the town with bands and full pomp was still a memory burned on his mind. Unknown to him it was also a vivid memory of a nine year old Osbert Sitwell, although he was privileged to watch from the balcony of the Pavilion Hotel opposite.

Now thirty two and a good deal wiser than he had been then, he wondered how he could have been so stupid as to volunteer for the army.

Here he was now; stuck with a menial job because of this bloody leg, digging in a sea of mud which old Mrs Kessler called a garden.

Terry was still a good looking man in a rugged sort of way. His thick blonde hair had a natural wave and bright blue eyes lit up his tanned face.

His upper body was muscular from hard manual work, tapering to a slim waist, and he had what the ladies might describe as a *tight little bum*. His slightly shortened left leg however gave him a rolling gait.

The damage to the leg was probably worse in the effect it had on his mind than any real constriction on him. Over the years he had convinced himself that any relationship would be marred by his injury, referring to himself as a cripple.

The sea of mud he was surveying belonged to old Mr Kessler, a very wealthy steel engineering works owner. He'd bought the large Edwardian house on Belvedere Road, situated on Scarborough's South Cliff, as a retreat from his business in distant Sheffield.

Terry had never decided whether old man Kessler really liked Scarborough, or if it was to keep his wife a suitable distance from his main base in Sheffield.

He never regretted coming back to live in Scarborough though, his home town, after his army life terminated so abruptly.

He loved the gorgeous stretch of Yorkshire coast with its bays and superb views from the high cliffs overlooking the North Sea. On hot sunny days the sea would sparkle and twinkle. The view from the South Cliff looking down on the old town was magnificent and he knew most of the locals from his childhood days.

On the far side of the South Bay stood the castle on its solid rock headland. It in turn looked down on the harbour, full of fishing vessels of every type.

He loved the sight of steam trawlers and drifters with wisps of blue smoke curling from their funnels, myriad smaller boats with red sails. Girls lined up on the west pier gutting fish and mending nets, and the red roofs of the old town at the foot of the castle hill, shone bright in the winter sunshine. This was the town of his childhood and he loved every bit of it.

He loved it all, except this bloody awful expanse of ground that the old dragon herself, Mrs Rosemary Kessler, wanted turning into a Japanese garden.

Mrs Kessler was a large overweight lump of a woman. Quite tall and with a bust that could match the cliff her house was on. Severe grey hair tied back in a bun, and always dressed in black like the late Queen Victoria.

In contrast Mr Leo Kessler was short and slim. A good nine inches shorter than his wife and still quite a handsome man even allowing for the fact he must be sixty. Wisely, he opted to spend the most of each week in Sheffield. This left the dragon lady, Terry's mental description, at home wondering what to do with herself.

It was the second time she had decided on a complete change for the garden, and Terry was her full time garden landscaper. All for fifteen bob a week with the occasional sandwich and cuppa thrown in.

He stood at the bottom of the garden looking towards the back of the house.

He'd cleared most of the vegetation now. A pile of shrubs and other burnable material to make future bonfire fuel, the other stuff piled up for composting.

A piece of paper sketched by the dragon showed what was required.

The hardest task was to be the large pond she required, in a kidney shape to the left of the garden as he looked at it. She wanted him to dig it out and eventually build an ornamental Japanese bridge over it.

The soil dug out would form the raised rockery to the right with a winding path to be built between rockery and pond. A summer house in the shape of a pagoda was to complete the effect at the bottom right.

It all sounded very nice, but Terry was under no illusions about the amount of shear hard graft required. He'd been working since eight that morning. Now it was turned twelve.

The rear door opened and Jane, the scullery maid, appeared with a tray containing a sandwich and mug of steaming tea.

'Lunch break Mr Sheader,' she called.

She was a wispy little girl of seventeen, thin in face and body with her hair taken up under her hat.

She quite enjoyed bringing a sandwich out to the gardener, seeing him stripped to the waist and looking rather tanned and muscular. She was quite titillated at the sight.

She always thought what a shame it was about his crippled leg, although he was of course quite old.

He was more than glad to pause for a moment and thanked Jane for the corned beef sandwich and cuppa. She gave a shy smile and scuttled back into the house. As he bit into the sandwich he saw the dragon observing him from the bay window.

He would often notice her watching him. He liked to think she was just seeing how hard he was working; any other reason sent a shudder down his spine.

It was at least a dry day. Typical cold December weather, but working hard with the poor tools provided raised the body temperature, hence no shirt.

The old wooden wheelbarrow took an effort to move empty, even more so full. Its worn wheel bearing would squeal like some demented animal.

Tools were expensive items and Terry certainly couldn't afford his own. Not on these wages. He reckoned it would take at least four days just to dig the pond out and move the heavy claylike soil.

It would be dark by four. He thought he'd crack on until then and call it a day. The shadow of the dragon flitted across the window again causing a slightly uncomfortable feeling in him. Bloody woman he thought, like a sodding spectre at the window.

Belvedere Road joined the main Filey road, and opposite on Filey Road stood the large imposing *Dunollie House*, the home of a wealthy York solicitor.

It was surrounded by one of the largest tree hedges Terry had ever seen.

The gardener there, old Bob Tanner, was employed full time on much better wages than Terry. And he was provided with the best of tools.

Like Terry, he would stop about four pm and then usually walked down into town with his mate Terry. There was an easy camaraderie between the two although he was the older by some twenty years.

They would stop at *The Black Swan*, known to all and sundry as *The Mucky Duck,* on the way into town. It was a hotel in name but nothing more than a pub basically, although one which did a good pie and pint.

Settled into the snug, nice and warm, a brisk fire roaring in the grate and with decent company, they could while away the evening. It staved off the return to a cold digs which they both shared above a shop on Victoria Road.

'What do you reckon to this war with Germany then?' asked Bob.

'Can't see it affecting us much here,' replied Terry. 'It'll probably all be over by Christmas. The Germans will get a bloody nose.'

'Aye, reckon you're right mate. At least neither of us will be needed. They'll need younger and fitter fella's than us.' Bob took a good slurp of his pint and stretched his legs out with a sigh.

'I think I'm getting too old for this bloody gardening lark never mind soldiering.'

'It's certainly a young mans game,' replied Terry. 'And look what I got out of it! It'll be a different war this time though Bob.'

'How's that then?' 'Mechanisation', replied Terry. 'Machine guns and the like. It's even said they may use aeroplanes to drop bombs.'

'Nah' the old gardener replied. 'Ah saw that Blackburn fella at Filey trying to fly one O those things. Bloody thing crashed inter sands.'

He took another slurp of beer. 'Had all on to lift a man. Put summat heavy on it like a gun or a bomb and the bloody thing wouldn't even get off the ground.'

He stretched his legs out further, slithering down in his seat. 'Take it from me lad. Strong men on chargers will sort out the Hun. Still the best way.'

Having delivered this sound advice he took another slurp, wiping foam off his droopy moustache with his sleeve.

Old Billy Pierce joined in the conversation from the corner close to the fire. 'I saw that French chap, Salmet or some such name. Flew a Bleriot plane off the beach last year. Took a passenger as well.'

Neither Terry nor Bob knew how Billy survived or where his money came from. No matter what time they went into the *Mucky Duck* Billy would be in the same seat offering comment on any subject under the sun.

'Toys fer rich boys,' sniffed Bob, his final comment on the matter.

Terry felt in his pocket and looked at what little change he had left.

Four pence for his pint and threepence for his pie. It was Tuesday today. He had one and six left to last until the old dragon paid him on Friday.

Bob looked at him sympathetically. 'I know mate, crap money aint it? But better than bugger all.'

Terry knew what he meant. Work in Scarborough was either with the fishing fleet or agriculture, labouring in the fields. Neither of them were known for paying well and the fishing relied on the season and the weather.

The only other work was in the hotels and holiday businesses, but that was seasonal also.

'Bloody Kessler's doing well out of the war,' Terry said. 'Kessler engineering works are pulled out with making gun breeches for the navy. He must be a very happy fella.'

'Bob gave a sardonic grin.' I'll bet he's got a woman in Sheffield as well.'

'Would you blame him?' smiled Terry.

They dragged out the time chatting with other locals, mainly about the war, until 7pm. Any later and the landlady would be getting stroppy.

Mary O'Brian was an attractive woman in her forties but she wanted customers, not people stretching a pint out all night. She knew them both and liked Terry in particular, but she still had a business to run.

They waved goodnight and wandered out. Bob had a wife, although he didn't know where she would be! But they would drift together before bedtime. A real love match!

Terry had his father in Scarborough's old town but that was his only living relation. The old man was a surly ex fisherman who never seemed bothered if Terry visited or not. And the woman who he lived with who was not Terry's mother! She never seemed pleased to see him.

His mother had died in child birth some twenty eight years ago, father preferring to remain single after that. His father was comfortable financially, just! Or so he said.

He had shacked up with a woman a good twenty years younger than him, a woman well-known to Bottom Enders as the old town dwellers were known.

This had caused bad feelings between them. His father had always had an eye for female company. The other unusual thing was his father moving into his current house. Larger than the previous cottage, and gradually giving up seagoing altogether. Terry was totally bewildered how his father could afford to do so but he was told in no uncertain terms that it was no business of his.

He and Bob wandered in companionable silence over the steel bridge linking the South Cliff with Scarborough town centre, passing over the valley that led down to the sea front.

The magnificent edifice of the Grand Hotel stood with all lights blazing on the cliff to their right. A clear reminder of the gulf between the haves and the have-nots.

When built in eighteen sixty seven, it had been the largest hotel in Europe. Designed around the theme of time it had four turrets to represent the four seasons. Twelve floors for the months of the year. Three hundred and sixty five rooms for the days of the year. Fifty two chimneys completed it, the entire plan view of the hotel in a 'vee' shape to pay homage to Queen Victoria.

Terry had often watched the wealthy clients rolling up to the front entrance in their carriages. Elegant ladies and well dressed gentlemen mounting the steps into the very grand interior. He wondered what it must be like to be in such a position.

The two small lodging rooms, the official description of a rough conversion they shared above a shop on Victoria Road, were just a ten minute walk from the Grand. However, the differences couldn't be more marked.

They shared a toilet and wash basin between them. Nothing at all that resembled a bathroom. Terry's was a single room and Bob had a room with a small offset kitchen.

Terry's room had a small cast iron fireplace set into the wall which he never lit because he could not afford the coal. A single gas mantle provided night time lighting. His bed was up against the outside wall, a single tiny window above it.

A large damp patch in the corner of the ceiling showed the roof needed repairing but no complaint about that was ever acted upon.

His landlord, Mr Reevers, who also owned the shop downstairs said the pittance he paid did not allow for anything fancy. Terry didn't know what *fancy* covered, but it certainly was the most uncomfortable place he could imagine, although he had to agree he could afford little else.

As he retired to bed that night he wondered if this life would ever change for him.

*

Many people in Scarborough that night had no idea that tomorrow would be any different from today.

In the Grand Hotel the crystal chandeliers sparkled and flashed. The five piece band played Strauss in the ballroom. Elegant ladies in beautiful gowns and men in evening attire swished around the room.

Only two guests were actually staying in the Grand at this time of the year but the Scarborough Masonic Lodge had booked it for tonight's ball.

Nineteen year old Fred Taylor, trainee barman, was run off his feet serving drinks. He knew he would be lucky if everyone had departed by one pm, and then the job of clearing up started.

In the Spa Grand Hall Alick Maclean conducted his orchestra in a selection of light classics. Another booking from the great and the good of the borough plus a few wealthy holiday makers. All of them in their finery and well into pre Christmas mood, politely applauding each item.

In the Royal Hotel across the road from the Grand elegant ladies and gentlemen sipped their cocktails to the accompaniment of a chamber orchestra. A similar scene in most of the upper class hotels where the wealthy were

16

able to indulge in seasonal parties. None of them thought tomorrow would bring anything other than a hangover.

On the sea front hard working fisher lasses supped pints of ale just like the men folk, the *Old Steam Packet* being a favourite watering hole.

A talented fisherman played the accordion so all could sing along, happily breathing in the thick blue fug from pipes and rolled tobacco.

Tomorrow would be another day of hard work but tonight it was time to let hair down and relax.

The men manning the war Signal station, situated within Scarborough Castle walls, were also settling for the night.

The castle, built in the reign of King Stephen in the twelfth century by the Earl of Albermarle and Holderness was now reduced to the outer walls and a partial keep. It was one of the ruins that Cromwell 'knocked about a bit.'

The barracks, built in red brick in stark contrast to the castle stone, were a much newer addition. Built in 1746 but not manned since 1878. The barrack building itself was being used for storage by the Yorkshire Hussars.

The men felt they were doing little of use whatsoever stationed in Scarborough. The war had started and they would be lucky to see any action. Like most people they firmly believed it would all be over by Christmas.

At least the ale that the local pub provided at a reduced charge was very welcome, it would help sleep that night.

*

Young Mary Duncan, one of the Scottish fisher lasses who followed the fleet from port to port, had decided to stay in Scarborough when the other girls moved on as the main fishing season ended. She'd found a nice little room on Quay Street with a landlady who treated her almost as a daughter.

Although work dropped off after the main fishing season a girl with swift and deft skills with a filleting knife would always be required.

On this evening of the 14th however she had no thought of the morrow whatsoever.

She was in the throes of rising ecstasy with her back against the rear wall of the *Old Steam packet* and her skirt up around her waist.

Tom Watson, the fit young fisherman she had met last night was thrusting into her with huge force. His right hand was in her blouse fondling her nipple.

She felt her orgasm rising with an intensity that took her by surprise as he gave a final grunting thrust and held himself erect against her.

She could feel the flood of warmth from him enter her very innards as she stifled her own gasping scream. It was almost like a wave of delirium washing over her. She had found the tall man, with curly dark hair and a slightly hard look quite mesmerising.

He had assured her that doing it standing up would avoid any chance of pregnancy, but at that moment she wanted the feeling to last for ever.

\*

Dickie Mainprize at Hayburn Wyke, a few miles to the north of Scarborough was also getting ready for bed.

As a farmer with a good herd of milk cows he knew his day would start at five thirty in the morning, and he had a milk round to complete. At the age of fifty six and not in the best of health, an early night was mandatory.

His beautiful dray, which had been his father's before him, was ready and prepared. Jenny, his faithful grey mare was warmly stabled for the night.

They would set off about six with full churns to serve his customers down as far as the village of Cloughton, on the road to Scarborough.

Most of the locals of Scarborough who had jobs which required early starts were preparing for bed. None with any worry that the morrow would be any different from today.

A war may have started in far away Europe but it was having no effect on them at all.

Thus was life in Scarborough and its surroundings that night of December 14th 1914.

***

# CHAPTER TWO

## 'Feuer Geben'

On the evening of 14th December things were very different in the German Jade Estuary.

Capitan zur See, Ludwig von Reuter, commander of *SMS Derfllinger*, the newest Battle Cruiser in the German fleet, stood on his bridge looking along the full 690ft of his charge.

Frantic activity was taking place completing last minute preparations and making ready for sea.

He was not a tall man, but with his wiry short cropped grey hair, small moustache and goatee beard he commanded respect.

His ship had only been commissioned in early September and it had taken a while to get the 44 officers and 1068 enlisted sailors up to scratch, able to work as a coordinated team.

His sharp eye was scanning the activity around while taking reports from his officers on the state of readiness.

He had immense pride in being the commander of the largest battle cruiser in the German fleet. Her eight 12inch guns and 12 5.9inch guns, plus eight 3.45 guns made her a force to be reckoned with in any navy.

Four twelve foot diameter propellers were capable of pushing her up to 27 knots (30.5mph) with a range of 5,600 nautical miles.

He and his ship had been assigned to the First Scouting Group, all of them now moored in the estuary ready for the early start in the morning.

She was due to take her first action of the war, along with Capitan zur See Max von Hahn in the battle cruiser

*Von Der Tann,* accompanied by the light cruiser *Kolburg* under the command of Fregattenkapitan Widenmann.

The overall command of the operation was under Rear-Admiral Tapken who had his flag in *Von Der Tann.*

It was now eight pm and wisps of dark smoke emitted from her two funnels as steam was raised ready for the 03:20am start in the morning.

Von Reuter scowled slightly as he looked at the smoke. He and the other commanders knew the weakest aspect of his ship was the very poor quality coal that they were issued with.

She had fourteen coal fired and eight oil fired boilers.

With all boilers operating she produced 77,000 Shaft Horse Power which was required for the top speed of 27 knots.   At this speed the poor coal produced vast quantities of dense black smoke. Not altogether desirable when an enemy was looking for you.

Von Reuter thought how lucky the British were with their plentiful supplies of good Welsh steam coal. However, choice he did not have.

His thoughts were interrupted by a sudden screech and awful clatter.

Young mess steward Helmut Weiss, bringing the captain a steaming hot coffee, missed his footing and slid backwards down the ladder cracking his head on a stanchion on his way.

He lay at the foot of the ladder looking dazed, splattered in coffee while a junior gunnery officer blasted him with abuse.

Young Weiss was in the navy against his own wishes. His father had been a sailor and he considered his son should be also.

A rather weak boy of seventeen with bad acne, and a built in clumsiness, he was the butt of other crewmen's jokes.

Even worse, he suffered from seasickness. All other crewmen said it would pass, but so far without any sign of it doing so.

Von Reuter couldn't help a wry smile. His ship was like a small village with the same percentage of characters and eccentrics to be seen in any walk of life. Young Weiss tried hard but seemed destined to be eternally clumsy. If anything could go wrong with him it most certainly would.

The ship had its share of clowns and others who stood out for one reason or another. They would be vilified and yelled at by the officers, but seemed unable to change.

The hiss of hydraulics caught his attention as the huge twin gun turret in front of his bridge rotated to the right. The giant barrels elevated up as the chief gunnery officer checked the workings of his baby.

The first officer raised his eyebrows, looked at Weiss shaking his head slightly, and then turned to Von Reuter and said. 'Most things seem to be ready and working sir.'

Von Reuter gave a tight smile. 'Good number one, if you will have the launch readied I'm expected on *Von Der Tann* at twenty one hundred for final briefing.'

'Aye sir.' He turned and issued orders for the launch on the port side to be lowered and duty men to stand by.

The launch slipped down with practised efficiency touching the water with a delicate slap. Four ratings climbed aboard, one of them starting the small petrol engine, a new feature to most of the older sailors who viewed it with some suspicion.

Von Reuter checked his pocket watch, twenty forty five. 'I'm off then number one. I should be back within the hour.'

He dropped nimbly down to the launch where the ratings stood at attention. '*Von Der Tann* lads, wait on the starboard side for my return.'

The launch slipped away with a whiff of petrol vapour, rocking slightly as it hit open water. A signaller on the bridge of *Derfflinger* clicked his Aldis lamp to let *Von Der Tann* know the captain was on his way.

The briefing confirmed Von Reuter's earlier one.

The fleet comprised of four battle cruisers, *Von Der Tann*, *Seyditz*, *Moltke* and *Derfflinger*, with the armoured cruiser *Blucher*, and four light cruisers. *Srassburg*, *Graudenz*, *Kolburg* and *Stralsund*, all accompanied by eighteen destroyers. They would leave the estuary at 03:20hrs.

They would negotiate the mine field, a tricky manoeuvre in the dark, and head out into the North Sea.

The *Seyditz*, *Moltke* and *Blucher* would head north toward the ports of Hartlepool.

*Von Der Tann*, *Derfflinger* and *Kolburg* would peel off and head south towards Scarborough and Whitby.

*Kolburg*, carrying one hundred mines would head for the area off Flamborough and lay her mines, extending out some thirty miles off Flamborough.

Any possible British naval interference coming up from the Hull area would, hopefully, encounter the mines.

*Von Der Tann* and *Derfflinger* would shell the port of Scarborough and then turn back up to Whitby to shell that port.

The briefing ended with port wine and a toast to the Kaiser. At twenty two fifteen Von Reuter was back on board his ship, satisfied that all that could be done was done.

Reports from his engineering officer and gunnery officer stated all was well. Chief engineer Schmidt had his usual moan about coal quality and said a boiler clean would probably be needed after their next operation. A filthy job which was hated by all involved. That job; and coaling the ship were the least liked tasks on board.

Von Reuter allowed Schmidt his moan. He was after all an excellent engineer and ran the engine room with a rod of iron. He was well aware that come the requirement, Schmidt would produce all the power needed at any time from his 'babies.'

He retired to his cabin at eleven thirty with instructions to be woken at two thirty am.

It seemed as though he had only just closed his eyes when his Steward was gently shaking him.

'02:30 sir, I've taken the liberty of bringing a coffee sir.'

23

'Thanks Johannes.' He slipped out of his bunk, quickly lathered his face in the small wash basin and ran his razor around to remove the stubble.

He gulped his coffee while it was still warm, donned his heavy sea going jacket and hat, and then headed for the bridge.

There was a decided chill in the air but it was fine with very little breeze. A strong smell of coal smoke hung in the air as all ships had steam up now. It hung in the air like a grey pall over the estuary.

Lamps were flicking messages from ship to ship, a pale moon making the image of most ships near them quite visible.

*Kolburg* had dirty smoke issuing from all three funnels. She was an older ship and was probably ready for the dreaded boiler clean.

Weiss appeared on the bridge carrying a metal tray with a coffee and some sort of sandwich for the first officer. He put it down, and in the process managed to spill a goodly amount into the tray.

Von Reuter heard the first officer curse, and Weiss mumble an apology before departing. 'All as normal then number one, should be a good trip.' His number one grinned. 'Aye sir, probably a good sign.'

The signal to up anchor came at 03:00 and the huge mass of ships started to move at 03:20.

Von Reuter was acutely aware of the need to keep a good lookout for mines. They had a nasty habit of breaking free of moorings and the 'biter' becoming the bitten.

He instructed his officers to station extra watchmen in the bows. The pale moonlight helped, but he knew his main attention was keeping station with so many ships sailing close together.

Until they were well into open sea the risk of collision was always present.

A swell was noticeable as they moved further out into the estuary at a steady eight knots.

*Kolburg* had taken the lead in his group, followed by *Von Der Tann.* He kept station on the dim red light on *Von Der Tann's* stern.

At the briefing, Rear-Admiral Tapken had insisted that they would fly no flags of identification. Thus, if spotted near the English coast they might be mistaken for units of the British Navy.

Von Reuter was a little uncomfortable with this. As an old fashioned sailor he thought they should take pride in the national flag, but had to admit he could see the reasoning behind it.

They had agreed a cruising speed which should see them arriving on target at aprox eight am. *Kolburg* would then proceed at full speed to Flamborough to lay her mines.

The mouth of the estuary was cleared without incidence, the sea now having a decided chop. Keeping station on *Von Der Tann* required regular adjustments of speed in the poor light and sea conditions.

All aboard heaved a sigh of relief when the minefields were safely negotiated and they made their turn to port away from the other units heading north. The die was now set. Only God could stop them.

*

Tuesday 15th 6:30 am. On the steam trawler *Our Lass,* first mate Tom Watson was on the wheel taking her out of Scarborough harbour.

The captain and owner was Bill Williams, a bluff old sea dog with a huge pockmarked red nose, the result of his love of a pint!

He had taken Tom on three years ago when he was seventeen years old.

Tom was a good seaman and natural fisherman but had a vicious temper and arrogance about him that worried Bill.

He had witnessed many occasions when Tom had flown at someone who had upset him, even for minor things, and he was a very dirty fighter.

He seemed to have more than a touch of cruelty in his makeup. He'd seen him throw a cat into the sea off the West pier once. 'Just to see if the bugger could swim.'

Bill had rescued Tom some three years ago from a fracas in a pub where he had been accused of stealing.

He knew from other fishermen that Tom was parentless and drifting from job to job, but he was fit and strong. And more to the point! He would be cheap to hire.

For some perverse reason which even he was unable to describe, he'd taken a shine to the lad.

Childless and unmarried himself, it may have been a substitute for the son he did not have.

Today they were heading to the rich fishing ground just to the north off Whitby.

*Our Lass* had been built in 1896 by the Hull shipbuilders Cook Welton and Gemmell. The boat was now eighteen years old, but Bill kept her well maintained and she was a good sea going boat.

Today she had a crew of seven. Bill, Tom, four hired hands from Scarborough, and Jack Campbell, the inevitable Scot in charge of the engine.

Jack Campbell he had known for years.

A tall rangy Scot with a shiny bald pate surrounded by a fringe of ginger hair, like so many of his countrymen before him he had a flair for engineering.

A fairly heavy sea mist, so common on the coast, hung in the air. Bill, luckily, knew the fishing grounds like the back of his hand.

He had fished these waters since his father first took him to sea in the 1890's.

They cleared the harbour and turned north at a steady four knots.

\*

6:45 and Dickie Mainprize had most of his milk churns loaded on the dray, heavy work indeed. And then Jenny to tackle up; he reckoned he should be away by 7:30.

Terry Sheader was up and dressed, having had his breakfast of a chunk of bread with a piece of hard Cheddar cheese which Jane the scullery maid had slipped him yesterday.

It was a good twenty minute walk for him from Victoria Road up to Belvedere Road on the South Cliff.

His gammy leg slowed his walk, and he liked to be at the Kessler's house to start work by eight. A day of hard digging was required on the pond. He knew he would have to pace himself to avoid being totally 'knackered' before finishing time.

*

By 7:35 *Our Lass* was three miles out from shore running north. The sea mist came and went in patches, the only sound being their own bow wave chuckling away and creaks from various parts of the boat, plus the hiss of the engine.

Both Bill and Tom were in the wheelhouse squinting into the mist.

The sky had lightened a little. They passed through a thinning bank of mist when Tom suddenly shouted. 'What the fuck!' and spun the wheel to port.

Rushing towards them on the starboard side was a huge grey shape with a bow wave that showed it was travelling fast.

Tom's quick action saved them from what would almost inevitably have been a collision as the shape very quickly materialised into a large warship steaming at high speed.

As quick as Tom straightened the boat up the ship was passing them. *Our Lass* rocked in the widening wake as it shot by, and then before they had chance to catch a breath another huge bow was bearing down on them from just off the port side.

'Another fucker!' cried the startled Tom, spinning the wheel again. This one looked even larger and seemed to be bearing straight at them.

Bill grasped the binnacle and closed his eyes in sheer terror. The giant passed them within what seemed inches throwing *Our Lass* onto her starboard beam. Bill lost his grip and crashed into the starboard side of the wheelhouse with a cry of pain.

A loud yell came from Jack Campbell below.

'What the hell are you fuckers doing?'

Before any of them were able to reply yet another huge ship appeared on the same side, but at least a little further to port and clear of them.

Tom got a good look at it as it surged by. Enormous gun turrets clearly seen, a startled looking sailor on the forward deck. Once again the passing rocked *Our Lass* like a toy boat.

Then just as quickly they had gone. The entire encounter had taken less than a couple of minutes.

Tom was gasping as though he had run a mile.

'Christ almighty! The fucking navy is supposed to protect us and they nearly killed us.'

He looked across at Bill who had a red gash across his forehead.

'Navy be fucked,' snarled Bill. 'Those fuckers were Huns.'

'What? How do you know that?'

'I saw a bugger on that last un,' he said. 'Only the bloody Huns have that sort O tally on their hats.' He spun round and yelled down the hatch. 'Jack, give us all you've got,' then he grabbed the wheel from Tom and spun it round.

'We need to get back bloody sharp, something nasty's about to happen.'

Jack's head appeared from below. 'What the hell's going on?' he demanded.

28

'Just give us all the speed you can,' replied Bill. 'Tom will fill you in on what's happening.'

'Check on them lads,' he said to Tom. 'Then fill Jack in on what's happening.'

The strong smell of coal smoke enveloped them as Bill reversed course. The passing ships were certainly burning lots of coal.

Within four minutes the old boat was doing nine knots and adding her own smoke to the air.

Having been apprised of the situation Jack was working flat out.

The elderly two cylinder reciprocating engine was going like the Devil, Jack squirting copious amounts of oil on the valve gear and watching the pressure gauge mount to its maximum of 220lbs.

The single Edison bulb in the engine room shone on a sheen of sweat on his head. Every time he opened the firebox doors to throw more coal in, the intense red flames added to the light making it look like a scene from Hades.

One of the young hands joined him to help with firing, the gleaming propeller shaft, covered in a slick of shiny oil, spinning like never before.

The old girl had the bit between her teeth, and Jack was enjoying the thrill.

*

07:55, although not having a watch, Dickie Mainprize did not know that. He was on the coast road heading down to Cloughton after serving old Mrs Welton at Welton farm. Jenny was trotting along without any input from Dickie.

She knew the routine as well as him. Indeed, had often brought him home from the pub when he had been well inebriated.

It had the makings of a fine cold day with tendrils of sea mist hanging over the sea.

He glanced towards the sea and was amazed to see three large grey ships, seemingly at rest, about a mile off shore.

Even as he looked, clouds of smoke billowed from the ship with three funnels and it started surging ahead.

The other two, which both seemed to be a little larger, followed suit. All of them were heading in the direction of Scarborough.

Dicky had never actually seen any large naval ships before and like Tom Watson assumed they were the Royal Navy.

He felt quite proud that such fine ships were there to protect them. 'Let the Hun meet them,' he said to Jenny. Confiding in Jenny was second nature to him.

*

*Kolburg*, on orders from the Rear-Admiral, surged ahead.

Her fifteen boilers all lit, four screws thrashing the water to froth at her stern, she built her speed up to the maximum twenty five knots.

Bypassing Scarborough she flew down the coast to Flamborough Head where she came round in a large arc to port. She then started laying her one hundred mines between Flamborough and the little town of Filey.

Having laid her mines, which would cause the Royal Navy problems for many years to come, she set course for the rendezvous at Whitby.

On board *Von Der Tann* five minutes later, Kapitan Hahn turned to Rear-Admiral Tapken and raised an eyebrow. The Rear-Admiral gave a brisk nod and Hahn gave the order, '*FEUER GEBEN*'

Hahn's gunnery officers, waiting for the order, opened fire with a tremendous crash of sound. The first eleven inch shells winged towards an unsuspecting Scarborough.

On *Derfflinger*, Von Reuter waiting for *Von Der Tann* to open the action gave the same order. Her huge twelve inch guns blasted forth, huge gouts of flame and smoke

30

emitting from the barrels. The Scarborough bombardment had started.

\*\*\*

# CHAPTER THREE

## Bombardment

As Dickie Mainprize watched the ships disappear in the mist towards Scarborough he heard the sound of a bulb horn coming up behind him.

Roger Ventriss who lived near Mrs Welton had bought himself a Stanley steam car. A 1913 model with blue coachwork and yellow wheel spokes.

Roger was a steam aficionado. Not for him the 'internal explosion engine,' his own words. Jenny never flinched at most things, but the hissing vehicle that issued clouds of white vapour really caused her to play up.

Jenny knew the sound of the thing straight away and veered into the side of the road.

Dickie pulled desperately on the reigns, but too late. The dray wheels dropped into the ditch at the roadside and they lurched to a stop with Jenny attempting to buck.

Worse, as the left rear wheel dropped into the ditch the rearmost churn toppled over, hit the ground and rolled a yard or so spilling a spreading white puddle of milk.

'Morning,' shouted Roger as he hissed by in a mini steam cloud totally oblivious to any problem caused. As he breasted the slight rise he coasted without a sign of steam or sound. Dickie cursed him roundly, and as he did so, he heard a deep rumble of thunder from the direction of Scarborough. 'Oh, that's all we need,' he said to Jenny. 'I think it's starting out to be a bad day old girl.'

\*

On board *Our Lass* a deep sense of disquiet existed.

32

Bill had suddenly become like a man possessed, urging Jack to produce more speed and sounding increasingly incoherent.

Thick smoke belched from the elderly funnel, but the trawler's makers had built a sound boat, she was flying along at a speed Tom would have thought impossible.

Jack had requisitioned one of the hired hands to help feed coal into the hungry boiler, the entire boat quivering like a living thing.

Bill, now on the wheel, wiped a trickle of blood clear of his eyes. He seemed to be talking to himself, alternately cursing 'the fucking Hun' and then mumbling incoherently.

He suddenly turned to Tom and said. 'I've made me will tha knows.' His shoulder twitched. 'If anything happens to me this boat's thine.'

'Makepeace and Flowers in town have it.' Mentioning a well know local solicitor. In his current state his Yorkshire accent had broadened and coarsened. Tom looked at him in amazement.

This was the first time Bill had ever indicated he even had a will, let alone the content.

The sky had lightened in the last few minutes and the mist was rapidly dispersing.

All of them were quite used to the way mist could disappear almost like magic on this stretch of coast. The weather patterns held no surprises for them.

Ahead, they heard a sudden huge rumble followed almost at once by another. 'Oh Christ,' shouted Bill. 'They're fucking guns.'

Tom had thought Bill was over reacting when he first said the ships were German, now he felt a sudden surge of dread.

What the hell were they steaming into?

He was suddenly unsure whether heading the same way that the ships had gone was the wisest action.

Even as the thought crossed his mind the deep rumblings had become almost continuous.

'Are we doing right sailing into this?' he asked Bill.

'Right, fucking right,' screamed Bill. 'We need to get into harbour as quick as buggery.'

The castle headland could be clearly seen ahead now. The old boat had a bow wave creaming back the like of which she had never seen before.

They could see a pall of drifting smoke rising from what seemed to be the South Bay area.

Even as they observed it, a further puff of blue smoke rose, followed a few seconds later by the rumble of what they now knew to be gunfire.

Ahead, the two battle cruisers were pouring a concentrated withering fire onto the town.

*Derfflinger* had limited the number of twelve inch shells fired, knowing they would need their high explosive and armour piercing shells should they encounter any units of the British Navy.

The twelve 5.9 inch guns were loaded with shrapnel shells, designed to explode while in flight.

Some of the twelve inch shells in fact, because of the very short range, were not in flight long enough for the fuse to set, arriving at target inert.

The townspeople were later to describe these as 'duds,' but in fact they had simply not activated.

One of the targets which Von Reuter had been briefed on was the Naval Wireless Station in the Falsgrave area of the town.

This and the barracks in the castle walls he reserved his twelve inch shells for.

The two ships steamed at three quarter speed across the south bay pouring relentless fire into the town.

At an area of coast known as White Nab, not far from the picturesque Cayton Bay, they turned rapidly to port to return on a second sweep.

*Von Der Tann* was still leading; with *Derfflinger* four hundred yards astern. Here, young Helmut Weiss met his nemesis.

*Derfflinger's* rapid turn to port, still at three quarters speed, caused her to heel over to starboard just as Helmut Weiss was exiting an armoured door on the starboard side.

His foot caught on the raised steel edge at the bottom of the door, and the next thing he knew he was sliding on his belly toward the starboard rail like a demented grey seal.

He issued a squeal like a stuck pig before shooting under the lower rail and out into the sea.

A torpedo could not have left the ship any more efficiently. He hit the water in a perfect swallow dive hat flying, swallowing a huge gulp of freezing sea water as he plunged under the surface.

Panic flooded through him as he sank his arms and legs flailing madly.

It was close to a miracle that he actually surfaced, with no help from himself.

He took a huge gasp of air, coughing and spluttering, unable to see anything with his eyes full of sea water and tears.

He had always been a very poor swimmer. Ironically like so many seamen.

Eventually, treading water, he managed to see the rapidly disappearing stern of his ship.

Had anyone actually seen him go overboard? He thought most likely not.

He looked desperately around, and then realised he could actually see the shore which looked not too far away.

The intense cold was now making his teeth chatter, but he had a sudden wish to survive. With his very poor breast stroke he started to head toward the shore.

Wavelets constantly splashed into his face. He was swallowing far too much water and a terrible coughing bout overtook him as he swallowed yet more.

The shore, no matter how hard he was trying, seemed to get no closer.

He realised he was rapidly flagging, then he saw a movement just off to his left, an object in the water.

As he lifted slightly he caught a glimpse of a buoy floating there.

Relief flooded through him. If he could just make the buoy he could hang on until he caught his breath and then swim steadily for the shore.

The cold was now so bad he had no feeling whatsoever in his lower limbs. He forced himself in desperation to swim toward the buoy.

Like the shore it hardly seemed to be getting any closer.

Amazingly, a small rising wavelet thrust him forward and the buoy looked almost within reach.

He redoubled his effort with a sudden spurt of hope. He would survive he told himself.

Suddenly, there it was in front of him. He made a final frantic effort and reached out to grasp a handle sticking out of the side.

The blast of the exploding mine could be heard miles away but was absorbed into the already frightful din of the gunfire.

A large and rapidly dying area of white water with an up turned hat bobbing in it was all that was left of poor Helmut Weiss.

To those attuned to such things, might just be heard the ghostly whisper of an officer berating the hapless lad!

\*

The two cruisers, making their second pass, were now hampered by their own smoke.

A pall of burnt cordite fumes mixed with coal smoke hung over the South Bay, making the sweating gunners lose sight of targets.

They instead fired on the lower part of the town, seemingly at random.

It was at the start of this second pass that the Harbour Master, flat out on the end of West Pier with his hands over his ears, saw the amazing sight of *Our Lass* shoot into the harbour at an illegal speed and fetch up against Vincent's Pier with an audible crunch before coming to a stop.

The harbour, like so many small ports, had two stone walls forming a basin.

The left wall or pier as known locally had all the fishing sheds and ice house. The right wall, known as Vincent's pier, had the historic light house, all as seen upon entering the harbour.

The Harbour Master saw two deck hands jump off at great speed; whip the boat's mooring ropes around bollards before running full tilt away from the pier.

Two other lads followed within a second.

'I don't bloody blame 'em for that,' mumbled the Harbour Master as another crash of gunfire sounded.

Jack, still in the engine room, muttered, 'good riddance the little cowards', before starting to pull the fire in the boiler, and venting excess steam in the process of shutting down.

Bill slumped onto the stool in the bridge house looking exhausted and slightly stunned, aware that his identification of the ships as German was correct.

Tom stood at the wheelhouse door looking at the mayhem in front of him, the strong smell of smoke and stench of burnt cordite swirling around.

He turned, just in time to see the last of the ships passing the end of the harbour. As it did so he saw a mighty blast from one of its guns, and then the lighthouse seemed to move as he looked at it.

A large round hole appeared in the structure just below the light proper. He was convinced he saw the offending shell come right through and spin away.

It was followed almost immediately by a resounding crash, and a chunk of masonry like a small boulder crashed on the deck just outside the wheelhouse.

It was at this point that he saw his opportunity.

Bill's comments about his will had squirmed around in his mind ever since he mentioned it.

Tom had lived on his wits for his entire life. He'd developed a cruel disregard for anything not in his interest.

He saw a situation now that could definitely be in his interest.

Bill was slumped on the stool looking as though all his energy had gone. Jack was busy below, no sign of anyone to be seen on or near the pier.

He seized the moment. An old belaying pin hung on the wheelhouse wall, a remnant from Bill's father's days.

He took another quick look around making sure no one was to be seen. He grabbed the pin in a flash and swung with all his might, striking Bill on the head with a sickening crunch of breaking bone.

He caught Bill as he dropped from the stool and dragged him to the wheelhouse door, dropping him close to the piece of masonry.

A widening pool of blood spread from the inert Bill, spreading under the masonry, and in a flash Tom had thrown the belaying pin over the side.

Adrenalin flowing, he screamed at the top of his voice. 'Jack, Jack, Bill's been hit.'

The old Scot came stumbling up from below. 'What the hells happened?' he gasped.

'A bloody Hun shell hit the lighthouse. A chunk of it hit Bill just as he was stepping out of the wheelhouse,' he replied in a voice of horror that would have done credit to a professional actor.

The old Scot felt Bill's pulse, and then shook his head sadly. 'He's gone lad,' he said. 'All this bloody way home for this?'

Tom gave a great sob the like of which amazed even him, and Jack put his arm round his shoulder to commiserate.

The old Scot looked out to sea. 'At least the cowardly bastards have gone.'

*

At eight that Tuesday morning, Terry Sheader had started the heavy digging, which he thoroughly hated.

He knew this was going to be a long job. He stuck the spade in just as an almighty rumble sounded at sea.

As a Boer War veteran he new the sound of big guns instinctively.

He new also it could only be coming from the sea. His first thoughts were that it was probably a naval exercise.

The sound of shells incoming and the mighty explosions that followed soon persuaded him otherwise.

He heard the screech of a shell pass overhead, exploding in the Filey road area. His first instinct was to go and look, thoughts of the safety of Bob in his mind.

Within a brief second however, his mind was made up for him when he heard an almighty thud, and he was struck by something hard and covered in a shower of earth.

Dazed and slightly shocked, he looked at his left shoulder and saw a gash from which blood was oozing.

Then he heard a scream and saw Jane, the scullery maid, running towards him. 'Mr Sheader, Mr Sheader,' she cried. 'You're hurt.'

The gunfire had built to a continuous barrage as Jane brazenly took his hand and led him into the kitchen.

She pushed him, with no opposition from him, into a chair.

The door opened and the dragon herself appeared, looking calm and collected amazingly enough.

She said. 'Get some warm water in a bowl Jane.' Never once taking her eyes off Terry she then proceeded to the first aid box on the kitchen wall.

She removed a roll of bandage and some lint, armed herself with a pair of scissors, and returned to him.

As Jane brought an enamel bowl to the table with warm water sloshing in it, she dipped a piece of lint in the water and started to gently wipe the gash, removing dirt to reveal a small cut, but one which bled profusely.

She stood behind him with one hand on his upper waist, leaning over him with her right hand to wipe his cut.

He could feel her large bosom pressing into his neck as she did it.

Her breathing was close to his ear and he could smell a waft of some sort of perfume.

Terry had a sudden recollection of seeing her observing from the bay window when he had arrived that morning.

His usual ritual of removing his shirt must also have been observed. It was clear she had seen what happened to have arrived so rapidly.

After cleaning the area of blood and dirt his wound didn't look all that bad. She gently drew the edges of the cut together and placed sticking plaster to hold it so. A wad of lint was applied, and then she started to wrap the bandage around his shoulder to secure it in place. She cut the bandage and applied a pin, all the while standing up close and pressing herself on him.

'We must check you have no broken ribs my dear,' she murmured, her voice sounding husky.

She ran her hands down his rib cage, pressing her fingers against him, making him feel decidedly uncomfortable.

Her right hand slid round and ran down his chest to the start of his trousers at the waist. 'No pain at all my dear?'

'None at all Mrs Kessler.' He shifted uncomfortably in the chair. 'I'm very grateful to you.'

She stepped back reluctantly allowing him to stand.

Her face looking slightly flushed she turned to Jane. 'Ask Mr Jameson to use the telephone to call my husband in Sheffield, we must let him know what is happening.'

Terry took the excuse to step back a little.

The sound of another loud bang from the Filey road area. 'Perhaps I should attempt to see if anyone needs help. That sounded quite close'.

'Yes, if you must, but exercise great care.'

He didn't know how, under the circumstances, anyone could exercise care, but he nodded and shot out to retrieve his shirt and jacket.

He had left both draped around a pitchfork thrust into the ground.

Fork and clothes were now across the other side of the garden. As he went to retrieve them he noticed what had injured him.

Almost exactly where the pond was required a large crater had appeared.

He couldn't help giving a grim smile. 'Well, I'll be buggered!'

He quickly dressed and set off for the Filey road.

As he got to the junction with Filey road he looked across at *Dunollie House*. He could see immediately that the porch area had taken a hit, and the glass in the front door was shattered.

A constable was bending over something to the side of the drive.

He could see Bob talking to the policeman as he limped across the road. He was horrified to see the object they were looking at was the postman.

It was apparent the poor man was dead; the entire surroundings looked as though they had been blasted by a giant shot gun.

Chunks of brickwork were scattered immediately in front of the door, the steps littered with at least a dozen pieces.

Bob saw him, murmured something to the policeman and then walked towards him looking very ashen.

'It's Mr Beal,' he said, indicating the postman. 'He must have taken the entire blast. Margaret's dead also.' Tears suddenly started streaming down his face.

Margaret was the maid and they had known each other a long while.

Terry put an arm around his friend, suddenly aware that the firing had stopped. He felt as though he were in some sort of dream and that this was not really happening at all.

He remembered exactly the same feeling when he was shot in the leg, as though it was happening to someone else and he was simply an observer.

He then noticed the postman's bag. Letters were strewn all around and blowing in the wind.

He made as though to start picking them up.

'Leave them sir,' said the policeman. 'We'll see to all that.'

He nodded, and then a sudden thought. 'I've got to go and see if dad's alright.'

Bob started, 'yes, go on, nothing you can do here.'

He squeezed Tom's shoulder, and then watched as his friend started walking. It would take him a good fifteen minutes to get to his father's house in the old town held up by his pronounced limp.

\*

Trainee barman Fred Taylor, was curled up fast asleep in his tiny top attic room at the Grand when it all happened.

He was snoring lightly, the party the night before had not finished until one thirty.

It took a good hour of hard work clearing the amazing amount of mess, glasses, napkins and assorted detritus that only people having such a good time could leave. He was having a delightful dream about one of the serving maids he had taken a shine to, his hand firmly clutching his manhood.

His dream was rudely interrupted by a huge clap of thunder.

He came awake feeling groggy, unsure what had woken him. Then another peel of thunder made him sit up in bed with the sheer volume of it.

He turned out of bed with some reluctance, staggered to the tiny window, which he had to stand on tip toes to see through, and peered out.

At first he couldn't believe his eyes. Were they actually ships firing guns?

He saw them passing from left to right in the bay, seeming to be moving quite fast. He dashed to the chair where his trousers and shirt were draped and struggled into them, hopping round the room as his left foot got caught in his trousers.

It seemed only a minute or two had passed when the intensity of fire increased. Peering through the window once again, he saw the two ships were now proceeding right to left.

A dense pall of smoke hung over the bay, and even as he watched, he felt the entire hotel vibrate and the sound of a huge bang from somewhere downstairs.

A feeling of panic overtook him. He started for the door and then felt the floor under him heave as a crash came from the room below. Multiple bangs then seemed to happen in quick succession and for the first time in his life he smelled the burnt acrid stench of cordite.

He could hear shouts and screams from the, mercifully, few staff in residence. They, like him, were now heading for the stairs and out.

He dashed downstairs at a rate never before achieved, and as he came down the grand staircase he heard a huge blast from the sea-view restaurant to his right.

This was one of the rooms in which he had spent so much time in the early hours clearing. Then, as though on auto pilot, he could not stop himself from going to look.

Mercifully the bangs and crashes seemed to have moved off a little. He dashed down the steps into the sea-view restaurant and shuddered to a stop, horrified.

The once magnificent restaurant, which stretched across the full frontage of the hotel, was now like a building site.

Tables were splintered and turned upside down. Chairs and chunks of the bar lay scattered about as though smashed by a giant hand.

Not a window looked intact, glittering shards of glass everywhere.

He wandered in a daze around the room. Broken bottles everywhere, liquor dripping from shattered optics.

It looked as though a hurricane had passed through leaving devastation in its wake.

Amazingly, a full decanter of port stood on the end of the shattered bar untouched.

He touched it as though doing so it would vanish, was it real?

He felt he was increasingly in a surreal world that would shortly right itself.

He took the stopper out and sniffed it, then raised the decanter and tasted.

Yes, it was real. He had never tasted port before and the sweetness was rather comforting.

Another sip, it seemed to steady his racing pulse a little. Perhaps another little sip would be good for him.

He noticed that large chunks of the beautiful stone arched windows were missing; it was almost as though he were standing partially outside. Another little sip. Yes, he was feeling much more relaxed.

As though by magic the decanter was suddenly empty, he couldn't believe it. Looking out of the window again he noticed the distant harbour was shimmering like a mirage. A great feeling of lethargy overcame him.

I must sit down, was the last conscious thought that slipped through his mind as he slumped to the floor.

Outside, the general manager was trying desperately to gain some semblance of order and attempting to take a roll call of his staff.

He was thankful to see no one was hurt; many badly shook up certainly, but no injuries.

'Is anyone missing?' he asked. Agnes Bradwell, the young maid who had caused Fred to sleep clutching his nether regions, piped up. 'Fred Taylor. I'm sure I saw him going into the restaurant as I came down.'

'Oh no,' exclaimed the manager. He turned and ran into the building, Agnes and two others hot on his heels.

As they burst into the restaurant and saw the devastation, they all paused for a moment, taking in the sight.

'Oh God no,' screamed Agnes. She pointed to the floor near the shattered bar. There, lying flat on his back was Fred.

They dashed across the floor to the prostrate body. The manager bent down over him. 'Is he dead?' stuttered Agnes, tears starting to well up in her eyes.

The manager felt his pulse, and then took in the sight of the empty decanter close by.

Leaning over the lad, he sniffed his breath suspiciously.

'No,' he cried in fury. 'The little bastard's pissed.'

For Terry, walking down the road into town, it all became rather surreal.

People were out of their houses and shops, talking excitedly, many looking panic stricken.

A number of people were appearing with items of hastily packed clothing.

He clearly heard one woman say she was off to her sister's in Leeds.

As he walked along Ramshill road where the small shopping area existed, he saw a large stout man flapping his arms like a seagull and proclaiming to all and sundry, 'we are about to be invaded.' He repeated it over and over, either in shock or really believing it.

A number of windows were broken, shards of glass glistening in the road and on the pavement.

As he passed the historic church of St Martins he could clearly see a large hole in the roof, and slates scattered some distance from it.

He dropped down the lower part of the road where it joined with Valley Road Bridge, the impressive iron work structure which joined South Cliff to the town proper, giving a panoramic view of the sea front.

Many people could be seen hurrying in the direction of the railway station. Thin wisps of smoke drifting up from the bay gave a blue tinge of haze to the scene.

He saw a man pushing a hastily loaded hand cart, his wife and three children in tow, going across the bridge as though the very Devil were after them.

Terry carried on down the road, past the bridge to the road underneath, crossing over to the turret shaped Rotunda Museum.

He negotiated the steep steps at the side of the museum which took him up to the Grand Hotel.

As he approached the impressive frontage a group of people could be seen milling around near the entrance. Clearly staff; as the girls were wearing uniform.

A young man was laid out on the pavement with what looked like a rolled coat under his head.

Terry was startled to see a person he took for the manager, as he was dressed in morning attire; dash a pitcher of water on the young mans head.

It seemed a very strange way to treat someone who must have been injured in the attack.

The water however seemed to do the trick. The young lad, (he was no more) rose to a sitting position, spluttering and looking totally bewildered.

The manager then started on the poor lad with venom, his face puce with rage, one of the chamber maids trying unsuccessfully to speak up for the lad.

To Terry it was a further indication of strange behaviour when people were in stressful situations beyond their control.

Carrying on past the Grand the path led to the impressive statue of Queen Victoria. The old Queen was totally untouched and looking down from her plinth at the side of the Town Hall to the harbour. A group of Town Hall staff were outside staring at a large hole on the corner of the building where a shell had struck, taking an area of brickwork out. The shattered bricks were spread in a fan shape some fifteen yards wide.

Terry intended to carry on down King Street, which went down from Queen Victoria's statue to the old town. Looking towards the harbour he was amazed to see a hole all the way through the lighthouse tower.

The old Queen on her pedestal, lovingly sculpted by Charles Bell Birch but not erected until ten years after his death, stood looking in haughty disdain at the events happening around her, the Orb clutched in her left hand as though about to hurl it at the aggressor.

Smoke hung over the harbour in patches, the acrid smell still hanging in the air.

Hurrying down King Street, one of the oldest in the town, he was horrified to see the devastation.

A number of buildings seemed to have received direct hits. One property had a huge hole in the wall, slates and broken glass littered the road almost the entire length.

Terry's father, Richard Sheader, lived in a terraced house on Overton terrace.

It was situated on the rising ground from the harbour, set into a grassy bank with a stout stone wall supporting the row.

It had a magnificent view looking down onto the roof of the *Three Mariners* pub. Lifting one's eyes slightly, the full stretch of curving coast line swept to the left giving a clear view right out to Flamborough Head.

To the rear of the house was a small yard, and then the bank swept up to the rest of the old town and beyond, rising steeply to the historic old St Mary's church with the grave of Anne Bronte.

Only the castle stood higher than St Mary's.

Richard Sheader had moved to this house from a tiny fisherman's cottage in 1905 or thereabouts.

Terry had no idea how his father had managed to obtain such a nice house on the money he earned as a fisherman. However, he dared not enquire as previous remarks had been rebuffed with a curt. 'No business of yours.'

This and his predilection for women caused the rift between them, hence Terry refusing to live with his father and ending up in the digs on Victoria Road.

However, the old saying *blood is thicker than water* applied, and Terry felt he needed to check the old boy had not come to grief in the shelling.

His mind was totally focussed on this as he walked, with increasing pain from his leg, towards his father's house.

All around, he saw people milling about as though not knowing what to do, which was probably the case.

He hurried along Princess Street in the old town, from which he could make his way to Overton Terrace.

Dropping down the steep flight of steps to the Terrace he heaved a huge sigh of relief. The street looked totally untouched, not even a broken window to be seen. As he walked towards his father's house he saw the door open, and out came Helen Standish, his father's current woman.

She saw Terry, uttered a startled little squeal, and then turned and hurried away as though terrified of him.

He was just starting to think that all the excitement of recent events had sent everyone totally bonkers, when the door next to his father's house opened and out stepped Jack Savage.

Jack Savage was the caricature of what the layman would expect an old sea dog to look like.

Short and squat, bandy legs, thick black beard rapidly going grey, and wrinkled and brown face from years of seafaring. From this face shone a pair of eyes of intense blue, topped by a totally bald pate that looked like brown wrinkled parchment.

'Oh Jack, can't tell you how glad I am to see no damage.' Jack stood looking at him, his body language and stance suddenly made Terry's blood run cold.

'Jack, dad is alright isn't he?'

The old seaman looked at him sadly. 'If it weren't fer yon bloody Hun I were coming looking for thee lad.'

'What are you saying, is dad hurt?'

'Nay lad, he's gone,' he replied sadly. 'Thi dad's gone lad; we've laid him out on't bed.'

'What?' stuttered Terry. 'But you haven't any sign of damage, how can he have been hurt?

'It weren't Hun what did him; he had a heart attack in't early hours.'

Terry felt as though an invisible being was drawing an icy finger down his spine. 'Bout one o'clock this morning, ah heard bangin on't wall,' the old man said. 'Knew summat must be wrong and went round.'

'Yon Standish's lass opened door.' The old man heaved a deep sigh. 'Looks as though thi dad was givin her a good seeing too when is heart gave out.'

***

# CHAPTER FOUR

## Aftermath

The immediate aftermath of the German raid on the Wednesday saw many people packing and leaving the town to stay with relatives or friends.

The feeling that it could either happen again, or that it was indeed the precursor to a landing was rife.

The damage to the town was wide spread, although the fact that more shells of the shrapnel variety were fired than high explosive ones showed in the large amount of broken glass and pock marked brickwork.

The very fact that shrapnel shells were specifically designed to maim people caused intense anger throughout the town.

Such an attack on an unarmed seaside town gave vent to fury right up to the Palace of Westminster.

The only target that might have been described as legitimate was the wireless station. This monitored signals from German shipping and allowed the Admiralty to plot the location of German ships.

It was estimated that some 6000 people had fled the town. Considering that the population in 1914 was around 38500, it gave some idea of the general panic that gripped the town.

In all, eighteen people were killed, although as we know, one of these was a murder victim.

A large number of people were injured, partly because a lot of the shells destined for the wireless station fell short and landed in the town.

Ironically, the wireless station escaped unscathed.

Considering so many shells of the shrapnel variety were fired it was a miracle that more deaths did not occur.

The Germans also thought the barracks in the castle grounds were in use. They hit this with remarkable accuracy, the imposing red brick building was hit a number of times, the roof and upper walls being totally destroyed.

The twelve feet thick castle walls, last under fire from Cromwell, were also struck; large holes being blown in them.

The war signal station in the castle grounds was hit and completely destroyed, fortunately with no loss of life, although the staff, thinking a landing was next, destroyed the official papers and code books.

Even the very old cast iron beacon, which used to be lit in the days gone by, flew into the air and crashed over the castle wall landing dented and battered in the dyke at the bottom of the castle hill.

The government were to use the attack to great effect as a recruiting tool, the slogan *Remember Scarborough* being used on recruiting posters.

As with most disasters though, some were to benefit from other's misery.

Bricklayers, glaziers, general labourers etc, were to get work for many weeks, and the poor old coroner was never busier.

The Scarborough Corporation decided that the lighthouse was in a dangerous condition and would have to be demolished to the lower level.

Young Fred Taylor, recently sacked from his job at the Grand, signed on with the work gang tasked with working on the lighthouse. He had to grasp at any work available. Going home to his parents in Whitby saying he had been sacked, and even worse, why, filled him with dread.

A very cocky Tom Watson hung around the pubs adjacent to the harbour waiting for the coroner's verdict on Bill Williams. He was confidant that Bill would be declared a victim of the German attack.

Ironically, he was supported by Jack Campbell who thought Tom would become the legal owner of *Our Lass* and continue to employ the Scot as engineer.

It was almost a week after the attack when Tom got the verdict he wanted and made an appointment to see the solicitors, Makepeace and Flowers on the morning of Tuesday 29th, the first available date after the bank holiday.

Armed with his seaman's docket as I.D; a large florid man who introduced himself as Mr Flowers took him into an office, asking his business.

Tom gave a succinct account of the terrible run for shelter they made in *Our Lass*, recounting the events leading up to Bill's death, giving the version that he wanted everyone to believe.

He even managed to give a very convincing sob when describing the million to one fluke that struck down his much beloved benefactor on arrival in the harbour.

His performance must have been very good.

Mr Flowers showed great sympathy for him and said the transfer of the ownership documents to Tom would be expedited as rapidly as possible. Furthermore, the will left the sum of one hundred pounds to Tom, a huge amount which caused him to exercise supreme control not to yell out loud.

As he came out of the office he saw Terry Sheader waiting patiently, seated on a chair in the corridor. He gave him a brisk nod of recognition. 'Sheader,' wondering as he departed what he could possibly be doing in a Solicitors office. He was confidant as he left the offices of Makepeace and Flowers that his star was rapidly ascending.

By five pm that evening he was in *The Three Mariners* celebrating.

He thought he was capable of achieving anything he wanted. At last, he, Tom Watson, was going to be master of his own destiny.

\*

52

For Terry Sheader the immediate aftermath was surreal.

His first thought was one of anger at his father for being such a stupid old fool. He was all of fifty four for God's sake! Surely the sex urge had diminished by then!

He entered the house with Jack Savage close on his heels.

The woman's touch was immediately apparent as he glanced around the room. His father never kept things as tidy as that.

Signs of a female 'home making' were everywhere.

He started up the steep steps to the bedroom, a feeling of dread stealing over him. He paused at the bedroom door, took a deep breathe, and then entered.

His father was lying on the bed with hands crossed on his chest. He seemed to be smaller than remembered and the stern look he usually had for Terry had gone.

A large scarf had been tied around his jaw and the top of his head, a tradition among the community to prevent the jaw sagging in death.

To Terry, it gave his father an almost comic look. He started to laugh, and amazed himself when it came out as a cry of grief.

He felt suddenly alone in the world. For all his faults his father was the only living relation he had, and now he was gone.

A mixture of emotions went through him as all who suffer the loss of a parent know. He thought of the times when as a child they went fishing together, dad showing him how to tie a fly and using the rod which he had made for him.

'Don't be mad at thi dad lad. Yon woman made him a happy fella.'

Jack's voice startled him out of his reverie.

'We all need a bit O comfort. I reckon he could have done a lot worse.'

He was lost for reply, then a thought. 'I don't even know who dad's landlord was, do you Jack?'

'It seems tha knows nowt lad. Landlord be buggered, thi dad owned this house imself.'

His eyebrows shot up in shock. 'He owns this house, but how the hell could he? Where had he the money to buy a house?'

Jack shrugged his shoulders. 'I can't tell thi abaht that, but I know he bought it from Solly Stein who ad it in't first place.'

To Terry, the world seemed to be going mad. The shock of the bombardment and the strange behaviour of people immediately after. The relief of seeing his father's street untouched only to find he was now dead in a totally unrelated way. And now, information that took him completely by surprise.

All this within the space of that one fateful morning in December. All these thoughts and feelings shooting through his mind while standing in his father's bedroom. He, lying in death on the bed with the ridiculous scarf around his head.

'May Allan has sent for the doc.' Jack's voice again. 'That's providing he ain't run in terror like some other buggers round here.'

Doctor Jameson had a practice in the old town. As far as Terry knew, his father had never ever used him, but a doctor would certainly have to certify death. Another glance at the bed, and then he turned slowly and made his way back down the stairs and into the tiny kitchen, sitting at the table he had eaten at so often.

'I'll put kettle on.' Jack's, answer to any crisis. 'If tha needs any papers like, thi dad keeps em all in't tin box under't bed.'

The tin box referred to was a battered old cash box that Terry remembered being in the house all his life. Any documents of any sort that needed to be saved ended up in it.

It made him very aware that he had no knowledge of any aspect of what might be required in an event like this.

Certainly, his father had never discussed anything about what to do if he passed on, or even if he had a will.

The battered kettle started to show signs of steam, standing on its single gas burner attached via a red rubber tube to an outlet on the wall.

He glanced around the kitchen as Jack poured boiling water into a plain earthenware tea pot.

The female touch was clear to see in lots of tiny details. The curtains were clean and of some bright blue cotton material.

Cleaning materials were tidied away in a pretty blue vase like container. Everything looked scrubbed and clean, a slight smell of soap in the air.

Another thought which flooded into his mind. A funeral would have to be arranged, how does one go about doing that? How would it be paid for? How much would it cost?

Once again, the calm voice of Jack stopped his rapidly rising look of panic. The old fisherman had obviously a shrewd idea of what was going through his mind.

'Nowt to rush for now lad. Wait until doc's been; if tha wants to do summat have a look through yon box.'

'I don't want to go back upstairs just now.' A feeling of dread stealing over him. 'Don't worry lad, sup thi tea, I'll fetch it.' The old man said gently.

He rose from the table and went upstairs. Terry had a grateful sip of the scalding liquid, aware that his leg was throbbing like mad. He'd been completely unaware of it prior to this moment.

Before Jack had come back downstairs, a knock at the door. He rose and opened it to see May Allan, a neighbour from Princess Street, standing there with a small man in a formal jacket and bowler hat.

'Hello Terry lad, so sorry about thi dad. This is Doctor Jameson.'

He was quite surprised the doctor had arrived so promptly. With the recent events he thought some considerable wait was in store.

The doctor changed his bag to his left hand to shake hands. Terry thanked May for her commiserations and help in running to the doctor's surgery and invited him in.

As he did so, Jack appeared with the tin box in both hands.

'Wud yer like me to show't doc upstairs lad?'

He was more than glad for Jack to take the doctor upstairs. He had a sudden irrational fear of going back in the bedroom.

Placing the box on the kitchen table Jack ushered the doctor upstairs. Terry could hear the mutter of voices, and at one point heard what sounded like a chuckle from the doctor.

He sat looking at the box.

Made from pressed tin and painted black with the slight remains of what had been a gold stripe around the lid with a brass handle on top that was almost green with verdigris.

The black paint was badly scuffed and scratched showing plain metal through in places. A key hole in the front just below the handle, but it was clear that it was not locked, bulging open slightly with the amount of paper inside.

Should he look now or wait for the doctor to finish upstairs? A sudden sharp laugh from the doctor made his blood boil. What was so funny about his dad lying dead up there?

He took a deep breathe and flung the lid open.

A wad, of what turned out to be receipts for stuff purchased over the last few years took up a half of the depth of the box.

He was still rifling through them when he heard footsteps coming downstairs. The strange irrational fear suddenly hit him again. He almost expected his father striding into the room and asking what he was doing there.

Jack and the doctor entered, Terry hastily shoving paper back into the box.

56

'A heart attack without much doubt,' stated the medic.

'Of course a post mortem will be necessary. No doubt some delay today eh? Not the most unpleasant way to pass though.'

Terry had no allusions that the reason for his father's demise would soon be common knowledge amongst all, probably the cause of the laugh he'd heard.

Again, a touch of anger mixed with shame running through him, and then guilt thinking the old man was dead.

'I will issue you with a death certificate after the post mortem,' the doctor said. 'It will cost four shillings.'

He held a hand up as Terry started to say something. 'Don't worry Mr Sheader; you may sort out your father's estate before I require payment.'

'I will arrange for your father's body to be taken to the Council mortuary on Dean Road. After the PM you will be able to arrange the funeral but there may be some delay under current circumstances you understand?'

Terry nodded, unable for the moment to speak. He shook hands with the doctor and bid him good day.

'I think you'll be needed here lad. Best thing, get your stuff from Victoria Road and come back ere.'

Good advice from Jack, a plan of action was what was needed. He'd go up to his digs and collect his few belongings, return here to his father's house, check the contents of the tin box for any clues as to what was what, and then see where he was at.

'I'll get Helen Standish to shift her stuff while you're gone.'

Terry had totally forgotten about the bloody woman. Under the circumstances that would probably be a good idea. He had no wish to set eyes on her.

Nodding agreement to that idea he took his leave of Jack after thanking him for all his help and advice, and started to walk to Victoria Road.

As he started his walk, he realised it was now turned three o'clock. Where had the time gone?

His tummy was also rumbling. He hadn't eaten since breakfast that morning. He thought a small piece of cheese and some bread was left in his digs.

As he walked the devastation all around was apparent.

The dazed state he had been in when first walking to his father's was now gone. He was able to take in his surroundings without feeling like an outsider looking in.

The most immediate sight was the large amount of broken glass everywhere. People seemed less aimless now. Some were out in the streets starting to clear up, others excitedly gossiping with neighbours, less signs of anyone attempting to flee.

By the time he'd walked, uphill all the way as his leg was telling him, to Victoria Road, the full horror of the attack was quite clear. As he turned onto Victoria Road it was apparent this was a road that had taken some severe punishment.

Victoria Road was one of the main roads in Scarborough, starting almost opposite the railway station and travelling deep into the town centre.

A road of shops and businesses, always busy with shoppers and the like, quite narrow. The shrapnel shells had destroyed the majority of windows along the road. Glass and slates could be seen over the entire street. The contents of one shop window were strewn right across to the other side of the street.

Chunks of brickwork littered about, with large holes in the walls of some of the shops, showing where larger calibre shells had struck.

It looked as though some huge tornado had run rampant through the street leaving chaos in its wake.

Mr Reevers, whose shop Terry lived above, was situated at the top end of Victoria Road near its junction with Westborough, the main thoroughfare passing the railway station.

As he approached it Terry could see that it was in a stricken condition.

The main window now glittered in fragments across the road. He could see his bedroom window was in the same condition; his curtains were blowing out in the breeze.

The shop door was splintered, and most of the woodwork on the frontage looked as though it had been blasted by a giant shotgun.

He had to put his shoulder to the shop door to open it, the top hinge was gone. Of Mr Reevers there was no sign.

The contents of the shop window were scattered at the back of the shop, the wall facing the window spattered with pock marks in the plaster.

As he ascended the stairs to his room above, one of the treads creaked alarmingly and almost at the top of the stairs he jumped like a startled deer when a gargoyle of a face appeared looking down at him. Lips turned down at the corners, nose wrinkled up as though detecting a bad smell. Mrs Agnes Tanner in all her glory.

'Oh it's you Mr Sheader,' she exclaimed. 'You startled me.'

Not as much as you fucking startled me thought Terry.

How Bob Tanner stayed married to this cow he had no idea. She must have attracted him at one time, but with the best will in the world, he was unable to see anything at all attractive in this ugly woman.

'Nothing left up there.' She tipped her head back in the direction of the two rooms. 'All smashed.'

She said it as though it gave her satisfaction that Terry had yet to see for himself. 'Every bit of pottery,' she exclaimed. 'Even the chamber pot.'

Terry had a vision of the dreaded pot under their bed smashed, and its previous contents now soaking into the bare floorboards.

He gave an involuntary shudder. He had an image for a moment of Agnes sitting on the said pot in all her splendour.

'We're moving in with my sister in Falsgrave.' She said this with such satisfaction he realised immediately the Germans had done her a great favour.

'I suppose you will be homeless?' She grimaced at him in what was supposed to be sympathy.

'I haven't even seen it yet,' he replied, nodding toward his room. 'But I've only come for my things. I'm moving into my dad's house.'

The disappointment on her face was plain to see. She obviously wanted to hear that he would be homeless.

'No one knows where Mr Reevers is.' She licked her lips. 'Might have been completely blown to bits.'

It seemed for a while as though she were savouring the thought; it would solve any rent payment that was for sure.

'Well, I need to get on.' He made for his door. 'I hope it works out well for you and Bob.' He inserted his key, swung the door open and gasped.

If he had been in this room when the attack happened he wouldn't have been here today.

Downstairs, the shop window had blown out into the street. Here, in strange contrast the glass from the window plus most of the room's contents was splattered on the rear wall.

Slivers of glass and other bits were embedded in the wall like some mad artist's idea of abstract art.

A coat and the only other shirt he had were shredded on the metal pole that acted as a wardrobe.

He took a step back and heard a cry of pain from Agnes as he stood on her toe. She'd followed him in to see his devastation for herself.

'As I said Mr Sheader, all smashed,' a shake of the head. 'All smashed.'

It was obviously the most exciting thing ever in her life. Getting his stuff together, working round her as she was determined to stay to the finish was no small feat.

In actual fact, all that was worth recovering filled a small woven shopping bag that had once belonged to Mrs Kessler.

Agnes's parting shot was. 'I can't find any rent books either Mr Sheader.'

She must have been hoping they had gone along with Mr Reevers.

He made his excuses and set off, not even finding it in himself to tell her his father was dead.

He would normally have strolled right through town and down Eastborough, which exited opposite the harbour, but Eastborough was now blocked off with sandbags and barbed wire. He returned the reverse of the way he came, still not having had any food.

It was five pm when he got back to his father's.

It was clear Helen had been in to remove her belongings. He felt slightly guilty. It was not his place to dictate to the woman, but Jack had obviously arranged for her to get in and out quickly and if she had anything to say to him no doubt it would happen.

He opened a cupboard in the kitchen and was surprised to find a fresh loaf of bread, butter, cheese, and sheer luxury, what looked like a jar of home made jam. In fact the cupboards seemed quite well stocked. A woman's touch again?

He had the kettle going again in no time, and with the delight of a huge doorstep of a cheese sandwich settled down at the kitchen table to look through the box.

The receipts which seemed of no interest or of little use he put on one pile. Anything else he set aside for further study.

One of the first items of interest, which he had never seen before, was his father's birth certificate.

It showed he was born in a little village called Sleights near Whitby in April 1860.

This was news to him. His father had never said where he was born, and Terry had always assumed it was Scarborough.

His parents were named as Hubert and Gertrude Sheader. He couldn't help wondering why he never knew them as grandparents.

A thick wad of papers in a brown envelope turned out to be the deeds of the house. Jack was right. They showed the house had been purchased from Mr Solomon Stein in 1906 for the price of £200. The sale had been completed in June of that year and the full amount had been paid in cash!

This bit of information he could not understand.

Prior to Terry going to Africa with the army his father was still working as a fisherman, scraping a living like everyone else.

He had lived in a rented cottage like most other men in that situation.

This had been so until, as he now realised, 1906.

To his knowledge, his father had no savings at all. So how could he lay out the enormous sum of £200 cash in 1906 for a house?

He rose, found a Vesta match in the kitchen drawer, and lit the gas mantle on the wall. It hissed, and then glowed brightly as he increased the gas flow.

A bundle with red ribbon tied around it was next, the name 'Makepeace and Flowers' on the front page.

A will no less. He felt his throat constrict, surprised that a will had actually been drawn up at all.

Not many fishermen could even afford the luxury of one, let alone actually have anything of worth to leave.

He untied the ribbon with trembling hands. It had only the one page inside, and stated very simply that all his remaining estate was to be bequeathed to his only son Terrence Sheader, with two codicils.

His gold Albert fob watch was to be left to his good friend Jack Savage, and his other good friend, Helen Standish, was to receive £100.

Gold pocket watch! Since when had his father had a gold watch? An expensive one at that. And leaving £100 to

62

Helen Standish, bloody hell! The slag had shagged him to death.

This last indignant thought probably made worse by the knowledge that he had never had sex with a woman in his life. Fumbles when in the army but nothing that was the real thing. And he was bloody thirty two now! And where had dad got a hundred pounds from to leave to her anyway?

He sat back stunned, his head throbbing. He looked at the ancient clock ticking loudly on the wall which was already showing seven fifteen. Where had the time gone?

A creak from the staircase. An icy finger ran down his spine. Was his father's ghost coming to remonstrate with him for rifling through his belongings?

His leg really throbbed. A feeling of exhaustion crept over him, and then a bang at the door which almost caused him to jump out of the chair.

Rising, with a heart thudding like mad, he went to the door.

Jack!

'Sally wants to know if tha might like some supper wi us?' the simple request warmed him and he realised he wanted to get out of the house for a while.

The thought of dad still laying upstairs troubled him greatly. He could feel a touch of claustrophobia. 'Oh that's nice, thanks Jack, I'd love it.'

Closing the door he followed him round next door, entering Jack's house to the smell of hot food the like of which he hadn't smelled for a very long time.

Sally, Jack's wife was a rotund cheerful little woman. Ruddy cheeks and with a smile that was a pleasure to see.

She put her arms around him and gave him a hug in a motherly way which he found quite comforting and touching.

The 'supper' was a huge fresh fish pie topped with a short crust pastry that had his mouth watering in no time at all.

She dug out a substantial portion and placed it onto a white enamel plate saying. 'There's plenty more if you want it lad.'

It was food the like of which he hadn't known for ages, and he scoffed a second helping with little persuading from Sally.

She looked on as the two men ate their fill, taking a pride in the look of gratitude and pleasure in equal portions on Terry's face.

After the meal she shooed them into the parlour to talk, making herself busy in the kitchen.

She refused Terry's offer of help, saying. 'Nay lad, tha needs to talk to Jack a dare say.'

The two men settled on the two seat woven bamboo settee. Jack produced clouds of smoke as he seemingly set fire to a large briar pipe.

'Nah then lad, where too from ere,' said the old sailor.

Where to indeed? He told Jack about the will and his loss of understanding how his father could be in such an affluent position.

Jack leaned back and said a simple, 'Aye.'

It was said with a deep sigh and touch of worldliness that had Terry sitting up to hear what was coming.

Jack related the story as he knew it.

'Ah can't giv thi details, but thi dad had a bit O luck in 1904,' he started.

'He were crewin on't old *Yorkshire Lass* wi Bob Pashley.'

Terry remembered Bob Pashley. He owned a steam paddle trawler called *Yorkshire Lass,* quite a common sort of vessel in those days.

'It were durin't fishin season, October.' Another deep draw on the pipe. 'Thi dad and Pash were out wi a crew O six.'

Another long pause as he applied more flame to the blackened bowl of the pipe. The dammed thing was starting to annoy Terry. He wanted Jack to get on with it.

Jack smiled as though he was enjoying the stretching of a good yarn.

'They come back late in't evening on't 22nd.' A suck and a glow across the top of the pipe. 'All O em seemed excited like.'

'They unloaded fish catch quickly like, nothing special. Some talk O bein' fired on by Ruskies, and then stuck ont' Dogger.' (Referring to the notorious Dogger Bank)

The old sailor stretched his legs out. 'They were huddled in't snug in't *Steam packet* that night heads close together an lots O whispering.'

'Lots O rumours a' course, but nowt certain. But thi dad never went out wi Pash again and he started actin secretive after that.'

'He didn't do much fishin after that either. We all reckon they trawled summat up that day, summat worth a bob or two.'

He sat back, tale told.

It gave Terry no further knowledge other than hints at some 'treasure' recovered from the sea.

'A bit far fetched don't you think Jack?'

The old boy shrugged. 'There's more wrecks around here than't parson preached abart' he said, quoting an old Yorkshire saying. 'Owt's possible from't sea.'

Terry in fact knew a little of the events of October 21/22 1904, it had been widely reported in the papers.

His dad had also mentioned the fright of coming under fire from Russian warships, spinning it out to a good tale, but no mention of being stuck on the Dogger Bank.

The Russian Baltic Fleet had been en-route via the North Sea to the far-east, the intention being to reinforce the 1st Pacific Fleet.

The Russo-Japanese war was under way. The fleet commander had received reports of Japanese torpedo-boats being in the vicinity, and on the evening of the 21st had mistaken a group of British trawlers as the torpedo-boats.

The resulting fiasco caused one British trawler to be sunk, the *Crane,* with the loss of three lives. The incident led to a huge diplomatic row with Russia, only being settled in late 1904 when the two governments signed a Treaty.

To rub salt into the wound, the Russian Navy suffered a humiliating defeat at the hands of the Japanese at the battle of *Tsushima.*

It became known as the *Dogger incident.*

Terry decided to call it a day. According to Jack's mantelpiece clock it was ten thirty, he was feeling exhausted. Then the thought, where to sleep?

He thanked Jack and Sally, refused an offer to stop for the night at first, then thinking of his father's body still and inert upstairs next door, had second thoughts and gratefully accepted the offer.

The tiny bedroom was sparsely furnished with a bed and set of drawers. That was it, but he slipped into bed and was asleep within minutes after extinguishing the oil lamp Sally had provided.

He dreamed heavily that night. Ghosts came to visit. Pirates and treasure chests, sunken ships, a huge battleship firing at him as he attempted to open the treasure chest. His father riding Helen Standish like a stallion.

He did eventually slide into deep sleep waking as dawn light filtered through the window.

The morning saw pale sunlight shining through the window, condensation running down it. The sound of gulls screeching on the nearby castle cliffs, a touch of normality returning to the east coast.

***

# CHAPTER FIVE

## A new day

It was the day after the bombardment, Wednesday 16th December 1914.

Terry had been provided with a breakfast of a pair of kippers and a chunk of buttered bread. The day was looking better already.

The people of Scarborough were awakening to trepidation and some fear.

Could it happen again? Was a landing on this part of the east coast possible? How vulnerable were they?

There were early reports of Whitby and Hartlepool also being attacked. Lots of residents still streaming to the railway station to get away.

Most of this passed Terry by. His immediate concern now was how long it would be before his father's body was collected.

He thanked Jack and Sally profusely, Jack telling him not to hesitate if he needed any help. A presence there next door for which he was deeply grateful.

He avoided going upstairs when back in his father's house. The thoughts of the body there gave him the creeps. He decided to settle with the contents of the tin box instead.

A bundle of receipts that he had discarded earlier took his eye.

A substantial bundle seemed to be from the same source. A gummed paper band secured them. A quick flick with a kitchen knife and they were spread before him on the kitchen table.

They all bore the same heading. *Isaac Steiner. Jewellers of Repute, Stonegate York.* York! Bloody hell that was forty miles away and there were a substantial number of receipts.

He looked at the first one on the pile. 8th August 1905. Received from Mr Richard Sheader item to the value of £185, paid, and his father's signature under it.

An ITEM! Worth £180. Not even a description of what this item was, and not as Terry had first thought, an item purchased by his father from this jeweller, but an item sold by his father to the jeweller.

He spread the receipts out in a fan. There were sixteen in total, the last one dated October 1913. All listed as items sold, the value of them all coming to £3200:7:8d.

That was an incredible amount of money. His head spun, what had he found? Was Jack right? His father and crewmen had dredged something up from the sea. The idea seemed bizarre. And why were the items sold not shown on the receipts from the jeweller? Why just listed as items?

He decided to conduct a search through drawers in the lounge and then the kitchen. Upstairs could wait! In the old sideboard he found odd bits of paperwork that had no bearing at all on the mystery, likewise the kitchen.

Make a cuppa! He did just that, cut a chunk off the bread and spread it thickly with the jam. Heaven! He was still not used to having decent food to eat. He was on the second slice when a knock came at the door.

The two strong looking men at the door announced they were from the town mortuary with instructions to collect a Mr Richard Sheader.

Although Terry had been expecting them at some time, indeed, willing them to come, now that moment was here he felt a great sadness. This was the final parting of any close relation, his emotions were totally confused.

He indicated where they would find his father but could not bring himself to go with them, remaining in the kitchen until his father had been brought downstairs and out of the door.

They had a struggle coming down the steep narrow steps. He had a sudden irrational fear they would drop his dad, but the task was accomplished, taking the old man out and placing him on a two wheeled hand cart.

They would use this to take the body along to Burr Bank at the end of Overton Terrace where they must have a vehicle of some sort.

Terry felt a mixture of sadness and at the same time relief. The corpse lying on the bed upstairs had really disturbed him more than he wished to say. Childhood stories of the dead and ghosts still whirled in his mind.

He sat heavily and drained the now cool tea, bit into the remains of the jam coated bread and then realised he could put off the moment no longer.

He really would have to look in the bedroom for any clues to his father's source of income. He still felt a strong feeling of discomfort at the thought, but putting off the inevitable was cowardly. He would have to do it.

He made for the stairs, started mounting them, and almost died with fright when the third stair up creaked alarmingly.

A pause, and glance at the top of the stairs to make sure no ghostly presence was waiting for him there. Heart beating loud enough to hear he stood for a moment on the small landing, then taking a deep breath, entered the room.

The room smelled musty and of death. Or was that his imagination? Moisture was rising in his eyes as he noticed the depression on the bed where his father's body had lain.

He could not remember ever actually having been in his father's bedroom before. A glance around. Once again the female touch evident. The sheets clean and flowery, certainly not his dad's choice.

The curtains were light blue with a similar flower pattern, no sign of dust or disorder. In fact totally unlike the disorder that used to reign at his digs.

A simple chest of drawers pushed against the wall under the window with a large framed mirror on a stand on top.

A pretty earthenware bowl and jug at the side, still with water in it. An uncomfortable looking straight backed chair placed in front of the drawers.

A wardrobe to the side of the bed, looking locally made from reclaimed ships timbers. He had seen these before in the fishing community, beautifully made by local craftsmen.

The floor was of pine boards lightly varnished. A couple of pegged rugs either side of the bed and one in front of the drawers.

The rugs, requiring long and patient work, yet another indication of the womanly touch. In the far corner a seaman's chest, a common sight in any seaman's house. A well executed painting of a fighting sailing ship hung on the wall opposite the window, probably the work of a local artist.

Where to start? He decided to investigate the set of drawers first.

The top drawer only revealed items of clothing, although neat and tidy. Ironed before being put away, the female touch again.

The second drawer also with clothing, but at the back of the drawer was a small polished wood box with a rather attractive inlaid lid.

He lifted the box out. It was about twelve inches long and eight or nine wide, with small brass hinges along the back. He gently opened it. The first sight on top the gold Albert watch mentioned in the will.

It was, without doubt a beautiful thing. He marvelled at the feel of it.

Next, an envelope which when opened revealed his father and mother's wedding certificate. Another item he had never before had sight of.

It showed Richard Sheader aged twenty one had married Marion Benson aged nineteen on 5th April 1881.

The venue was shown as South Cliff Methodist Church on Ramshill Road, amazingly close to where he worked now.

He had never known his mother's maiden name. She had died in childbirth when he was only five.

A small guilt framed sepia photograph wrapped in a piece of cloth was next.

It was of a pretty young girl with long fair hair, probably about seventeen or a little more. A lovely smile on her face which was most unusual for photographs in those days.

Her eyes were mesmerising, and something about the skin beneath them, identical to what he saw in the mirror made him realise this must be his mother.

He sank into the chair clutching the picture. The loss of his father, the events of the bombardment, and now a picture of his mother overwhelmed him.

The tears came uncontrollably. He was wracked with great sobs. His shoulders heaved; he felt like a little boy all over again.

A timid knock at the door brought him upright. Oh no, he thought, not now Jack.

He descended the stairs, wiping his eyes on the back of his sleeve just as the little boy would have done. He opened the door and froze in shock.

Helen Standish, blushing slightly, trembling a little. 'I know I'm the last person you want to see right now,' she said, 'but I just had to come round to see you.'

He looked hard at her. She seemed to be rather vulnerable looking. He paused a moment, then without speaking, indeed, was unable to say anything, stepped back and invited her in with a lift of the chin.

She followed him into the kitchen. Terry sat at the kitchen chair and flicked his eyes at the other one.

He could not trust himself to speak, instead waiting for her to make the first move. Her eyes were moist. It seemed she was fighting away tears. She had obviously seen his state also. A moment passed while she stood there wringing her hands, then she sank into the chair.

They both sat in silence, and then,

'I must apologise first for running from you yesterday.' She shifted uncomfortably on the hard chair. 'I was in shock and terrified.'

Her head slumped forward. 'I didn't know what to say to you. I know you don't like me Terry but I want you to know I really loved your dad.'

'I know what the gossips say about me, and I was a bit of a wrong un before your dad met me.' Her eyes lifted to meet his. 'But your dad made me feel wanted. He treated me like a real lady.' Tears were running unashamedly down her face now. 'I've never been happier in my life. I didn't want anything to spoil it.' She sniffed.

'I was always afraid when you used to visit you would turn your dad against me.'

She fished a handkerchief from her sleeve mopping up tears. His eyes also were starting to swim again.

He eventually met her eyes. It was the first time he'd really had a proper look at her. She must be about thirty five or so, but was rather pretty. Very dark hair and brown eyes with a neat little figure, almost a touch gypsy like.

He admitted to himself that it was possible to see what had attracted his father.

He managed to find his voice. The tidiness of the house and the little touches that had made it a home had impressed him more than he realised.

'I don't hate you Helen. I thought at the time you were using my father for your own ends.' He held up a hand as she made to speak.

'I was probably cross because I felt pushed out myself, but I can see you're sincere. I wish now I hadn't been perhaps so childish.'

As he said it the truth of it hit him. He had only seen the relationship in the way it affected him. Seeing a parent with someone so much younger never feels right to the child, no matter how old the child!

Tears were flooding down her cheeks now.

'Terry, will you let me come to the funeral?'

She looked really desperate sitting there. Her distress was obvious and genuine. He was crying again openly now.

'Yes, yes of course I will, how could you think any different.'

She reached across the table and placed her hand on his. It was strangely comforting. The anger he thought he would feel for this woman had evaporated. All he felt now was some comfort in the person who had been so close to his father.

He realised with some shock she would only be two or three years older than him. The hand on his was slim and brown with beautifully tapered fingers. He pulled his hand back guiltily. What was he thinking of?

The contact with this woman's hand had actually been pleasant. Once again, a feeling of guilt.

After another almost uncomfortable silence. 'I've been looking at dad's will Helen. He wanted you to have something. Had he mentioned it to you?'

She looked startled that he would mention something like that at this time.

'No, never. I didn't know your dad had such a thing. We never ever talked about things like dying.' Tears flooded her again.

'Would you like to see it?' He indicated the envelope on the table at the side of the box.

'Oh no.' She blushed slightly. 'Truth be told,' hanging her head. 'I can't read and write, never learned you see.'

She paused for a while, then as if an explanation was required.

'I had a terrible childhood. My dad always wanted a boy. I was a great disappointment. As I got older he would knock me about when he'd been drinking.'

'He always said a girl had no need of learning, just how to cook and look after a man.'

73

The words were spilling out now as though they had been bottled up for far too long.

'I was sixteen when he came home one night. I was in bed. He came in drunk, said this is how you look after a man.'

She was gazing at a spot on the wall behind him, her eyes seeing nothing, only the internal picture that she alone could see.

'He raped me,' she said simply. 'I left home two days after that.'

'My mum knew but was too frightened of him to stand up for me. I had nowhere to go, left just with the clothes I had on and a few belongings in a bag.'

This was the woman he had already judged as using his dad for her own ends.

'You don't have to tell me all this Helen.' He said gently, the distress on her face showed how difficult it was for her.

Her large moist brown eyes looked up at him. A little electric spark went down his spine, what the hell was he feeling?

'I want you to know.' Emphasise on *you*. 'I was so alone, ended up taking up with a seaman who offered me shelter, but of course, with strings attached.'

'The story of my life is a grim one. I flitted about a bit, got pregnant, had a miscarriage, even at one time thought of doing away with myself.'

She gave a little self deprecating shrug of her shoulders. 'I climbed the railings on Valley Road Bridge intending to end it all. A man ran up and grabbed me before I could do it.'

Once again her eyes bored deep into his. 'That man was your father.'

Terry had never had any inkling of how she and his father had got together, in fact had never thought of it. He had simply condemned his father for 'shacking up' with a younger woman.

'Your dad took me in, treated me with kindness and never condemned or criticised me. He became the father I never had. A friend, and yes, a lover.'

She said the last with a touch of defiance.

'He allowed me to run the house. He bought things for me. No one had ever bought me anything before,' the last said wistfully.

She slipped her hand in the neck of her dress and pulled it down slightly to reveal a gold chain with a cross. It looked chunky and expensive.

'He bought me this,' leaning forward for him to see. He also saw the tops of two brown breasts which caused him to sit up with a flush rushing to his cheeks.

'The neighbours and people who know me probably think I'm a loose woman.' She gave another shrug. 'I don't care what they think; only I know the facts.'

'My mother is a gypsy.' Ah! This confirmed what he had thought, her dark looks and brown eyes.

'It's probably she who gave me my love of sex.'

She was looking deeply at him now to see what his reaction was.

'You're shocked Terry?' Shocked! He could feel his face burning, he was sure he could light the gas mantle from it.

'I realised making love was a very pleasurable feeling. Very little of anything pleasurable ever happened to me so why shouldn't I enjoy it?'

The defiance in her voice again, even a little confrontational. His face on fire, and, Oh God! Not now, a hardening in his groin.

Change the subject, bloody hell, change the subject. A full hard on now. Why did the sodding thing always act as though it were not under his control?

His voice came out in a croak, a quick cough and clearing exercise.

'I didn't know any of this Helen. I'm sorry if you think I was one of those judging you.'

Why did her lips look so moist and parted? Get a grip lad.

'I promise what you've just told me will not be repeated to anyone.'

She shrugged again as though she didn't care.

He told her that he had been upstairs trying to find a clue to a mystery when she came to the door. Anything to change the subject. Christ! Why had he still got a hard on?

'I didn't know for instance that dad had bought this house outright for cash.'

She looked so surprised that he knew she had no idea either.

'I just can't work out how he was seemingly so flush for money.'

'I always thought he must be renting like everyone else,' she said. 'He never told me anything about money matters, although,' she sat up as though it was just coming to her. 'He never quibbled about anything I said we needed he just bought it.'

She smiled at him in a way that made his pulse increase. 'I'm not very bright with money, just never thought of questioning it.'

'Did you know about the little wooden box in his chest of drawers?'

'Oh yes, your dad had some papers in it, never looked though.' She smiled again. 'Wouldn't know what anything said anyway.' Her admission that she couldn't read or write gave the truth to that.

'Am I stopping you getting on?' She made as if to rise.

'No, no,' he stuttered quickly. He suddenly didn't want her to go.

He didn't even want to be in this house alone. 'No, I know it must have been hard for you to come round. It's cleared the air. I'm glad you came.'

'Does Jack know anything? They were close mates. Perhaps your dad let him know his affairs.'

'No, I've already asked him. He told me what the locals think but it's mainly rumour.'

'Oh! Like what they think of me then, can't beat a bit of rumour.'

She said it quite bitterly. Bearing in mind what she had so openly told him about her life he couldn't blame her.

'Where have you moved to now?'

He didn't know where she had gone when Jack had told her to move her things.

'May Allen is letting me stay in the spare room for the time being.'

Guilt flooded him again. She had made this house a real home, he had ejected her from it without a thought.

She saw his obvious discomfort. 'Don't worry Terry. I understand, I'll be alright.'

'No, it's not alright. I didn't know any of the circumstances before. You've made it your home, please come back. I'll go back to my digs.

He didn't dare mention that his digs were a blasted mess of rubble; he just wanted to put his guilt at ease with this enigmatic woman.

'There's a spare bed in the attic,' she said. 'That would be fine.'

She gave him a smile that melted him. 'Have you had anything to eat yet?' She nodded in the direction of the clock. Good gracious, surely not twelve thirty already. It seemed only a moment since breakfast with Jack and Sally.

'No, I hadn't even realised what time it was. I've not even thought about food.' She nodded at the kitchen cupboards. 'There's plenty of food in; would you like me to make a meal?'

'Oh, that sounds the best idea yet, I'd love that.'

She rose gracefully from the table. As she stretched, he caught a glimpse of her breasts pushing against the thin dress. It did nothing to solve the problem of the bulge in his trousers.

'Could you reach me the plates?' she said, pointing to the shelf at the side of the kitchen sink.

This was it! The ultimate embarrassment. How the hell could he stand in this state. His face almost burned him, he felt like a school boy caught out in a misdemeanour.

She had seen something was troubling him and raised her eyebrows in query. He gave a very Gallic shrug with both shoulders, and slowly stood, trembling slightly and hanging his head in shame.

He was unable to say a word, tears of shame on his eyelids.

She saw immediately the problem. It was difficult not to, he was a well hung man. 'Oh Terry love,' she smiled, looking him right in the eye. 'I'm very flattered. Such a result for an old lady like me.'

She said it with kindness hoping to ease his embarrassment.

'I'm so sorry Helen; I don't know what to say.' He looked so distraught her heart melted.

'Nothing to apologise for love its nature at work,' she grinned at him. 'Sit down before I molest you.'

'No one is going to molest a bloody cripple like me.' His bitterness and anger clear to see.

'Thirty two and still a virgin. That's me, must be a world record.'

The embarrassment and feeling of shame had the desired effect. His stiffness had returned to normal.

'Ever since that bloody Boer shot me people will have looked at me and said look at that poor sod.' He was feeling really sorry for himself now, all other current problems pushed into insignificance.

She walked round the table and stood before him.

'Terry love, you mustn't say that, you're a very handsome man. A gammy leg is not the be all and end all.'

She took his face in both hands and planted a kiss firmly on his lips. It was like tasting wine; his heart did a full somersault.

'And that,' she grinned, pointing at his crotch. 'Is the biggest bloody thing I've ever seen.' Still holding his face in both hands and looking straight into his eyes. 'We've both been to confessional today. Now let's concentrate on what needs doing, the plates eh?'

He laughed briefly, the tension removed. 'Yes; the plates before I make another fool of myself.'

But of one thing he was certain; he was well and truly smitten.

Using three eggs and some of the cheese she made an omelette that had his mouth full of saliva before it was on the plate, a chunk of bread and butter to mop up the remains. What Heaven!

As she washed the pan and plates he stood at her side with the tea towel.

He could feel the warmth from her closeness. He dried the last plate. She turned to him her brown eyes looking into his. 'So, what's next?'

Croaky voice again. 'I was looking through the wooden box in dad's drawer, hadn't finished it when you came round.'

She smiled at him. God! How could a woman who he had thought he disliked have this fluttery effect on him?

'I think it might be a good idea to change your dad's bed. Open the window, let some air in; then you can carry on sorting the box.'

She turned and headed for the stairs. He followed her as she ascended noticing the shape of her buttocks through the dress. Was this what was known as instant love? Or just the accumulation of a lifetimes frustrated lust?

He had no idea, an area in which he had no experience at all. He just followed her blindly.

She stripped the bed with practised ease replacing it all with fresh linen out of the bottom drawer of the chest, and then pushed the sash window up to its maximum. The sea breeze flooded in.

'That's better.' She gave him another bewitching smile. 'Do you want me to stay while you look at that,' nodding towards the box.

'Oh yes, yes of course. You might even be able to help sort the mystery.'

He didn't know if she could help at all. He just knew he didn't want this alluring creature to go, ever!

He showed her the picture of whom he was certain was his mother. She looked at it with interest. 'She's a very beautiful woman.'

'Yes,' his eyes slightly wet again. 'She was wasn't she? I never really knew her; she died when I was five in childbirth.'

She was sitting on the corner of the bed looking at him with compassion and tenderness. It was as though she were a giant magnet and he a piece of steel.

He placed the photo frame down on the drawer top; walked a little towards her.

'I....I,' he started stuttering.

'Shush,' her finger on her lips. Still sitting, she raised her right hand and placed it on his lower chest. It was as though she knew exactly what was in his mind and his great need.

Her hand slid up his chest to the top button on his shirt and then undid them one by one. The hand felt as though it were a flame travelling down his chest. She eased his shirt open, looking at his muscular body.

'Oh wow Terry, you are a fit lad.'

The bulge in his trousers that had caused so much embarrassment before was back with a vengeance and he didn't care.

Her hand was on the top of his trousers. Five buttons, dealt with one by one, and then both hands quickly sliding them down, his freed swollen member standing out like a soldier at attention.

'I was right,' she whispered. 'That is big.'

Her hand closed around it. His head was spinning; his breath coming in short stabs. And then, very gently, she started to masturbate him, looking up at him with those big brown eyes.

He didn't know such a feeling was possible. She was increasing the speed of her erotic massage; this was not going to take long!

He was jerking back and forth with her actions and then the inevitable. With an uncontrollable yell he ejaculated, the stiff rod twitching like a living animal.

He stood trembling like a man in the throes of a fever. It felt as though his legs were going to give way.

'Sit on the bed,' she commanded. He did so gladly before falling on it.

She stood and slid his shirt off then knelt and removed his trousers.

He sat, totally naked, watching her as with one fluid movement she removed her dress. No undergarments! She stood before him in absolute splendour.

Her breasts were small and firm with prominent brown areola around erect nipples. A flat belly with a delightful curly black triangle at the base of her tummy, long slim legs completing this vision.

And those mesmerising brown eyes boring into him. He was already hard again as she knew he would be.

Leaning forward, placing her hands on his shoulders she lowered her face to his and kissed him. He could feel her tongue slip between his lips, totally helpless in her control. She was stroking his chest and then slid her hand down to grasp him again.

He slid his hands onto her waist, then up to cover her magnificent breasts, the nipples hard against his palms.

He was shivering uncontrollably. Her hand guided his to those delicious black curls. He quivered as he felt the mounds either side, slipping his fingers into her. He was living in Aladdin's cave. Treasures and magic he had never known before, experiences he thought a 'cripple' like he would never ever know.

She pushed him gently down on the bed; lying at the side of him, fingers caressing his chest, belly, and the now huge throbbing member.

With a swift movement she rolled him onto her, legs wide and inviting. He was gasping like a man who had run a marathon.

With her left hand guiding his erection she placed his swollen head at the entrance to her moist cave, and with no further guidance necessary he was sliding in with shudders of ecstasy.

'Slowly, slowly my darling,' she murmured, slowing down his urgent thrusts. 'Take it gently.'

It took immense effort to 'go slowly' but he did as she said. And then, with both hands grasping his firm muscular buttocks and said with urgency. 'Now, fuck me, fuck me.'

The sudden coarse command drove him to frenzy. He thrust and plunged like a man possessed, the pair of then groaning and squealing like a couple of animals.

The mightiest orgasm wracked him and he drove deep and held himself rigid against her. She was digging her nails into his buttocks and holding him tightly to her, legs wrapped firmly around him.

It seemed ages that they remained locked together like that before he subsided onto her, kissing her eyelids, nose, mouth. Great feelings of love, warmth, tenderness. Emotions the like of which were alien prior to this amazing moment.

She smiled up at him, those big brown eyes moist with tears. 'You're a good pupil Terry Sheader,' said with kindness and a touch of humour.

He rolled to her side lying there holding her hand. 'I never thought I would experience anything like that,' he murmured. 'I always thought this leg would destroy any chance of any sort of relationship.'

She rolled onto her side and looked at his left leg. It was clear that the bone below his knee had been badly broken, and the flesh around it was slightly withered and purple. She placed her hand gently onto it and stroked him. 'It didn't stop you performing my love did it?'

Placing a finger on his lips as he made to speak. 'You have a beautiful body my darling, and this fella,' touching his now deflated member. 'This fella is magnificent.'

He lay back fully on the bed still holding her hand.

'I don't want this moment to go. I wish I could freeze it in time,' said wistfully. 'Do you know what the worst thing has been for me all my life? The sheer loneliness of it.' Stating what all single and lonely people could empathise with.

'Coming home after work to a house that is empty and lifeless. No one to welcome you home, knowing that the last person to touch anything was yourself.' He locked eyes with her. 'No female touch to make a house a home. No one to talk to, and even worse, when the urge is great, nothing but a furtive wank to relieve it.'

He could be as direct as her. 'The thought of going back to a life like that terrifies me,' he said simply.

'Helen,' gripping her hand tightly. 'Will you stay here please?' The please imploringly said.

'If I did the tongues would wag like sails in the wind,' she replied. 'Could you cope with that?

'The locals already think I'm the loose slag of the town.'

'I don't care. I'm used to coping with what other people say. Let the first man cast a stone etc. If you could cope with them Helen then stuff em.'

She thought about it while running her fingers through the hairs on his chest. She was a very physical creature and used to having to get from life whatever she could. This naïve and unworldly man attracted her in so many ways.

The leg apart, he had a beautiful body. And the biggest, most virile cock she had ever encountered. It was an important part of her life as she so readily admitted.

She also, and this took her by surprise, felt a great tenderness for him. His simple naivety and trust in her appealed. He did not treat her like the 'Bottom End slag' that the locals did. He really desired her company, treated her in fact like his father before did. Perhaps this was a family trait?

He was on his side now facing her. He couldn't resist gently caressing her left breast, the feel of her flesh a constant excitement.

She looked into his trusting face. 'All right, but one day at a time eh? Let's see where it takes us.'

A great and overwhelming feeling of ecstasy overtook him. He grasped her in a huge bear hug, his obvious delight making her smile. Her closeness making him begin to swell again also.

'Down boy,' she laughed. 'We have some sorting to do don't we?'

'I'd love you to stop like that all day,' he replied lustfully.

She rolled off the bed and slipped her dress back on.

'Come on big boy,' holding out her hand. 'Get dressed.'

They wandered downstairs to make a large pot of tea, refreshment was definitely needed. While she poured boiling water onto the leaves in the pot he told her about the weird sales his father had made in York and the large sums of money involved.

She seemed amazed at what he said. 'But your dad did go to York now and again, he went on the train.' This in itself an event. You needed money to take a train ride.

'He has some posh clothes in the wardrobe as well. He always dressed up when going to York.'

His father with 'posh' clothes! An ex seaman. He raised his eyebrows at that bit of information. The mystery deepened.

She poured a mug of tea for them both, then fished in the cupboard under the sink and retrieved a piece of waste cloth. She soaked it in water, wrung it out and then said. 'Come on, bring your tea with you,' and headed back up the stairs.

He wondered what the cloth was for; then saw to his horror, on the pine floorboard at the side of the bed a thick streak of white semen. The result of his first pent up ejaculation.

His face flushed with embarrassment as she bent to wipe it up, she laughing at the schoolboy look on his face,

'Oh my darling,' giggling. 'Look at that. A better shot than those big guns on the Hun battleships eh?'

She tossed the cloth onto the pile of bedding she had removed earlier. 'Let's look what else is in this box shall we?'

They sat side by side on the bed, the only comfortable seat in the room, Terry with the box on his knees.

He retrieved the next item, a rather crumpled dirty envelope. In it, his mother's birth certificate.

Marion Benson, born January 4th 1862. Father David James Benson, mother Marie Benson. Christened at South Cliff Methodist Church on 10th January. So that is why they were married there!

There was only one other item in the box, a small square of paper with 17 right, 13 in, written on it in pencil.

What the devil did that mean? Was it some sort of measurement or instruction? It was probably his father's hand writing, although he hadn't seen enough of that to be sure.

Helen looked equally blank. He returned all items to the box, stood up and put it back in the drawer.

The next drawer down was the one Helen had drawn the fresh linen from, nothing else in there. The bottom and final drawer had some old bills, paid in full! It contained a couple of old newspapers. Why had he kept them?

At the back of the drawer a large cloth bag, heavy to pull out, and then, the greatest shock of the day.

He tipped the contents of the bag onto the bed. It was full of sovereigns and half sovereigns plus a number of half crowns and florins.

They both stared in amazement. 'Had you any idea these were here?' to Helen. Her face told him the answer. 'No, not a clue. But as I told you, he always had money for anything that was needed.'

He counted the coins. £102 and 5 shillings in total. Where oh where had his father acquired cash like this?

'I always saw to the clean bed linen and such,' she said. 'He never said don't look in the drawers or anything of that sort.'

'I knew he had some old newspapers and bills in there, but,' she shrugged. 'As I told you, can't read so of no interest to me.'

The last comment made with a touch of shame.

'Let's have a look at these posh clothes,' opening the wardrobe door. Again, startled to see among everyday fare, a dark blue striped suit. A couple of very expensive looking shirts and on the shelf across the top a bowler hat of all things!

In the bottom of the wardrobe a pair of good leather shoes, polished to a shining black and sitting at the side of three pairs of clogs. Typical wear for the local folk.

'Well, this cash will be of great use for our immediate needs. I think at some time I'll have to make a trip to York and seek out this jeweller. Perhaps he could throw some light on matters.'

The old clock in the kitchen chimed five. Wow! Where was time going today?

'I think I'd better get my things from May's house before doing anything else.' She smiled sardonically. 'That should get the tongues wagging.'

'Won't be long.' She left and immediately he felt the absence, a sudden irrational thought. She will come back wont she?

Helen climbed the steep steps up to Princess Street and made her way to May Allan's house. Tapping on the door she looked around to see if anyone else was watching; it seemed pretty quiet.

May opened the door. 'May, thanks for everything. Terry has kindly said I may stay in the attic bedroom until things are sorted out.'

'Oh, that's good of him. That sorts Christmas out for you then.'

Christmas! She hadn't even though of that.

The look on May's face showed the sails were full of wind already. As soon as she departed May's house, May would be spreading the gossip with glee. Such excitement in two days. She would hardly be able to contain herself.

May helped to get her belongings together in record time. The urge to spread the tale was already pulling at her.

A large canvas holdall held all. Rather sad that her entire life could be contained in such a little space.

As Helen descended the steps back to Overton Terrace May was already exiting the front door. Arriving back, the door opened before she touched it. Terry had obviously been looking for her. She was crushed in a huge bear hug.

'Oh God that's good. I had an awful feeling that you might not come back.'

His obvious delight, worn so plainly on his sleeve, warmed her more than she realised.

'Shall I take this up to the attic?' looking at him quizzically.

'Only if that's what you really want.' The disappointment plain on his face. He had a face that was so open and guileless she had to smile.

'What do you want?'

Her large brown eyes burning him; a laugh, slightly nervous. 'What I want is you by my side all the time, preferably naked.'

She laughed with him. 'As said before, one day at a time.'

They had a dinner of fried cod followed by a slice of fruit cake which she produced from the wall cupboard, delicious.

After the meal, she said. 'Now we need a plan of action.' For one who professed to have no formal education she was doing a good job of taking charge.

He nodded. 'Yes, perhaps first I'll have to ask Mrs Kessler if it's alright for me to have some time off to sort dad's affairs.'

He laughed and told her about Mrs Kessler peeping at him when he was working.

'I think she likes to see me shirtless digging in the garden.'

'You work without your shirt on?'

'Well, its dammed hot work. She has me completely transforming the garden including digging out a huge pond, although,' another laugh. 'The Hun has helped me dig that.'

She eyed his muscular torso and neat waist. 'No wonder she spies on you, God! The old bird must be drooling.'

She asked him what he meant when he said the Hun had dug the pond for him. 'Dropped a shell right where the pond is intended to be,' he laughed. 'Almost got me too.' He told her of Mrs Kessler's first aid and the way she touched him. Helen had noticed the red scratches on his shoulder. It was not much, but must have bled somewhat.

'I hope she never saw you with that bloody bulge in your pants,' she laughed. 'No, only you create that,' looking at her longingly.

They drank some tea in companiable silence, then. 'Yes, that's what I'll do first, see the old bat, then we need to sort through the house starting in the attic and working down. See if any more clues await us.'

'And we need to get in touch with a funeral director,' she murmured softly.

God! How could that have slipped his mind?

'Yes,' His head in his hands. 'We'll do that first thing in the morning.'

So much to do. His head still swimming with all that had taken place in a matter of two days. It seemed an eternity.

'I wonder if Jack might know anything about that scrap of paper.'

'Only thing to do is ask him,' she replied. 'And,' looking at him in her intense way. 'You need to tell him I'm staying here.'

'Oh hell! How to broach that without the old boy blowing up. Perhaps he aught to go round now and tell him and Sally. They'd been so kind, he should make a clean breast of it.

'Think I should do that now?'

'The sooner the better love, one less thing to worry about.'

He was already asking her for advice but she was right. Taking his courage in both hands he went next door. Jack answered at his knock.

'I thought I should let you know Jack. I felt guilty about Helen. I've told her she can stay in the attic room until all is sorted.' It sounded lame even as he said it, and his rapidly rising colour didn't help.

'The attic ye say?' The old boy's eyes twinkled, a tiny smile hovering on his face. 'Very civil of ye lad.' He turned to go in, then. 'I'll not be hearing any bangin on't wall then?

'Err, no.' Face red and the stutter back.

'I'll wish yea a very good night then lad.' He heard a chuckle as the old man went inside.

Well I bloody handled that well he thought crossly.

Helen had a fit of the giggles when he told her what Jack's reaction was.

'No pulling the wool over his eyes,' another giggle, and then looking at him with deep smouldering eyes. 'And just where are we sleeping tonight?'

He looked at her so longingly she hadn't the heart to tease him any more.

'It can get cold at night. Perhaps we should snuggle up together, just for the warmth.' She grinned as his face lit up.

'I see your friend thinks he's invited to bed too,' giving a lewd look at his crotch.

'He has a mind of his own. I never said a word to him,' he grinned.

He found he was much more at ease with her now, could exchange banter just like she did. Perhaps some of it was rubbing off?

He looked at the clock, ten fifteen. 'It's time all good people were in bed.' He said it lightly, but excitement ran through him like an electric charge. 'Hope you picked up your nighty.'

'Nighty, Never wear one of those.' Her eyes sparkling like lights. She put the kettle on for hot water for a wash, filling the huge jug.

'There master, carry that aloft.'

He did just that, drawing the pretty blue curtains and lighting the single gas mantle.

It gave a soft warm glow casting their shadows on the wall.

The large bowl on the chest of drawers in the bedroom was filled, cold water being added from the jug already there. Then she performed the same lithe movement as earlier, disrobing with no hint of embarrassment in front of him.

He looked at the beautiful brown body as she washed herself down as though completely unaware of his presence. And then after drying herself, turned to him. 'Now your turn.'

He disrobed in a trice washing himself down as she stood behind him looking at his firm buttocks with admiration.

He dried, and then a firm command. 'Turn round,' her voice breathy in his ear.

He did as told. His 'friend,' like all good soldiers in the presence of authority, standing rigidly to attention.

90

She placed both hands in the bowl and worked up lather from the block of green soap, and then proceeded to apply the lather to the soldier sliding both hands up and down.

Her fingers worked soap on his velvety helmet; drawing the skin back firmly to do so.

'Oh God Helen, I'll come in no time if you carry on like that,' shudders running through him. 'Helen, oh Helen, Heleeeeen.'

Once again a huge spurt of semen. She kissed him firmly and then wrapped the towel around soldier to dry him.

'Come on my man, bed time.'

She had called him 'my man.' It could just be the way this fascinating girl spoke, but it sent a thrill of pleasure through Terry.

Feeling wanted was something he could never recall from anyone at any time, it was a feeling he was loath to loose.

In bed she teased him back to hardness, stroking and caressing, kissing him passionately. She showed him how to proceed less frantically, delaying his entry, and then teaching him to pace himself. She drew out the inevitable climax to a great shuddering explosion that wracked them both.

Jack, standing on the doorstep next door having one last pipe full of aromatic smelling tobacco, thick blue smoke rising as he sucked on the briar, rolled his eyes up to the still wide open bedroom window next door.

The gasps and cries floating from it self explanatory. A deep grin spread on his weathered face. 'Oh fer days like that agin,' smiling as he finished his pipe, knocking it out on the wall. 'Attic be buggered.' He turned and went in for the night.

The two lovers, the experienced and the inexperienced, slept like logs, curled up in each others arms. Tomorrow was a good night's sleep away and for our hero, well, he was floating in dreamless bliss.

***

.

# CHAPTER SIX

## Two as one

The morning of Thursday the 17th December was dry but overcast.

A battalion of the Leeds Rifles had arrived in Scarborough from York Barracks, steaming into Scarborough railway station.

Their instructions to keep order in the town; and to help resist any enemy attempt at a landing. This latter was not believed by anyone in authority, it was put about simply to reassure a nervous population, although the tough Yorkshire spirit of the majority of Scarborough folk was quickly getting back to normal.

A huge clearing up operation was starting, neighbours helping neighbours. Community spirit coming to the fore.

Condolence messages were arriving for the Mayor from the King and the First Sea Lord, Mr Churchill. International condemnation of the Germans for an attack on an unarmed seaside town.

The Germans claimed the wireless station made it an official target.

The controversy was to rage for a long time.

*

All this passed Terry Sheader by on that morning. He woke feeling like the cat that had got the cream. This beautiful creature at his side still asleep, long eyelashes and dark hair spread out on the pillow. He pinched himself to make sure he was not dreaming.

He slipped out of bed quietly, pulled his trousers on, and then went downstairs to put the kettle on.

He poured boiling water into the pot, cutting two slices of bread and buttering them. A coating of jam, tea poured into two mugs, and then balancing all on the piece of board that served as a tray. He carried them carefully back up to the bedroom, the badly creaking third stair waking Helen.

She gave him a radiant smile as he entered the room his pulse quickening with delight. Could he ever get used to this?

'Breakfast my lady,' giving a mock bow. 'Would madam like me to leave while she dresses? Not that he will,' he grinned evilly.

'You're a naughty boy Terry Sheader.' She slipped the covers down stretching seductively, taking in his gorgeous muscular torso. He with eyes popping at the vision of beauty before him.

She sat up, her breasts standing out firm, grinning at his salacious looks. Swinging her legs out of bed he caught a glimpse of the triangle of black curly hair. 'Let me get dressed you randy devil, we've much to do today.'

They sat on the edge of the bed to eat and drink, she dictating the running again, he quite happy for her to do so.

'I'll need to stock up on provisions, and,' a look at him as she said it. 'face up to any locals who make comments.'

'You need to get up to the Kessler's to explain the situation and then we can start our search for clues.'

Plan of action agreed he took his leave of her.

'I'll call at Victoria Road on the way; see if Mr Reevers has turned up.'

He kissed her passionately. 'We make a good team.' She smiled. 'Yes, a good team my love.'

He set off; she collected a straw bag and opened the door to go to the town market, just as Jack was coming out of his door. Their eyes met.

'Morning lass, shopping for two are we?'

He looked intently at her. 'Yes Jack, shopping for two.' She looked back at the old sea dog determined to stand her ground.

'No judgements from me lass, but just one thing. I have a fondness for the lad, don't hurt him.'

'I won't hurt him Jack; that I promise.' and then giving him a cheeky look. 'But I might just exhaust him.'

He gave a loud guffaw. 'Aye, I think tha's made a good start on that lass,' raising his eyebrows and looking pointedly up at the bedroom window.

She was the one who blushed brightly this time taking in the still wide open window; she shrugged her shoulders. 'Well, he's a bonny lad.'

'Aye, he is that.' The old man gave her a smile and turned down the street.

That could have been worse. She smiled ruefully, as she had said to Terry; Jack was no fool. Slipping the bag over her arm she set off to shop.

Terry retraced the route to Victoria Road once again. This time people were moving around as though they had a purpose in life. Glass being swept up. Girls already chatting to the soldiers at the bottom of Eastborough.

Victoria Road was one that had suffered most. Hardly a shop window on that street had escaped. The blast of lead balls from the shrapnel shells playing havoc with glass. He dreaded to think how many people would have been killed or injured if had been later in the day when more people would have been on the streets.

On arrival at Mr Reever's shop it was clear nothing had changed. No sign of life. He entered as before and made his way upstairs, wary of seeing the dreadful Mrs Tanner's head popping round the door at the top of the stairs.

His room was exactly as left. Bob's room had been stripped. Obviously Mrs Tanner had moved to her sister's with great speed.

He wondered if her sister would really be pleased to see them both move in.

He went down and tried the door to Mr Reevers' living quarters. The door was not locked, all the furniture etc was still in place, but of Mr Reevers there was no sign.

As he made to leave he almost bumped into a burly figure in blue uniform standing at the doorway.

'Nah then lad, what's your business here?' the constable asked, looking at him suspiciously. Terry explained that he lodged here, that he was now living at his father's house but he was unable to find Mr Reevers to settle his bill.

The policeman seemed satisfied with that. 'Oh, right lad, ah can tell thee a few are looking for yon fella. It seems he owes a lot O money.' He winked at Terry. 'Reckon he's done a runner.'

Terry knew that Reevers' shop had not been doing very well. A factor he would moan about whenever Terry mentioned any work that needed doing.

Perhaps he had indeed used the German attack as an excuse to disappear.

Well at least I tried he thought, and set off for the Kessler's.

On arrival, he was amazed to see Mrs Kessler herself rush to the door on seeing it was him. 'Oh my dear, we have been so worried. What news? What news? My husband's on his way, he was told by telephone.'

A jumble of words, all spilling out, and the reference once again to the fact they had a telephone.

Then, standing close to him, he hadn't even had chance to speak yet, and placing her hand on his shoulder. 'And your shoulder my dear, is it alright?'

She paused for breath.

'It's absolutely fine thank you. A scratch that bled a little but I have some very distressing news.'

She looked expectantly at him, Jane hovering in the background.

He drew a deep breath. 'My father is dead. I have a lot to sort out and I hoped you might allow me a little time off to attend to things?'

'Oh my dear how dreadful, those dammed Germans. Of course you can, take whatever time you need. I'm here if you need any help.'

The offer of help came out hot and breathless. He had no intention of letting her know his father's death had nothing to do with the Germans.

'I'll clear things away in the garden first. Leave it tidy, please give my regards to Mr Kessler.'

Her face clouded slightly at Mr Kessler's name. 'Of course. I hope all goes well for you.' She gave him a longing look and then went back inside.

'I'm so sorry about your dad Mr Sheader,' little Jane moving forward.

'Thanks Jane. I'm sure I'll be back soon.'

He went into the garden. It seemed such a long time ago when he had left. He cleared the few tools into the small shed and then frowned as he took in the hole where the shell had landed. He'd seen many shells land when in the army, this hole just didn't seem right for an exploding shell of large calibre. It looked more like the depression a heavy falling boulder might make.

He looked into it, but no sign of any object. He tried to remember the incident. He remembered hearing a huge thud, not an explosion, or had the explosion affected his hearing?

The impact had been enough to throw considerable amounts of soil about. It was probably soil or a stone that had struck him.

Another mystery; too much to do to worry about this, he took his leave of Jane. She gave him a shy little smile and said she hoped he would soon be back.

\*

He suddenly seemed to be very popular. He started off walking slowly, conscious that his leg was throbbing now, various thoughts flitting through his mind.

His mind inevitably flitted to the sheer ecstasy he had enjoyed with Helen. Warm and erotic thoughts, then, like a bolt from the blue! Had his father had an experience like that just before collapsing?

Oh God, his father! His bloody father had done what he had. The thought filled him with repugnance. This was his father's girl. He was taking over his father's girl. Taking over? No, falling in love with. Yes, it hit him hard, he was in love with her.

He stopped and sat on the edge of a horse trough. His legs felt suddenly weak, feeling breathless. Was she using him to continue the lifestyle she had made? Was he a convenient extension of his father now he was no longer here?

She had been frank about her childhood and how she had to do whatever it took to survive.

Doubts and frightening thoughts filled him, he was suddenly so confused.

'You all right mate?'

A man stood looking at him with concern. He realised tears were running down his face. 'Yes, yes, just had some bad news after - you know what.'

The first thing that had come into his head; the man looked at him with sympathy. 'Aye, bad do all round, but we'll whip the buggers in the end.'

He nodded and raised his hand to the man. The man looked at him again to convince himself this chap was indeed alright, and then went with a sympathetic nod.

He had to get back. He just had to get back. Would she be there? Would she have had trouble with neighbours? Were they even now laughing at him? Oh Helen, Helen, Helen.

He set off again in a stumbling run cursing the aching leg. Could she really ignore the leg. Was she just saying that? Run, run, must get back.

It was an exhausted, confused and terrified man who arrived back at Overton Terrace that morning, sweat dripping from his face, hair askew, wild eyed.

The door to the house was shut. Oh God no; she's gone, she's left me. He turned the knob and almost fell in as it opened.

Helen looked up with a start as the door burst open and a wild eyed and sobbing Terry burst in.

She rushed to him. 'What is it love? What is it?'

He saw her standing before him through a veil of tears. He sagged to his knees clutching her legs, great wracking sobs shaking him.

'Don't leave me Helen, don't leave me.'

She pressed his head into her belly, stroking his hair.

'Terry, Terry my darling, what's brought this on? I'm not leaving you. I'm here, here for you. Oh my darling, shush, shush.'

He felt almost faint, breathing starting to return to normal. She continued to stroke his hair brushing her lips against his forehead. He felt the warmth of her up against his face, her smell, her everything. He wanted to draw her into him, meld her into his very being.

He started to calm, beginning to feel foolish. He looked up at her with tear streaked face. 'It was awful. I was wracked with doubt. I had awful thoughts, can't even tell you about them,' shaking his head.

'Thought you would have gone when I got back. So confused, so confused, I love you so much.' There, he had said it.

She took his face in both hands, smothering his face with kisses.

'Oh you silly boy,' said kindly and with affection. 'I'll always be here for you while you want me.' She lifted his face further and kissed him passionately on the lips. 'My lovely boy, come,' she drew him to his feet and led him into the little lounge.

He allowed her to manoeuvre him just like the little boy she had called him. He was totally hers to command.

She sat him in the wicker settee sitting at his side. She undid the top three buttons on her dress exposing her left breast.

She drew his lips to it, allowing him to suckle like a child, all the while stroking his hair and whispering. 'Darling, darling', rocking slightly back and forth.

She felt a huge flood of warmth for this beautiful man child, feeling instinctively his distress. It brought out all the motherly feelings in her.

He felt tremendously comforted. All the panic and doubts faded as she caressed and held him. For the first time in his life he had someone who said they cared for him. The first time in thirty two years. So much catching up to be done. He couldn't lose this, the thought of losing it was what had terrified him.

Her nipple was hard in his mouth and instead of immediate eroticism he really felt like a child being comforted.

After a while he drew back, feeling embarrassed and ashamed for such a show. He started to apologise. 'Shush, shush my darling. Nothing to apologise for, shush.'

She smiled at him. 'Jack collared me this morning. We left the bedroom window open my love, he certainly knew I wasn't in the attic.'

She laughed. 'But the nice thing was he made me promise not to hurt you.'

She took his face in both hands again, those mesmerising eyes looking straight into his. 'And I promise you my darling. I will never cause you any hurt.'

His eyes flooded with tears again.

She chuckled. 'But I did tell him I might exhaust you.'

He looked up at her with big puppy dog eyes. Her heart melted. What was going through this poor lad's mind to get him in such a state?

'I was so frightened Helen. It was as though I was having a brain storm.'

'Shush, shush, it's alright darling.'

'I thought terrible things,' he continued shame faced. 'I had visions of you and dad together. You know, together,' he looked bereft. 'It's a terrible feeling. I felt confused, jealous and frightened you might leave me. Oh! I just don't know how to explain.'

She drew him closer to her, her dress top still gaping open. She pulled his head down until his cheek was resting against the warm brown flesh.

'Now my love, listen to me. I've told you about my life, how I had to live on my wits just to survive. Your father was the only other person I've ever told.'

She continued stroking his hair. 'If it hadn't been for him I would have killed myself that day.' Her eyes took on a far away look. 'He became the father I never had. He comforted me when I was so depressed and suicidal. He was totally non-judgemental of me, a friend I could spill all my worst fears to. He deserved comfort in return.'

'But,' and she looked deep into his eyes. 'It wasn't like the experience we have now. I would never have known you, known you for the lovely person you are if events had been different. Tragedy has drawn us together,' kissing him gently now. 'I promise you I'll never go behind your back or be insincere. You'll always be the first to know my thoughts and troubles and I want you to be the same with me.'

A deep well of contentment and warmth swept through him. How could he have entertained such thoughts? He pressed his head against her breast.

'And,' she continued, giving him a lecherous look. 'You know the saying that children are always bigger than their parents,' she grinned evilly at him, reaching down and stroking his crotch. 'Well, lover, you have proved that point.'

And then, before he started to get excited again. 'But you haven't asked me yet how my morning has gone.'

Oh! He sat up straight.

'Oh, I'm sorry, so full of my own stupidity, how could I be so selfish? You didn't have trouble with anyone did you?' he asked anxiously.

*

'Not trouble as such. Some dirty looks from the usual people, women mostly. They have always been the first to gossip when they really know nothing of the facts.'

She sighed. 'Story of my life really, the slag of Scarborough.'

She said it bitterly; it was his turn to comfort her.

'The good thing about that is you're my slag,' kissing her passionately. 'If anyone has anything to say let them say it to me.'

'And, before telling me any more,' pointing at her dress. 'Button that up before you get into trouble of a different kind.'

She laughed out loud, all tension finally evaporating.

'Well, you'll be pleased to know master,' grinning cheekily now. 'That we are fully provisioned, and I have been to see Masterton's, the funeral directors.'

She picked up a folded piece of paper from the table. She opened it. He saw 'Geo Masterton' on the heading.

Helen gave it him to read. Once again, this had been pushed to the back of his mind. A list of prices, £7:17s for a single pine coffin with a one horse drawn hearse, the prices going up then with quality and number of carriages required.

How many people would attend his father's funeral? Jack and Sally certainly, perhaps the immediate neighbours. Himself and Helen. Possibly two carriages would be enough, a better oak coffin? He did a quick bit of mental arithmetic. The total would be £19:10s.

They would have no trouble covering that from the bag of cash, one of his big worries removed. He heaved a sigh of relief. They'd started to make progress, or, more to the point, Helen had.

He looked at her. 'You see, I can't do without you.'

She smiled at him. 'And, look at this.' She went to the little gas oven, threw the door open, and inside he saw a delicious looking pie with a crisp brown crust.

'Meat and potato pie,' she declared. 'Big enough for a hungry man. Of course if you don't like it you won't want to keep me will you?'

She thrust her breasts out provocatively at him as she said it an impish grin on her face. He stuck his tongue out at her.

'I could eat those,' laughing.

'Right my man, plates and cutlery while I get it ready,' looking over her shoulder at him. 'You can reach the plates with no embarrassment this time?'

'Can't guarantee it,' grinning. The happy repartee lifting his gloom completely. How lucky he was finding this enticing creature.

The pie, accompanied with carrots, cabbage and thick gravy, disappeared with no effort. A fresh fruit salad and cream to follow.

He sat back, tummy full, contentment on his face. 'I think I'll keep you.'

She gave a little mock curtsy. 'Thank you, oh master.'

They cleared away and washed the pots like a couple joined at the hip.

'We're both working as one,' he murmured in her ear.

'That sounds good,' she replied. 'I could get used to us both as one.'

'Lets go and practice being one, I've so much to learn.' He took her hand and led her to the stairs.

She laughed, 'only if I can be teacher; and you the pupil.'

He pulled her to him, kissing those sweet parted lips. 'Lead on teacher.'

*** 

103

# CHAPTER SEVEN

## A touch of domestic bliss

The following morning, Terry, happy and sated, prepared breakfast once more in the kitchen. Helen had bought bacon and eggs, bread, butter. An abundance of food which left him feeling like a rich man.

This sort of fare he had never been witness to for years. In fact the last time he had tasted bacon was with his father years ago before their drift apart.

He placed strips of bacon in the frying pan, a dollop of lard, and got cracking.

Cutting some bread as thinly as the rather blunt bread knife would allow, buttering it; keeping an eye on the pan as he filled the kettle.

To say he'd never had any practice, he managed to produce bacon and eggs, bread, and a couple of mugs of tea without any catastrophe.

He carried his creation aloft proudly, all balanced on the board which served as a tray, pushing the door open with his foot, placing all on the chest of drawers.

'Wakey, wakey sleepy head,' he said, planting a kiss on the head buried under the sheet. Two dreamy brown eyes fluttered open.

A warm smile that touched him as always. 'Come on breakfast is ready.'

He pulled the bedclothes back, grinning lustfully as her superb naked breasts were exposed. Would he ever get used to such beauty?

She slid out of bed, sniffing the tempting aroma. 'You've actually cooked a breakfast without disaster?' She was tormenting him. 'Wow, a really useful man. They're in short supply you know.'

'I wish I were a sculptor or famous painter. I would love to do you.'

'I thought you'd already done me.' The banter, even the fact someone was there to talk to, so rare for him before, was like manna from Heaven.

He couldn't imagine ever going back to his previous life. How had he missed out on this for so long?

They sat on the bed side by side eating bacon and eggs, the board balanced across both their knees, she still stark naked. 'It's a wonder soldier doesn't push this tray up and onto the floor.'

She giggled through a mouthful. 'Save that energy lover, we've work to do today.'

It was ten before they finally were dressed and ready for the big search.

The attic was the obvious place to start. Terry looking at the tiny single bed there, the dusty and very plain surroundings.

'Crikey, this would have been awful if you had really stopped here; basic doesn't even begin to describe this.'

It was obvious that it was never used. The bare floorboards, pine by the look of them, the tiny single bed, and a two drawer set pushed tightly under the eaves.

'Not much to search by the look of it.' Helen looking round the room. 'No hiding places in here.'

The two drawers were completely empty. Nothing under the bed, the floorboards creaked alarmingly.

'Not much point looking any further here,' Terry said. He went over to the window and looked out.

The magnificent sweep of coast up to Flamborough, a superb view by any standards. He turned to go, stepping forward about two paces. The loose floorboard under his foot creaked, and then as he put his full weight on the edge of it a section about three foot long shot up and cracked his left leg, the damaged one.

He let out a yell of pain. The wood had hit him just below the knee, the worst area possible. The pain was indescribable and he sat on the floor with a thump.

Helen rushed to him in alarm. 'Oh God darling, how bad is it? Can I do anything?' Her concern was certainly a great help. In the past, when he caught the dammed leg he had to suffer alone.

He was rubbing it ruefully. 'No, it'll ease in a while. I'm used to it. Bloody typical that it would be that leg though.'

Helen was looking at the cavity exposed under the loose board. 'There's something in there.'

He swivelled on his bottom to look. Sure enough; in the cavity was a small cloth wrapped parcel.

She bent to retrieve it. The material looked like oilskin.

'Can you get up darling?

'Yes, it's just dammed painful.' He got to his feet, staggering a moment. 'Lets see what it is.'

She carefully un-wrapped the parcel. Contained inside it was a pristine blue bank book with the words. 'Williams and Deacons Bank' on it.

Terry's eyebrows shot up. His dad with a bank book? And hidden under floorboards.

She handed it to him. 'Reader needed,' she said simply.

He took it from her and opened the front cover. Inside were shown a number of deposits over a period from 1905 onwards. No withdrawals, and the balance, the bloody balance! Was £2700:8:4d.

He stood stunned, the pain in his leg forgotten. 'Oh my God Helen. I can't believe this, there's £2700 in this account.

She looked as startled as him. 'It's a fortune',' she whispered. 'An absolute fortune.'

'Come on, I need a drink.' He turned and limped to the stairs, Helen following in stunned silence. They proceeded to the kitchen, Helen putting the kettle on.

He sat at the kitchen table and threw the book on it.

'You know what this means?' He said sadly. 'I wondered when we found all that cash, but this confirms it for me. Dad must have been into something crooked. No ex fisherman can accumulate this sort of money legally.'

She didn't know what to say to him. In fact, that seemed the most likely scenario to her too. However, with the struggle to even exist which had been Helen's life prior to Richard Sheader rescuing her, it seemed an opportunity not to be lost. Her scruples she could overcome for that amount of money.

'It is in your dad's name?' she queried hesitantly.

'Yes, Richard Sheader, no doubt about that.'

'And all is left to you in his will?'

'Yes, but do I want the proceeds of crime?'

They sat in silence, he didn't know what to think. How could he mention this to anyone? Did he want his dad's name dragged into disrepute now he was dead?

'What do we do Helen? What the hell do we do?'

She, as ever, the practical one.

'I think the first thing you need to do is go to the will solicitors but you can't do that until we get a death certificate.'

'In the meantime, keep silent. We don't know what we're dealing with here.'

As ever, good sound advice. Why couldn't he think clearly and logically like this?

A knock at the door startling both of them. Helen answered it. Jack!

'Come in.'

She needn't have said that because he was in as soon as the door was open.

Terry casually slid a plate over the book on the table.

'I've brought yea latest paper,' he started, putting the Scarborough Mercury on the table. 'All't latest news abaht attack.'

He looked shrewdly at them both. 'Owt to tell me?'

'Bloody hell Jack, you don't beat about the bush.'

Terry straightened his leg, wincing, Jack spotting it straight away. 'Having trouble wi it lad?'

'He had a fall coming down the attic steps,' piped up Helen.

A huge guffaw came from Jack. 'Attic steps! Attic steps! Bollocks.'

Typical old seadog, never call a spade anything other than a spade. Even Terry had to laugh. 'Yes, alright you old bugger. Helen and I are going to make a go of it, but I really did hurt my leg in the attic,' holding his hand up as Jack made to speak. 'We were looking for clues to that mystery that I mentioned to you. Thought it would be a good idea to start at the top and work down.'

The old dog leered at him, looked at Helen, and then said.

'Aye, I'll bet tha started at top and worked down.'

He sat back.

'Alright you two, jokin done, am right glad for't pair O yea.

Did yea find owt on't search then?'

'No, nothing so far,' Terry deciding, as Helen advised, to say 'nowt' as Jack would say.

'But we have something that dad left for you.' He made to get up, but Helen beat him to it.

'Sit and rest that leg, I'll fetch it.'

'That your dad left fer me?' asked Jack in surprise.

'Yes, he left a will and wanted you to have a watch.'

Helen returned with the Albert pocket watch and handed it to the old man.

He held it in his hand looking at it in amazement. For all his perceived toughness his eyes glistened.

'It's beautiful, av never seen owt like it,' he whispered. It was clear he was touched, 'Well, I never.' For once, the old boy was without words.

'What's next then?' he asked.

'Well, we're stuck until the PM lets the doctor issue a death certificate. Once we have that we can plan the funeral.'

'Aye, reckon it might be a while. People killed int attack, and all t'other normal deaths,' he nodded his head wisely. 'Right, I'll leave ye two,' a big grin. 'Have a good night, and shut yon window or gag her lad,' the last said with a great guffaw. He took his leave, still chuckling.

'Cheeky old sod,' said Helen. 'Gag me eh, that's bondage.'

A look at Terry. 'We haven't been there yet have we?' She laughed.

Terry couldn't help laughing either. 'You my girl will be the death of me.'

The clock chimed twelve. 'Can you manage the remains of that pie for lunch?' 'Yes, fine.' He shifted the plate and picked up the bank book again.

One thing which caught his eye, the amounts he had seen on the receipts from the jeweller in York matched the deposits in the book.

He mentioned this to Helen.

'Are you thinking your dad has committed some jewel robberies? I know he was a bit of a character but I can't see him doing anything serious like that.'

'I wish I could be sure. At the moment I'm at a loss to think of anything legitimate.' He sat back a worried frown on his face. Helen lit the oven and placed the pie remains in.

As she prepared the meal she said. 'Do you think any of your dad's old crew are still about? Would they know anything?'

'That's a thought. I could make some enquiries, in fact Jack might know of them.'

Another line of action to follow. Helen served the pie with hot gravy and they both tucked in. After eating, she said. 'A job for you.'

She went to the cellar head and pointed to the huge copper used for providing hot water in quantity. It had a gas burner built in underneath, a rubber pipe sticking out for connection to the gas tap on the wall.

'I want that up; and the zinc bath tub.' He lifted the copper into the kitchen, a heavy device on three legs, and then hefted the large zinc bath tub.

Helen pushed a piece of hose onto the cold water tap, stuck the other end into the copper top and proceeded to fill it. When three quarters full she connected the rubber gas pipe.

'All ready my love, bath time tonight.'

Terry looked at the bath. She saw the expression on his face.

'When did you last have a proper bath?'

He looked shamed faced. 'I only had room for strip washes in the digs. I didn't have a bath or anything to fill one with.'

'So! We can both have a proper bath. We'll feel better for that.'

'Both?

'Oh yes my love, both. You can wash my back,' she said giggling.

Things were looking more interesting. He couldn't yet believe this could possibly be happening to him. Helen naked in a bath tub. His thoughts ran away with him.

He opened the paper Jack had brought. An excuse to come round and nosey if ever there was one! He saw that the official inquest for the war victims was announced.

They were disturbed once again by a knock on the door. May Allen, sporting a black eye! Helen had to practise extreme control not to smile. May was the one who was taking delight in gossiping. She had been all chummy when Helen saw her in the Market hall, but other women around had been giggling and casting furtive glances between May and Helen.

Helen had met May's husband, a big tough fisherman with a thick full face beard. He was of the era when it was thought good to give 'the woman' a clout now and then. 'Just to keep em in line.'

'I've been to the doctors,' she announced, not saying what for. 'He asked if I would drop this note off for you.' Her eyes flitted around taking all in, resting on the bath for a moment. Helen was sure she could see the gleam in her eye.

'Thank you May.' She took the proffered note before Terry could even rise. He could feel the tension radiating from Helen. Had a suspicion why too.

'That's very good of you May.' He being all sweetness and light. 'Will you stop for a cup of tea?'

He pretended he couldn't see Helen glowering at him.

'No thank you Terry.' She smiled at him in a way that had Helen's blood boiling. 'He,' a thumb over the shoulder. 'Will want to know how I've gone on.'

'Nothing serious I hope?'

'Not if you don't call another bloody kid serious,' she replied, scowling.

'Oh, well, thanks again May.' With that she took her departure.

'Another kid,' sneered Helen. 'That will be number five.'

'Has something gone off between you two?'

'She couldn't wait to point the finger and gossip when she saw me in the market. Probably couldn't wait to tell all that the slag was shacked up again.'

He rose and slipped his arms about her hugging her tightly.

'That sounded very bitter my love. It matters not a jot to me, ignore them. They've nothing better to do.' He gave her a squeeze. 'Although I suspect May will have plenty to do shortly.' She laughed, the tension dispersed.

'Let's have a look at this note.'

The *note* in fact was an official document from Doctor Jameson's surgery in St Sepulchre Street. It stated that word had been received from the mortician at Dean Road confirming that Mr Richard Sheader had died of coronary arrest. If Mr Sheader junior would care to call at the surgery in person, Doctor Jameson would issue him with a death certificate.

This had come far earlier than he expected. He told Helen what the doctor had said, she replying simply. 'Then you must get up there.'

'Yes, won't be long then.' She laughed as he stood. 'And I will be still here when you get back.'

He flushed; memory of his panic the last time he left the house alone. He couldn't resist giving her a hug and kiss before leaving, taking one of the half sovereigns from the bag. He still felt uncomfortable about using this money.

Helen sat down as he left needing to get her thoughts into order.

So much had happened in such a short time. She had never for one moment thought she would now be involved in a passionate affair with Richard's son. Even as that thought flitted through her mind a mental image formed of his muscular chest, the deep blue eyes and shock of blonde hair. His amazing 'soldier' and his total innocence.

As the image formed she felt a stirring in her loins. Always a very physical girl, like the gypsy mother before her, he excited her beyond measure. The thought that she had full control over him. And she, Helen Standish, was teaching him all about sex. Him, at his age, a total innocent. And yet there was more. She realised she loved him as a person. His sincerity and lack of guile was very appealing. The way he was completely non judgemental of her, treating her with respect and concern for her well being. Was she starting to fall in love with him?

And what about the mystery of Richard's wealth. The bank book and the amount in it left her speechless. She was unable to contemplate such an amount. Would Terry really relinquish it if he thought it was tainted?

She had to admit to herself she would be very loath to see that opportunity of financial security slip away. The difficult survival she had practiced just to keep going, would she be tempted to look the other way if required to keep such wealth? Yes, she probably would.

Far too many thoughts to cope with. She rose and busied herself in the kitchen, cleaning and preparing the meal for later, a beautiful bit of steak. She was sure Terry would like that. An apple pie with custard for after. Pie made by Mrs Bullimore in the market - something she was famous for.

She was not sure enough of her baking skills to make one herself perhaps that might come with practice.

She threw a shovelful of good Welsh steam coal on the little kitchen fire, obtained like all the other locals from the harbour.

A collier visited regularly to provide coal for the ships. Much better quality than the stuff sold by the town coalman. A quantity always found its way to the Bottom Enders.

She needed the kitchen to be comfortably warm by evening, bath time!

She new exactly what was going to happen. Had planned it to happen, part of his awakening. The delicious thought sent a thrill through her. Oh was that moment going to be special.

Her domestic work was completed by the time Terry arrived back, clutching a large brown envelope.

'Is that it?' He just nodded not speaking. The document in his hand was written confirmation of the end of a chapter in his life.

She drew him to her ruffling his hair. 'Next job is to make some arrangements then.'

A deep sigh from him, 'Aye.' Sounding almost like Jack.

'Not now love, leave it until Monday. Too close to the weekend anyway. You've done enough for now.'

'Yes,' glancing at the clock. Three forty five, no time now anyway. He sat at the table and massaged his leg.

'Is it all right?' looking in sympathy at him.

'Oh it's alright, nothing I haven't felt before.'

He looked tired. A lot of stress and mixed emotions in such a short space of time.

He looked so vulnerable and helpless in that brief moment. She wanted to scoop him up and tell him all was well.

'Well I hope you're not too tired,' she ruffled his hair again. 'After bath time teacher has a special lesson in store for pupil.'

'Oh, who said I was tired?' Grabbing her hand and kissing it.

'You know I'm madly in love with my teacher. Should I bring you an apple?'

They laughed together like young school children. He pulled her down onto his knee and hugged her enough to stop breath.

'Have I told you I love you?' She surprised herself, feeling tears come to her eyes. 'Yes, and I think it might be catching.'

He floated in a sea of pure delight, all that he wished for. He wanted to spend the rest of his life with this alluring creature, and she had just said she was falling in love with him. Him! The cripple lad. He had seen himself in that light for so long, could this actually be true? This vision actually caring for him?

'Now', she said, dragging him from his reverie. 'Plan of action. First thing Monday morning we'll go to the funeral director.' She noticed his look. 'Yes, we, I'll come with you. I can tell just from looking at you that you'll need moral support.'

'You can already read me like a book,' he grinned. 'So Monday it is.'

She looked serious. 'Yes, we need to get on with it. It will only be after the funeral that we can attempt to sort everything else.' She stood up and threw a pose, breasts thrust forward and arm held aloft, and said in a theatrical voice,

'Monday, action this day.'

He laughed. 'You sound like a politician. Can't see that phrase catching on though. Just imagine, standing in the commons,

Helen Sheader MP.'

She dropped her arm. 'You said Sheader.'

'Oh yes. I'm working on it.'

Eyes looking moist again, she hugged him.

'I thought we said one day at a time?'

114

'Forward thinking, that's me.' He looked like a cheeky schoolboy with a grin that said challenge me.

'Next,' she continued. 'Is to find you something to wear,' eyeing the weather beaten trousers and shirt that had once been blue, but now looked a faded white with a hint of blue.

'It's what's known as a working wardrobe,' he said.' In fact, two pairs of trousers and shirts, some socks and a seaman's hat which I think might have been dads at one time.'

'You'll need to look decent when we go to the funeral director. Perhaps if you look in your dad's wardrobe you might find something that will fit.'

He looked uncomfortable at the idea but accepted his current clothes were scruffy to say the least. She decided to leave that for the moment seeing the look on his face.

'Oh! Look at the time! Go and do something useful and let me get started on dinner.' Seeing he looked lost. 'You can start by filling that coal scuttle.'

'Yes teacher, did you say you wanted an apple?'

They passed the rest of the afternoon in domestic simplicity, Terry happy to do anything asked of him. By six o'clock he was tucking into a piece of steak with obvious delight. The gas mantle was casting a glow, bolstered by the flickering coal fire. Little jets of blue flame spurted from the gas rich coal. The apple pie disappeared as though he had never tasted one before.

They cleared away after the meal, washing and drying the pots together. Helen slapped his bum as he reached up to put the plates back.

'Naughty teacher, I've been a good boy, no need to chastise me.'

'Sit down,' she commanded; pointing to the kitchen table, he did just that.

She sat opposite him. 'Now darling, read the paper to me.'

A simple request which took him by surprise, her warm eyes locked on his.

115

He started on the front page and read aloud. She asked clarification when needed, exclaiming at some features, attentive as he spoke in a soft voice.

'I wish I could read,' she said wistfully.

'If you want I'll teach you my love, in return for all the lessons you're giving me.'

A huge grin at that. She laughed, rising to turn on the gas burner under the copper boiler. She pulled the zinc bath closer to the fire. He watching in fascination and rising excitement.

'Let's have some more reading while that warms up.'

He read the paper from back to front, even some of the adverts. She was interested in the reports of sympathy from politicians and heads of state regarding the attack on Scarborough.

She rose at intervals to check the temperature of the water in the copper. And then, when satisfied, turned to him. 'Lock the door,' smiling. 'We don't want Jack barging in again.'

The rubber tube from the cold water tap to the boiler she now transferred to the boiler output tap, the other end in the bath. Warm water flooded in while she drew the pretty blue curtains. She stopped it when three quarters full, withdrawing the tube. She picked up the large block of soft soap from the sink placing it at the side of the bath on the floor. Then placed a large fluffy towel from the kitchen cupboard at the other side.

Terry watching in rising anticipation. She then stripped naked with no further ado. She knew what the effect would be and so did he.

The firm up tilted breasts, long brown legs and tiny rounded bottom having the usual result on him and soldier.

She lowered herself into the water with a sigh of delight, ducked her hair under and came up streaming and laughing.

'Come on lover, soap my hair.'

He needed no second bidding. Picking up the soap bar he rubbed it into those lovely black locks.

She threw her head back, breasts standing out. Standing behind her it was like looking into the Valley of the Kings. He couldn't resist leaning forward and cupping both in his soapy hands.

'Steady boy, hair first.'

Reluctantly, he did as told until she dipped her head back under the water to rinse it.

'Now you can soap the rest of me.'

Oh Heaven! How could he contain himself? He leaned forward, hard soldier pressing into her neck as he slid soapy hands around her breasts. He slid his hand down her belly, her back, and then washed each long leg as she lifted each one clear of the water.

His breath was coming in gasps, face red and flushed. And then sliding his hand down to the magnificent curls as she lifted one leg lewdly out of the water.

He was close to premature ejaculation when she slid under again to rinse off, rising like a shining goddess out of the water, pushing him away laughing.

'Let me get dry impatient lad. Get those clothes off, your turn next.'

She hooted with laughter as he got his foot tangled in his trouser bottom in his haste and went crashing to the floor.

'What have I told you? Slowly, slowly my darling.'

'Get in.' A strict command. He did as instructed, a pleasant feeling immersed in warm water. Like her he ducked his hair under.

She was behind him now, soap being rubbed into his thick blonde hair. And then a vigorous rubbing before the command. 'Duck under now.'

Her hands following his head under rubbing the soap from his hair. It was a replay of a few moments before only he now being the recipient.

She stroked soapy fingers down his chest giving little grunts of pleasure. In fact he was joining her in the grunt department.

She continued down his back reaching right down and grasping his buttocks. Then, Heaven of Heavens, reaching with freshly soaped hands to his throbbing soldier. He almost screamed as she soaped it with long strokes.

'God Terry, that is so thick my love, oh so thick.'

She cupped his testicles with one hand while sliding up and down his shaft with the other. He was squirming and gasping, and them she stopped and straightened up.

She gave a little chuckle. 'Don't want you coming too quickly do we? Get out and get dry.'

She smiled at the disappointment on his face.

'The best is yet to come,' she whispered. 'I told you it was lesson time tonight.'

He climbed out dripping water all over the kitchen floor. She wrapped the towel around him helping to rub him dry.

'Let me dry my little friend.' Her eyes were on fire as she took the towel from him and started to dry his manhood. His eyes popped as she grasped a handful of towel around it and squeezed.

His erection felt as though it would burst. He didn't know how he was holding himself back. She completed the drying and then turned away from him walking to the kitchen table.

He watched the lithe figure. Long legs, bottom swaying as she walked, and then she suddenly stooped forward legs splayed apart. She bent from the waist and lay fully on the table with both arms spread and clutching the sides.

'Now,' she cried in a hoarse voice. 'Now darling, take me from behind.'

He thought his heart was going to burst it was pumping so hard. The long brown legs splayed, with her curls and sweet entrance on display almost made him feel faint. He staggered forward, placing the velvety head against her entrance. He pressed, and felt his shaft slip in as though it were its' permanent resting place.

She gave a loud whimper as the thick member entered her. 'Slowly darling, slowly.'

He did his best, withdrawing almost all the way out before slipping back to where his belly was pressed hard against her buttocks.

She was gasping and yelping, or was that him? Both of them! He grasped a buttock in each hand. 'Now,' she cried. 'Now, fuck me hard.'

Once again the crude exhortation did the trick. He pumped for all his worth. At one point the table moved with a grating scrape on the floor. He was yelling incoherently, she letting out a piercing scream.

He climaxed in a huge shuddering jolt that sent an electric charge through his entire body. He leaned right over her with his belly pressed tight up against her buttocks.

She was writhing and groaning under him like a thing possessed, saying over and over again. 'Oh God, oh God.'

He leaned right forward, laying on her with his arms outstretched to cover hers, kissing the back of her neck. Enjoying the feel of his belly against her buttocks. This was bliss of a sort he could never have envisaged, oh how he loved this woman.

He withdrew reluctantly, helping her to her feet. The table, to his amazement, was only a couple of feet from the door. She turned and flung her arms around his neck kissing him passionately.

'I've never known anything like that,' she murmured, her face as flushed as his. 'Oh my lovely man.'

He was floating ten feet high. Whatever happened in the future he was determined to make this woman his wife; he would work on it until she agreed.

Next door Jack and Sally were listening to loud screams and yells, the sound of some piece of furniture being dragged across the floor.

Sally, looking concerned, turned to Jack. 'Do you think they're fighting? I really hope not.'

'Fighting lass,' he gave a loud guffaw. 'If that's fightin I wouldn't mind a bit meself, nay lass, their shaggin.'

Sally's face flushed. 'Men,' she muttered.

***

# CHAPTER EIGHT

## A useful weekend

Saturday morning, late Saturday morning. He was always reluctant to get up with her lying on the pillow next to him. After breakfast he allowed Helen to draw him hesitantly to the wardrobe with his dad's clothes in.

His father had not been as broad in the shoulder nor as tall as him, but they eventually found a pair of grey trousers that looked reasonably his size. A shirt that was too tight across the chest, but new. Helen thought the tightness suited the figure under it to a tee.

A dark blue seaman's type jacket that would have been three quarters length on his dad but came just below the waist on him. Luckily, and to his surprise, he found his dad's shoe size was the same as his, a nine and half.

A pair of very expensive looking black leather shoes fitted perfectly, and the outfit was complemented by a black cap that looked as though it may have been German in origin.

Helen made him put the lot on to check the result herself. as she said. 'Men have no idea about clothes; it needs a woman's touch to guide them.'

She was very satisfied with the result. The jacket was too tight to fasten but looked good unfastened, emphasising his figure. And the hat set at a jaunty angle finished the job.

'You look good enough to take out now,' with a big grin. He doffed the hat with a flourish, making a sweeping bow. 'Thank you kindly madam.'

The banter came freely between them now, Terry feeling he had known her for years.

They were joking and larking about when Terry had a sudden thought.

'Helen! That piece of paper with the strange code or whatever. I've had an idea.'

She looked up at him expectantly. 'What's that then?'

'Follow me,' he headed for the stairs. 'Leading me into evil are you,' laughing. She followed behind, intrigued. He went into the bedroom and opened the box, retrieving the piece of paper with the 17R 13IN written on it.

'Right, the attic.'

Heading up the steep stairs and entering the attic he went across to the cut out floorboard. He studied it for a while and then said. 'Yes, I'm right, look at this.'

'That board is the seventeenth from the right as we look at it from the doorway and the thirteenth in from the window.'

She studied it for a brief second. 'Well, you clever thing you.'

'I can't see why he needed to write it down though,' he said.

'Probably waiting for his son to find the box then,' she laughed. 'At least that's one mystery solved, although, he was getting very forgetful. I did wonder if he was starting with some form of dementia. Yes, thinking about it, he may have been afraid of finding things again, he knew he had a problem.'

'I didn't know that,' he replied, a little wistfully. 'I wish I'd made up with him before he disappeared from my life.'

'I know love,' she hugged him and they went back downstairs.

One thing the 'Bottom Enders' were never short of was really fresh fish.

The fisher lasses and other workers on the pier were not officially entitled to it, but it was always considered a perk of the job.

'I've made friends with one of the fisher lasses called Mary,' Helen told him. 'For a few pence she gets me some good fish, so tonight my love we are having fried cod.' They were back in the kitchen; strangely it seemed to be the room they spent most time in. Helen showed him a huge fish wrapped in a sheet of newspaper.

'That sounds pretty good to me. Ah! It's moving,' he jumped back a foot. Helen yelled and did the same.

He grinned at her, the naughty little schoolboy grin. 'That made you jump didn't it?'

'You bugger!' She chased him round the kitchen, which ended in a laughing tussle that finished in hugs and kisses. He couldn't ever remember being as happy as this. He placed a strong arm around her waist.

'Marry me Helen Standish. Change your name to Sheader, it sounds a lot better.'

She looked up into his eyes. 'Oh impatient one, ask me again when we can see an end to all this uncertainty.'

'But before anything else you have an appointment,' she announced.

'I have?' he looked puzzled.

'Oh yes. Sit in that chair and take your shirt off,' pointing to the kitchen chair near the window.

'Shirt off?' Eyebrows raised in question.

'Yes, can't do this with it on, far too messy.' She was teasing him again. In typical male style he dragged it off over his head. Producing scissors and comb from the drawer in the table she declared.'You are now about to meet the demon barber of Overton Terrace.'

'You're a barber as well, are there no ends to your talent?'

She stood behind him running her hands through his hair. 'How much would sir like off?'

He twisted his head giving her a provocative look. 'I would like it all off.'

'Having my hair cut with a nude barber would be something new. Just think, if you set up a barbers shop like that you would make a fortune.'

The laughter was free and easy and she proved to be a very good barber. His hair had been looking thick and unruly. She produced results that would not have been bettered in a professional barbers shop.

She finished with a flourish, wafting bits of hair in all directions with the tea towel. 'There, you look less like an ape now; that will be nine pence.'

'Can I pay you in kind?'

She grinned at him. 'Oh, alright, but later,' she pouted her lips at him. 'But I will need payment in full.' More laughter from them both.

'Have we got a mirror?'

'Only this.' She reached into the kitchen cabinet and producing a tiny bit of glass with browned edges.

'That will do.' He took it from her and checked the 'barbers' results. 'Amazing, that is amazing.'

Helen actually blushed at the praise. She had always cut his father's hair but thought now was not a good time to mention that, but there was no doubt he was transformed. With the clothes they had sorted out, and now a neat haircut, it would be a very smart young man who presented himself at the funeral directors on Monday. Smart and very handsome. She startled herself with the thought that slipped unbidden into her mind. She had built up a hard shell of protection during her life but this lovely man had cut straight through that.

'Helen.' His voice snapped her out of her reverie. He was suddenly very serious. 'What have you got to wear on Monday? All this effort over me. I want my girl to look nice.'

She felt tears mist her eyes; he had called her my girl. She realised it was very comforting. No, more, it was bloody wonderful.

And, smiling inwardly self deprecatingly. Calling her girl at bloody thirty five, yet seeing in his face he really meant it.

She drew a deep breath. The effect of his words had touched her more than she realised.

'I've got a fairly decent dress in the bag,' shrugging at him. 'It should do the job after ironing.'

He gazed at her to a point where she felt uncomfortable.

'After the trip to the funeral people on Monday we're going shopping.' He reached across and held her hand. 'We'll spend some of dad's ill-gotten gains and buy you some clothes. Some pretty dresses that will make you look like the princess that you are. It can be your early Christmas present.'

She wanted to laugh at him, make a joke about being a princess in her typical downright way. The way she was before coming into contact with this lovely man she would have been really coarse and said something like 'bollocks.'

And yet, as he said that she felt butterflys flutter in her stomach. Warmth and a feeling of being wanted travelling the length of her body. A sudden yearning to be loved and pampered by someone who really did care for her.

Her experiences with men in the past, with the exception of Terry's dad, had been hurtful. They had wanted her for one thing alone, and she had played on that to survive in what could be a very cruel world. She never thought for one minute love, true love, the sort of love that the Bronte's wrote about would touch her.

Those deep blue eyes looking at her with such intensity and love. Yes, she could see the love shining there, his chest still bared. Her tummy fluttering, she said simply. 'I think I'd really love that.'

'You'd love some new dresses?' A challenging smile from him.

'Yes, and,' she whispered, 'I would love to be your princess.'

That old saying, 'a moment frozen in time' was an accurate description of what passed between them at that point, sitting holding hands like young star crossed lovers. Just happy in each others company.

The moment was broken by Terry when he suddenly said. 'You'll have to marry me if you're pregnant.'

As soon as he said it he realised he had said the wrong thing. Her face clouded with what seemed like pain.

'No chance of that lover,' she said with pretence at lightness, but he saw the underlying bitterness. 'The miscarriage I told you about put paid to my chances to be a mother.'

'Oh darling, I didn't mean to upset you. I just thought, you know, with all that sperm flying about,' trying to make light of it. 'At least that which wasn't wasted shooting across the bedroom floor,' ironic laugh. 'Well you know.' He ran out of words, feeling dreadful that he had caused upset to her.

'Its alright love,' she clutched his hand. 'You weren't to know. If I were to ever have a child I could think of nothing better than it be yours.'

Cheeky little schoolboy look again, smiling at her. 'Who knows, miracles do happen, perhaps we just don't try often enough.'

That broke the gloom.

'Don't practice enough you cheeky man! You're on a steep learning curve; much more is to be revealed.'

She pouted and fluttered her eyes at him in a deliberately posed sexy way. It made them both giggle, but he shelved away the information that children and pregnancies were a subject to skate around delicately.

The thought of spending the 'ill gotten gains' as he called them troubled her a little. An idea came. 'I know a girl who has a sewing machine, one of those Singer ones,' she announced. 'Boyes remnant store has some beautiful ends of cloth. I could make some dresses myself.'

Ruefully, 'When I was at home I was quite good at sewing.'

'Instead of me buying you a nice dress?'

'Oh no,' she laughed. 'As well as. But seriously, I could make four or more dresses for the price of a bought one. You would be proud of me.'

'I am proud of you,' those intense eyes looking at her. 'I think you could do anything you set your mind to and do it well.' Once again the little fluttery feeling in her tummy. Oh this lovely man.

'Thank you for such confidence in me,' said slightly mockingly. 'And you my man,' pointing at him. 'Put that bloody shirt back on.'

More hoots of laughter. Jack, knocking his pipe out again on the outside wall next door, blowing bits of debris from the stem, shook his head, went in and said to Sally. 'Sounds like a bloody kinder garden next door.'

'That lad's had a bit of a rough life up to now,' replied Sally.

'Aye that he has. Bloody makin up fer it now though, lucky bastard,' he replied.

'Jack,' raised voice. 'You've had your fill of fun and fireworks in your time.

'Aye thart right lass,' and then with a grimace at Sally. 'Bloody old age tho, crap aint it?'

For Terry and Helen the rest of the day passed in pleasant companionship. The fried cod with boiled potatoes went down a treat. He was starting to get used to good hot food, such a luxury! The plan for Monday now was to be at the funeral directors by nine thirty and then they would go shopping for clothes.

Terry suggested they have some lunch in town at the little stall in the Market vaults; and then go to Makepeace and Flowers to make an appointment about the will.

Having decided an actual way forward felt very satisfying. The start of some progress at last, something positive. Admittedly, with a great deal of input from Helen.

A sudden commotion and shouting outside had them both at the door to see what was happening. Jack was out pointing into the air. Most of the other members of Overton Terrace were out too.

A rattling crackle was coming from an aeroplane fluttering over the bay. It looked so frail it seemed impossible it could remain in the air.

'It's that Blackburn chap,' said one of the neighbour's knowledgably. 'He's got that machine stationed at Scalby Mills now. They reckon he's employed by the admiralty to scout the coast.'

'Looks as tho he should be paid danger money,' said Jack. 'It looks bloody dangerous to me.'

He had a point. The machine dipped and the wings waggled enough times to make it look a highly dangerous enterprise.

'Brave man flying that,' remarked one of the watchers.

'Aye', Jack again. 'If yon fella falls from that height he'll end up lookin like a lump o strawberry jam.'

Laughter all round. 'That's the first time I've ever seen an aeroplane,' marvelled Terry.

'Not had much time to see owt outside lately,' sniggered Jack.

Terry blushed vividly. Helen gave Jack a scowl that would have dropped a donkey. The neighbours were grinning at the repartee as she steered Terry back indoors with a final angry look at Jack.

'I'll swing for that old bugger.' She was furious, not for herself but for Terry's sake. He hugged her. 'Shush, nothing to worry about. It doesn't bother me and they'll get used to us being together eventually.'

'Besides,' grinning at her. 'I quite like you when you're angry. It makes your eyes flash.'

She looked up into his face his arms still around her. 'You know we'll get a lot more of this don't you?'

'I don't care. As long as you're with me they can all take a running jump, we just need to stand firm.'

'Her anger drained away slowly. 'Well, all right, but you'd best show me what firm is later,' she chuckled.

They retired to bed at ten. A gentle rain had set in, running down the window in long streaks. The gas mantle hissed, casting its glow over the room.

They both undressed slowly, watching each other. To Terry, the sight of Helen stripping off was one he was sure he would never ever tire of.

She oozed erotica. The usual reaction was evident and she gave him her best lewd grin.

'I think I owe you nine pence madam.'

'Let's make it half a crown,' she replied.

Laughing, he picked her up in both arms and threw her onto the bed. There was an almighty crash as the two legs on that side collapsed and she was dumped on the floor, legs akimbo.

They both howled with laughter, and then with no further ado Terry yanked the mattress off onto the bare boards.

Grasping her ankles he dragged her forward until her bottom was at the edge of the mattress. Then kneeling before her he lifted both legs until they were resting on his shoulders, leaned over her, and with a mighty thrust was into her.

Helen was used to taking the initiative, now it was he doing so. She gave a gasp as his stiff member entered, then he started to pump like a man possessed, her gasps rising in volume with his frenzy.

They both achieved a climax together, Helen shouting. 'Oh God.'

In the bedroom next door the crash of the collapsing bed sounded clear through the wall. The sound once again of something being dragged, and then the creaking of floorboards accompanied by Helen's rising yells and gasps.

'Oh Christ, oh Christ', mumbled Jack. 'Sally, their bloody fightin agin.' Before sticking his head under the blankets.

Sally lay on her back looking at the ceiling. 'Oh for those days again,' she murmured. 'Although I can't remember it being that good.'

The two lovers laid in each others arms, totally spent.

'I think that was three shillings worth my love.' She kissed him deeply. 'I thought I was supposed to be the teacher.'

'Well, you've made most of the decisions all day, it was time I contributed.' 'Besides,' touching one of the broken bed legs. 'It was an emergency. I had to make a snap decision.' They fell asleep in deep contentment, the gas mantle left unattended and still hissing.

*

Sunday morning Terry was awakened by a shake from Helen.

'A thought came to me in the night.'

He groaned. 'You've woken me to tell me that?'

'What you said about them getting used to us,' she continued. 'There's to be a special service at St Mary's this morning. If we went as a couple everyone would see we're not being swayed by any condemnation from them.'

He clasped her hand. 'The roof might collapse if we go. I'm sure God will think we're a couple of fornicators.'

'Well, everyone else thinks it, so nothing to lose.'

'What would you wear?'

'That dress I told you about, soon get it ironed.'

'Right, let's shock em.' He shot off the bed/mattress pulling her to her feet. 'You're getting very forceful my love.'

'Oh yes, you've lit the fuse now watch the fireworks.'

They were up washed and dressed in short thrift, Terry starting on breakfast. Helen set the iron on the grid attached to the fire in the kitchen, and then took over from him while it heated. He cut ragged slices of bread with the blunt knife, buttering them thickly. When the iron was hot, she produced the dress. A deep mauve that looked a little faded, with a white lace collar.

'Get this first.' He pushed a plate of egg and bacon before her, a mug of strong tea each, and they both sat down to enjoy it.

After breakfast, while Terry put the pots into hot water in the sink, Helen laid the dress on the kitchen table using it as an ironing board, whooshing round with practised ease. She soon had it wrinkle free. She hung it on a wire hanger from the door to cool then slipped off her current dress and tried the mauve one on.

It had shrunk slightly, evidence of many washes, but it suited her figure being slightly tight and emphasising her shape.

Terry gave a whistle of appreciation. 'A little risqué for church I think?'

She slipped a knitted black shawl over her shoulders. 'There, that better?'

'Yes, that'll do my girl.' He had put on his new/father's outfit. She looked for a moment. 'Hang on, I know what that needs.'

She disappeared upstairs and returned with a black cravat, slunk up to him and tied it around his neck. 'Oh yes, very presentable.'

They made their way up the steep hill to St Mary's arm in arm, ignoring raised eyebrows from some as they passed. The service was due to start at nine thirty; they were seated for just turned nine. Deliberately choosing a seat not too far from the front Helen clutched his arm as they sat in the middle of the uncomfortable wooden pew. The church was filling up. Lots of glances and surreptitious looks. If they had come to make a statement then that was certainly happening.

The service started promptly on time. The minister, a large fearsome man with an all face beard and a voice that was difficult to ignore, gave a booming sermon from the raised pulpit. Then the usual singing of well known hymns, and prayers for the dead and injured of the dastardly German attack. The minister called down God's wrath on the unrighteous, meaning the Germans, and was convinced that he would smite the aggressor. Terry was not a religious man. He had seen too many events in the Boer War that defied, in his mind, the presence of a caring God, but was prepared to live and let live. He had an irreverent vision for a brief second of flashes of lightening blowing up German battle ships.

However, some good came from it when the minister announced that all monies from the collection would go to the families of the dead and injured. With the glances of some of the judgemental neighbours on him, he made sure they could see the half crown he dropped into the box.

The minister stood at the church door as the congregation filed out; greeting regulars with bonhomie. As they drew level with him he shook Terry's hand. 'New to this area are you my boy? I think this is the first time we've met.'

'I've just moved into my father's house on Overton Terrace,' replied Terry truthfully.

'Ah, then I look forward to seeing you and your good lady wife in the future.' He clearly heard the rustle of sound as those around heard the conversation.

'Yes indeed.' he nodded at the minister. Helen giving him her most charming smile which had the minister beaming. As they walked away three of the local women could be heard chattering agitatedly, glancing at the couple, making it quite clear they were the subject of conversation.

The rain had passed, a pale glimmer of sunlight reflecting off the wet paving slabs. A scent of salt in the air. Terry, breathing in pleasurably.

'Well my love, I think we have well and truly made a statement.'

Their chuckles, and the fact they were walking arm in arm bringing scowls of condemnation from the three hags.

'Well, the roof didn't fall in, is that a good sign?' She giggled. 'I'm now your lady wife. I thought those three were going to choke when the minister said that.'

'Just a matter of time.' He slapped her bottom to a chorus of sound behind. A loud voice raised, obviously to make sure they heard.

'Disgusting.'

'I don't think your bottom is disgusting at all,' he grinned. 'Perhaps they don't have the same perspective as me.'

The walk back down the hill was done in high spirits ignoring anyone who allowed displeasure to show.

Tomorrow they would make progress he was sure. Anyone who had complaints about either of them could like it or lump it.

***

# CHAPTER NINE

## A trip to York

They were both up early Monday morning.

Terry feeling nervous. Helen, sensing that, being as supportive as she could.

Nine o' clock; dressed as smartly as possible, no rain thank goodness, they set off for the undertaker. Situated in the centre of town Masterton's funeral directors were long established. They entered into a little vestibule where a middle aged woman sat behind a desk.

'Good morning, how may I help you?' Terry, feeling more than a little nervous now, said. 'I think my wife called in Friday to inquire about funeral costs,' avoiding Helen's eye. 'I need to make arrangements for my father's funeral. The death certificate has only just been received.'

'Yes indeed, I remember your wife coming in. I'm so sorry to hear about your loss, please, take a seat.'

She indicated the two upright chairs to the left of the desk. They sat, Helen giving him a 'you little bugger' look.

'May I take your name?' smiling warmly at him.

'Yes, its Mr and Mrs Terrence Sheader.' He didn't dare look at Helen.

The woman introduced herself as Mrs Womack, and then proceeded to take details of the date of his father's death. She asked to see the death certificate, which Terry had only thought to bring with them when Helen said it would be required. She produced a list of prices for different caskets, number of horses required for the hearse, and asked if they would need any carriages.

Terry found it all a little unreal, as though they were in a shop arranging the purchase of large items. She asked if they would be proceeding from his father's church.

He looked at Helen desperately. He hadn't a clue if his father had attended any church.

Helen retrieved the situation with her customary aplomb.

'My father-in-law was not a church goer unfortunately. We thought perhaps a service at Dean Road Chapel,' mentioning the town cemetery.

'Yes that can be arranged. The address you will be starting from?' Her eyebrows raised. Terry supplied the address.

Mrs Womack produced a large diary from under the desk.

'The only problem we have at the moment is the first available date will be Wednesday 30th at ten thirty.'

She looked up at them. 'I'm sure you realise the difficulties. With the devastation that was unleashed on the town by the German attack and the intervention of Christmas the book is rather full.'

They accepted the date. No choice really, although they would both have liked it to be earlier. Both decided Richard Sheader should have a good send off. They picked an oak coffin, the hearse to be drawn by two black horses and with the provision of a four seat landau for them, Jack and Sally. Others could make their own way there.

The negotiations made, Mrs Womack added up the cost, looking at them with a touch of uncertainty. 'The total Mr Sheader will be twenty guineas.'

She said it as though really wanting to say, *can you two pay that much?*

She was unable to hide her surprise completely when Terry said, 'May I pay now in cash?'

He handed over the cash, obtained a receipt, and then they thankfully escaped to the fresh air.

'I hate the smell of those places,' he said with a shudder. 'If ever a place smelled of death they do.'

'So Mr Sheader, are Mr and Mrs Sheader going now to the solicitors?'

Heavy emphasis on Mr and Mrs as she looked into his face in her typical forthright way. Colour coming to his cheeks. 'Sorry love, in a place like that,' shrugging. 'Well, you know.' She grinned at his discomfort.

'Forgiven, naughty boy, I think I could actually get used to it.'

They made their way to St Thomas Street, a main thoroughfare through town where the offices of Makepeace and Flowers were situated. The office was bright and well furnished unlike the last place they visited. A cheerful young man greeted them on entry.

Terry explained the reason for their visit, showed the young man the copy of his father's will, asking if they needed to make an appointment to see anyone or if having the will was enough.

'No idea squire,' the young man said candidly. 'But if you just take a seat I'll find out for you.'

They did as bidded while he disappeared down a corridor at the rear.

He retuned after about ten minutes. 'I've had a word with Mr Flowers. He has looked up your father's details Mr Sheader; he will need to see you. Your father had substantial funds apparently. Mr Flowers will need to see the death certificate and need to write a letter to the bank for you. Has your father's funeral taken place yet?'

Terry explained they had just left the undertakers and it was arranged for Friday. The young man, he still hadn't introduced himself, looked in an appointment book. 'Would eleven o'clock on Tuesday 29th be alright?'

'Yes, perfect, thank you Mr, errr?'

'Oh, sorry, Jonathan Makepeace,' he blushed slightly. 'Rather remiss of me wasn't it?'

They bid good day and left.

'Spoilt son of daddy eh?' said Helen.

'A lot to learn I should say but pleasant enough,' he replied.

'Now, sandwich in the vaults and then?' her eyes gleamed. 'You can dress me like a lady.'

She pulled the knitted shawl further around her shoulders. 'God it's nippy today.'

Making their way to the popular indoor market hall the signs of the big clear up were evident everywhere. Council dust men busy loading swept up glass and brick debris into carts. The sense of panic previously dominating now replaced by a sense of purpose. The market hall was as busy as ever. It was not only a place to shop but a great meeting centre for the exchange of news and a good gossip.

The eyes of a number of the Bottom Ender's followed them as they made their way to Betty Metcalf's little tea and sandwich stall.

A scattering of half a dozen rough chairs made it, in Betty's eyes, a café.

There was no doubting the quality of the food though, and she always had home made cakes as tempting afters.

Both of them indulged in a hot pork sandwich with crackling followed by a large slice of Victoria sponge, a thick coating of jam and cream inside.

Tucking into food like this was still a luxury Terry was finding hard to get used to. The meagre wages from his job at the Kessler's didn't allow much for food.

They were totally oblivious to the fact that their presence in the market hall had contributed to an increase in the gossip level.

The recent German attack was the most exciting event most locals had ever seen in the little town. Most of them led a boring humdrum life, gossiping about who was having *it off* with who, was usually the only entertainment for working people who couldn't afford to go to shows or the Spa concerts which were reserved for the well off and privileged.

In fact, right up to the start of the century, the Spa had been the playground of the minor aristocracy. The snob's playground as some locals called it.

Helen, sat there, her tight little dress showing off her curves to advantage.

It brought forth scowls, sniggers and snide remarks in equal portions. The odd man whose partner caught his eyes straying to the girl brought the temperature up further.

The interest caused by the pair passed them by. Helen was chattering excitedly about the forthcoming shopping trip, Terry basking in the pleasure it brought her.

Having finished their lunch, Helen clutching his hand in excitement, they set off, Helen leading.

She knew exactly where she wanted to go first. The classy Marshall and Snelgrove store on St Nicolas Street. The store was an exclusive one catering for the more affluent client. She wafted through to the ladies dress dept almost leaving Terry behind. Various dresses were on display, some on manikins, but her breath was taken by a dress on display on a prominent part of the floor near the counter.

An extremely elegant assistant who had upper-class written all over her, eyed them carefully.

The manikin on display looked about the same size as Helen. The dress was stunning. A long slim creation of soft cream, the top fashioned in a tunic style, all the rage at that time, with a matching lace collar.

A bow at the neck in deep burgundy was matched by a belt in the same colour. A row of eight elegant buttons extended down the front in cream.

The tunic ended just below the manikin's bottom creating a feminine curve. The front of it flowed away in an inverted vee with three-quarter-length sleeves and a thin strip of burgundy lace at the wrist and shoulders.

A beautiful hat in the same cream with burgundy band, and the final effect! Shoes, also deep burgundy in colour with a small heel completed this vision of elegance.

Helen stood looking at it with desire written all over her face. The assistant, taking in her current faded dress probably thinking, *we have one here, look and touch but no sale.*

'Oh Terry,' her voice dripped desire; she had no need to say another word. Terry had already observed the fact that no price was displayed, meaning it would be expensive. The look on this beautiful girls face overcame his discomfort at the source of the money.

'Would you like to try it on?'

A loud sniff from the assistant, who then said with reluctance,

'Can I offer any assistance madam?'

The *madam* was said in a way that made Terry bite his tongue. With his anger rising, 'yes, she will try it on.'

Helen was startled at his forcefulness. She'd been taken aback at the sight of this exquisite creation, but thought looking was all she would manage before moving on to something practical and cheap.

'Madam is aware that this should be worn with an appropriate bodice?' She looked slightly uncomfortable in Terry's presence.

'I'm sure you can advise on a suitable garment.' His deep blue eyes locked on the assistant's with an intensity that had her scurrying from behind the counter to do his biding.

Helen could hardly believe this display of determination on his part. The unworldly man she'd guided and schooled up to this point seemed transformed.

'Darling are you sure? It will be very expensive.' She thought it might be wise to steer him away from it.

'I'm absolutely sure.' He turned to the assistant. 'And the hat and shoes if you have the appropriate sizes.'

The assistant led Helen to a booth at the rear of the shop, casting a glance back at him. His mouth was in a firm line and authority oozed from him. This was a Terry she had never seen before. For the first time she wondered what she'd started here.

He sat at the chair provided near the shop counter. Although looking composed anger seethed through him. The shop assistant's attitude, the way she had looked,

139

almost with an insolent sneer at the pair of them had his blood boiling like never before.

His discomfort at using what he had decided was dishonestly obtained money was overcome by his desire to see Helen, his Helen being spoiled for the first time in her life. Well! His dad may have spoilt her, a little. It was a thought that he firmly pushed to the back of his mind. He sat dreaming a while until a cough brought him back to the present. He turned in the direction of the interruption. Helen stood before him like a vision from a movie film.

The dress had looked good on its display but she filled it with an elegance and beauty that took his breath away. She had a touch of colour in her cheeks, her tanned skin against the soft cream of the dress mesmerising.

The assistant had loaned her a string of beads in the same deep burgundy that set it all off to perfection.

He was already in love with her, but his heart did somersaults seeing her like this. This was the most beautiful woman he had ever seen and now she looked like royalty.

She looked at him her face glowing. He said simply. 'You look ravishing my darling; you must have it, all of it.'

He took delight in seeing the snooty assistant's face drop in surprise. She looked at him, a little cough. 'And the undergarments sir?'

'All of it.'

She scuttled behind the counter, took her receipt pad, and did some hurried calculations, and then looked at him with a *this will shock him* expression.

'The full amount will come to ten pounds,' she declared, and then watched with amazement as he produced a little cloth bag and tipped a number of sovereigns onto the counter. She had been fully expecting him to declare the amount beyond his reach. Was this one of those rich eccentrics who dressed like peasants?

She had heard other shop girls tell of such.

'Thank you very much sir,' deep servitude in her voice now. Even Helen looking shell shocked. She placed the

140

cash into a small brass cylinder, attached it to the overhead rail system and off it whizzed to the cash office.

'I'll help Madam undress and pack it all for you sir.'

That was more like it. He basked in the changed attitude. *That's shocked you, you snooty bitch* smiling at her and hiding his thoughts with great expertise.

Helen was lead away completely speechless. The brass cylinder came shooting back on its wire while they were away, Terry finding this device of wires and rail like track fascinating.

By the time Helen and the assistant returned loaded with a large hat box, shoe box, and very large box containing the dress, he had another surprise for them. He well and truly had the bit between his teeth now.

Before Helen could even speak he turned to the assistant, now all grovelling servitude, and said. 'We'll now need a couple of everyday dresses. Perhaps a warm coat and a couple of pairs of sensible shoes. I'm sure you can advise my wife?'

Helen's eyes looked as though they were about to pop out of her head.

'Yes indeed sir. If Madam and sir would like to follow me I will show you suitable items.'

She was convinced now these two were eccentric rich people who took a delight in not dressing accordingly.

Helen caught his eye. He put a finger to his lips and gave a wink. She followed helplessly as the assistant lead them into another part of the shop.

He ended up paying another ten pounds ten shillings for two dresses of everyday practical nature. One in beige with lace collar the other a very dark blue.

'That will also be suitable for the funeral,' he informed her.

Two pairs of stout but stylish shoes in black and a warm woollen three quarter length coat. A little dark blue hat to match the blue dress completing the purchases.

He accepted the offer of free delivery for all the items. He had to, there was no way they could carry all those boxes.

When they finally stepped outside the shop a good hour had passed.

Helen gazed at him with misty eyes. 'I don't know what to say. I don't think I even recognise the man who was in that shop with me. So much money Terry, so much money.'

'Every bit of it was worthwhile my love. Happy Christmas. Besides, when I saw you in that dress I was overwhelmed. You looked stunning.' He gave an evil grin. 'And the attitude of that cow pushed me,' he admitted.

'You were so forceful.'

'I can be when needed, you thought you had me in the palm of your hand,' laughing at her. 'Just shows you can't take things for granted.'

'I haven't got you in the palm of my hand then?'

'Not at the moment my love, can't feel a thing.'

She giggled. 'You know what I mean, and those other two dresses. I could have bought material from Boyes and saved a lot of money.'

He squeezed her waist regardless of passers by in the street.

'I know you could love, but I wanted you to have them without all that effort. Its time you had something good in your life without wondering all the time if it could really be happening to you.'

She gripped his arm tightly, overwhelmed and lost for words. He was going through a great awakening after many years; it rather looked as though she was doing the same.

'Where are we going now?'

She was being steered across the road onto St Thomas street, taking them away from the homeward route.

'To Barney Cohen's on Castle road,' he replied.

Cohen's was a tiny tailor's shop, hardly seeming big enough to carry on the trade of a tailor where large bolts of cloth would be stored.

'While I'm in this expansive mood I thought I would see if I could get a suit and hat so that I can match your elegance,' looking at her with a self deprecating smile.

'I thought it would be nice if possible to go to the funeral wearing clothes that are actually mine rather than clothes belonging to dad who we're seeing off.'

He attempted to say it lightly, but she sensed the underlying disturbance he was feeling.

'Yes, yes I'm glad you're doing that. You're right my love and besides,' she gripped his arm even tighter. 'I want you looking good, just for me.'

Castle Road was the continuation of Victoria Road. As its name suggests, heading in the direction of the castle. As they turned left onto the street at the end of St Thomas street some of the damage caused by the German attack was clear to see, mainly in the shape of broken windows. Cohen's shop was a couple of hundred yards on and mercifully, looked undamaged.

They turned into the shop, the old tailor himself greeting them.

After commiserations about the general damage in the area Terry explained his dilemma. 'I need a suit, if possible in time for Tuesday 30th. I know that sounds short notice but it's my father's funeral.'

Cohen scurried round the tiny counter tape measure in hand. 'Just let me measure you up sir and then we will see what can be done.'

Helen looked away with a huge smile on her face as the old man took Terry's inside leg measurement. He had to hide his own smile; he could read her mind.

After taking all the measurements he required the old man said. 'One moment please,' and scurried into the rear of the shop.

He returned with a three piece suit in worsted cloth, dark grey with a very fine stripe.

'This was made for a gentleman who has passed on before taking delivery,' he said. 'Fortunately larger than you. I could make the necessary alterations in the time you require and include a fine grey bowler to match for fifty five shillings.'

'I seem to be stepping into dead men's shoes in so many ways,' murmured Terry. 'But yes, that's a very good offer, deal done.'

He shook Cohen's hand who looked delighted he was no longer stuck with an expensive unsold suit. Cohen said he would have it ready by Saturday morning. Terry felt it was a good deal struck.

He was to have another lesson immediately however. He was to learn that a comment made without thought could backfire in a spectacular way. A lesson in the rapidly shifting mercurial ways a woman's mind works.

As they stepped out of the shop Helen rounded on him in fury, her face flushed with anger.

'So, is that how you see me, dead man's shoes? 'Stepping into a dead man's shoes are you? Taking over a bit of property?'

Her voice was raised and tears streaming down her face. A man and woman across the street, standing by a lamp post watched hoping to see some exciting action.

Terry was taken completely by surprise. He took her by the shoulders with both hands.

'Helen, Helen darling, what're you saying? You know how much I love you. I think of you as the woman I've fallen in love with, not a piece of property. I didn't mean you darling when saying that in the shop.'

She was trying to shrug him off, her full gypsy fury now directed across the road as she saw the couple openly watching in anticipation.

'What do you two think you're staring at? Go on, bugger off.'

The man, who received the full weight of Helen's screech turned so rapidly that he bashed his face against the lamp post, blood spurting from his nose.

They both looked at the unfortunate man and then Terry's shoulders started shaking.

Helen was unable to keep her fury going as she saw the look on Terry's face. They both cracked up laughing, breaking the moment of upset.

The couple opposite hurried away, the woman calling him all the names under the sun, all revolving around the word 'stupid'.

Terry drew Helen into his arms. 'Oh you silly girl. I'd never do anything to hurt you. If what I said came out wrong I apologise my darling, do you forgive me?' He wiped her tear streaked face stroking her hair softly. She clung to him.

'Yes, I'm sorry too. I must be getting very sensitive. Me, the Bottom End slag getting sensitive.' She shook her head in mock derision.

'If I ever hear you use that expression again I'll take you across my knee and spank your bottom.'

She gave him one of those looks. 'Ah! Now things are getting interesting. Would it be my bare bottom you're referring to?'

They both laughed, the tension and sudden flash of female *paddy* gone, but he was sure he'd learned another lesson in life.

'Come on. Far too much excitement for one day,' taking her hand. 'Let's call it a day. Tomorrow we're going to do something you've never done before.

'Oh, what's that?'

'We're going to take a train trip to York. I want to seek out this jeweller, see if he can tell us anything about the *items* dad sold him.'

'Atrain!' She sounded awed. 'You're right that's something I've never done before.'

The walk home was conducted in relative silence holding hands. Terry thought it was like leading a spirited thoroughbred horse. They arrived home feeling exhausted but ultimately feeling much had been accomplished. Terry slipped next door while Helen started preparing dinner to let Sally and Jack know of the arrangements for the funeral.

They had dinner at five pm, both feeling it had been a long day and then retired to the little lounge with a mug of tea each, sinking onto the wicker settee.

'I still can't believe you spent so much on my clothes. It's like a dream that dress. Oh Terry, that dress.'

'That dress, yes,' he smiled. 'I've never seen anyone look more ravishing.' You'll be horrified to know Madam; we spent thirty two pounds and sixteen shillings today.'

She gave a little gasp and put her hand to her mouth. 'And I repaid you by going at you like a tigress. I'm so sorry for that darling, forgive me?'

Her big limpid brown eyes looking at him. 'Look at me like that and I could forgive you anything.'

She drained the tea and snuggled down, her head on his shoulder and he putting an arm around her. The gas mantle hissing softly, the fire crackling and spitting in the hearth, the room giving off a warm glow, he wanted that moment to last and last.

It lasted ten minutes when Helen suddenly sat up with a start.

'Terry, have you forgotten? The bed's broken.' Yes, he had forgotten, so much else on his mind.

'Bugger! Can't do anything tonight though, and that's if it is repairable,' he grinned. 'looks like mattress on the floor tonight.'

'You know how to make a girl comfortable,' she laughed, and then serious. 'We need to put a notice in the Mercury too.'

'Oh blimey! Yes, so many things to think of. Well, here's what we'll do. First thing in the morning we'll call at the Mercury office to put an announcement in, then to the train station for York. When we get to York we'll head for Stonegate wherever that is. Do you know York?'

'No,' she admitted. 'Never been there but I'm sure we can get directions.'

'That's the plan for tomorrow then. Let's hope we can get some information from this jeweller chap. Short of that I don't really know where we go.'

Bed time came around remarkably quickly. Helen had done some sandwiches to take with them in the morning. Ever the practical one she knew they couldn't carry on spending lavishly and she reckoned York would be an expensive place to eat. They could buy a *cuppa* somewhere she was certain.

She boiled some water on the kitchen gas ring to take up with them, pouring a mixture of hot and cold into the bowl in the bedroom as Terry lit the mantle and pulled the mattress clear of the broken bed. They both stripped without any hesitation now, comfortable in each others presence. Terry of course had an immediate erection.

He was convinced he would never get used to seeing this gorgeous creature in the nude. Helen was washing unconcernedly. She finished and indicated it was his turn.

'Do you want any help?' She whispered.

'Hussy.' He hurriedly got washed. Helen delightedly insisting in washing 'soldier.'

She dried him tenderly. 'You know you said if you ever heard me say I was a slag again you would spank my bare bum,' she said, looking at him brazenly.

'Yes.'

'Well I'm a slag.' Giggling and laughing he chased her round the room, grabbing her and pulling her onto his knee on the chair by the drawers.

He slapped her buttocks gently. She was wriggling and squirming. It was highly erotic and again he thought he would burst. She had her legs slightly splayed displaying the delights that he enjoyed so much.

She slipped off his knee.

'Considering you've broken the bed we need a different way. Sit still boy.'

He did as told and then, with no further ado, she straddled him grasping his erection in her hand and lowering herself onto him.

147

With both hands on his shoulders she rose up and down with increasing speed, both of them starting to gasp and shudder. Terry fondled the magnificent breasts and nipples like a man possessed.

They reached orgasm almost simultaneously, Helen with head thrown back and a loud 'ahhhhh.' Another highly satisfying lesson for him. Was there no end to this girls revelations? They slept soundly that night wrapped in each other's arms sleeping the sleep of exhaustion.

Tuesday morning came with a touch of frost and patterns on the bedroom window. A good encourager in getting out of bed and dressing quickly.

They breakfasted on kippers with chunks of buttered bread all washed down with mugs of scalding hot tea. It was one of those crisp clear days when one's breath could be seen indoors. Terry had not bothered lighting any fires as they would be out soon. He wished they had taken Helen's new coat with them from the shop. She didn't posses a coat at all, just the thick knitted shawl.

They left the house at nine thirty heading straight to the newspaper offices to insert the funeral date announcement.

The railway station was a new environment for Helen. The last occasion Terry had ridden on a train was when he returned home after being invalided out of the army, and that was on a railway warrant supplied by them.

He asked at the ticket office for two return tickets to York.

The next train to York was at eleven. As it was only ten fifteen Helen wanted to have a look at the hissing monster that would haul them there having never seen a locomotive up close before.

The superb locomotive was painted a light green with dark red under frames and polished brass dome and fittings. Its number, 1541 proudly displayed in brass numerals on the cab side took her breath away. It seemed the height of modernity. So different to the horse draw carriages she was used to.

Her fascination for this hissing machine rendered her oblivious to the return interest shown by the fireman, who was getting a good eyeful of this attractive creature looking at his locomotive.

She insisted on climbing into the carriage at ten to eleven, frightened the train would depart before they got on board, all excited like a school child on a first outing.

'Can I sit by the window?'

Terry, laughing at her giddy enthusiasm, 'Do you need to hold my hand? We'll be travelling very fast.'

'Any excuse,' and then, thinking about it, a little alarmed. 'Will we be going really fast?'

'Oh, they fly along these modern locomotives. The entire carriage will sway from side to side it's a miracle they stay on the track. You might have to cling onto me for safety.'

'You're pulling my leg you sod,' she said realisation sinking in.

'I'd like to.'

Promptly at eleven the guard blew his whistle. Helen actually did clutch his hand. A little jerk as the loco took up the slack in the linkages then a very smooth movement. A few yards and then the first 'whoosh' from the locomotive's exhaust. As the train started slowly picking up speed the whoosh became a regular whoosh, whoosh, whoosh. She was gripping his hand without realising how tightly her grip was.

'Oh, this is exciting,' sounding girlish, Terry loving the look of excitement on her face.

After passing Seamer the train really did pick up speed, the exhaust a steady beat and the diddly dum of wheels passing over rail joints. To her alarm the carriage was swaying a bit too. The countryside seemed to be flashing by. She'd never in her life travelled at a speed like this. In fact she'd only ever travelled in horse drawn vehicles prior to this.

Pointing excitedly out of the window, 'oh look at that,' she said when parallel with the road on one stretch.

'Look how we're passing everything how we're flying. What speed are we doing Terry?'

He estimated they must be travelling at somewhere near forty five miles per hour. Her eyes widened with amazement. This sexually sophisticated woman who had the ability to make him feel like an innocent schoolboy was now the child. The first stop en route to York was Malton, an upmarket town with a reputation for race horse breeding. A few passengers alighting; many more getting on.

The journey carried on then non stop finally steaming into York at twelve ten. The size of the station and bustling activity bewitched Helen. A buzz of excitement existed about the place, whistles blowing, people hurrying to and from trains, and trains pulling away. The high canopied roof amplifying the blast of steam exhaust.

A heavy smell of coal smoke and steam oil hung in the air. The chatter of many voices, noisy vendors selling drinks newspapers and snacks. It all gave an air of bustling excitement that was the reverse of Scarborough.

She watched in fascination as a troop train with eight carriages pulled away slowly, the soldiers leaning out waving and shouting to their loved ones as they departed. She couldn't help thinking they all looked incredibly young.

'Cannon fodder,' muttered Terry. 'I wonder how many of those lads will be coming back injured and maimed and then thrown on the scrap heap without anyone caring a bugger what happens to them?'

She looked at him concerned at his tone. 'Is that what happened to you love?' 'Yes, boat ride to Hull, a free rail warrant to Scarborough. Thank you very much see you around mate.' It was said very bitterly. She wondered if he would tell her more as their relationship blossomed.

He looked incredibly handsome standing straight on the platform watching the troop train depart; a far away look in his eyes. She felt a familiar flutter in her tummy. I'm falling in love with this man. The thought took her by

150

surprise, she analysed it mentally. No, I am in love with him. Yes Helen Standish, it's happened to you my girl, I'm in love.

Her mood must have communicated itself to him, he was looking at her. 'Is everything all right love? You look pensive.'

'Yes, I don't know if it was watching those boys going off to war or not but a great realisation has just come over me.'

'It has, what's that then?'

'I've realised I'm in love. Me, Helen Standish of all people. I'm in love with a handsome beautiful caring man.'

His mouth dropped open in astonishment and then a look of fright.

'Don't look so worried, I'm talking about you silly lad, my wonderful lover.'

'Helen, you're actually saying you're in love with me?'

'Yes darling that's exactly what I'm saying.' There was a moment of stunned silence as she looked up into his eyes.

'So the next time I ask you to marry me?'

'I'll say yes my darling.'

A yell of sheer exultation escaped his lips. 'She's said she'll marry me.' Then extreme embarrassment as he realised all around were looking at the pair of them. Laughter, and then passengers shouting to him. 'Good luck mate, good on yer.' An elderly man with a morose looking wife. 'You don't know what you're letting yourself in for matey.' Winks and thumbs up from a group of soldiers nearby. 'Nice Christmas present mate,' shouted one of them. Everyone joining in the congratulations, smiles and wishes of good luck. It seemed to have been just the tonic for a country at war. People watching troops depart, now a little light relief. Something good happening to someone.

Both of them were bright red in the face but elated. They escaped towards the exit then Helen pulled back. 'Err, I think,' pointing to the sign 'LADIES.'

He laughed. 'Yes, good idea. Before we head out into the city.'

He insisted on taking her into the station café before departing ordering coffee with cream and a slice of sponge cake. She confessed she had never had coffee before.

'Oh, I have,' he grinned. 'About twice before.'

More chuckles between them. He was on a high floating on air. 'Put some brown sugar in,' when the coffee arrived. 'Now, pour the cream in over the back of your spoon; sip the coffee through the cream.'

'I never realised you were so sophisticated.'

'Neither did I.'

This was all a new experience for her. Riding on a train, drinking coffee like a lady, and the best feeling of all. Being in love.

'Its lovely,' she sighed sipping the coffee slowly. 'I can't believe this is happening to me.'

When they finally tore themselves away from the cafe Terry asked a porter if he had any idea where Stonegate was.

'Oh, sure squire. Turn left out of the station; follow your noses over the bridge. Lendal Bridge that is, second right is Blake Street next left is Stonegate.'

As they stepped out of the station premises onto the famous frontage Helen couldn't believe the number of Hansom cabs and four wheelers filling the road with traffic.

The city was teeming with people. Double Decker motor buses passing. Brewery wagons with four in hand horses, everywhere bustling activity.

They set off; arm in arm, walking over the bridge. Lendal Bridge as the porter had told them. Both of them fascinated with the myriad river traffic on the river. Working boats of all sorts mingling with pleasure boats taking punters for a trip. Unlike Scarborough signs of Christmas were everywhere.

There were decorations at shop windows, people bustling about with parcels, a cheerfulness all around.

'What did the porter say the name of the second street was?'

'Blake Street,' replied Helen. 'This is it coming up.'

Stonegate when they found it was an ancient street. It was full of a mixture of timber framed buildings, red brick ones, and some stone properties. Some of the buildings looked medieval. Most of them were shops or businesses of some sort. The street was bustling. Strolling along, arm in arm Helen suddenly said. 'There.' In one of the black and white timber framed buildings, a single window and doorway. A sign above. *ISAAC STEINER.*

The shop looked very worn and unloved. In the window were some faded green felt boards with items of jewellery displayed upon them. A grubby card in the corner of the window declared, *Unwanted jewellery bought. Silver and gold best prices given.*

'It doesn't look the sort of place the wealthy and rich frequent.'

'No,' Helen agreed. 'It all looks a bit down trodden.'

Terry pushed the faded brown door open, standing aside to allow Helen to enter ahead. A brass bell on the rear of the door jangled.

The interior was gloomy and smelled fusty. A mahogany counter ran across the back of the shop with a glass display case on the top. A wizened looking little man sat on a tall stool with an eyeglass screwed into his right eye peering at a necklace in his hand.

Not a single word of welcome but a rather brusque. 'Yes, can I help you?'

The yes uttered in a manner that said *what the hell do you want?*

Not a good start. Terry took the bull by the horns.

'I hope so. My father died recently and I'm trying to sort out his estate.'

The eyeglass had come out as Terry started speaking and he was looking at Terry intently. 'We've found a number of receipts in my father's possession that indicate he sold a number of items to you over quite a period of time. Yet we have no knowledge of what they were or where my father obtained them.'

He scowled at Terry. 'What was your father's name?'

'Richard Sheader.'

'Sorry, never heard of him.'

Terry was stunned, a tiny bubble of internal anger starting to grow. He felt in his pocket and produced the first receipt he had seen in the tin box.

'I have the first receipt here, dated 8th August 1905. It clearly says received from Mr Richard Sheader an item to the value of £185, a huge sum and it clearly has your shop address on it.'

Helen had sunk onto an upright chair at the end of the counter taking all in.

'There are sixteen receipts like this in total, the last one dated October 1913. When I added them all up the value was £3200, seven shillings and eight pence. And yet you say you have no knowledge of them?'

Steiner looked at Terry shiftily. 'I always respect customer confidentiality. It's very important in my trade and I'd need a signed letter from the customer to disclose information.'

'But I've just told you my father is dead, a signed letter would be impossible.'

'Can't give you any information then can I?'

Terry felt fury inside. This man's very demeanour made it clear to him that he had something to hide.

'Are you in fact Mr Steiner? Is this your signature on the receipt?'

'Yes, I'm Steiner but you keep saying your father. You haven't told me who you are, you could be anybody for all I know. Have you got any identification?'

'I'm Terrence Sheader, Richard Sheader's son. I have this receipt. How would I have access to this if I were not his son?'

'You could be a thief who's stolen it. I'd need positive proof of who you are before I'm even prepared to discuss this any further.'

Terry was angry with himself. He didn't think he would run into this sort of intransigence. The only proof he could have brought would have been a very tattered birth certificate or a letter from the solicitor, but he'd not be seeing him until Monday.

Helen, who had sat quietly through the exchange, dropped her bombshell.

'Come on darling we're wasting time here. And I'm sure Mr Steiner would not want any more of those items.'

Steiner almost fell off his high stool as they turned to leave. Terry had picked up straight away on her tactics and played along.

'You've more to sell! Have you inherited your father's supply?'

He stopped as Terry turned and gave him a stare.

'Well.' he stuttered. 'Perhaps when you've sorted your father's estate, and of course proof of identity, if then you think you've anything of interest to me well; perhaps we could do business.'

'I'll bear you in mind Mr Steiner,' he gave him a nod and escorted Helen out.

On the pavement he took a huge breath. 'God, fresh air. If ever there was an obvious devious crooked character that was it, but well done darling that was a brilliant intervention.'

She smiled. 'I've met a few men who sail close to the wind but he's sailing so closely his sails are in the water.'

He gave a sigh. 'It just convinces me all the more that dad was selling expensive items. And from the place we've just been in, items of jewellery. Dad must have obtained them by foul means. I reckon Steiner is what the criminal world call a fence.'

'We haven't learned much coming here, he said. 'A bit of a wasted trip,' and then brightening. 'But I've found my priceless jewel,' giving her a hug.

She smiled up at him. 'It's not all been wasted. It's clear he knew your dad. As soon as he thought more stuff might exist he gave the game away. No doubt at all that he

155

buys stuff of doubtful provenance. I'll bet most of the petty thieves in York know him.'

'Let's go back towards the river, find a seat and have those sandwiches.'

'Come on then lover I can see you're wasting away.'

They made their way back, found a wooden bench at the side of the river underneath Lendal Bridge and ate cheese sandwiches, enjoying watching the river vessels passing by.

'I wonder if we'll ever get to the bottom of this business.' He said gloomily. 'We still have nothing but suspicion and nothing of fact.'

'Well, those receipts are fact. After visiting Steiner we can be pretty certain that is where your dad's fortune came from. It's what your dad had and where he got it that's the difficult one.' She took a last bite of cheese sandwich.

'I think the answer lies with the crew your dad sailed with on *Yorkshire Lass*. That has to be the answer. The answer lies in Scarborough.'

She snuggled up to him. 'The ride on the train was fun though, and the sight of this busy city, it's exciting, I love it. It has a nice feel to it. But, right now I'm freezing.'

She pulled the shawl tightly round her shoulders.

'Oh love, come on back to the station. Sod the expense we'll have another coffee and piece of cake,' pulling her to her feet. 'In fact when I see you needing something I feel like saying sod the worry, just accept the money dad has left and to hell with it.

I could provide you with a super wedding. A better house or perhaps set up our own business.'

She slipped her arm through his.

'Naughty man, don't tempt me. I've lived so close to real poverty all my life that I'd give in to that idea without too much of a struggle.' He gave her a wry look; they hurriedly retraced their steps to the warmth of the station café.

The café had a roaring fire, waiting passengers sipping tea and coffee. A melting pot of travellers. The affluent and the not so affluent, cigarette smoke swirling in the air. The pungent smell of pipe tobacco, a buzz of conversation, a cocoon of warmth and bonhomie.

Helen was just starting to thaw out. Terry came back from the counter with two mugs of hot sweet cocoa made with milk, and two slices of rich fruit cake.

She sat back with a sigh. 'I could get used to this, 'she said dreamily. 'I know you haven't got what you wanted darling but today has been heavenly for me, such luxury.' she held the mug with both hands either side enjoying the warmth. He felt a flood of protective love. Should he stop being so upright and righteous? Was it about feeling just a bit rebellious about his father? He could provide such a life for her if he ignored his inner man. He pushed the thoughts to the back of his mind. Far too much confusion.

The return train left at three ten. Once again Helen wanted to board as soon as it arrived. It steamed in belching steam, squeals as the brakes were applied, doors slamming as some passengers disembarked and others boarded.

She bagged the window seat again snuggling down into her seat.

'This is the way to travel,' she sighed contentedly.

Three ten, spot on with the big station clock. The blast of the guards whistle followed by the much louder one of the locomotive. The same jerk and then a smooth take off. Whoosh, whoosh, from up front.

Helen was as much mesmerised on the return journey as coming. Eyes glued to the window they made good time and hissed into platform A at Scarborough at four fifteen.

She paused as they walked down the platform beside the hissing locomotive.

The fireman had the firebox door open throwing coal in. The bright red glow and sheen of sweat on his face was testament to the heat being thrown back.

Even standing it hissed and clanked like some living prehistoric beast. He caught the eye of the pretty girl observing. 'How do love, enjoy the trip?

'Yes thank you it was wonderful.' He watched her walk away with her man. He turned to the driver. 'Lovely arse on yon Bill.'

'Aye, I'll say.'

They were back at Overton Terrace in no time, Helen walking as quickly as possible to keep warm. As they arrived at their door Jack's door opened. How did they know they were back?

Sally! 'I've been keeping an eye out for you two. A man from Marshall and Snelgrove has delivered a load of parcels for you, a right load,' said almost accusatory. 'Been spending have we? Early Christmas presents?'

Well, that was obvious surely. A touch of jealousy there perhaps.

'I'll come and collect them,' said Terry.

'Oh I'll help.' Meaning I want to see what you've bought.

Terry had a broad grin on his face as he carried the three large parcels in, Sally scurrying behind with the two smaller ones. He gave Helen a wink as they dumped them on the kitchen table saying. 'I must get some fires going it's perishing in here. I think we might be in for a cold snap.'

'Are you not opening them now?' asked Sally looking disappointed.

'Got to get some warmth going Sally. Helen's freezing.'

Sally looked at Helen expectantly. Terry lighting fires was no reason for her not to start opening these intriguing parcels.

Helen decided to put her out of her misery. She took the hat box, unwrapped it and withdrew the cream creation with the burgundy band.

There was a gasp from Sally. 'Oh my,' Hand to mouth. 'Oh Helen, that's so lovely, oh it's gorgeous.' She looked stunned and envious all at the same time.

The residents of Overton Terrace were not known for shopping in Marshall and Snelgrove's store. Having parcels delivered from there even rarer. Having five parcels delivered! Well, unique. She wanted to be in at the unveiling.

Terry screwed up balls of the Mercury newspaper placing them in the grate. Then putting chopped sticks on top followed by selected pieces of coal. Helen decided to relent and allow Sally to help in unpacking.

Flames were taking hold of the coal assisted by Terry putting a sheet of newspaper across the grate opening supported on the back of the coal shovel. The inevitable happened! The sheet burst into flames and disappearing up the chimney but the fire was well alight now adding its warm glow to the hissing mantle. He turned from the fire to see what was causing a sudden degree of mirth from the two women. Helen had lifted out the bodice supplied for her exquisite dress.

It was the latest piece of silk under wear. A product of the French designer Poiret whose designs were making waves on both sides of the Atlantic.

It was in soft pink. Side panels of elastic but designed to gently pull the waist in instead of the ghastly tie strings at the back, a feature of most previous under garments. It had pink fabric covered buttons, tiny and dainty. The upper part of the bodice supported the breasts from underneath in a cup cake like frilly shelf leaving the upper part of the breast uncovered from just below the nipple.

Delicate stocking straps dangled from the base, and it had an elasticated panel to hold the tummy in. Only a Frenchman could have designed such an erotic piece of under wear.

Helen held it up for Sally to comment on which she did in typical manner.

'That Helen Standish is disgraceful.' Said with a chuckle. 'If you wear that in front of yon fella,' nodding in Terry's direction. 'You'll have no need of lighting fires, the heat from him will be enough.'

They both broke into a fit of giggles. Terry had visions of Helen wearing it.

'I'll let you know Sally what the result is,' he grinned at her.

'I'll light the fire in the lounge,' turning away toward the lounge. The mental vision of Helen wearing that creation was having its inevitable effect and he didn't want Sally making any lewd remarks about that.

He could hear the delighted and excited voice of Sally as the two of them carried on opening the parcels.

He repeated his exercise with paper wood and coal in the lounge to get a roaring fire going. The superb Welsh coal burned with tremendous heat, no wonder it was described as steam coal.

Gas rich, little spurts of blue flames shot out as it burned. It was the sort of fire a person could stare dreamily into. Rather like watching the shapes in clouds, little scenarios in flame.

The house was only small. The roaring fire in the kitchen and now the lounge started permeating throughout. He was particularly concerned about Helen saying she was frozen. At least she now had a warm coat. The thought that previously she only had a shawl was disturbing.

He went back to the two in the kitchen both happily clearing up cardboard and tissue paper. What was it about clothes that got women so excited?

'I can't believe how much you've spent on this girl,' said Sally in mock admonishment.

She had a shrewd idea of some of Helen's background. She actually knew her mother, saw her occasionally in the market.

Rebecca Standish would ask Sally, nervously, if Helen was alright. She had heard on the gossip chain that Helen was living with Terry's father and knew Sally lived next door.

'Can you not ask her yourself?' Sally had once asked her. Tears had flooded Rebecca's face. 'No, too much bad blood between us, it's my fault too. When I should have been there for her I let her down.'

She wouldn't explain any further and Sally didn't push her for explanation. But it also made her less judgmental of Helen as most of the neighbours were.

One thing was immediately obvious to Sally however. Helen had never been happier. Her cheeks glowed, her eyes sparkled. She showed all the signs of a person who had finally found true fulfilment.

Terry's story she did know.

Richard Sheader, Dick to her, had often talked about his son. About his injury in the war and his feeling of being worthless.

He also felt angry that things had gone so sour between them. Sally knew in reality that they were very much alike, never a good recipe for smooth relationships.

'Are you going to try that one on?' said Sally, pointing to the expensive, very expensive, cream dress. 'I've never seen anything so beautiful. It's like the dresses you see on the posh ladies going to the Spa.' To Sally, all ladies who went to the Spa were posh.

'I just love it. I still can't believe Terry has bought this for me, although,' laughing. 'It was partly to rub the nose of a snooty shop assistant.'

'No it wasn't', protested Terry. 'I really wanted you to have it.'

'In any case,' said Helen. 'I would have to put that bodice on to wear it and we don't want this lad getting all excited before bedtime.'

That prompted giggles from the two women.

'Oh, hell, the bed,' Terry smacked the palm of his hand on his for head.

'I've forgotten about the bed again.'

'What about the bed?' Sally asked with raised eyebrows.

'Err, it's broken.'

This thought Sally is getting better. 'Broken, how did that happen?'

'It just collapsed', he replied lamely.

'Looks as though you will be sleeping on the floor again then,' said Helen. 'I'm glad my bed's alright in the attic.' She was grinning from ear to ear.

Sally hooted with laughter. 'You two will be the death of me. I think I'll say goodnight and leave you both to it.'

She gave Helen a warm hug. 'Night dear, hope it's not too cold in the attic.' There were chortles of laughter from her as she left.

'Right big boy, while I get on with dinner you can dispose of this rubbish, fill the coal scuttle and', laughing. 'Have a look at the bed.'

'Right teacher,' he replied.

He took the cardboard out to the steel bin and rammed it in, filled the scuttle from the cellar then went to have a look at the bed. The wooden legs on the collapsed side had snapped clean off where they fitted into the cast iron base, the broken stubs still in place.

It would require the making of two new legs. The original ones were turned ornamental ones; he thought he might manage to make suitable replacements but they would just be a square practical job.

Perhaps in the meantime he could find something to prop that side up.

Could he remember seeing some bits of timber in the cellar?

Go and look Terry lad he thought.

There was a mouth-watering smell of frying steak and onions coming from the kitchen.

'God, that smells good.' Sliding up behind her and nuzzling her neck.

'Down boy, can you do anything with that bed?

'Just going to see if any bits of wood in the cellar could be used.'

He lit one of the little paraffin lamps, used for stopping the cistern in the outside toilet from freezing, and descended the cellar steps.

It smelled damp and fusty, quite unpleasant. A rack screwed to the wall in the cellar had a saw, screw drivers and other assorted tools. But the only wood was firewood or odd bits that would be useful for small jobs.

He looked around holding up the lamp. He was looking for anything that could be used to build up a pile of support.

There was a pile of coal under the grate. Various bits of detritus that most men kept because *it might be useful one day*. A hobbing foot used for repairing shoes, odd pieces of leather at the side of it. A rudimentary work bench made from reclaimed timber, rough but solid. A rusty old tin casket that looked ancient.

He pursed his lips. Nothing that looked as though it could be used for what he required. In fact most of it was rubbish. He made a mental decision to clear it all out after the funeral.

The casket caught his eye again. Pure curiosity made him go to it and prise the lid open, holding the lamp to cast light into it. In the top was a tray with some rusty spanners and other tools that had not been used for years.

He lifted the tray. It was empty underneath except for an object wrapped in oilcloth in the bottom. It measured about eighteen inches by ten. He placed the lamp on the floor before reaching in and lifting it out.

It was surprisingly heavy for its size. Lifting it out he carried it to the work bench. He placed the lamp on the bench and then un-wrapped the object revealing a wooden box with a hinged lid.

Curiosity well alight now he prised the lid open. His mouth dropped open with shock as the contents were revealed.

It was full of gold coins. Lifting one out he looked closely at it. Written around the top, KONINGRIJK DER NEDERLANDEN.

There was a crown in the centre of the coin with 10 to the left and G to the right. A date on the bottom, 1867.

He was stunned, and then after a moment.

'Helen, Helen, come and looks at this.' And then. 'No, in fact stay there. I'll bring it up, better light.'

He carried the box up into the kitchen placing it on the kitchen table.

Blowing out the flame in the paraffin lamp, a spiral of blue smoke curling upwards, he opened the lid as Helen looked on.

She looked as stunned as he must have upon seeing the contents.

'Where, what, are they gold coins? Where did you find them?' Her words rushed out in shock. So much had happened in the last week, now this find in the cellar. 'I can't believe this. The world is going mad.' She sat down heavily on the kitchen chair.

'No, neither can I. This was in an old tin tool box.' He tipped the contents onto the table gold coins spilling out in a glittering array.

They were all the same as the one he had looked at; all dated 1867.

Forty six coins were counted altogether.

He sat down at the side of Helen.

'This might be the source of dad's wealth,' he breathed. 'Probably the last of the supply, bloody hidden in the cellar.' 'Well, no one but him would go down there so I suppose they were in as safe a place as any.'

'Nederlanden, that's Dutch isn't it? Number ten; must be ten guilder coins, gold guilder coins.'

'How would a load of coins explain the items listed on those receipts from Steiner? they just said an item.' asked Helen.

'Perhaps dad took so many each time and our crooked dealer gave him a price for the lot. A lot lower than the true value you can bet, listed as a single item. He obviously didn't want to identify what the transaction was on a bit of paper it could be incriminating.'

'That makes sense,' she replied. 'Oh bugger; the steak!' She shot up and dashed across to the frying pan.

'I think we'd better eat before any more brain storming. Unless you like burnt steak.'

She dished up steak and fried onions with slices of pre-boiled potatoes finished off in the frying pan, all followed by apple pie and custard. What a boon that tin of *Birds* powder was.

They cleared the dishes and washed and dried them as a team, working in silence, thoughts busy. Terry had a far away look on his face. Reaching up and placing the plates on the shelf, no incident this time, he turned and looked at the golden hoard on the table.

'Oh hell, I just don't know what to make of all this.'

'No, me neither. I suppose it's possible they dredged something up from a wreck.'

He shrugged. 'Who knows,' a sudden thought. 'That cross dad gave you; do you know where he bought it?

'No, he just presented me with it one day and said he had a present for me. I was too delighted to ask where he got it. As I told you, being given a present was something new for me. It was such a lovely thing; I was just bowled over by it.' She gave a deep sigh.

'Where is it love?

'It's on the drawers in the bedroom.'

He got up and went upstairs, coming back down with the cross in his hand.

He placed it on the table and studied it closely. It was a beautiful thing about two inches by one. Very thick and of very fine quality, but it looked, to him anyway, as though it was much older than the chain.

He turned it over. A hallmark was pressed into the centre of the cross. It seemed to be in the shape of a shield, a mark, or date?

'I think it might be an idea to get a local jeweller to look at this. See if he can throw any light on it. My gut feeling is that it may have come from the same source as the coins.'

'You mean he didn't actually buy it for me?' a touch of indignation in her voice. 'I just don't know love. But if you

165

look at it closely this chain is a slightly different colour to the cross and just looks newer.'

Another deep sigh from her. 'Well, the bugger,' she said in an unfathomable tone. 'The absolute bugger.'

Terry gave a deep chuckle that bordered on a downright laugh.

'It's not bloody funny.' She snapped.

He reached across and took her hand. 'Its wonderful, do you know why? Because the first piece of jewellery to be bought for you will be bought by me, the man who loves you more than life itself. I'm glad if I'm right that dad didn't buy it. I want to be the first man to buy you something special.'

'Silly romantic.' But her eyes were misty when she said it and her squeeze on his hand belied the words.

'I can't put into words what you mean to me Helen. Perhaps I allowed the leg wound to embitter me for so long. No real friends or company. In fact I lie; I did have one very good friend in the army, a chap called Bruce Campbell. He saved my life when I was shot. He pulled me to safety while still under fire. He got a medal for it, sadly I lost contact after de-mob. I wonder where he is now.'

'So I owe your existence to a man called Bruce, your best friend.' She gave a huge gusty laugh. 'From now on then I'll call your best friend and my best friend Bruce,' stroking her hand provocatively up his thigh.

He burst into laughter. 'Trust you, you little minx, and we still haven't got the bed repaired. Let's put these away,' scooping the coins back into the box.

'I think you were right love. As you said on the train, the answer to all this is here. We need to try and find any of the crew that Pash and dad sailed with.'

He gave a yawn. 'Wow, it's been a long day. I've just realised how tired I am.' 'Me too but I would like to go to York again one day. Perhaps in summer, I really enjoyed York.'

'We will love, promise.' He rose and inserted the big key in the old clock winding it up to the top.

'Strip wash in the kitchen. Don't feel like traipsing upstairs with hot water tonight.'

'No, you're right,' he agreed. 'Its too much effort; I think we're both shattered.' Pouring hot water into the big white pot sink was much easier then carrying it upstairs in a jug. 'You first.' She commanded.

He stripped to the waist and had a good all over wash. Helen fishing a big fluffy towel out from the cupboard. Whilst he was drying himself she undid his trouser buttons with great dexterity, slipping his trousers down.

'Bruce needs a wash,' she grinned, proceeding to do just that.

He made it easy for her by standing to attention. She dried his friend carefully, and stopped him from grabbing her. 'Off upstairs big man. Get the floor bed ready', laughing. 'I'll be up as soon as I've washed.' He did as commanded bounding upstairs naked. He lit the gas mantle turning it up full, and then went to draw the curtains but was mesmerised by the view.

The moon was casting a silvery light on the sea. Surf showing silver white in the distance, a vision of natural beauty. It was almost like a painting. 'Perfect,' he breathed.

He closed the curtains and sorted the mattress on the floor. Must get that seen to tomorrow and find a jeweller who might be able to tell them something about the cross. He realised ruefully that he really wanted proof that the cross had not been bought by his father, mixed emotions flooding through his mind.

He heard Helen coming upstairs. He was waiting for her comment about the still broken bed. The door opened and his breathing almost stopped.

She was wearing nothing but the pink bodice, a salacious smile on her face.

Her long brown legs stretching up to the hem, just a glimpse of tightly curled black hair below the centre line. And her breasts looking like an offering to the gods,

167

supported from below, her hard nipples pointing at him like a pair of pistols.

She'd excited him from that first day when she came to the house to make her peace with him but this was the most erotic sight ever. He reached out for her but she dodged playfully.

'Not yet my love, you've another lesson from teacher waiting.'

He quivered with excitement. If this was a return to school then he would be the most attentive pupil ever.

She sat on the chair by the set of drawers, legs parted provocatively, crooking a finger at him.

'Come to Helen darling.'

He almost fell in his rush to her. She held a hand against his chest as once more he made to take hold of her.

'Now my darling. Kneel down and eat me.'

She sat back in the chair lifting her legs slightly. He was overwhelmed by her request. He knelt and looked at the erotic sight of her moist fleshy mound, lowered his head to her and nuzzled, quivering with the sheer excitement of doing something he could only have dreamt of.

She gave a loud gasp as his tongue entered her. Both of her hands clasped his head and pulled him in. She started bucking and writhing like a woman possessed, gasping and making animal like sounds. He felt as though he were in the lap of the gods.

She reached orgasm with an almighty scream, clasping his head to her so tightly he almost suffocated.

He couldn't wait any longer; he was aroused as never before.

Shooting to his feet he grasped both of her legs just below the knees, lifted and parted them. Then his good friend Bruce was in and he was thrusting into her like a starving man tasting his first good meal.

Helen started to groan as he went at it full tilt, his energetic and rapid performance awakening her to arousal again.

He had the mightiest orgasm yet, thrusting deep and holding himself erect against her as his ejaculation took over. She quivered and wriggled against it until she had her second orgasm, both of them locked together in a brief frozen moment of time.

The chair, tilted back on its rear legs, started to creak. A sudden crack like a pistol shot and then both legs snapped and they were deposited unceremoniously on the floor.

Laughing and giggling, still locked together, they rolled off the chair sideways.

'Oh my darling,' he said. 'If you thought before that I was a Hun battleship I can tell you that was a full broadside.' Another fit of giggling as he helped her out of the erotic bodice, then the pair of them collapsed into bed and slept the sleep of the exhausted.

In the bedroom next door, the crash of the breaking chair, and the squeals and giggles floated through the room wall.

'Christ almighty,' muttered Jack. 'I know that young bugger's got sum catchin up ter do but carryin on like that will shorten is life a bit.'

'A touch of jealousy Jack Savage?' said Sally with a smile.

He grinned at Sally. 'Aye, well, a touch perhaps. The young bugger,' and then, after a pause. 'Lucky young bugger.'

*

The two lovers awoke Wednesday morning to a day of relentless rain. It streamed down the window like a waterfall driven by a strong north easterly whipping in off the sea. The curtains twitched and moved as draughts found there way through the ancient window frame.

'Listen to that?' Said Helen. 'Don't feel like getting up to that.'

'Me neither.' They wrapped arms around each other and nodded off again.

It was ten thirty by the time they got out of a warm bed and staggered downstairs although they only knew that on arrival in the kitchen. That was the only clock in the house! At least it was warm downstairs. Terry had banked up the fires last night before they went to bed so a poke and shovel full of coal soon had kitchen and lounge fires roaring nicely.

Kippers and chunks of buttered bread for breakfast. Large steaming mugs of tea. 'I needed that, need to rebuild my energy', putting on a little boy voice. 'Teacher's driving me too hard.'

A laugh from Helen, 'You've been a good little boy. You might just have earned your first gold star.' The kitchen door rattled as a gust of wind whistled down the terrace.

'Do we have to go out in this today?' she asked.

'I know what you mean. Did dad have any wet weather gear? I haven't a thing for this sort of rain.'

'Oh yes, his oilskins and sou'wester are in the wardrobe. Smelly old things though', she said, wrinkling up her nose.

'Are we desperate for food or anything,' he asked.

'Not really. Provided the milkman calls we should manage until tomorrow.'

'Good, have you any idea if Chippy Jones still lives up on Princess Street?'

He was referring to the local carpenter and odd job man.

'Oh yes, we had him recently to fix the door.'

'Right, I'll borrow dad's oilskins and call at Chippy's house. I'll ask him to have a look at the bed. And then call at that little jeweller in Westborough. Ask him to look at the cross, should be back for lunch time.'

'Don't run off with any strange woman', she laughed.

'Don't need to I've already got one.'

'You've just lost your gold star,' she hissed.

'No matter, it's the gold cross I'm interested in.'

'Out man before you get walloped.'

She was right about the oilskins; they were probably his dad's original fishing gear. Like a man who has a favourite pair of trousers and is unwilling to part with them they were well past best but should at least protect him from the driving rain.

He stepped out and was immediately hit by the squally rain, gusty wind off the sea driving it almost horizontally. He climbed the steep steps up to Princess Street, turned right and went along to number fourteen, Chippy Jones house. He banged on the door to be heard above the wind. It was a few moments before it opened and the monkey-like face of Chippy peered round the door.

'Bloody hell! Terry Sheader, not seen you for a long time mate. Sorry to hear about your pa.'

'Thanks Chippy. I wondered if you could help me out. Two of the legs on the bed have snapped off, must have been woodworm or something. I wondered if it were possible to make a couple?'

Chippy looked at him suspiciously. 'Snapped off you say, never come across that before.' He sniffed, a little candle disappearing back up his left nostril. 'I'll come round and have a look. Nothing on just now.'

'Oh thanks for that Chippy. I'm just off to sort out some stuff, Helen's in. Just tell her I've asked you to come round.'

'Helen Standish?' He looked startled.

'Yes, she and I are a couple now.'

Chippy opened his mouth and then wisely shut it again. Terry turned as though to go. 'Oh, we have a broken chair in the bedroom as well. Don't think it's a repair job but if you know anyone who has a sturdy chair to sell I'd be grateful.' 'Aye, I think I know where I could pick one up. Might be a bit difficult like being as it's so close to Christmas.'

Meaning an excuse to charge a bit more thought Terry. He took his leave, Chippy still watching as he departed. Well, he thought, that's given him something to think about.

He knew they would get a chair. Chippy would buy one off one of his many contacts, add a percentage, and sell it to them. It was the way of the world.

He set off for Westborough and the jewellers. The German attack had seemingly knocked some of the stuffing out of the residents of Scarborough. Considering it was close to Christmas, there were few signs of decorations or festivities although the foul weather was probably keeping people in.

Back at the house Helen answered a brisk knock on the door. It was the milkman, drenched to the skin, even though he was wearing oilskins and hat.

'Foul morning missus.'

'It is that.' She turned into the kitchen and took the two pint jug off the shelf, returning to the door. 'Two pints please. Will you be coming Christmas Day?'

'Oh aye missus,' he said. 'Nowt much to celebrate this year anyway.'

He lifted his measuring ladle off the churn dipping it in twice to fill her jug. Helen thanked him, paid her four pence, he tipped his hat to her and trundled the barrow next door.

Sally was just sticking her head out as she was going in. 'Morning Helen, good night was it?' a big smile on her face.

'Morning Sally. You were right about the bodice,' giving her a wink. Hoots of laughter from Sally as she went back indoors.

She hadn't been in more than five minutes before a knock came on the door again. It was Chippy Jones. 'Terry asked me to come round and see if I could make some new legs for your bed.' He leered at her. He was an obnoxious little man, not someone she was really comfortable with when alone in the house.

She decided she would not accompany him upstairs.

'It's at the right at the top of the stairs,' she told him.

He hesitated for a brief second. 'I'll go and have a look then.'

He set off up the stairs. She had a sudden moment of panic. The box of coins were in the drawers. Was he likely to look around? He was a shifty little character; she decided to follow him up after all.

He'd lifted the bed up onto its side, not an easy task for a little bloke like him; it had a heavy cast iron frame. She had to smile when he said looking slightly disappointed and surprised at the same time. 'There's signs of woodworm, yes, definite in this one,' pointing to the bed head one. 'Good news is they're standard turned spindles. I can get four matching ones from the joiners.'

'You'll need four so they all match.' He added hurriedly.

'Terry said you needed a chair as well.'

'Yes, that's broken.' He looked hard at the shattered chair. 'How'd that happen then?

'Terry stood on it to reach the curtains,' she lied smoothly, 'he's a big man.'

'Aye, I dare say.' He leered again and then produced a wooden rule, pencil and pad from his pocket. He measured the socket size and leg length, writing it down on his pad after giving the pencil a good licking.

It reminded her of a grass snake's tongue flicking out.

'Suppose you'd like it fixing for tonight?' Openly looking at her bosom.

'Yes, that would be good if you could do it by then.'

He licked his lips like a man tasting a treat. 'Right, I'll be off then.'

She turned quickly and led him downstairs wishing him good morning as he departed. As the door closed behind him she breathed a sigh of relief. Bloody little weasel she thought.

Terry meanwhile was entering Seizers jewellery shop in Westborough. The door bell tinkled as he entered A

173

pleasant looking young man greeted him with a cheery. 'Good morning, not the weather though', with a chuckle.

'No, not indeed. I'm looking for some enlightenment actually,' he confessed. 'I've inherited a gold cross from my father, it seems rather old. I wondered if you might be able to tell me anything about it?

'Not much else to do on a day like this,' he grinned at Terry. 'Let's have a look at it then.' Terry handed him the cross. The young man took one look and then said. 'Well. It's immediately obvious the chain doesn't go with it. The chain is nine carat, rather cheap if I may say so. The cross is twenty two carat and of extremely fine quality.'

He turned it over. 'Ah! A nice hallmark.' He reached into a drawer and produced a hallmark recognition chart, screwed an eyeglass into his eye, and looked closely at the mark.

'Dutch', he announced after consulting the chart. 'Amsterdam assay mark.' Another look at the chart. 'And the year is 1600.'

'You can tell the actual year? Asked Terry.

'Oh yes, a very clear date mark. It's a very fine piece of workmanship. Superb craftsmanship, it'll be quite valuable. If you should wish to sell it I'd be happy to give you a valuation.'

'I'm very grateful for your time,' Terry replied. 'I rather think it would look very nice on my wife.'

'It would look good on any lady. But please, put a chain of equivalent quality on it I beg of you. That chain does not do it justice.'

Terry thanked him again and said he would be the first jeweller he would contact if he decided to part with it.

It was a very thoughtful Terry who set off for home. Dutch and an early date. The coins also were Dutch. It would seem to indicate they all came from the same source. The source of his father's wealth he thought was now certain. He had sold coins and items of jewellery over a period of time, and to a 'dodgy' buyer at that, indicating he didn't want anyone in authority to know of his sales. He had so much to ponder on.

He arrived back home sopping wet; the oilskins were definitely due for dumping. He stripped off the useless outer garment; his shirt was wringing wet, his trousers dry from waist to knee only.

'Get em off,' grinned Helen. The big fluffy towel was produced and she rubbed him down vigorously.

'Go and get some clothes on before I molest you.'

'I could get so used to that.' He shot upstairs to change. She called after him. 'And I'll tell you about that little weasel you sent round.'

He came down looking concerned. 'What do you mean love about Chippy?'

'Oh, no real problem it's just that he gives me the creeps. He looked at me as though he was undressing me. I'd prefer you to be here when he comes back.'

'The bugger, do you want me to have a word with him?'

'No, we need him to sort the bed; he says he can get legs from the joiners shop. They're a standard pattern, should be back this afternoon. Oh, and he says he should be able to find a chair.'

He laughed. 'He'll find a chair no doubt; it will be at a good profit to him though.

'And another thing,' she grinned. 'Believe it or not the legs that collapsed actually did have woodworm.'

'Well, what do you know; it wasn't just my fault then?' He took her hand. 'Now then, sit down and let me tell you about the cross.'

'Ah, the cross.' Said in a neutral tone.

He gave a little shrug and raised his eyebrows.

'The jeweller was very helpful. In fact I think he welcomed someone to talk to. The weather was so foul I was the only person in the shop.'

He placed it on the table.

'He said the cross was of very fine quality. Twenty two carat gold and, as I expected, of Dutch origin.' He turned the cross over.

'He examined this hallmark and identified it as an Amsterdam mark and he was able to date it exactly to 1600.'

'However, he said the chain was only nine carat gold, of average quality and certainly didn't go with the cross.' Helen picked it up and held it.

'As said before, Richard Sheader you little bugger.'

He gave a tight little smile. 'What can I say Helen?'

'You don't have to say anything love it's not your doing. I'll still be sad at the funeral. As I said to you, your dad was a bit of a character and yes,' a little laugh. 'A randy sod, but he saved my life and was good to me. It really is a shame you and he never made up your differences. I suppose I was even the partial cause of that but he was a good man. If it were my father being buried I would dance on the bastard's grave.' The last was said with such venom it was painful to hear.

'Helen darling, the one thing we can all be certain of is that the past can't be changed. But we dam well won't let it colour our future. We need to look forward now. To hell with the past the future is ours.' He held her hand tightly.

'On Tuesday we'll give dad a good send off. And then no looking back.'

Terry spent the rest of the day clearing junk from the cellar while Helen tidied the kitchen and generally played happy homes. And it really was starting to feel like *their* home now to both of them. A comfortable feel of domesticity after so much upset and disorder.

Chippy came round mid-afternoon and replaced the bed legs and also brought a sturdy but plain chair. Terry thanked him rather brusquely, paying the inflated price of £4:10s.

It was a tired couple who climbed the stairs to bed that night, Terry asking if she were going to hang her stocking up tomorrow night. She laughed. 'Don't posses a pair.' It was the first night they had snuggled together without making love and they fell asleep within minutes of retiring.

Thursday morning, Christmas Eve was overcast but fine. A welcome sight as they were going round to Sally's for pre Christmas drinks and a meal. They had both been very touched when Sally asked them. At least they were welcome there. No sniggers and snide remarks. Not unless Jack pulled their legs, but it would be good humoured. It turned out to be an extremely laid back enjoyable day. Sally was a superb cook and Jack produced a bottle of sherry after dinner. Helen had never tasted sherry. She decided she liked it, and with a wink from Jack to Terry, her glass was refilled a couple of times resulting in a merry and giggly Helen.

They stayed until midnight, no-one noticing the time. It was one of the most convivial days the two had spent since the bombardment. It was a very happy and slightly inebriated couple who staggered back home that night. Helen so much so she collapsed on the bed fully clothed and was asleep immediately. Terry undressed and lay at her side following suit.

The Friday morning, Christmas Day was cold but bright. They didn't surface until eleven am, Helen waking to a thumping headache.

'Oh God Terry,' she said. 'Is this what's known as a hangover?'

'Serves you right for drinking too much sherry. Drink is supposed to make you randy. It didn't work for you did it?' He was laughing as he said it.

'In fact, you were so drunk I'll bet you don't even remember me taking advantage of you.'

'She sat upright sharply. 'What? You didn't? Then a pause, 'Did you?' He burst out laughing. 'I knew that would wake you up. Come on, wash your face you'll feel better then.'

They washed and dressed slowly neither having much energy. Terry suggested they have a walk after some breakfast. Helen declined the idea of breakfast but decided a walk in fresh air was a good idea. They wandered hand in hand down to the harbour. Terry was fascinated to see a huge steam crane on Vincent's pier at the lighthouse, the demolition of the top section of which was well under way.

Few people were about and rolls of barbed wire were on the beach. A sad sight to the delights it offered before war was declared. They sauntered onto West pier, some work taking place there. Christmas Day or not, boats still went out and needed help unloading and filleting fish stock. Helen waved happily to a slim young fisher girl who was chatting to one of the men; she didn't seem to be very busy.

'That's Mary the girl who I get fish off,' Helen said. 'Come on, I'll introduce you.'

She walked up to the girl. 'Hi Mary, let me introduce you to my lovely man,' Terry going bright red. 'This is Terry,' turning to him. 'This is Mary my friend I told you about.'

'Hello, pleased to meet you Mary. It's nice to meet the girl who helps keep my tummy full.' He gave her one of his most infectious grins to which she responded. He noticed she was a petite little thing with a pretty elfin face, freckles across a little upturned nose giving her a cheeky look. Even though it was quite chilly on the pier she had bare arms.

'It's a shame to be working Christmas Day Mary,' he said.

'Oh, this is just pottering about plus a bit of company. Mrs Evans, my landlady fed me so well I need to get some fresh air.'

She gave him a big beaming smile which lit up her entire face. 'Are you two doing the same?'

'Yes, this one,' he said, indicating Helen with a grin from ear to ear. 'This one got a bit tiddly last night. She needs a blow to clear her head.'

She gave a girly chuckle. 'Oh Helen what are you like?'

'They filled me up with sherry,' protested Helen. 'We went round to our neighbours. I've never had sherry before and I think I only had three glasses.'

Terry winked at Mary who looked into his face laughing. Helen, girl alarm bells ringing, decided it was time to move on. They said goodbye to Mary and strolled back towards home. As soon as they were out of hearing Helen said.

'Hit it off rather well didn't you?' Terry, working hard to keep his face straight. 'She's a very pretty girl isn't she?'

'Don't you dare start fancying other women,' she snarled. 'She's far too young anyway.' He burst out laughing. 'Helen Standish are you jealous? I have the loveliest creature in the world, and she thinks I'm going to look at other women. It's only a week ago that I thought I would never have a girl.'

She gave him a rueful look. 'Just remember you're mine. Besides, we girls know when a girl finds a man interesting and Mary was giving off all the signs.'

He shook his head and was still chuckling as they walked home.

They had a relaxing lunch. Helen had invited Jack and Sally round for dinner that evening to return the pleasure the older two had given them. Helen had cooked a chicken for Christmas lunch, Sally offering to do her version of Christmas pudding. Both Jack and Sally seemed to accept they were settled and making a great start at a relationship, offering a stabilising friendship that was very comforting.

It was a late night again. Jack had brought the remains of the sherry with him. Helen was wary, but the bottle emptied quickly enough. When the older couple made their departure at twelve thirty, both looking remarkably fresh still, the younger pair crawled into bed, arms around each other and were both asleep in a trice.

Saturday morning, Boxing Day was cold but still clear and fresh. A day spent pottering, as Terry called it, happy in each others company. He took some time showing Helen how to write her signature which she practised copying over and over. The day passed in remarkably quick time, although, talking about it afterwards, they could remember little of what the day had involved. Terry may not yet have achieved married status but they acted like an old married couple that day.

*

They shocked everyone again by going to church on Sunday morning. But this time Terry wore his new suit and Helen wore the dark blue dress he had bought her. The bowler worn at a rakish angle he looked the very essence of sophistication. Both of them making a handsome couple, and they made sure all saw them as a couple.

The minister welcomed them warmly gazing a little too long at Helen. The blue dress showed off her figure to perfection. When they were seated in the pew Terry whispered. 'Some need to talk about me and the little fisher lass. I think you've just won over a man of the cloth.'

'Phooey! Man of the cloth indeed. He'll still have a cock under that cassock,' she said crudely. They drew angry looks as they gave way to barely suppressed giggles.

The day was spent lazily, pottering about sorting out his dad's wardrobe, putting a pile on one side to throw out. Helen altering the layout of ornaments in the lounge, putting their own touch to the house, and then after dinner discussing the morrow.

They planned hopefully, to collect Terry's suit. Helen had also persuaded him to see if he could buy a warm overcoat; and they needed to buy fresh food. It was a new and rather nice experience for Helen to have *her man* accompany her on shopping trips. Richard had certainly never done so. It was *woman's* work.'

They decided they would go to Castle Road first and collect the suit. Terry was worried if it was not right could it be made so in time for Tuesday? And then they would buy groceries on the way back.

He needn't have worried. The experienced old tailor had made a superb job of alterations. It was impossible to tell it had not been made for him and he was able to supply a warm grey wool overcoat for only £2.

It was then that Mr Cohen made a suggestion that was to have a profound effect on Terry. He had parcelled up their purchases. The suit and overcoat in two brown paper parcels, the hat in a cardboard hatbox, and explained he had made a subtle alteration to the left leg of his suit. On measuring Terry when they were in the shop previously he had noticed Terry's left leg was shorter by half an inch. He had made the necessary adjustment accordingly.

'An accident was it sir?' as they were about to depart.

'No, a Boer bullet,' replied Terry. The old tailors face clouded.

'Oh, I lost my son at Balaclava.' His face showed intense sadness.

'I'm so sorry to hear that Mr Cohen we lost a lot of good lads.'

'I hope you don't think I'm interfering Mr Sheader but I know a chap who had a similar injury causing a slight difference in leg size just like you. Mr Daniels the cobbler up the road made a small cork insert for his shoe. It made all the difference to the way this chap walked he was almost back to normal.'

They thanked the kind old man gratefully, and as they exited Helen turned to him and said. 'We aught to call at that cobbler's it sounds worth exploring.'

'I don't know,' he replied doubtfully. 'The army surgeon said nothing could be done.'

'Perhaps nothing could be done for your actual leg but this isn't surgery, it's about making an adjustment to your shoe to compensate for it.'

'I don't want to look like one of those people with a club foot,' he said. 'I couldn't stand that.'

*

181

'Silly lad. It's just a small insert in your shoe, it won't be noticeable. In fact you would probably walk without a limp.' She hitched up the parcel on her hip which was getting heavy and cumbersome. 'Look, it's only three doors up let's just call and have a word.'

He agreed with some reluctance. He had spent his entire life deliberately ignoring his injury, only Helen could push him into taking this sort of action. The shop was similar to Cohen's with the exception of a sheet of wood replacing the window which had been shattered by the shell blasts. Helen took the initiative explaining to Mr Daniels how her husband's leg had been injured, and how Mr Cohen had mentioned he might be able to make compensatory foot ware.

It lifted Terry's introspection immediately when she referred to him as her husband. He couldn't help grinning like a Cheshire cat at her as in fact she knew it would!

Daniels was very helpful and sympathetic, soon putting Terry at ease. He asked Terry to remove his shoes and then stand as straight as possible, allowing his right leg to take his weight. He then carefully measured the difference in leg length.

When satisfied with his measurements he straightened up.

'Yes indeed Mr Sheader. I can make special shoes that will compensate for your injury. They'll be of finest leather and will give no indication of any difference in appearance to a normal pair. I could do you a pair for £1:5s or two pairs for £2.'

Terry hesitated. 'If you're not satisfied that they're an improvement to you I'll take them back free of charge. I'm so confidant they will be of benefit to you.'

Helen,as always the decisive one said, 'Yes Mr Daniels, please measure my husband's feet. He'll take the offer of two pairs, one pair in black and one in brown please.' Terry looked at her speechless. 'Decision made for you darling. This is so important.'

He looked at this amazing woman. Lover, teacher, mother and carer all rolled up into one. Looking so concerned about his welfare, making decisions on his behalf. He wanted at that very moment to just scoop her up into his arms.

He sat meekly while Daniels produced a wooden foot measuring device, placing his foot on it and sliding a wooden stop up to his toe. A leather strap went around his foot to measure the height, all the time, Helen observing every move.

By the time they left there it was already eleven thirty. Daniels had promised the shoes would be ready in a week.

'I can't believe I've agreed to all that. I feel as though I was just pushed along by the tide.'

'Quite so,' she said. 'And the tide as you know is unstoppable. This tide certainly is.'

'I think it'll be nice to have a sandwich at Betty's again. These parcels are a struggle and we can get just the essentials in the Market and then stagger home.' Once again she was in charge.

Their arrival at the market hall, laden with parcels, caused the usual commotion. A number of gossipy females nudging each other and making remarks that were clear to Helen they were the butt of conversation.

'It seems my darling, that when we walk in here we take precedence over the Germans,' she whispered. 'I wonder if they'll ever get used to us.'

'I couldn't care less I'm happy,' he gave her hand a squeeze. 'Very very happy.'

They bought fresh veg and meat at the stalls, and then well and truly laden up to the gunnels headed for home.

On arrival back home Helen insisted he try on the suit. She dragged him up to the bedroom and ordered him to strip.

'Well that suit's a beauty,' she grinned. 'Come on then. The blue shirt will go very well with grey.'

He quickly donned the clothes. The three piece suit in its dark grey. Matching waistcoat, blue shirt and the bowler worn at a jaunty angle transformed him. Helen took a deep breath.

'God you look handsome. Good enough to eat. Oh yes my darling, you'll do.'

Her delight in his appearance, the look in her eyes, caused a flutter in his tummy as always. He wished for no more.

'Keep those clothes on.' Taking his hand she led him back downstairs. 'I want Sally to see this.'

Leaving him standing in the kitchen bewildered she shot out of the door, and was back in no time with Sally.

'There Sally, what do you think to my lovely man?' she said proudly.

Sally looked open mouthed. 'Oh my, Terry you look gorgeous, absolutely gorgeous.' The two women gazed at him in admiration. He felt like the mannequin in Marshall and Snelgrove's store.

'Do a turn; commanded Helen. He duly obliged. 'Can I swap him for Jack,' giggled Sally.

'Sorry Sally, this one is definitely mine.'

'You'll do your dad proud Tuesday.'

Sally brought him down to earth with a bump. Tomorrow, the funeral, only a couple of nights away. Helen saw the look that flitted across his face. She gave him a hug. 'It'll all be alright Tuesday love. You won't be on your own. You and me, Jack and Sally, we'll all stand by your side. It'll all go well.'

'Aye, we'll all be there for you lad.' Said Sally kindly.

They had one of Betty Metcalf's steak pies for dinner and a piece of her famous sponge cake. Their mood was solemn. The thought of the funeral spoiled the atmosphere slightly.

'An early night tonight I think,' Helen said. 'You can forget that young girl on the pier, this one has something for you.'

They were in bed by ten, a proper bed again with legs! They cuddled naked, fondling each other and then Helen brazenly rolled onto her left side and pressed her naked buttocks into him.

Erotica again! He slid into her with his right hand caressing her right breast, long slow strokes as she had taught him, and then Helen urged him on.

'Go on boy, go on.' He did just that, and as sensations increased he released her breast and clutched both hips with a firm grip. And then pulling her into him he plunged in and out. The inevitable result as they both achieved orgasm in a bucking thrusting climax, a sure precursor to a good night's sleep.

\*\*\*

# CHAPTER TEN

## Solicitors, a funeral and an assault

Tuesday 28th, they both knew the appointment with the solicitor at eleven was the most important event of the day. Helen thought it better if he went alone. She would buy some groceries and meet him half an hour later. She also suggested, which he had not thought of, that he take the bank book with him and his birth certificate.

The morning was again a fine one, overcast but mild. A breakfast of toast and marmalade, Helen holding the toasting fork in front of the kitchen fire then handing Terry the toasted squares to butter and spread thickly with marmalade. They washed and dried the plates, and then set off for the appointment. Terry dressed in the smart suit, Helen in the beige dress and wool coat. He kissed her warmly as she peeled off to the market, and he carried on to St Thomas Street and the solicitors. He was early. Punctuality had always been important to him, a remnant of army life. It was about ten fifteen as he approached the office and as he did so was amazed to see a figure he knew also entering the office. None other than Tom Watson.

He knew Watson as a young man with a short temper when in drink and knew he was an odd jobbing seaman who had been in trouble for stealing. He had had a run in with him one night in the *Mucky Duck*. It was very rare that Terry went in a pub at night. He couldn't afford it for one thing, but the night in question, some six months or so ago, had been Bob Tanner's birthday. He had agreed to meet Bob in the pub for a drink with him. Watson was already there when they entered and it was clear from his loud manner that he had already supped a fair bit.

Terry and Bob settled in their usual spot in the snug, chatting with some of the regulars, when a loud argument broke out at the bar. Watson was arguing fiercely with an older man. What about they could not hear but they both saw Watson throw a punch at the other man. The punch connected with the older man's cheek and he staggered back. Mary O'Brian, the landlady, tried to intervene but was pushed roughly by Watson who told her to *fuck off* at the same time.

Terry was furious at her being treated like that but as he made to rise a full blown fight started.

Punches were thrown by both men, but it turned ugly when Watson produced a knife from a pocket. Ignoring his gammy leg Terry shot to his feet and strode forward, grabbing Watson's arm just as he made to strike.

He twisted it savagely and Watson dropped the knife with a cry of pain.

Watson turned on him furiously attempting to throw punches. Terry blocked them, and then slapped him across the face with an open hand. The crack of flesh on flesh was loud and clear. It seemed to incense Watson even more. He'd been slapped like a girl, the ultimate insult.

Terry's army experience and muscular torso won the day. He twisted Watson's arm up his back and escorted him to the door. Watson found himself sprawled on the pavement.

'Come back in and I'll break your neck.' Terry's tone of voice brooked no argument. Like all bullies, Watson backed off, but he was incensed with rage and as he staggered away shouted. 'I'll remember you, you fucker.'

Terry just smiled grimly and went back inside.

Mary O'Brian rushed up to him and threw her arms around his neck giving him a resounding kiss on the cheek. 'My hero, bless you Terry.' It brought the colour to his face with embarrassment but it also saw him with free drinks for the night.

He'd seen Watson occasionally after that around town. His presence always brought a scowl to Watson's face but he had never had cause to speak to him.

And now here he was going into the same solicitors that Terry was visiting.

Terry gave his name to the lad at the desk and was asked to take a seat. The same lad provided a cup of tea while he waited which was very welcome.

It was just turned his appointment time of eleven when the office door down the corridor opened and out came Watson. He looked as though he had made an effort to look smart, and it was impossible to hide the look of elation on his face. Terry thought he looked like a man who had received some very good news.

He seemed momentarily startled to see Terry there and acknowledged him as he passed with a curt, 'Sheader.' Terry couldn't bring himself to speak, simply nodding in return.

A few moments later the door opened and a large man with a shock of white hair and florid face stepped out. He took in Terry's smart attire; and stepped forward with out stretched hand.

'Mr Sheader, I'm Jonathan Flowers please come in.'

Terry followed Flowers into the office, an expensively furnished room with a large mahogany desk dominating in the middle.

Various framed certificates hung on the wall, no doubt testament to the qualifications of Flowers.

'Please be seated.' Flowers nodded at the well padded chair in front of the desk. 'I believe you're here in regard to your father's will?'

'Yes, that's so.'

'It seems to be a morning of dealing with wills.' Flowers said expansively.

Terry ferreted away that comment. Was that what Watson was doing there?

'I take it you've brought proof of identification?' Flowers asked his eyebrows lifting. 'Yes, I've my birth certificate and copy of father's will; also my father's bank book.' Helen had prepared him well he thought.

Flowers already had the original will in front of him.

'It's a straight forward will Mr Sheader no complications. Your father did indicate a substantial bank sum was involved.' He raised eyebrows again and looked up from the will to Terry. Bright sharp eyes looking straight into his, perhaps expecting Terry to comment on this huge sum. It would not have been lost on Flowers that this was an ex-fisherman's will. The huge sum was unusual to say the least.

Terry decided to remain neutral. 'It was a surprise to me to see this amount I must confess. Regrettably, my father and I have been estranged for some time. I wasn't aware he even had a will.'

Flowers grunted. Make of that what you will thought Terry.

'Your father has left all his worldly goods to you Mr Sheader with two codicils. An Albert gold watch to be bequeathed to Mr Jack Savage, and the sum of £100 to be bequeathed to a Miss Helen Standish.' Eyebrows up again, big bushy things thought Terry.

'Miss Standish was my father's live in carer, in fact we have formed a relationship leading hopefully to marriage. Mr Savage is father's friend and next door neighbour. I've already presented the watch to him.'

'Fine, all seems well then. If you would just let me look at your documents.'

Terry passed his little bundle across the desk. As Flowers looked at them he said. 'I will need to write a letter to the bank on your behalf and implant our official seal. That should be ready by Wednesday morning. If, after getting access to your father's account you would ask Miss Standish to put her signature to a letter saying she has received the £100, and perhaps one similar from Mr Savage. They then will be attached to this original and kept by this office as proof that all your father's wishes have been carried out.'

Terry decided at this point not to tell him Helen could neither read nor write. He could do that for her and save her any embarrassment.

Flowers stood up and offered his hand again. 'The letter will be ready Thursday morning. As it will be New Years Eve we'll be closed after lunch. It will be with the receptionist who will accept the small charge involved. It just remains for me give you my best wishes in your marriage prospects my dear chap.'

Terry shook the proffered hand and made his way out, nodding to the receptionist on the way.

Helen was already waiting outside shopping bag full.

'How did it go?' she asked anxiously.

He told her the gist of it. 'And he says when we get access to dad's account I have to give you a hundred pounds, and you have to write and sign a letter acknowledging it.'

He had to smile as he saw the cloud pass across her face.

'And before you ask, no, I didn't tell him you couldn't read. I'll write it for you darling and you can practise your signature.'

He made pretence of signing in the air, big flourishes. 'Helen Sheader.'

'You don't miss a chance do you,' laughing. 'Here, take hold of this bag it's too heavy for me.'

'I'll tell you what was strange. As I went in Tom Watson was coming out. He's a right villain if ever there was one.'

'Tom Watson, that little swine.' She said.

'You know him?'

'Oh yes, when I was being dragged from pillar to post by Jim Swift, that seaman who took me in when I first left home,' she explained seeing the quizzical look on his face, 'but we won't go there.' she said hurriedly. 'He took me in the *Old Steam Packet* one night. A night out for the slag.' She said bitterly.'

'You realise that's another slapped bottom,' he said, trying to lift the tension.

She gave him a wry smile. 'Well, as I was saying, we were in the *Packet*. Young Watson was at the bar semi-drunk as usual. Banter from the men in there, and then Watson saw me and Jim. He came across and stood in front of me. He said. 'What a lovely pair of tits.' With no further ado he reached down and grabbed my right breast.'

Tears misted her eyes as she told him. 'He squeezed really hard and hurt me. I slapped his face and he just laughed and staggered away. What made it really bad was Jim thinking it was a great joke. Just like all the other men in there.'

'Bugger.' She fumbled for her handkerchief as tears came. 'I told you I had a past.'

He put the bag down and put his arms around her ignoring the looks of passers-by.

'And I've told you the past is the past. We're starting afresh love, don't distress yourself. You'll never ever be treated like that again; it's gone never to return.' She looked up at him with damp brown eyes.

'I love you so much.' His heart did a flip.

'I love you more than words can describe. Nothing will come between us now, push the past away darling,' he said. 'But,' and his eyes were icy cold as he said it. 'Tom Watson needs to steer clear of me.'

They made their way back down Eastborough. As they did so a cheery voice called out. 'Hello you two.'

It was Mary Duncan the fisher girl, wearing a pretty blue dress, wicker basket over her arm. 'Are you alright Helen?' noticing the damp eyes. 'Yes, nothing to bother about. Just a nasty memory from the past.'

'Oh, right. I thought you had man trouble that's all,' with an impish grin at Terry. Helen laughed.

'No, no trouble with this man. This man's very special.'

Mary allowed her eyes to linger a little too long on Terry, making Helen purse her lips.

'Have you got a boy friend Mary?' he asked.

'No one currently,' impish smile again. 'Why are you offering?'

'No he bloody isn't, he's got more than enough with me.' Helen laughing as she said it but with a glimmer in the eye.

'Well, we need to get on,' she tugged on his arm. 'We need to prepare for the funeral in the morning, lots to do. See you Mary; enjoy the rest of the day.'

Terry smiled and winked at her as he tipped his hat and they left the small figure as she turned towards the market. Helen's *enjoy the rest of the day* was to prove anything but for the unfortunate girl. Her day was to end on a horrifying note.

Arm in arm they walked back home.

'She quite fancies you,' said Helen. 'I can tell in the way she looked at you. It's a girl's second instinct.'

'Rubbish, she probably sees a father figure.'

'Girls don't stare at their dad's crotch and she had a good look at yours.' They wandered home the easy banter flowing between them.


Tom Watson was on cloud nine, he was going to be a boat owner in his own right. He celebrated in the usual way, getting drunk.

It was when exiting the *Three Mariners* much the worse for drink that he saw Mary Duncan. Mary lodged with a woman on Quay Street at the back of the pub. She was in a blue dress with her auburn hair hanging long down her back. Her attractive face with a dusting of light freckles over her pert little nose and intense green eyes caused him an instant hardening in his groin.

'Mary me girl.' He called.

She turned at the sound of the voice. It sounded slightly slurred and she recognised Tom Watson. She realised he was the worse for drink, something that she found awful in a man. The smell of ale on the breath she found obnoxious, and as she looked at him he seemed different to the young man she had found so attractive almost a fortnight ago.

His lips looked to be compressed in a very thin line and he had a slightly wild look in his eyes.

'Well, well my love, just the tonic for a young seaman.'

He leered in a way that made her feel a little touch of fear.

'I'm on my way in. I've to get this parcel to Mrs Evans,' she said, holding the paper wrapped packet out. 'She's expecting me back before nine.'

'Plenty of time for a cuddle me girl.'

He'd moved closer to her and the smell of ale on him was overpowering.

'No, no, Mrs Evans sent me to Shirley's especially for this lace. She's expecting me back with it directly.'

She made to move away but he shot his hand out and clasped her wrist.

'In too much of a rush lass,' he murmured. He made to kiss her, his stinking breath making her heave.

She pulled away, but it seemed to enrage him.

'Bitch, stop messing about.' He tightened his grip on her wrist.

'Come on let's have a walk.'

He was pulling her towards the steps leading to the steep path which climbed upward at the side of the castle dyke, by now very dark and totally without any lighting.

She was furious. 'I won't go and I'll not be called such a filthy name.' She felt anger surge through her, and then suddenly and with no warning he gave her a hard slap across her face.

She yelped stunned, and felt herself being pulled along. She stumbled and almost fell but with incredible strength he yanked her upright.

For the first time she felt real fear. His face was contorted with anger. His whole demeanour had changed making her feel highly threatened.

She started to gasp in short little breaths seeming unable to say anything, and he was literally dragging her up the path now.

The only light came from a pale moon casting a ghostly light that made the brambles at the side of the path take on weird shapes.

Her face was burning where he had slapped her. She couldn't believe he had done that.

'No, no, no.' She managed to stutter.

'Shut up you little cow.' The intensity of his voice struck terror into her. They were a good thirty yards up the path, no one to be seen. He suddenly thrust her off the path into the rough growth at the side.

The move threw her off balance and she stumbled and fell to her knees. In a swift move he grabbed her hair and yanked her head backwards. It made her gasp with pain and she saw he was fumbling with his trousers.

She realised he'd released his swollen member. As her mouth opened to shout for help he thrust forward and drove it into her mouth.

A terrible feeling of gagging, unable to breathe hardly. He was thrusting in and out of her mouth like someone mad, grunting and muttering 'bitch, bitch,' over and over. She could feel the world starting to swim and a feeling of faintness coming over her. He seemed completely oblivious to her being unable to breathe.

Just as she thought she was going to loose consciousness he yelled something unintelligible, and as he did so a flood of hot liquid flooded her mouth.

Then he was out of her and stumbling away.

She fell forwards on to her belly coughing and heaving, spitting his awful sperm out, the stink and saltiness of it suddenly making her violently sick.

Tears flooded her eyes. She was gasping for air and then was convulsed by huge sobs. It felt as if she would never get the awful taste out of her mouth. Then she realised she was partially lying in nettles the stinging only just starting to register.

Her head resting on the damp grass. She was violently sick again feeling too weak to even move or get up. She had no idea how long she lay there.

After a while, and with immense effort, she forced herself to her knees and managed to stagger to her feet. Swaying and almost falling back to her knees but remaining upright with great effort, feeling sick again but nothing left to come.

It took a great effort to start walking back feeling all the time as though she would fall. Another great shudder overtook her. She had no idea how long it took to get back to Mrs Evans house and then she was unable to open the door as her entire body started trembling. The door opened, Mrs Evans standing there.

'Oh my God lass look at you, what's happened?'

*

Terry and Helen enjoyed a lazy dinner. Helen had found a couple of candles which she lit after pouring melted wax into two saucers to hold them firm.

They added a romantic air to the meal and she loved the way the soft flame seemed to make Terry's blue eyes sparkle.

'I quite envy Mary.' said Helen suddenly.

'Oh, why's that?'

'She's a bright girl; she can read for one thing. She told me she spends a lot of her time reading books from the penny library. Sherlock Holmes detective stories are one of her favourites.'

'You're letting this get out of proportion love. I promise, when we're over the next few days I'll start teaching you to read and write. Of course, I'll expect you to keep teaching me.'

She giggled. 'That's a deal then.'

After the meal she put out the clothes they'd wear in the morning.

'I think that dress could do with ironing and while I'm at it I'll run the iron down the creases in your trousers. Should we nip next door and make sure Jack and Sally know the times for tomorrow?'

He readily agreed to that. He wanted to keep busy tonight, the thought of the funeral in the morning was weighing heavily on him. He knew he'd be glad when it was all over.

They had another early night both of them not looking forward to the morning. As had become custom now they both slept in the buff, curled up together in happy unity.

Funerals are gloomy affairs. As though to emphasise that fact the morning broke with a steady drizzle and sullen dark clouds.

They were up at seven thirty, Terry feeding the banked up fires. He shaved and generally kept busy, gas mantles hissing on full to help dispel the gloom. Terry had mentioned to Jack and some other neighbours who'd enquired that he didn't think his father would have wanted everyone in black. He said he welcomed less formal attire. It was just as well because he certainly didn't have a black suit and Helen didn't have anything in black.

He'd wear the new dark grey suit. Just a hint of a fine stripe in a lighter shade of grey. Helen would wear the dark blue dress covered by a grey cape she had produced from the wardrobe.

They had breakfasted and got ready well before time. Jack and Sally came round and sat with them, waiting for the knock on the door to signal the arrival of the cortège.

As the terrace was inaccessible to vehicular traffic the plan was for the cortège to come to Burr Bank situated at the end of the terrace. They'd then walk from the house to the cortège.

The knock came at nine fifty. The butterflies in Terry's stomach worked overtime. Helen squeezed his hand and gave him a smile of encouragement.

Two formally dressed men in frock coats and top hats conducted them to the carriage. Fortunately, the drizzle had stopped although looking capable of restarting any moment.

As they approached the hearse Terry felt tears pricking his eyes. The rift that had divided him and his father now seemed so ridiculous. He felt such deep regret at not having seen his father before his death.

Helen also looked deeply moved. She was quite pale and clung to his arm.

They climbed into the landau, Terry and Helen sitting facing forward. Jack and Sally with their backs to the hearse.

The two top hated men boarded the hearse and the cortège moved off. The clatter of horse's hooves rang clear in the murky morning.

The slow stately journey was a blur for Terry. He was to remember afterwards people removing hats as they passed. People standing with bowed heads showing respect to a total stranger.

With great efficiency the cortège arrived at the little chapel at Dean Road at ten twenty. They alighted and watched as the coffin was lifted from the hearse, and then they all followed it into the chapel.

Terry was surprised to see that the little chapel was packed. Obviously his father had commanded more respect than he thought. The funeral director conducted him and Helen to a front pew, Helen sobbing quietly now at the sight of the coffin on trestles placed before the altar.

For him the service passed in a blur of hymns and prayers, none of which meant much to him. After the service the coffin was placed on a large two wheeled cart and they all followed to the grave side for the final internment.

He felt guilty when Helen whispered. 'Terry, you're hurting love.'

He hadn't realised he was crushing her hand so tightly.

'Sorry.' Face flushing. The last handful of soil was thrown into the grave and they turned to leave. It was as though it was happening to someone else. All slightly unreal like in a stage play.

The journey home brought on the most intense relief. It was over, he could breath normally again. Helen gave his hand a little squeeze.

'Are you all right love?'

'Yes, fine now, just glad it's over.'

'A gud service,' said Jack. 'Dick wud a bin pleased wi it.'

Helen had prepared some sandwiches and cake before hand. They invited Sally and Jack back for refreshments, the worst part of the day over. Now they could move on.

\*\*\*

# CHAPTER ELEVEN

## Investigations

Thursday, New Year's Eve. Awaking with a feeling of a weight lifted from his shoulders. He felt slightly guilty to even feel that way, but knew getting the funeral over and done with had a huge psychological effect on him.

His father's death. The circumstances of the death. The relationship he now had with what had been his father's girl had all spun around in his mind like a spinning top.

The funeral had removed some of the many aspects of uncertainty. He could concentrate on solving the mystery surrounding his father's wealth, ever hopeful of a satisfactory conclusion.

Rain once again was streaking down the window. Typical weather for the coming weekend he couldn't help thinking.

What was it about the British weather that always seemed to turn vile at weekends and bank holidays?

He lay on his back looking at the ceiling. At his side Helen was still fast asleep an occasional little whimper suggesting she was dreaming.

He knew little would be achieved in the next four days. Tomorrow was New Years Day and then the weekend again. Perhaps they might try to see if any of his dad's old crew could be tracked down on Saturday? Monday he would need to present the letter to the bank. The letter, yes, he needed to collect it this morning before the solicitors shut.

He decided he would question Jack. See if he could remember who the crew members were. That was of course if he knew in the first place.

Another little whimper from Helen. She turned and slid an arm across his chest. He found it incredibly comforting. All these years alone and now this amazing creature asleep at his side.

He determined that he would do everything in his power to make sure no one rocked this particular boat.

A sudden gust of wind and rain rattling on the window. He closed his eyes again nodding gently. Then his eyes flew open as unbidden, the image of Tom Watson flitted through his mind.

Now why the hell is that bastard in my mind he thought. How strange the mind's working when on the borders of sleep.

*

A movement from Helen. Her hand slid down to his belly, she still fast asleep.

An instant twitch in his groin, God! Would he always react like this?

He must have nodded off again for the next recollection was Helen's hand firmly grasping his manhood and whispering, 'Are you awake lover, Bruce is.'

His eyes flicked open. 'We both are now.'

A little giggle from her, her hand grasping firmly, the other one rubbing his helmet with the palm.

'That's so velvety.' She murmured.

'I can't ever remember being woken like this,' he giggled. 'At least when the hand didn't belong to me.'

'Start of a new year tomorrow lover perhaps we aught to see this one out in style.' He turned to her caressing her hard nipple, the feel making Bruce harden even more. The rain rattling on the window falling now on totally deaf ears.

He rolled onto her kissing her lips, breasts, then making love slowly and easily as she had taught him. He paused as his ejaculation approached allowing it to die down, and then increasing again until she was bucking and gasping under him.

'Now, now,' as she arched her back. He duly obliged with an increase in prolonged hard thrusts. The inevitable cry from her, and his deep final thrust and hold tightly up against her, both of them shuddering in ecstasy.

'Don't take it out.' He did as told and held himself tight against her until he felt the inevitable shrinking, only then rolling off her perspiring body, both of them fully sated.

'You're proving to be a very good pupil.' She whispered.'

'Well, my education has been so delayed. I have to try extra hard to catch up.'

'My love, you're doing very well in the extra hard department.'

They had a relaxed breakfast of boiled eggs followed by toast and marmalade, Terry told her his plans for the weekend.

'If we can get in touch with any of dad's crewmates they might just spill the beans, although Jack mentioned they were all acting secretively so we may have to tread carefully.'

'Do you think Jack actually knows the names of any of them or was he just repeating rumour?'

'There's only one way to find out.'

'Would you like a walk up town with me? I've to collect the letter from the solicitors.'

'Yes, nothing else pressing. Will the bank be shut do you think?'

'Probably open until lunchtime. If they are I'll most likely need to make an appointment to see the manager. I don't think he'd see me there and then.'

Breakfast dishes dealt with, warmest clothes donned, they set off to collect the letter. Surprisingly few people about again. Poor weather and most people probably having done all the preparation for the coming evening. They walked quickly arm in arm through the town.

Good as his word the letter Mr Flowers had promised was waiting at the reception desk. Terry paid the three shillings requested and then the pair of them hurried along the road to William and Deacons bank. Luckily it was open, but due to close at lunch time.

Terry explained his business to a wizened little teller who asked him to wait while he made enquiries. He came back within minutes.

'Mr Johnson will be able to see you on Monday at ten o'clock Mr Sheader if that would suit you?'

'Yes, that would be fine thank you.'

It didn't matter whether he thought it was fine or not. He wasn't going to be seen before Monday; that was that he thought.

They made the journey back down Eastborough once again, the rain now a fine drizzle. As they approached the coiled barbed wire that blocked off the bottom of Eastborough Helen shouted. 'Mary.'

A figure hunched in a fisherman's type cape and floppy souwester was crossing the road.

The figure lifted a head and Terry saw it was indeed Mary Duncan.

*

She looked startled that her name had been called, turning as though to move on.

'Mary, it's me, Helen.'

Mary paused. She had a strange look on her face. As they walked up to her, her face quivered as though about to break into tears.

Helen could see immediately that something was wrong. Female instinct to the fore yet again.

'Mary', she said very softly. 'What's wrong love?'

Mary stared at them both as though they were strangers. She looked as though she were about to speak but nothing came, just standing helplessly looking at them in utter misery.

Helen placed a hand on her shoulder. 'What is it love?'

The dam burst. The girl broke into a frightful wailing, clutching herself to Helen, Terry looking on helplessly. This was a situation he suspected that required female input. He'd be of little help here.

Mary was wracked with sobs. Helen consoling her very much in the way she had Terry when he returned from the Kessler's in a distressed state.

He caught Helen's eye and nodded at the nearby Merchants row, a small loop of road off Eastborough that gave a view of the sea. It had a convenient seat for the use of visitors and locals to sit and take in the view.

Helen led Mary gently to the seat. It was wet of course but so were they by now, it would make little difference.

They sat down Helen pulling the girl's face onto her shoulder, holding her tightly until the sobs started to ease.

'Now love, take it easy, tell me what's wrong.'

The words came out in a great gabbling rush. She recounted the events of that Tuesday. How after seeing them she had gone home for tea. She had run an errand for her landlady, Mrs Evans that night. How she had been accosted by a seaman whom she had had a brief fling with previously. She told Helen how he had dragged her up the Castle Dyke path where he had thrown her in the shrubs and assaulted her. Both Helen and Terry were horrified.

'You mean he raped you?' asked Helen.

'No, no, not rape.' She said the tears flowing freely again. 'No, he forced his thing into my mouth. He almost choked me. He only stopped after, you know what,' shrugging.

'Have you told the police?' asked Terry.

'No, no, I don't want police involved,' she shuddered. 'They'd make me give evidence in court. No, I couldn't stand that and I don't want everyone to know.'

'But you're not going to let him get away with it Mary love. He mustn't be allowed to get away with it.'

She went quiet curled up against Helen as though she were a mother figure.

Helen squeezed her. 'Do you know his name love? You said you'd known him before.' The girl looked shamefaced and coloured up.

'It was Monday night before the German attack. It was silly I know but I let him make love to me at the back of the *Steam Packet*, rutting up against the wall like an animal,' she said, self-disgust in her voice. 'Just that one time. He seemed a really fit lad and,... well,... you know.'

Helen thought yes, I do know.

'But do you know his name?' asked Terry again.

'Oh yes, it's Tom Watson.'

Helen made a choking sound and Terry gave an incredulous, 'What? That bastard? God almighty Mary, not that bastard.'

Mary looked at Terry for the first time. 'Do you know him?'

'Know him! He's a nasty piece of work, a really nasty piece. You couldn't have picked anyone worse love. He's got a real evil streak in him.'

She gave him a beseeching look. 'But what can I do? I just don't know what to do. I couldn't even tell Mrs Evans what he did. I just told her he'd interfered with me.'

'You really should tell the police love. They're the only ones who can bring him to justice,' he replied.

'No, I couldn't. I know you think I'm a coward not doing that but honestly, I couldn't do it.'

Helen looked at him and shrugged. She could visualise herself in that situation especially as she had been in her previous life. The police would think she was a bit of a slag, probably asking for it. She'd have led the lad on wouldn't she? Helen could see exactly the girl's predicament.

Terry gave a deep sigh. 'So love. What are you going to do?'

'I really don't know. Just try and get on with life and avoid him if I see him again.'

'New Years Day tomorrow,' said Helen suddenly. 'What are you doing for that?'

Mary gave a shrug. 'Nothing. Nothing to do.'

'Right, tell Mrs Evans you've been invited out for New Year's Eve Dinner tonight at our house. We'd love your company.'

'Really, you really mean that?' Helen caught Terry's eye, he nodded.

'Yes, we'd both love you to come. We'd only be on our own anyway. You can see in the New Year and then Terry will walk you home,' said Helen.

Mary looked sad. 'Oh, that'd be lovely. But New Year or not, Mrs Evans locks the door at ten and that's that. She wouldn't let me in, I'd be locked out.'

'Then tell her you're stopping the night at our house. You can go back anytime tomorrow.'

'Do you really mean it?' She was looking directly at Terry now.

'Yes, we do. Go home now and tell her. You know where we live, No. 6 Overton Terrace.'

They sent a much happier girl away Terry saying to Helen. 'We'd better do a bit of shopping before going home eh?'

It was two thirty by the time they got home loaded down with extra provisions and three, yes three, bottles of sherry. And, as a surprise for Mary a large teddy bear.

'What the hell,' said Terry. 'It's the start of a new year. We'll push the boat out tonight.'

They struggled in loaded down and sopping wet.

'First job,' declared Helen. 'Get changed and then try to make that attic a little hospitable.'

'Yes, you're right; it won't do as it is.'

After having a very late lunch, if it could be called that, of cheese on wedges of buttered bread; they set too on the attic. One of the rugs from their bedroom was placed at the side of the single bed, Helen making it up with fresh sheets and blankets. A new mantle was fitted to the light. The old one was broken and hadn't been replaced for ages.

The spare pair of clean curtains for their room was put up. A large bowl from the kitchen with a matching jug was supplied for washing. And the chamber pot under the bed was given a good wash and replaced.

Helen set out the spare towels. The fluffy ones she had insisted on buying when she lived with Terry's dad. A small face towel and a bigger bath towel. Terry inspected, making sure the rug covered the loose floorboard.

'All in all that's not too bad.' He announced. 'Probably better than her room at Mrs Evans.'

'Yes, she should get a good night's sleep. God, when I think of that swine.'

'I know,' replied Terry. 'Would you believe it, last night I actually dreamt about the bastard. What should we do about him love? Can't believe he's just going to get away with it.'

'God only knows,' she replied moodily. 'What the hell can be done? Short of using some of your dad's money to pay a villain to give him a good working over.'

'Don't tempt me,' scowled Terry.

They went downstairs, Terry getting all the fires roaring. Helen started to prepare the meal for tonight. They really had pushed the boat out having purchased a large pork joint, an expensive item. Lots of potatoes and vegetables. One of Betty Metcalf's famous puddings, a rich fruit sponge. And, luxury of luxuries, a box of crackers.

'Should we invite Jack and Sally round?' asked Helen eyeing the amount of food. 'We have loads here.'

'That's a good idea. Yes, it will make up the numbers but just prime them to be a bit discrete about Mary.'

She checked on the gas level in the oven. The piece of pork was well basted, and then went next door. She returned after a few minutes.

'Sally says they'd love to come. They weren't planning anything special tonight. But they'd prefer to go before midnight,' she gave a grin. 'Getting old, need their beddy-byes.'

'Nothing wrong with an early night. Jack might want to get Sally in bed early to let the New Year in.' she hooted with laughter.

'Some chance. He gets a bigger thrill these days setting fire to that briar than setting fire to Sally.'

They chuckled the day away, Helen just having enough chairs by bringing the bedroom one down to allow five around the kitchen table.

There was no table in the lounge, although that was pretty common in the terrace. She put a cracker at the head of each plate.

'I'll bet the Kessler's are having a posh do,' she said wistfully. 'Silver cutlery, wine and all the trimmings. All dished up by the servants.'

'They'll be no happier than us though. In fact I don't think Mrs Kessler gets much in the way of happiness.'

A beautiful smell was starting to drift from the oven.

'That pork is already making my mouth water. You're proving a good cook as well as a good...' He stopped at that point and gave her his best lewd grin. She responded by throwing the dish cloth at him. Helen looked at the clock, five fifteen.

'Go and make yourself look presentable, out of the kitchen man.' She said, pointing to the stairs. He stuck his tongue out at her and did as told. He decided to put the suit trousers on with the blue shirt. He knew Helen was putting the blue dress on. We'll match, he thought.

He came back down looking transformed. A big smile of approval from Helen.

'Oh! I've just thought, have we any sherry glasses?' He asked.

'No, but we have some wine glasses. None of them match but I don't think anyone will mind.'

She fussed around, lighting some more candles and placing them where their flickering glow added warmth to the house.

There was a timid knock on the door at five forty. Helen winked at him and opened the door for Mary. 'Come in love, we're all ready.'

She gave her a big hug drawing her in and removing the rain cape in one swift movement. Terry had a quick thought which made him smile. She's good at whipping clothes off fast.

Helen hung the cape up, Terry stepping forward and also giving her a hug. 'Welcome love; so glad you've come.' She had a simple light blue dress on with a matching ribbon in her hair.

The long auburn locks hung down her back. She looked pretty and demure, just a little shy. A touch of colour came to her face when Terry hugged her.

Helen already had the kettle on.

'Soon have a warm cuppa love. Are they your night things?' picking up the tiny basket with a wicker lid.

'Yes.' Even more shyly.

'Take them up to the attic love,' to Terry. She winked at him and nodded. He knew what she was alluding to. They had both been appalled by Mary's story, and on Helen's idea, had bought a teddy bear in the town which was now sitting on the bed.

'Come on,' he said to Mary. 'I'll show you your room. It's nothing marvellous but we think you'll be comfy.'

She followed him upstairs, the first flight and then the steeper one to the attic.

The door had a simple latch. Terry flung the door open, stood to one side giving a flourishing bow. 'Your room madam.'

She giggled and went in. The very first thing she saw was the teddy; lying on the pillow a big pink bow around his neck.

'Oh, a teddy,' she whispered, turning to look at Terry as though to ask what can it be.

He answered her unspoken question. 'Yes love it's for you, he's yours. We were both appalled by what has happened to you; we thought that little chap might bring a bit of comfort for you.' She gave an almost childish gurgle and ran to the bed scooping up the teddy and hugging it.

'Oh he's lovely. I've never had anything like it; I don't know what to say. He's lovely, thank you thank you.' She ran to Terry, threw her arms around him and planted a kiss on his cheek, teddy squashed between them. His turn to colour slightly. Still clutching teddy she ran to the stairs.

'I've got to say thank you to Helen.'

She scooted downstairs like an excited child, ran into the kitchen clutching teddy in her left arm, threw her right arm round Helen's neck and kissed her.

'Helen, I'm so happy. I've never had a doll or anything. Is it really mine to keep?'

Helen took in the excited child like young woman. She knew what it was like to miss out on so many things when still young. She also had a bad sexual experience when she was only sixteen. She had enormous empathy for this girl.

'Yes love, we both thought you'd like him. It's yours with our blessing.'

Mary's eyes were wet and shining. She hugged the teddy as though it were her own child.

'He's just so cuddly, I love him. I don't know how to thank you enough.'

'Just looking at your face is thanks enough; we're going to have a smashing New Year's Eve.'

A knock at the door signalled the arrival of Jack and Sally. Helen introduced Mary to them and vice versa, Jack giving her a hug like a real live version of the teddy she was hugging.

'Nice ter meet yer lass. What's name o this fella then?' grinning at her.

'Oh, I haven't thought of a name. Terry and Helen have bought him for me, isn't he lovely?' Sally hugged her also. 'He looks a real cuddly chap, I'm quite jealous.'

Jack sniffed. 'By, that smells good lass,' to Helen. 'Hope the cracklin's crisp.' They all laughed at the old man. He was beaming joviality. Just what was needed and when he turned to Sally and said,

'Show em what we've brought lass.'

Helen yelled. 'We're all going to be drunk tonight.' Sally had produced a bottle of sherry, identical to the three that Terry and Helen had bought.

Helen had primed both Jack and Sally to Mary's plight. Jack's typical retort when told it was Tom Watson. 'We'll have ter have that bugger sorted.'

The dinner was a great success. Mary was soon made to feel at ease. Plenty of good food, a superb pudding with lashings of 'Birds' custard, and then a glass of sherry each. Mary, like Helen before her had never tasted sherry in her life.

They enjoyed the pulling of a cracker each. Mary, to her delight, getting a silver sixpence in hers arranged previously by Terry.

Helen piled all the pots in the sink.

'They can wait until tomorrow. Come on everyone bring your sherry into the lounge.' They retired to the lounge, Terry bringing a kitchen chair with him as they only had seating for four.

Wearing paper hats, the fire roaring and gas mantle turned up full, they played party games and guessing games. Jack proving for all his Yorkshire common man persona to be very bright and *with it*.

The teddy never wandered more than arms length from Mary, the purchase of which had been an inspired decision.

There was much merriment playing charades, the merriment rising with the consumption of sherry. Helen was merry but not drunk She knew what the effect of too much sherry had now and wisely paced herself. The stuff didn't even touch Jack. Sally was red of face but well in control.

It was eleven o'clock when Jack and Sally took their leave of them. Kisses and best wishes all round for the coming year. Mary was in the same state as Helen had been before becoming wise to the effects of too much drink. The room was really warm, the result of the roaring fire and five bodies until recently. Terry undid a few buttons on his shirt and sat back.

'Wow, it's warm, or is it just me?'

'It's warm all right,' said Helen.

'Look at Terry showing his muscles,' slurred Mary. She was staring goggle eyed at Terry.

'Enough of that girl,' said Helen. 'He's an old man.'

'Hey, less of that,' grinned Terry. 'This old man is more then enough for you.'

'Oh, look its three minutes to midnight, stand up and get your glasses ready,' said Helen. She only knew that because Terry had brought the kitchen clock into the lounge for just this purpose. Mary stood, staggered, and promptly sat down again. 'Oops,' she giggled, sherry slopping from her glass.

They both laughed at her. Terry grasped her hand and helped her to stand. She swayed. He put his arm round her waist and held her upright. She leaned into him which brought a slight pucker to Helen's lips.

'Midnight,' announced Terry. 'Happy New Year,' he leaned across and kissed Helen warmly and passionately and then bent his head to kiss Mary on the cheek. She was having none of it; turning her head she met his lips with her own and gave him a real smacker. 'Happy New Year.'

Helen was off the mark like a greyhound.

'I think its time for bed now young lady. You're just a wee bit tipsy.'

There was no doubt about that. It was only Terry's steadying arm keeping her upright. She looked up at Terry's face, slightly unfocused.

'Are you putting me to bed Terry?'

'No he bloody isn't, teddy's putting you to bed,' said Helen.

'Come on Terry; help me get her upstairs.'

Terry had to almost carry her up her legs now like jelly. He shuffled her into the attic bedroom sitting her on the bed, and then going back downstairs to fetch some hot water on Helen's orders.

He stuffed the teddy under his arm, grasped the bowl with both hands and went back upstairs. He entered the room and placed the bowl on the drawers.

'Can you manage?' he asked Helen.

'I'll manage, you can float.' Giving him a knowing look. He grinned at her.

'Here we are young lady you've left teddy.' Handing it to Mary.

'Oh thank you. Do I get a kiss night night?' She looked up at him, face flushed and eyes unfocused.

'You'll get a smacked bottom behaving like that,' said Helen. 'Off you go,' to Terry. 'I've to get her undressed now.'

'Terry can undress me,' she giggled. Terry went as Helen gave him a drop dead look.

He put out the mantle in the lounge and banked the fire, smiling as he took in the sight of three empty bottles. The remaining one was only half full, and then he started on the pots in the sink.

He was putting the last plate away when Helen joined him.

'I was going to leave that job until morning but thanks darling, that's a great help.'

'I've told you before. I'm a very useful man; you can't do without me.' She put her arms around his neck.

'No I can't, you've really grown on me Terry Sheader,' she murmured as she kissed him.

'Is the little madam asleep?' he asked.

'Not yet. She was talking to teddy when I left her. Randy little bugger, or is it just the drink?'

'The latter I think,' he laughed. 'She was like you when you had sherry for the first time. You were so far gone you couldn't even remember me using your body.'

'You liar, you are lying aren't you?' He laughed out loud. 'You'll never know will you.'

'Strip wash here in the sink?' he asked. 'Don't feel like carrying water upstairs now. I'm well and truly ready for bed.'

'Yes, same here. While the fire's still throwing some heat out.'

They stripped off, completely unselfconscious in each other's presence now and had a good wash. Even Bruce seemed ready for bed. No twitching at the leash tonight, or rather, morning.

Towelled dry, they turned to go upstairs when Mary appeared at the door.

Her eyes almost popped out of her head as she stared openly at Bruce.

'What the hell are you doing Mary?' yelled Helen.

'I was coming down to ask for a glass of water,' she replied, steadying herself on the jamb. Terry grabbed the towel holding it in front of both of them.

'Get back upstairs Mary. I'll bring you some water as we come up.'

'Shorry,' she slurred, turning and almost falling.

'Bloody hell Terry, help her up,' snarled Helen. 'Wrap the towel round yourself.'

He tied the towel round his waist, turned Mary towards the stairs, and grasping her around the waist pushed her up the stairs. They made it to the attic without incident. He guided her to the bed, whipped the sheets back and said. 'Get in.'

She slid down the bed ruckling up her nighty on the way and exposing a very shapely leg. He pulled the covers over her quickly and placed the teddy at her side.

'Want a kish night night,' she mumbled. He bent to kiss her forehead but she threw both arms around him and pulled him down, kissing him passionately on the lips. As he pulled away she ran her hand over his chest.

'Mary, that's enough of that, now go to sleep. Helen will bring you some water.' As he straitened up Helen came in

213

with a glass. Mary had her eyes shut. Had she crashed or was she acting because Helen was there? He rolled his eyes at Helen and left the room. Helen followed him down after turning Mary's gas mantle down to a dull flicker.

He got into bed rapidly, Helen turning the gas off and following. A dim glimmer of moonlight lit the room.

'The little minx, did you see the way she stared at your cock? I could have slapped her.' She said indignantly.

'She's had too much to drink. We should have stopped her when we saw she was getting tipsy.'

'I told you at the harbour that she fancied you. Women sense things like that. We invited her because we felt sorry for her and now she's after my man.'

He chuckled. 'Helen love, no one but you is going to get this man. She's a young impressionable girl who's had too much to drink and had an exciting time, although, I'd expect any girl would be impressed by Bruce.' He laughed.

'You bugger.' They had a mock fight, romping in the bed and finally cuddling into each others arms. 'God I'm tired,' she said.

'Me too, the start of a New Year. This is going to be our year love.' They fell asleep, curled up together.

In the attic Mary lay with her eyes wide open. She couldn't get the sight of Terry naked out of her mind. His cock looked huge, and that muscular chest and slim waist. She felt hot and definitely randy. She slipped a hand down to her crotch, rubbing and inserting fingers into herself. Eyes shut now visualising it was him doing it to her. Visualising that beautiful cock, how hard; entering her. She brought herself off to a shuddering orgasm, and then put her arm around teddy snuggling her head into it and drifted off into sleep.

The slightly drunk randy girl had enjoyed the best day for a long time. Thankfully, she was unaware of the devastating events that would befall her in a fortnight's time.

*

214

New Year's Day 1915, a crisp bright day. Pale wintry sunshine dispelling the gloom of the day before. Terry rose and looked out of the window, sun dappling the sea and lighting the distant cliffs at Bempton. He thought the change in the weather could only be a good omen.

Helen was still fast asleep her right arm thrown back on the pillow. Her delicious right breast, pulled taught, peeped above the sheets.

He walked across to the sleeping form, leant over and kissed her nipple teasing it gently between his teeth. She moaned and her eyes flickered open.

'What time is it?'

'I thought you might just wake up,' he grinned. 'It's a beautiful day. Welcome to 1915 my love.'

She sat up rubbing sleep from her eyes. To Terry she looked like a picture of perfection. He would never get used to seeing this vision in his bed he was sure.

'Any movement from upstairs?' she asked.

'Nope, she must be dead to the world. I'll bet she has a thick head when she does awaken though.'

A chuckle from Helen. 'If its anything like the one I had she's welcome to it.'

She slipped out of bed, kissed him, and then the pair of them wandered downstairs naked, clothes over their arms to rinse at the kitchen sink and dress having taken no water up the previous night.

They washed and dressed leisurely.

'I don't feel like much breakfast this morning,' said Helen.

'No, just a slice of toast and marmalade will do me.' He poked the fire and threw some coal on. Helen took hold of the toasting fork after putting the kettle on. She sat on the chair and pulled up to the fire with outstretched fork. A delicious smell of toasting bread wafting through the kitchen. A couple of slices each and a steaming mug of tea washed away the lethargy of a late night.

'I think I'd better go up and check on Mary. See if she's in the land of the living.'

215

'Good idea,' he replied. 'Go easy on her.'

'Go easy on her! After last night I could slap the little devils bottom. She couldn't take her eyes off you for all her drunken state. I hope she's got a thick head.'

He shook his head laughing. 'Women, what're you like?'

She bounded up the stairs to the attic, listened for a moment at the door and then lifted the latch and entered. Mary's head could just be seen above the sheets, face turned into the teddy bear. The two seeming to be cuddling each other. Helen stood at the side of the bed looking down at her. She couldn't help thinking how childlike she seemed, fast asleep with a teddy.

She placed a hand on the girl's shoulder.

'Mary, it's time to get up, wakey wakey.' She would have had more success waking the dead. Not a movement from the girl. Helen decided to leave her. She could surface in her own good time.

In reply to Terry's raised eyebrows she said. 'Dead to the world. I couldn't get her to even stir. That young lady is going to have the devil's own hang over when she wakes.'

'Leave her be. She'll come down when she's ready, nothing spoiling.'

It was eleven twenty when they heard unsteady footsteps coming downstairs. A head poked round the kitchen door, still in her nighty and clutching teddy.

Terry couldn't help chuckling. 'You look rough Mary lass. Definitely too much sherry last night.'

'I feel funny and I've got a headache,' she said in a weak little voice.

'Nothing a wash and bit of breakfast won't cure,' said Helen briskly. 'You can wash here in the kitchen and get dressed. I'll turn master here out.'

'I don't want to be any trouble; Terry can stay if he wants.'

'Like hell he can,' scowled Helen. Terry held up a hand in supplication.

'I'm off for a breath of fresh air outside. Welcome to nineteen fifteen young lady.' She gave him a weak smile. He put on a coat and giving them both a wink, stepped out of the door.

Jack was sitting on his bench at the front door puffing clouds of smoke up into the heavens.

'Morning lad. You two aught ter av somebody stopping more often, quietist night av ad,' he said with a gruff chuckle.

'I'll bet,' grinned Terry in reply. 'Mary has only just got up and she looks a bit fragile.'

'Ahm not surprised. She must av supped half a bottle o' sherry.'

'Mind if I join you? Helen's trying to get her washed and dressed. She's in the kitchen now so I was ordered out.'

He sat at the side of Jack, quite enjoying the fragrant smell of pipe tobacco.

'Jack, can you remember any of the crew that dad sailed with on that last time?'

'Well, it was Pash's boat. Not sure if he's still alive, might av snuffed it. The two Thomson brothers ah remember. Billy Jackson, don't know who t'others were. But there were a young lad. Relation O one O em, bout ten years old then. Seen him knocking abart now. Bloody tearaway, Tom summat.'

Terry drew in a deep breath.

'Not Tom Watson?'

'Aye, ah think that's is name. Alus in bother.'

'That's the bastard who assaulted Mary,' said Terry. 'The bugger's name seems to be cropping up everywhere. So if he was on the boat he should know what happened. But there's no way I could bring myself to ask him or even speak to the bastard,' he said grimly.

'You'll av ter ask around't arbour lad. I thought I'd eard Pash ad snuffed it, but can't be sure.'

Terry sat back, deep in thought. Watson! He seemed to have entered his life with a vengeance. He certainly

217

couldn't bring himself to approach that man. Perhaps Jack had the best idea, make some enquiries around the harbour. In fact, he would start tomorrow, Saturday, as it was back to a normal working week.

The door opened next door, Helen stuck her head out.

'Morning Jack, not teaching him bad habits are you?'

'Nay lass, I'll leave that to thee.' Both men laughing.

'You can come back now Terry madam is looking human.'

Terry gave Jack a wink and returned next door. Mary was sitting at the table looking slightly better. At least she was dressed and Helen had combed her hair. She had a steaming mug of tea from which she was taking the occasional sip.

'You look a little better now love. You've learned a lesson about the demon drink I think?' He gave her a warm smile. 'Did you sleep all right?'

'Oh yes,' she said in a breathless voice giving him a demure look. 'Yes, I slept very well.' She looked at him with wide green eyes making him feel just slightly uncomfortable. It was almost as though she was telling him something.

'I'm glad you're back. You could have brushed my hair while Helen got breakfast ready,' with a little giggle. Behind her back Helen stuck out her tongue and made a face.

He could imagine what it would be like if this girl were lodging with them. He was sure Helen would throttle her. He willingly accepted another mug of tea from Helen. Mary never took her eyes off him and they chatted about matters of total irrelevance until Helen said.

'You must be ready to get off love. Terry will walk you back home.'

She had Mary's little basket already packed, teddy's head peeping out. Placing it on the table in front of her, Mary took the hint rising to her feet.

'I've had such a lovely time. I can't thank you both enough and I just love teddy, thank you Helen.' Helen was taken completely by surprise as Mary threw her arms around her and kissed her full on the lips.

She picked up the basket and slipped her arm through Terry's. 'I'm ready.'

He and Helen exchanged glances.

'Right, come on then young woman, let's get you home.'

'Straight there and back,' murmured Helen making him smile. All those years of no one caring a toss to this. He could hardly believe it.

He stepped out of the door, Mary hanging on his arm tightly, Jack still puffing on his pipe.

'Off then are ye lass? Well all the best to yer.'

'Thank you Mr Savage, I had a lovely night.' Jack nodded and waved with the pipe as they walked away. 'He's got is ands full that lad,' he muttered.

Mary seemed to have recovered remarkably rapidly hanging onto his arm and chattering away ten to the dozen. She kept looking up at him as she chattered, her green eyes seeming to bore into his. He kept reminding himself that she must be a good fourteen years younger than him. He was picking up on the same disquiet that Helen was. It was only a ten minute stroll to Quay Street. She stopped short of Mrs Evans door, turned to him and said.

'I've had such a lovely time Terry. You're really a special man, thank you for caring about me.'

She put the basket down and put both arms around his neck. He was waiting for it, but it was still testing. She kissed him warmly on the lips, but at the same time pressed her entire body against him. It was impossible to not respond to a lithe young body in that situation and Bruce did his own thing as usual. There was no doubt that she felt his erection. She pressed even harder against him. Her face was flushed and her breathing rapid. Oh Christ he thought, what a bloody situation. He broke away.

'Mary, that's enough. Off you go in.'

'It's all right,' she whispered. 'Shan't tell, thank you for bringing me home.'

As she turned away he felt her hand brush across his erection sending an electric shock through him.

She opened the door and went in, turning on the threshold and blowing him a kiss.

He was trembling with annoyance at his own lack of control and the stupid situation. What's bloody wrong with me he thought. Letting a bloody schoolgirl excite me like that.

He walked back at a brisk pace furious with himself. The power that women have over men, he shook his head. They had felt dreadfully sorry for the girl when inviting her to join them and stay overnight, but God! What a dangerous situation.

As he opened the door back at home Helen was waiting by the table.

'Got her home safely?'

'Yes,' expressing surprise.

'And?'

'And what?'

'Did the little minx try it on? No, I can answer that myself. She did try it on.'

He was the world's worst liar, his face bright red in any case. He couldn't lie to this woman.

'Well, I knew she'd give me a kiss, just didn't realise how she'd do it.'

'And how did she do it?' Her eyes boring into him.

'She put the basket down and threw both arms round my neck.' He felt his collar uncomfortably. 'But then she pressed herself tight against me.' He stopped, gazing at the floor.

'And Bruce performed his usual trick?' she snarled. He gave a helpless shrug. This woman could read his mind, what could he say.

'I suppose she was well aware of it?' Once again he gave a helpless shrug.

'What happened then?'

'I broke away from her and told her to go in.'

'And did she? Just go in that is.'

'Yes, she went in after thanking me for caring for her and bringing her home.'

'I'll bet she thought you were caring for her, pushing a big hard dick against her.'

'I didn't,' he protested. 'She pushed herself on me.'

She suddenly laughed. 'I believe you my innocent. I knew she had the hots for you back at the harbour. Young she may be but bloody innocent, no. You might believe me in future. I told you it's a woman's sixth sense.' She drew close to him and put her own arms around him and kissed him. And then, in a flash, she dropped her hand and grabbed his testicles.

'But if these ever discharge anywhere near her I'll screw em off,' giving a little twist that made him yelp.

'Take it as another lesson from Helen,' she said softly.

*

The Saturday morning was identical to Friday's, crisp and fine. Terry was up early and making breakfast in record time. He had a lot of guilt to assuage.

Helen had teased him last night. Played and toyed with him but not given in to sex. She was going to show him who he belonged to.

Man's eternal question. Would they ever understand a woman? Not a bloody chance.

Helen had said she needed to buy provisions today; they'd gone through all fresh food stuff on last night's dinner. Terry seized the opportunity. He said he'd meet her later. If she could manage the shopping alone he'd see what information he could find around the harbour. Helen knew he had to try to find the source of the windfall; that was how she saw it! He'd not rest until finding answers, and to be fair, she understood his need. For her part, having to fight in the past even to survive she would have been very happy to simply accept the money. It would be a

221

godsend to them. Terry ultimately would have to go back to work in a job that wouldn't support them. In her opinion he had a lot to learn about life.

However, she agreed to his request and he duly made his way to the harbour.

He knew one or two of the fishing community. Some by name, some just by nodding acquaintance. January was not a busy time for the fishing boats so there were fewer men knocking around the harbour. Finding someone of the age who would remember events of six years ago would be hard.

It was largely a fruitless search. The only bit of information he did get, from an old chap he didn't even know, was that Bob Pashley was indeed dead.

He'd died some three years ago and that his wife and four children had upped sticks after his death and left Scarborough. The old paddle trawler had gone to the breakers yard.

Terry thought that Bob's wife would have needed substantial funds to just leave like that. So perhaps that pointed to the likelihood of the *windfall* being something that involved the entire crew of that day.

He was returning from the pier when a hand tapped his shoulder. He turned to see the beaming face of Mary, green eyes glowing.

'Are you looking for me Terry?' Shit!

'No love, I was looking for anyone who might have known my dad's crew in nineteen-o-four. I'm doing a bit of research into his last sailing.'

'Oh,' her face fell. 'I see, well I've got some good news. I've just got a job working for Madge Shelley on her shell fish stall. It'll be nice to get away from stinking fish and lousy weather. I'll be in the little kiosk under cover.'

'I'm so glad for you. That's really good. Well done love.' She glowed under his praise.

'You'll know where to come if you need anything.' The emphasise on *anything* obvious.

He glanced across at the lighthouse pier, seeing the huge steam crane lifting the entire glass and steel top of the lighthouse in one lift. He was brought back to the here and now by a hand stroking his chest.

'Where's Helen? I thought you two went everywhere together.'

'She had some shopping to do. In fact, I need to go and meet her. I said I'd only be down here a short while,' he said guiltily.

He hadn't said anything of the sort, but the temperature was rising too much for him here and they were starting to attract looks from some of the men around.

He took his leave of her, wishing her well in her new job and hurried up into town. He and Helen had made no arrangements, but he might just catch her coming from the market.

He did see her, walking down Eastborough with two very heavy looking bags and was glad he'd decided to go and find her. She was equally glad for help with the bags.

'Did you find anything out?'

'Not much, Bob Pash is dead as Jack thought. His wife and kids upped sticks and left shortly after. And I saw Mary, or rather she saw me. She tells me she is just starting a new job on one of the shell fish stalls.'

Now one thing his learning curve had taught him was, mention another woman's name to your partner and it would switch a light on in her eyes that would match the lighthouse.

She turned to him with a look that could have burned through armour plate. 'She just happened to see you did she? Wanted to tell you her news?'

'Seemed like it. She did say I would know where to come if I needed anything.' He was grinning internally, knowing exactly what that comment would bring.

There was a minor explosion at his side.

'I'll swing for that fucking little cow. If you need *anything* it will be supplied by me.' He burst out laughing.

'Tut-tut, naughty language, did I wind the clock up fully just then?'

She glowered at him. 'You're playing with fire matey. Just make sure you don't get your fingers burned.'

They walked home, Helen exuding a touch of frostiness. By the time they'd finished lunch she'd thawed enough to ask,

'Do you think you'll ever get to the bottom of your mystery?' (it had become his mystery now!) 'On Tuesday, hopefully, the bank will sign over your dad's book to you. You'll be getting it legally from his will. Does it really matter if you don't know how he got it? And if you did, what then, would you give it away?'

She had a point. Why was it of such concern to him? was he doing it for the right reasons or was it all about the guilty feeling he still harboured at not making up to his dad? Was it more about his confusion? Not thinking clearly. Oh bugger! So much to sort out in his head:

'If I'm truthful love I don't know why I'm so concerned. If I can find where the money came from, perhaps at that stage I can think more clearly. Plus, I don't like being beaten. It's not my style.'

'Well, think about us love. How we'll live if you only have the Kessler job. You've asked me to marry you. Can you keep me?' He looked worried at that. Was she saying she wouldn't think about marrying him if his prospects were so poor?

He hadn't even put any thought into that aspect of life. He'd been so obsessed with his new found lifestyle and, he had to admit it, his mind was on sex every few minutes. The thirty two years of abstinence was not one he could contemplate going back to.

'Let's see what happens Tuesday. If the bank transfer goes through without problems we'll have to dip in just for living expenses. But as you said to me previously, one step at a time.'

She looked at him with those appealing brown eyes.

'Spend next week trying to find out what you can. If you still haven't found anything after that call it a day. You could be taken over by it if not.'

It was good advice, perhaps that was a sensible way forward.

'Besides, most of our local fishermen consider anything of worth that's found at sea is finder's keepers. If it was dredged up or whatever is that the same as stealing?'

'In a way it is,' he replied. 'But,' holding up a hand as she made to butt in. 'Treasure trove I think it's known as is supposed to be declared to the government. But after my treatment at the hands of authority I would be happy to say balls to them.' They left it at that, a sort of understanding between them. However, the Watson connection was still niggling him.

As it happened the bank transfer went through with no trouble, and all he was able to establish on his enquiries was that the two Thomson brothers were twins. That came as a surprise to him as they didn't look alike, and no one knew of their whereabouts now. Not a single enquiry could establish who the other two crew members had been, or indeed if it had been the one with the very young Watson along for the ride.

The end of the week came with no further information. He decided to keep his bargain with Helen and start thinking of their life together. He could always keep his eyes open for anything that may crop up. There was also the issue of the coins in their possession. Helen, practical as ever said they could always have another ride to York (which she would relish), and get rid of them in the same way his father did.

They did start using the funds for themselves. Helen bought items for the house, and both of them bought many new items of clothing. One of the most important purchases was the collecting of the finished pair of special shoes. They felt strange and uncomfortable at first, but as he got used to them he realised he was walking much better and the ache that usually accompanied much walking was gone.

Helen noticed the difference immediately. His rolling gait was much less pronounced. As the shoes bedded in he wished he had found them much earlier.

They saw Mary a few times at her stall and bought lobster and crab at knocked down prices. Mary was always delighted to see them, and Terry in particular, much to the annoyance of Helen. It wasn't that Helen disliked the girl, quite the opposite. But Mary wore her feelings on her sleeve. She was like a schoolgirl with a crush on teacher and Helen found it irritating. Mary had settled into her new job with gusto enjoying making new friends. Her bubbly personality was a great asset in selling.

Terry seemed a little less obsessed with the finding of his father's wealth source. Life had settled into a pleasant time of togetherness with moments of intense passion, much to his approval, but as they drifted towards the end of February an event was to occur that would bring intense grief and upset for both of them, more so for Mary.

\*\*\*

# CHAPTER TWELVE

## Mary Duncan

Mary Duncan gave a sobbing account of her ordeal to Mrs Evans after Watson's assault. She was unable to put into words the actual detail of what Tom Watson had done to her, saying he had interfered with her.

Mrs Evans immediately said she should report it to constable Grayson, the local Bobby.

'No, no, I don't want the police involved.' Mary had the typical fisher girl's distrust of officialdom. They were used to sorting out problems themselves. Getting police involved was definitely out.

She was angry and frightened. For the next few weeks she wouldn't go out at all after dark. At least she was relieved to see that *Our Lass* had gone to sea taking the ghastly Watson with it.

She was aware however, working during the day on the fish stall, that she'd see him when his ship came in again.

The invitation to stay New Year's Eve with Helen and Terry had come just at the right time. Her mind was diverted from her ordeal and she had the delicious mental image of Terry to comfort her at night.

She even started calling the teddy, 'teddy Terry.'

The new job also suited her. She found it a pleasant change from filleting and packing fish. One of the other girls on the stall, Shirley, became a good friend. She was settled and enjoying the job, at least until the end of February.

Just when she had thought the worst was behind her and all was going well she started being sick in the mornings.

Some of the other worldly girls who knew Mary were nudging each other knowingly, and having an idea herself she asked her best friend Shirley if this indeed was a sign of pregnancy.

She was terrified of a positive answer but Shirley confirmed that it was highly likely.

Her world was collapsing. She had family only in Scotland, and her strict Protestant parents would be the last people she could confide in.

Mrs Evans, for all her sympathy would turn her out if she knew she was pregnant. She wouldn't tolerate a single mother in her lodgings.

A sudden flood of anger. Dam him! She'd confront him when he came back to port. All that rubbish about not being able to become pregnant if they did it standing up. It was his entire fault; he should just face up to his responsibilities.

She felt better for having made a positive decision. Let him come back, she'd tackle him.

Only two days later *Our Lass* sailed into the harbour with a full hold of fish and started unloading at the fish dock.

It was close to mid-afternoon before she saw Watson leaving the ship, striding down the pier as though he owned it.

Taking her failing courage in both hands and drawing a deep breath, she stood in front of him. He looked up as he strode along the pier; saw her, and then in a moment which made her blood boil he said. 'Mary lass; waiting for some more are we?'

The fury and anger in her almost boiled over. What had she ever seen in this awful man? The nervousness she had felt at her original decision to confront him evaporated. She flew at him like a tigress striking out with both arms, he simply catching them and holding her helplessly.

'You bastard', she hissed at him, 'you horrible selfish bastard.' Temper caused her voice to rise ever louder, oblivious to all around.

'I'm pregnant! Yes, you heard, pregnant.'

Fishermen and lasses working on the pier also heard, it was a bit of entertainment. They watched eagerly for the next bout. An event like this helping liven up a dull existence.

Tom Watson brought his acting skills to the fore, internally he was seething.

He'd set himself up as the responsible ship owner. Emphasise on owner, and this stupid girl could bring him into disrepute.

He grinned and played to the watching and rapidly gathering crowd.

'Look at this lads, she can't wait to get at me.' Ribald jeers from the men.

'I think she's saying she wants me to make her pregnant.'

Yells and laughter drowning out Mary's increasing fury. He quickly grabbed her arm, 'everyone's watching love,' making his voice sound concerned.

'We can sort this out but not in front of all this lot eh? 'Come on, let's talk where they can't hear us. We don't want everybody knowing our business.'

Did he really mean this? Could it all be made right? How could he make it right? She found her hopes rising. Perhaps he did want to do the right thing. She certainly didn't want the publicity they were getting at this moment.

He led her away with gentle pressure on her elbow, winking at a seaman as he passed.

'Woman trouble mate.'

More laughter from the men. Domestic strife was common in the local community. Most of the seamen there had witnessed relationship upsets. His comment caused more laughter and 'sort her out mate.'

'Woman trouble,' she spluttered furiously.

'Only joking with 'em love, you know what they're like. It'll stop 'em copping what's happening eh?'

He had concern in his voice. 'We can sort this out don't worry.'

She thought he sounded fairly sincere. Perhaps he really was going to take responsibility; she really wanted to believe him. It would be so much better if that were the case. She allowed him to lead her off the pier and towards *The Old Steam Packet*, faltering a little as she remembered the last time he had led her in that general direction.

As though sensing her concern he turned and winked at her.

'We can talk at the back of the pub, nobody listening eh?'

It made sense. She certainly didn't want any more ribald comments; the rumour mill would already be buzzing.

He led her gently to the very wall where he had made her pregnant.

'Now lass are you sure about being in the duff?'

'Yes,' indignantly, 'I wouldn't joke about something like that.'

'Well it's easy to sort.'

'It is?'

Still smiling at her, 'oh yes, very easy.'

Without any warning he drove his right fist into her stomach with immense force. She collapsed gasping with pain onto the floor. He leaned over her.

'There, told you it could be sorted. Now bitch,' sudden savagery in his voice. 'Tell anyone or try reporting me and you'll end up in the harbour, understand? You know I mean it, a bloated corpse in the drink.'

He kicked her viciously then strode away.

She was unable to move clutching her stomach with both hands, gasping for breath. The intense pain was like nothing she had ever experienced before.

It took a while to even breathe, and then again at the hands of this monster she was violently sick. She heard a movement behind her. A feeling of terror. Had he come back? Then Shirley's timid voice.

'Mary, oh God, what has he done to you?'

\*\*\*

# CHAPTER THIRTEEN

## Mary's revenge

Shirley had followed at a distance, she didn't trust Watson. She'd witnessed his loutish behaviour when in drink. She'd been surprised to see Mary allowing herself to be led away by him and was now horrified to see her friend writhing in agony on the floor.

'I'll get help,' she gasped, turning and running to the front of the pub.

The first people she saw were Helen and Terry walking arm in arm towards the stall that she and Mary worked at. She recognised them as friends of Mary and ran up to them in panic.

'Please come quickly, Mary's been hurt.'

Terry knew her from the stall. 'Where is she?'

'She's behind the *Steam Packet.*' They followed the frightened girl to where Mary was still lying on the ground clutching her stomach and crying.

'God almighty, what's happened?' asked Helen, stooping over the stricken girl. Mary unable to speak, Shirley saying,

'She's been beaten up by that bloody sailor she knew.'

Terry felt a fury the like of which he had never known. If Watson had been there at that moment he'd have strangled him with his bare hands.

He took decisive charge.

'Helen, get up to doctor Jameson's and ask him to come to our house, tell him it's an emergency. I'll carry Mary up home.'

He stooped and picked up the injured girl with ease holding her to him like a child. Mary was whimpering and sobbing. She'd gone a deadly pale colour. 'Shirley, will you

232

let Mrs Evans know what's happened. Tell her she'll be staying with us until the doctor has seen her.'

Helen left at a trot. Shirley saw them out from the back of the pub, and then set off for Mrs Evans house.

'It's going to be alright love,' he whispered to the girl. 'We'll look after you.'

She clung to him as he carried her up the hill towards Overton terrace, he thankful for the new shoes. He made home in record time. Upon seeing Jack puffing on his pipe on the bench, he shouted as he approached,

'Jack, need some help. Mary's been hurt.'

The old man jumped up. 'What's happened lad?'

'She's been beaten up. Key in left pocket,' turning to let Jack get the key out of his pocket.

He opened the door for Terry. Terry carried the stricken girl in and straight up to the attic bedroom. Thankfully, the bed was still made up.

He put her down gently on the bed, Mary immediately curling into a ball.

'The doctors on his way love; hold on.'

He stroked her hair trying to calm the little gasps and sobs. She was still clutching her stomach, obviously in severe pain.

'Look out for the doc coming Jack.'

'Aye lad,' the old boy went downstairs. Terry was still trying to reassure and calm the girl.

She suddenly let out a scream that frightened the hell out of him and he was horrified to see blood staining the centre of her dress.

He had no knowledge of first aid. He felt totally helpless, stroking her hair and repeating over and over. 'It'll be alright love. Don't worry, all will be alright.'

It seemed an eternity before he heard footsteps coming up the stairs and Doctor Jameson and Helen came into the room.

At a nod from Helen he left Mary in the hands of the doctor and Helen, going back down to the kitchen where

Jack was waiting. He realised he was trembling with delayed shock, and sat down with a thump.

'What the ells appened?' asked Jack.

He told him that Helen and he were going to the stall that Mary worked at when her friend had come running up to them to tell them Mary had been hurt.

They'd found Mary collapsed behind the pub and her friend had said Watson had done it.

'That bastard, agin. We need to do something about yon,' said Jack.

'Well, like it or not, I'm going to let the police know. See if we can get him locked up,' replied Terry.

They waited anxiously for the doctor upstairs. After a while Helen came down. 'Put the kettle on we need some warm water,' she looked grim.

Terry jumped up, happy to do something useful. 'What's the doctor say?' he asked.

'I was terrified. She was bleeding from you know what.'

'It seems she was in the early stages of pregnancy,' said Helen, 'although not anymore.'

'Oh God, the poor lass. Will she be alright? It won't mean permanent damage will it?' Helen gave a shrug. 'Don't know we'll have to see what the doctor says.'

She poured a mixture of hot and cold water into the bowl, took a clean face towel from the cupboard and returned upstairs.

'Nowt I can do,' said Jack. 'But if ah can do owt tha knows where to find me.' 'Thanks Jack. I'll let you both know what the verdict is.'

The old man went leaving Terry sitting anxiously, the clock in the kitchen seeming to sound louder than ever. He could hear the occasional voice float downstairs but was unable to make anything out. The most terrifying moment came when he heard Mary scream again. He felt tears for her prick his eyes. If I really believed in a God he thought, I would pray now.

The time seemed to drag. He made a cup of tea just to do something, and then left it untouched on the table.

After what was probably half an hour, but seemingly six times that to him, he heard them coming downstairs. The bowl of water in Helen's hand's; its contents bright red, frightened him. The look on the doctor's face was grim. 'What?' he asked. He couldn't get the rest out for the life of him, but they knew what he was asking.

The doctor went to the sink to wash his hands. As he was doing so he spoke to Terry over his shoulder.

'A very nasty assault Mr Sheader. Miss Duncan was about nine or ten weeks pregnant. The blow to her stomach has caused her to miscarry. How this may affect her future child bearing I don't know at this stage. She will need a long period of rest. For the moment I have given her an injection that will make her sleep.' He turned from the sink.

'Your wife assures me she may stay here as long as necessary. If any further bleeding takes place call me at once.'

My wife! Once again Helen had the element of surprise.

'Thank you for coming so promptly doctor. I'll meet any expense for Miss Duncan,' he said.

'In that case I will bid you both good day. I will call in the morning on my normal patients rounds.' He saw the doctor to the door; saw Jack hovering next door, gave him a brief account of what was happening then sat back down opposite Helen.

'Christ, what a day,' he said savagely. 'That poor kid up there suffering twice at the hands of that monster. We should call the police.'

'We need to be careful on that,' said Helen. 'They'll see it as a domestic. They don't have a good record on matters like that and Mary mumbled something about him threatening to kill her if she reports him. He'd be quite capable I should think.'

'Rubbish, that's just bully boy tactics. He's an out and out coward trying to frighten her off. He needs locking up.'

'That's as may be, but we should wait until she's fully able to let us know what she wants. In the meantime we need to concentrate on her recovery.'

He was unconvinced but decided to wait until Mary was speaking again.

'Is she asleep now?'

'Not fully, at least she wasn't when we came down. She's going to be in pain for some time but the injection should make her very drowsy.'

'I'll have a look in on her.' He got up and went to the stairs, leaving Helen with a neutral expression. He opened the door quietly. Mary turned her head as he entered; a weak little smile as she recognised her visitor. 'My hero,' she murmured softly.

'How are you my love?' He knelt at the side of the bed and held her hand.

'I feel a long way away. I'm glad you're here. I've never been so frightened.' Tears glistened again in her eyes. 'My tummy really hurts.'

'You're stopping here until you're better. Helen and I will look after you.' She looked up at him. 'Thank you,' said so softly he had to strain to hear.

'Is there anything you'd like, anything we can get for you?'

'I'd like teddy.' Her eyes were fluttering, she seemed to be close to nodding off.

'I'll get him for you.' Her eyes closed.

He remained holding her hand until he saw she was asleep, and then returned to Helen. 'She wants teddy,' he told her. 'She's sleeping now. I'll go round to Mrs Evans and let her know she will be staying here until better, and bring teddy back of course,' with a smile at her.

'Yes, you go and do that. I'll start some dinner,' she said very blandly.

He took her face in both hands and gave her a passionate kiss, looking into her eyes. 'We can't leave the lass you know that. She's helpless at the moment. But I tell you now, she's no threat to you darling. I know you think the enemy is in the house but you are and always will be my only love.'

She clung to him tearfully. 'I know you think I'm being silly, but from my point of view I've always had to fend off danger. And I'm sorry if I seem neurotic but she has such a crush on you.'

'I love you and adore you. There's nothing to fear from that little girl upstairs.' He gave her a squeeze and wink. 'Just be here when I get back.'

'I'll always be here for you.'

He left Helen at the sink and set off to Mrs Evans house. Helen was left in a welter of emotion. There was no doubt that she was, for the first time, deeply in love. He meant so much to her now it was almost painful thinking anything could disturb it.

She felt ashamed of herself for the feeling of jealousy the little girl upstairs aroused but was unable to fully control it. She gave herself a mental shake. Get a grip girl, Terry is right. We can't abandon the girl in her time of need. But the nagging feeling wouldn't go away.

Terry arrived at a worried looking Mrs Evans. She'd already heard on the super-efficient grape vine some of what had taken place.

'How is the girl?' she asked.

'Very poorly and in a lot of pain. We think she should stay with us until she recovers. Of course, I'll pay her lodging bill until she's able to return to you.' 'Mrs Evans face lit up noticeably at that comment.

'That's very good of you Mr Sheader. I'll keep her room in good order.'

Terry explained she had asked for her teddy. She asked him to wait a second and she would fetch it for him. She returned with teddy and a couple of the detective novels that Mary so liked.

'When she's a little better she might want something to read.'

'Oh, lovely, yes, just the ticket.' He paid her two weeks rent money there and then. He had made a friend he noticed as she simpered at him. Taking his leave he hurried back home to find Helen making some beef broth.

'She probably won't feel like eating just yet, but this should keep her strength up.'

He slipped his hands around her from behind and cupped her breasts.

'You're a good woman Helen Sheader,' nuzzling her neck.

'Silly bugger,' but she didn't remove his hands.

'Take teddy up to your girlfriend then and make yourself useful.' He kissed her neck and took teddy up to the attic. Mary was fast asleep, hair spread out in a fan on the pillow. She looked so young and vulnerable. A huge surge of anger flooded him, the vision of Watson's sneering face drifting into his mind. He placed the teddy on the pillow at her side, bent forward and kissed her brow. 'Get better soon little one,' he whispered.

He went down. 'Fast asleep now, the injection must be working. I wonder if that bastard is back on his boat?'

'Leave it for now; he'll get his come uppance sooner or later.'

They had dinner quietly and contemplatively, both lost in their own thoughts. He lit the mantle and turned it up.

'What a bloody day this has turned out to be. I still can't quite believe it.'

'I can believe anything of Watson. We've both seen what he can do, but I'm just as sure that good will triumph eventually,' said Helen. They sipped tea together. 'I've been thinking,' she announced.

'Bloody hell, is that dangerous?'

'No, seriously, about our earning a living. I've always fancied the idea of setting up a tea room. Not any old tea room but a high class one. One with really good quality and sensible prices, with, of course, excellent service.'

'Wow; where did that come from? How long have you had that idea?'

'It was one of those things that you dream about. I never thought it'd be possible but we could actually do it now. Don't you think it's worth a thought? There are always posh people in Scarborough who will spend money in a place like that.' He sat up and looked at her deeply. She was constantly surprising him. Teaching him new ways of love making was one aspect, but here she was coming up with a business idea, and, a good one at that.

'Do you know love, I think that's a pretty good idea. But we'd need premises in a nice part of town and a damn good cook.'

'Do you think it's a possibility though? You'd be good with the paper work. I'm sure I could practice being a good serving girl. If we found a really good cook and perhaps another girl to serve we could make a go of it.'

'Helen my love you're a constant surprise. Yes, we'll give it some serious thought as soon as our guest is up and about.' She leaned over and kissed him.

'You see; beauty and brains.'

'I've never doubted it love. Come on then dreamer, let's do the pots.'

'Well, that's a romantic proposition,' she laughed. She picked up some of the dinner pots and took them to the sink, Terry bringing the rest. She filled the bowl from the kettle, added a dash of cold and bent over the sink with a cloth. While she had both hands in the water he went up behind her and pressed himself against her. 'About the beauty bit,' he said, gently rotating against her bottom. 'Who said pot washing couldn't have a touch of excitement.'

'You devil, taking advantage of a girl while she has her hands in dirty dishes.'

'I like a bit of dirty.' He reached down and with a quick movement lifted her skirt exposing her shapely bottom in all its glory, pressing a now hard Bruce against it.

'Brains and beauty. Well Bruce thinks you have a gorgeous arse, is that dirty enough?' He quickly freed the straining Bruce, slid him between her legs so he stood proud at the other side. Helen was giving little gasps. He toyed with her for a while and then drew back slightly;

placing Bruce's head against her moist passage and inserting with a long steady thrust.

She gave a long 'aaahh,' as he withdrew and then thrust back in, pushing hard and lifting her slightly off her feet. Her hands splashed into the bottom of the bowl as she stooped forward water going everywhere.

He grasped both hips firmly and then started to pump with vigour. Helen flopped forward almost on top of the bowl as he increased speed, and she yelled in ecstasy at almost the same time as he ejaculated in a gushing spurt, pressing hard and firmly against her. He held it for a few seconds before gently withdrawing. 'God; If that's pot washing we should do more of it you randy sod,' she giggled. He turned her round; her dress front water stained and kissed her passionately. 'That's how much I love you.'

'That's just full on lust,' she giggled. 'Put that thing away and dry the pots.'

In the attic, Mary, drifting in and out of sleep thought she heard a yell from downstairs but she felt so woozy she may have been mistaken. She turned her head and saw teddy Terry, smiling as she clutched him to her. Terry, I'll be safe now Terry is here. She drifted off to sleep.

*

Helen looked in on her as they made ready for bed that night. She was fast asleep, one arm thrown up the other clutching the teddy. It was almost like looking in on a child and it brought a sudden pang to Helen's heart. She left the gas mantle on low, a soft hissing and dull warm glow just as she might have done if Mary were a child. She reported back to Terry.

'Sleeping like a babe. In fact I was quite touched she looked like a child.'

He kissed her gently. 'Still think she's a threat?'

240

'Not as she is certainly. When she's recovered and back to normal I'll let you know.' He shook his head and ruffled her hair. 'Come on; let's get some sleep.'

Terry slept lightly. He was really concerned about Mary. He heard her whimper a few times and he found he was listening just to reassure she was alright. He did eventually nod off but it was in the early hours.

Helen had no such trouble. She was off as soon as her head touched the pillow, on her side with one arm thrown across his chest.

The following morning he was up early, Helen still fast asleep. He nipped up to the attic lightly and peeped round the door. Mary was fast asleep but the badly rumpled sheets were testimony to a disturbed night. He went downstairs and got the fires blazing, leaving the doors ajar to allow heat to seep upstairs. He started getting breakfast things ready, cutting some bread finely, thinking Mary might manage toast for her breakfast. It was over an hour later that a sleepy eyed Helen popped her head round the door.

'What time were you up?'

'Well that's nice, not good morning my gorgeous lover.'

'That as well,' she laughed. He grinned at her. 'I was up at seven thirty actually. I wanted to check on Tinkerbell in the attic.'

'And?'

'She's sleeping. But looking at the state of the sheets she's had a disturbed night.'

'What would you like for breakfast, toast or something cooked?'

'I'd like Bruce lightly grilled between two slices of bread,' keeping her face straight.

'Right, you're just going to get toast then.'

They had toast and marmalade together banter flowing lightly, both keeping an ear for signs of Mary waking. Terry was just about to sip a second mug of tea when there was an almighty scream from the attic. It startled him so much he dropped it on the table, a hot pool flowing onto the floor. They both jumped up and dashed to the stairs, Terry taking them three at a time. He flew into Mary's room. She was sitting bolt upright in bed a sheen of sweat on her forehead, eyes wide and staring.

'What is it love, for God's sake what is it?'

Mary looked around the room in panic and then seeing no one but Terry, with Helen standing behind him, sank back down on the bed.

'I thought he was here, he was going to hit me again.' Her breathing was ragged, 'I must have been dreaming.'

Terry felt a huge gush of relief wash over him. He thought she had been having some sort of medical emergency.

'It's alright love, he can't get at you here you're safe.' He hugged her. 'You're safe love, safe.' She put both hands around his neck sobbing. Helen in floods of emotion, watching helplessly. Feeling for the girl, but hating seeing this pretty young creature hanging on to her man.

'How's the pain?' he asked gently. She looked up into his face with tear streaked eyes. 'Better than last night but I feel very stiff, and it hurts down there,' eyes dropping momentarily to her nether regions.

Helen, woman of the world, could see the love shining in those eyes. Something men can be so oblivious of she thought. As soon as this girl is fit enough she's out of here.

'The doctor's coming again this morning. You'll soon be back to normal,' she said to the girl.

Mary released her grip on Terry reluctantly as he straightened up.

'I think I need the toilet,' she whispered.

'I'll leave you two,' he said, turning to Helen. 'You'll be alright love?'

'Yes, off you go. Make some toast and warm a glass of milk.' As he left, Mary's eyes watching his departure. Helen couldn't help thinking; he gets the hugs and loving looks. I'm left helping her to shit.

242

She was right about men, simple creatures that they are. Terry was happily slicing bread and pouring milk into the pan without any idea of the turmoil of emotion upstairs.

Like all the houses on the terrace the toilet was across the yard in a separate brick building. Night time needs, or in this case invalid needs had to be catered for by the dreaded chamber pot. It was just manageable for *tiddle* needs, but the other was an unpleasant job indeed.

Helen had nipped down while he was getting breakfast to collect a bowl of warm water and a cloth, glaring at his back as she went back upstairs. Terry, whistling happily, relieved that it was not a medical emergency just annoyed Helen even more. Helen felt a little guilty when she saw the widening purple bruise on the girls stomach, it was clear this had been a very savage blow.

The poor girl cried out in pain as she tried to stand, clinging on to Helen, bringing the maternal instincts out in Helen as she helped her to crouch over the pot. Helen was not used to caring for others. Her entire life had been a battle to survive against a cruel world. Over time she had built a hard shell to protect her from the sneers and looks from people who were quick to condemn, but who, in the same circumstances, would have probably done the same.

She felt concern and sympathy for this naïve girl, helping her to crouch there in agony. But at the same time she couldn't help taking in the fact that she had a beautiful little bottom and long shapely legs. She wondered how Terry would react doing this job now? And then crossly to herself. I know how he'd react, he'd have a bloody hard on.

Helen came downstairs with the chamber pot grimacing, and opened the door and went across the yard. Two slices of toast and marmalade and a glass of warm milk prepared, Terry took the breakfast upstairs unaware of Helens mood.

Mary's face lit up when he entered the room after first calling. 'Are you decent?'

'Yes, come in,' she called, her face lighting up as he entered. She was sitting up, or rather propped up with the aid of two extra pillows. One sleeve of her nighty was pulled (or slipped?) down to expose a naked shoulder.

I've brought you some breakfast love. You need to eat something to get your strength back.' Liquid green eyes fluttering up at him.

'Thank you so much Terry.'

He placed the tray, a piece of flat wood with beading tacked round it; on the bed in front of her. She leaned forward before he had time to step back, the night dress gaping open giving him a brief view of a firm little breast.

He noticed her eyes switch to his crotch. Bloody hell! Helen was right. This little minx definitely knows what she's doing.

'I'll leave you with it love. Try and eat it and drink the milk. I'll go downstairs and wait for the doctor coming.'

She pouted. 'You don't have to dash off Terry.'

'So much to do today. I'll pop up later when the doctor's been.' He hurried down before any further temptation was placed before him. Helen looked at him with raised eyebrows.

'What's that look for?' he asked.

'You have that flustered look of a man who's just been offered a big fat cake knowing he shouldn't really have it,' she said. 'So what did the little minx offer?' There's no pulling the wool over her eyes! 'She didn't offer anything,' attempting to sound surprised. He didn't convince himself, certainly not Helen. 'So why the fluster?' Bloody hell, just tell her.

'She showed a good bit of titty pretending it was by accident,' he sighed. 'You're right, she's trying hard.'

She had a look of triumph on her face. 'You're realising at last I'm right. She's definitely trying hard, just make sure she doesn't harden anything else.'

He grinned at her. 'You're the expert on that my darling. I'll attempt to be more aware and on my guard in future.'

'I'll tell you something about life,' she said, looking hard at him. 'I found out long ago that the old saying, *a standing cock has no conscience* is right. If you ever get into a position where that happens, turn away quickly before it over rides your brain.'

He shook his head. 'Helen love, you come out with some cracking expressions.'

The lesson was disturbed by a knock on the door, the doctor had arrived. Terry welcomed him in and sat down as the doctor and Helen went upstairs. He was still convinced, even though it was flattering, that Mary had a teenage type crush but it was starting to get embarrassing. Should he try and have a *fatherly* style word with her? Or would that make matters worse? Perhaps he should discuss it with Helen. She was far more world wise than him in these area's he had to admit. He could hear the sound of voices upstairs. Impossible to make anything out, he would just have to wait patiently.

Helen and the doctor came down after fifteen minutes or so, Jameson addressing Terry.

'I think, Mr Sheader, with no stress and plenty of rest and good food our patient should make a good recovery. Physical recovery that is. Her mental recovery may take a little longer. If you have any concerns don't hesitate to call me but I think at this stage no further visits are necessary. I will send you the bill via the post.'

'Thank you doctor. We're both relieved to hear that.' He shook Jameson's hand and saw him to the door.

'That's it then,' said Helen as the door closed on the doctor. 'Feed her up, get her well, and get her out.'

'You sound so hard when you say it like that,' he grumbled. 'The lass has suffered badly at the hands of that monster, show some compassion.'

'I do feel for her. She really has suffered no doubt about it. And I, as much as you, would love to see Watson come a cropper. But, and this is a big but for me, she's a very pretty girl and she has a crush or something more for you. You're my man and I don't want someone making a play for you under my very nose.'

He smiled at her comments. She was right, and he was so touched that she really saw him as *her man*.

'Just think love,' she continued. 'If it was a handsome young man up there, same age as her, and every time I attended to him he fluttered his eyes and made it clear he would like to shag me, how would you feel?'

He held his hands up in surrender. 'I've already accepted you're right. We'll do as the doc says, get her well as quickly as possible and then get her back to Mrs Evans.'

'Helen gave him a knowing look. 'Can you remember telling me that your leg would prevent you from ever having a relationship with a girl. What do you think now?'

'I think I'm the luckiest man in the world and one who still has a lot to learn.'

'Well, here's another lesson. Go up there now and have a long chat to her. Put her straight without hurting her if possible. It's no good me saying anything to the lass. I'm the opposition.'

'Do you think that's wise? Won't it make it worse? She'll be convinced you've sent me up.'

Helen shrugged. 'We can't allow the girl to think you really might be available. She's living in a bit of a fantasy land. She has to face the facts, has to learn real life is difficult at times.'

'Go on,' she nodded at the door. He took a deep breath, and went upstairs knocking on the door. 'Are you fit for a visit?'

'Of course I am.'

She was still propped up on the pillows a detective novel in her hand. She placed it down on the bed smiling at him.

'You can visit any time Terry; you don't need to knock.'

'You might be in disarray.'

'Would that frighten you off?'

He pulled the chair up to the side of the bed.

'Mary love, you're a beautiful girl and any red blooded man would be turned on seeing you lying in bed looking vulnerable. And I have to admit I'm no different. But it would be wrong of me to even let you think I, a man fourteen years older than you, could ever be right for you.' He put a finger to her lips as she made to speak. 'You deserve a man of your own age who loves you and wants to care for you and I'm sure you'll find a man like that.'

Tears in her eyes; 'Terry.'

Once again he put a finger to her lips. 'Let me tell you something about myself. I don't know if you were aware that I was wounded in the leg during the Boer war? It made a hell of a mess of my leg and for years, right up to now in fact, I was convinced that it would stop me from ever having a relationship with a girl. That was before I met Helen.' He placed a hand on hers.

'She made me realise that a lot of the problem was in my head. She taught me how to love someone, and I really love her passionately. I want to spend the rest of my life with her. Marry her, but at the same time I don't want to hurt you. I can't believe you can think anything of me and I hate Watson for what he's done to you. I just want to see you better and leading a happy life.'

He sat back, that must be one of the longest diatribes ever for him. She was looking at him with those intense green eyes, a tiny glisten in them.

'I know you're Helen's and yes, I'm jealous. You're a lovely man Terry. Age differences don't mean a thing when the person is right and you could be so right for me. It's not going to happen I have to accept. And I couldn't hurt Helen after the friend she's been to me but Helen is right, the leg doesn't matter at all.' She gave a little chuckle. 'Not that leg anyway. The middle leg I saw in the kitchen was outstanding. Helen's very lucky.'

She took his hand and gently placed it on her breast.

'If you hadn't met Helen could you have loved me?'

247

He felt highly uncomfortable. He was more than aware of the feel of that firm, very firm, breast. He withdrew his hand and held hers instead.

'Yes, I most certainly could but it's wrong to go there. I want to see you well, and what I would really like is for you to allow me to tell the police what happened. We'd both like to see that monster behind bars.'

She shuddered. 'No, no police. I've seen how they treat cases like this. If it got to court I would be made to look like the slag who seduced him. Perhaps I was. I enjoyed that first time, just didn't realise what a wrong-un he was.'

She held his hand and looked into his eyes again. 'We all make mistakes don't we? But as far as Watson's concerned, I have plans for him.' The last was said with such bitterness it startled him.

'Mary, you don't even want to go anywhere near him. Promise me you won't.'

'So you do care for me a little?'

'I care for you a lot, I've told you. I want to see you happy more than anything in the world. Don't let that monster rule your life, put him behind you.'

'Oh I'm going to put him behind me I promise you that.'

He felt somehow that she said it with a double meaning but was unable to fathom it. He had so much to learn about the workings of a woman's mind.

'Did you see what he did to me?' she suddenly whispered and with no further ado, pushed the sheets down and pulled her nightdress up.

The huge purple bruise on her stomach made him feel sick, but the long shapely legs and triangle of auburn hair brought instant colour to his face.

'Mary,' he croaked. He took hold of the hem of her nightdress and pulled it down closing his eyes. I must retain control. Bruce said bollocks as always. She smiled a secret little smile.

'You said you were a red blooded man Terry. I can see you are. I'm not going to make life difficult for you darling. I love you too much. Yes, I love you; love you enough to let you go. You and Helen must think I'm an immature girl with a crush, but I know different.' This young girl suddenly seemed very mature to him.

'Will you always be my friend Terry? Be there for me if I'm in trouble?'

'Yes, I will, never suffer alone again. If you need help we'll both give it. I promise you that.'

She put her head back on the pillow with a sigh.

'Kiss me,' she said with closed eyes.

He bent over and kissed her gently, her eyes open now and looking directly into his, and then her eyes closed again.

'Now go down and tell Helen all is well.'

Helen was sitting erect on the chair in the kitchen when he returned looking tense. 'Tell me all,' she said quietly.

She put a mug of tea before him.

'She's a very complex girl. She frightened me a little when she said she had plans for Watson. I told her to steer well clear of him and get on with her life.'

Helen was looking at him intently.

'Just like you said, she wouldn't even entertain the idea of telling the police. She can be very forceful.'

'Oh yes,' she whispered softly. 'Did she tell you she loved you?'

Good old Helen, straight out with it.

'Yes, and I told her I loved you. I didn't have to because she knew. She said her love was such that she was not going to make any trouble, would just let me go. But, would we both remain friends and be there for her if she was ever in trouble. I told her we would.'

She was looking hard into his eyes. 'And did she make Bruce stand up?'

'God Helen, you're starting to sound like the inquisition.' His colour gave him away as always.

'And how did she achieve that?' she continued, as though he had not interrupted.

'She pulled her nightdress up to show me her bruise.'

'And it wasn't her bruise that turned you on; it was the sight of her fanny.'

'You can be so coarse love. Yes, alright, but I pulled it down immediately. Although I suppose you would say she had her moment of triumph.'

She smiled sadly at him. 'I know you think I'm neurotic love but I know how men work, and I know how we women work too. I'm not worried, because any other man just wouldn't have told me what went on like you've just done. You're such an innocent still and I love you for it. I'm glad you told her you love me. That will have far more effect coming from you.'

He leaned across and kissed her.

'It's not difficult telling anyone I love you it's simply the truth.'

'Has she had any breakfast did you see?' and then laughing. 'No, it's the last thing you'd have noticed.'

'I think you know me better than I know myself,' he smiled.

'I know I do and don't you forget it. Drink your cuppa and I'll go up and see if our patient wants anything. Apart from you, that is.'

She went upstairs, tapped on the door and went straight in. Mary was studying a passage in her book with a frown. She looked up at Helen; smiling a knowing smile. 'Have you come to read me the riot act?'

'We're both women aren't we Mary? Terry can be very un-worldly. He's got a lot of catching up to do. He still wears all his emotions on his sleeve.'

'I know, that's one of the lovely things about him isn't it?' She smiled at Helen.

'Has he reported back to you? No, don't answer that, I can see he has. You know how lucky you are finding a man like that don't you Helen?'

'You know I do and I would fight any one who tried to take him from me.'

Mary chuckled. 'You always come straight out with it, don't worry about me Helen. I love you both enough not to even try to spoil what you have. I told Terry as much although I was naughty. I had a bit of fun with him.'

'Yes, he told me.'

'He did! Well, there you go Helen you have a man in a million. Not many men would confess to getting a hard on looking at another woman.'

They both laughed, the air cleared somewhat.

'Did he tell you about trying to persuade me to go to the police?'

'Yes he did. I'd already told him you wouldn't want that. Men don't understand how badly we girls are treated in cases like this; the woman is always the loser.'

They both sat in contemplative silence for a while and then Mary took hold of Helen's hand. 'Will you both still be friends with me. Help me if ever I really need help?' Helen picked up on some inflection in the voice.

'What are you really asking love?'

'If you were in my position Helen would you try to get even with a man like Watson?'

Helen didn't like where this was going.

'I know we girls have to stand together sometimes but be very careful love. Don't put yourself in any further danger from that man, think carefully. You're young with many years to go, don't do anything rash.'

Mary pressed the back of Helen's hand against her cheek.

'You're a very beautiful woman Helen. I'm glad I've got you for a friend.' She looked up at her and with a sudden giggle. 'Do you think Terry would be capable of two in a bed?'

Helen burst out laughing. 'I'm bloody sure he would but he's not going to get the sodding chance.'

They had a fit of girly giggles, and then Mary said.

'I promise, as soon as I can stand without pain I'll go back to Mrs Evans. You'll have your man all alone again.' She pulled Helen forward and for the second time, taking her by surprise, kissed her full on the lips, one arm around her neck stopping her from pulling away. It was Helen's turn to go bright red. Even worse; it aroused her. Bloody hell, what's going on here?

As Mary released her, she looked up and said. 'I told you I loved you both.'

Helen scooped up the tray with empty plate and glass on it and headed for the door.

'I'll come back up in a while to see how you are, try and get some extra sleep.'

It was Helen's turn to look flustered when she got back downstairs.

'God, that girl is complicated.'

'That's the sort of thing you'd accuse me of saying. What's gone on up there for you to say that?'

Helen just shook her head. 'I'll pop up later to check on her. I've told her to try and get some more sleep.'

Upstairs, Mary lay wide awake looking at the ceiling hatching a plot that had been forming for some time. One great thing about being incapacitated. It allowed time to get her thoughts in order, time to think through in detail what she was going to do to exact her revenge on Tom Watson!

*

Helen busied herself getting lunch prepared. It wasn't time yet but she needed to be busy. Mary had disturbed her. Firstly, she was certain the girl was planning to get some form of revenge on Watson against both Terry's and her advice. Secondly, that kiss! Mary's tongue just probing her lips she had found highly erotic. It frightened her. She shouldn't be aroused by a girl kissing her should she? That wasn't normal surely. She was a *normal woman*, so why had it affected her so?

Terry was totally unaware of her quandary. As both women had agreed; he was just a simple bloke!

She made a bowl of nourishing thick beef broth for Mary, with chunks of thickly buttered bread to soak it all up, poured a large mug of tea and took it up.

The complex girl had reverted to being a little schoolgirl thanking Helen demurely, sitting up in bed and patiently letting Helen place the tray on her lap. 'I think it might be an idea if I get up this afternoon and try walking a bit. I need to move before I get too stiff.' Helen wasn't sure.

'Go very carefully. We don't want any sort of relapse, a little at a time.'

She told Terry. He was concerned. 'Can she do any harm trying too soon?' 'We'll have to watch her closely, make sure she doesn't over stretch herself.'

They both sat down to the same broth as Mary. It was as good a lunch as any, tasty and nourishing.

'I've been thinking about your idea for a café,' he said. 'As soon as Mary is well enough to leave we'll start putting some thought into it.'

Helen's face glowed. 'That's wonderful. I'm certain we could make a go of it.'

Upstairs, Mary leaned out of bed and placed the tray on the floor.

She was feeling much better. The pain in her stomach was now just a dull ache. She'd concentrate on getting up and about, had much to do, a lot of detail to work out. Her interest in detective novels had given her a good grounding for what she planned to do.

She spent another three days with Terry and Helen. Getting up, and staying up more often building up her strength. Wandering around the house in a nightdress that left little to the imagination, and jolly well knowing it caused both Terry and Helen, yes, Helen; increasing feelings of desire in one way or another.

They had not indulged in any sex while Mary had been there. Another reason Helen couldn't wait for the day of departure.

It was the fourth day after her ordeal; that Mary announced she was fit to go back to her digs. Helen decided they would both accompany her there. She didn't want Terry to experience any more passionate goodbyes.

Mary walked slowly and kept stopping for a rest. But the pain was minimal now and she made it to Quay Street with no great difficulty. They said they would accompany her in, carrying her few belongings up to her room. Terry slipped some cash to Mrs Evans when Helen wasn't looking.

Mary broke down in floods of tears when they departed, clinging to them both in turn, kissing each one of them passionately and leaving Helen once again reeling.

They made their way back home hand in hand, chattering about the business they were going to set up.

Mary immediately, after reassuring Mrs Evans she didn't need any nursing care, put the first bit of her plan into action. Her room at the back of the house looked out onto a yard. Immediately below her window was the slate roof of an outhouse. She forced up the sash window which squealed alarmingly, and started rubbing candle fat onto the runners, gradually moving it up and down until it moved easily and most importantly without sound.

First bit accomplished. The next job would be more difficult and would have to wait until she could walk further without effort. She spent the rest of the day carefully working her plan out in her head, having a mid-afternoon nap on the bed. Mrs Evans cooked a filling roast beef dinner which she struggled to finish, but was grateful for. She told Mrs Evans she would go to bed early and possibly read a little.

'A very good idea dear. You need to go slowly and build up your strength.' Everyone was telling her to build up her strength! Well, she intended to do so. Strength would be needed for what was coming.

She changed into her nightdress and stretched out on the bed with the gas mantle on full, reading some more of her novel until she started to feel drowsy.

Eyes closed, she allowed her mind to wander. It inevitably went back to Overton Terrace. A lovely vision of Terry naked in the kitchen flitted through, and then the deep brown eyes of Helen, erotica growing in her vivid imagination.

She formed a mental image of herself; face between Helen's splayed legs and Terry pumping into her from behind with that huge penis. She fingered herself to a gasping climax and then slipped between the sheets and was asleep in a trice.

She forced herself to walk a little further each day gradually returning to normal. She even started back at the stall after a week. Shirley in particular welcoming her back.

'I've been so worried about you Mary,' she confided.

She reassured everyone that she was fully recovered, but as the doctor had mentioned, the mind was something else.

Inside, her mind was a seething turmoil of fury and revenge. She lived each day now for the action she was about to take.

She visited the market. The second hand stalls were her target. Making sure she saw no one who knew her, she bought some well-worn seaman's trousers, a smock and a cap, all of approximately her size. She had her hair cut by Norah Jean in the market into a bob-cut telling Norah it was getting bothersome being too long.

In the sanctity of her room that night she altered the clothes to give her a passing resemblance to a young man. She'd do more work on that shortly.

During her lunch break from the stall she had wandered onto the pier often, always making sure Watson was not around, fixing in her mind the mooring which he brought *Our Lass* to.

Room in the harbour, with the number of boats using it was always at a premium. Watson would moor at the same berth but three boats deep, his being the outer one.

She next checked out the shed at the end of the pier. It was unlocked and used to store all the rubbish which men thought might come in useful one day but never did. Typical bloody men she thought scornfully, but it was ideal for her requirements.

She 'borrowed' a large canvas holdall which some unsuspecting seaman had left lying around far too trustingly, and sneaked it back home.

The one tool she had kept from her previous life as a fisher girl was her razor sharp filleting knife. Fisher girls were known to be able to gut fifty fish a minute, a skill built up with much practice. Mary was no exception.

Now to rehearse the vital bit of her plan she waited until nightfall. Then, dressed in the fisherman's garb and hair tucked up in the hat she slid the window up and climbed out, dropping lightly onto the outhouse roof.

It was a very short drop from there to the ground, but could she do it in reverse?

Making sure no one was around, she jumped a short way to grasp the gutter and tried to pull herself back up onto the outhouse roof.

It was much more difficult than she thought it would be putting enormous strain on her arms. She looked around. Ah, a fish crate in the corner. She pulled it up to the wall and used it as a step. She was able to spring from that to the gutter edge, hauling herself onto the outhouse roof.

The climb from there back into her room was even worse, but she managed that also giving her great satisfaction. If this hadn't been possible her plan was doomed.

She quickly changed back into her nightdress and went down stairs demurely asking Mrs Evans for a glass of water. This also was vital, that Mrs Evans was unaware she had been out and to establish an alibi that she had been in all night.

As she retired to bed that night she had a huge feeling of satisfaction. So much so that she treated herself to an even more bizarre scenario with her two imaginary friends achieving a satisfactory orgasm.

\*

Two days later all was set, Watson was in port.

He slept on his boat. It was the centre of his universe, his pride and joy, and she had observed his return and routine carefully. He would inevitably spend the evenings in the pub returning to the boat about ten, but never leaving for the pub before seven thirty or eight.

She had previously dropped off the canvas bag in the shed, slouching along the pier dressed as a seaman. To her great satisfaction arousing no interest whatsoever.

This was the night! It was only six thirty, but dressed in her nightdress she told Mrs Evans that she was going to her room early as she had a thumping headache.

The old lady even gave her a glass of warm milk to take up with her.

Once in her room she dressed with great haste into the seaman's outfit. She tucked her hair up under the cap and exited via the window, dropping the bag down before her.

She checked the coast was clear and then sauntered onto the pier, head down, making her way to the shed. She did it unobserved. Quickly slipping her clothes off she donned the blue dress she had brought in the bag. The same dress she had been wearing on the night he dragged her up the castle path and assaulted her.

She ran a hand through her hair and checked the knife was secure in the little pocket she'd made. She had on a matching blue belt, and pulled her dress up a little to show a goodly portion of ankle. All set, her heart beating furiously she peeped out. All clear, she made her way to the boat. This was the difficult part, she had to cross two others to board his.

The two inner boats seemed deserted. Very few men actually slept aboard most having family in town.

She stepped carefully; and quietly across, setting foot on his boat lightly.

She could hear him whistling below sounding cheerful. The entrance to below decks was a covered flight of steps just in front of the bridge house. She slipped silently down the steps making her way forward to where his little cabin was.

'Hello Tom.'

He turned startled. He was just in the process of pulling on a pair of trousers. His mouth dropping open when he saw her there.

'What the hell are you doing here?' he snarled.

'I heard you're a boat owner now, that's very attractive to a girl,' she simpered. 'That looks attractive too,' nodding at his nether regions, giving a little girly giggle.

'Would you like me to give it a proper suck?'

He couldn't believe his ears. Stupid women, they thought you'd got a bit of money, thought you'd *arrived* and they were prepared to prostitute themselves for it.

She put on a lewd look.

'Would you like me to take it right down my throat Tom?'

This was too good an opportunity to miss. The little cow was really going to get it, he grinned at her. 'Come on then love, let's see what you can do.'

His erection was large and throbbing. He thrust it forward and she obligingly went down on her knees before him.

'Close your eyes big boy,' she giggled. 'That's really going to be swallowed.'

He was quivering with excitement. Firstly, ownership of the boat, and now this dirty little cow. He was going to enjoy this; all his chickens had come home to roost.

They had! He felt her hand close around his erection. He felt it sliding down to grasp his testicles closing his eyes in anticipation, and then they opened in surprise as he felt a sudden stab of intense pain.

A quick flick of the razor sharp filleting knife, the best bit of filleting she had ever done. She jerked back rapidly as blood spurted dropping the disgusting sack of flesh on the floor. Jumping to her feet in a flash, she sprinted for the steps rushing up them and lightly jumping the boats onto the pier.

A high pitched screaming followed her as she made the shed in record time, retrieving the fisherman's outfit from the bag and doing a quick change.

By the time she emerged, once again looking like a young seafarer, a crowd was starting to form opposite Watson's mooring. All eyes were turned towards the boat from which the terrible screams were emerging.

She was able to slink past unobserved and within fifteen minutes was scrambling back up into her room.

Nightdress donned again she made her way downstairs to Mrs Evans, telling her she felt quite faint.

Mrs Evans fussed over her, pouring boiling water on crystals and holding a towel over her head, telling her to breathe in the vapours.

Under the towel her face beamed. Mission accomplished, alibi established. Mrs Evans would testify she had been in all night. In fact had been quite unwell, requiring her to administer help to the poor girl.

\*\*\*

# CHAPTER FOURTEEN

## A business venture

The intervening days after Mary had returned to Mrs Evans was spent constructively for Terry and Helen. They visited the girl regularly at the stall just to make sure she was alright. Mary was always glad to see them, although at times seemed to be preoccupied.

Helen had viewed an empty shop property in Westborough which she thought would be ideal for their venture. It was not far from an already well-established restaurant, Rowntree's, but she thought what they wanted to offer was unique and could be successful.

Terry contacted the landlord of the property, found the rent to be satisfactory, and put a deposit on it. They had received some good news; they had finally got the probate sorted on 6 Overton Terrace. The house deeds were transferred into Terry's name.

Helen had suggested they have a word with Betty Metcalf in the market. She'd built up a huge following for her home baked cakes and pies; and Helen thought they would make the ideal basis for establishing their own café.

Her idea of offering an outstanding quality of service with excellent home baked food and attractive pricing seemed a sound formula to Terry. The quicker they could start the better. They poured over plans for the internal features of the café. It was large enough to provide twenty comfortable seats set in an Edwardian up-market setting. There would be pretty lights on each table, with attractive coloured glass shades, and they would be electric!

The seats were to be sumptuously upholstered deep velvet buttoned cushions. The latest fitted kitchen, and a window display that was inviting and attractive. The entire café was to be designed to appear very exclusive, meaning it would always attract customers who could afford to spend money.

They had enlisted the help of an up and coming young designer named Jonathan Edwards. His water coloured sketches formed the basis for their plans.

And Terry still had to go up to the Kessler's to arrange for someone else to take on the Japanese garden. Now that would be an interesting confrontation, not one he really relished.

It was while the two of them were studying the latest batch of drawings that a knock came at the door, and before they could answer it, it opened and in came Jack all hot and bothered.

'What's up Jack?' queried Terry. He knew the old man wouldn't enter like that unless something serious had happened.

'Ave, just eard,' he puffed. 'Watson's in ospital, he's ad is balls cut off.'

'Christ,' they almost said it together, 'Mary!'

They looked at each other. 'Do you know any more Jack?'

'They reckon he were found on is boat screamin like. Bloke's on't pier went ter see what's appenin, and found blood everywhere an Watson rollin abaht on't floor. Reckon he was only got ter ospital before he died er blood loss.'

Terry puffed out his cheeks. 'Have they got anyone for it Jack?'

'Can't tell thee that,' he replied.

Terry looked at Helen. 'We need to get down to Mrs Evans, see if Mary's there or if Mrs Evans knows anything.'

They set off quickly, both of them worried for Mary. They were both convinced it was Mary who'd done it. Neither of them could care a toss about Watson, but they would hate to see Mary end up in prison.

As they approached Quay Street they were both worried to see one of the local constable's bike propped up against the wall.

Terry tapped at the door. It was Mr Evans who answered the door. It was the first time they had ever seen him. He had no idea what he did for a living but he was rarely at home.

He introduced himself and 'Mrs Sheader,' saying they were the couple who had looked after Mary recently, and were just calling to see how she was.

'You'd better come in, seems there's some trouble brewing.'

He took them into the lounge and asked them to wait there. He came back almost immediately, asking them to come through to the room at the front.

As they entered the room they could see Mary and Mrs Evans sitting side by side on a settee, a large policeman was standing before them. He turned at their entrance.

'Mr and Mrs Sheader come in. You've both come at an appropriate time; you may be able to help with some enquiries I'm making.'

Mary sat, looking very demure and childlike. She smiled up at them as they came into the room.

The *copper*, Helen's view of all policemen said. 'We have a report of a serious assault on a fisherman. He's in hospital badly hurt. He claims his injuries were inflicted by Miss Duncan here. Mrs Evans has assured me that Miss Duncan was in her house all night when the incident took place, and in fact was being treated by her for a bad headache and feeling of being faint.' He paused for breath. Why were *coppers* always such windbags? Thought Helen. 'I must admit,' he continued, 'I've known Madge Evans for many a year and find her word adequate, and no one can recall seeing a girl on the pier on the night.'

'What night was this incident?' interrupted Terry.

'Night before last sir,' he said, looking at Terry keenly.

'And what are the man's injuries?' he asked. The policeman coloured slightly and rocked up and down on the balls of his feet.

'Errrrm, he; errr, had his nether parts cut off with a sharp knife.'

'He had his balls cut off,' chortled Helen. The *copper* sniffed and gave a slight smile.

'Quite so madam.'

'And he says this little lass here is the one who did it?' continued Helen in faked astonishment.

'Who is the man constable?' asked Terry, face totally neutral.

'A man called Tom Watson, 'he replied.

Helen felt Terry's hand brush her thigh.

'Ahh! Watson, that blaggard. He's the man who caused this young lady serious injury for which we nursed her for some four days. She was reluctant to report it to you, but this assault by Watson was witnessed by one of the fish stall girls. It was an assault so bad it caused her to lose the child she was carrying.'

'I had heard on the grapevine some such, 'said the *copper*.

'I have to admit Watson is well known to us. Trouble maker who can't hold his drink but you realise we have to follow up an allegation of this nature.'

'And where was Watson when this attack took place?'

'He was on his boat sir.' It was Terry's turn to chortle.

'His boat is the one that moors three deep is it not, the outer one of those indeed?'

'Yes, that's correct sir.'

'And we are led to believe that this young lassie walked the length of West pier, no one having seen her, jumped over two other boats to get to Watson's. Then attacked a big strong lad and removed his laughing tackle and disappeared. Still seen by no one, and all the time being here in the care of Mrs Evans? Really constable, I think you should be looking to charge Mr Watson with wasting police time and making false allegations.'

The constable gulped. 'Put like that sir it does indeed seem ridiculous.'

Terry was on a roll. 'Watson obviously bears this girl a grudge. Certainly he's been injured, but by this girl? More like a prostitute whom he'd refused to pay. That would fit better with the type of person he is.'

Mrs Evans snorted. 'As I said, its rubbish. Mary was with me all that night and in her nightdress. The poor child was quite poorly. That Watson man should be strung up.' The policeman put his pocket book away.

'I think I've enough information to exonerate you Miss Duncan. I'm sorry you've been put through this entire trauma. I'll be asking Watson to withdraw this allegation or face the consequences.' He turned to Mary. 'You should consider laying a charge against this man about the assault upon you. I would urge you to consider it.'

'Thank you for being so considerate constable,' she said in a little girly voice, fluttering her eyes at him. He gave her a beaming smile.

'I'll take my leave of you all, thanks for the help Madge.' He tipped his helmet and went out.

'Of all the terrible things you've gone through my dear, put it behind you now it's good you have such friends,' said Mrs Evans smiling at Terry and Helen. 'Such evil in the world,' she said shaking her head. 'Such evil.'

Terry stood up, Helen doing the same.

'I'm glad we came when we did,' he said, smiling at Mary who returned his look unblinking. 'We'd love you to come and see us when you can,' his eyes searching hers but finding no clues.

'I'd love to come and see you both. Thank you for saying such sweet things about me. It's terrible to be accused of such a thing.' Her eyes sparked for a brief millisecond as she looked at him. They made their goodbyes and left. As they got outside Helen said,

'Well, I don't know how she did it but it's far too big a coincidence to be someone else don't you think?'

'That's one clever girl. God, how she put on the little girl act, that's been an eye opener for me.' Helen looked just a little smug.

'I told you didn't I. You my love will never understand a woman.' He laughed. 'That's true, never in a million years. I must make sure you never fall out with me, I don't think I'd like to be without my dangly bits.'

They made their way home discussing how she could possibly have done it.

Terry had an appointment with the bank manager the following morning. He and Helen had discussed financing the café venture. Doing it all from their newly acquired bank balance would deplete it far too much. It would make sound business sense to arrange a bank loan to part fund it.

They had made Makepeace and Flowers their legal representatives and they had helped to draw up a business plan for them. This he was to present to the bank manager that morning. The meeting went well. By the time he left the bank at eleven thirty he had security for one thousand pounds, a sum that he found hard to visualise.

He was meeting Helen in Rowntree's café for lunch. Not a normal lunch stop for them but as a way of celebration, and a sneak look at the opposition.

He was walking up Westborough towards Rowntree's when he received a tap on the shoulder. Mary!

'Hello Terry, where are you off to?'

He looked hard at this demure looking girl. He felt he no longer knew her.

'Is this coincidence or have you been following me?'

'My, you are sounding like Helen but you're right. I saw you going into the Bank earlier and hung around waiting.' She touched his hand. 'You said you'd be my friend didn't you? I need some help.'

She gave him a beseeching look, green eyes flashing.

'What help do you need love.'

'I'd like to go up to Glasgow for a while to see my parents. I haven't seen them for more than a year, and when Watson is out of hospital you know he's going to come looking for me don't you?'

'Was it you Mary?'

'He thinks so doesn't he?' she replied non-committedly.

'What help do you need?'

'Would you buy me a train ticket to Glasgow? I can't afford one.'

'Yes,' he replied softly. 'Let me know when you want it and I'll get it for you. Will you be coming back?'

'Eventually, yes. I'd like to leave on Monday.'

It was Wednesday. 'I'll get it for you, come round and see us both on Friday night. Good luck love.' She put a hand to his cheek, leaving it there far too long. 'Thank you, I love you,' a glisten in her eye and then she turned and hurried away.

He watched her for a moment mixed feelings going through him, and then carried on walking to his meeting with Helen.

When they were seated in Rowntree's café, delicate sandwiches in front of them and a silver teapot on the table, he recounted his information. Firstly, the success with the bank loan and then the meeting with Mary.

'So she's coming round on Friday? That should be interesting,' she said.

'The next job, which I've been putting off, is to see Mrs Kessler to tell her I'm packing in as her number one gardener. I can't believe I'm in such a position. I thought I was stuck in that rut for life.' Helen laughed. 'She's going to be upset. Her free naked thrill leaving her.'

As they walked back home Helen asked.

'Did Mary give any indications about Watson's misfortune?'

'Not in so many words but she said she knew he'd come looking for her when he was out of hospital. I asked her if she did it. She simply said he thinks so doesn't he.'

'I can't think of anything more fitting for that swine, but if she did it I'm damned if I can see how,' mused Helen. 'I wonder if she got any ideas from those detective novels.'

'We'll have to give her a bit of a quizzing on Friday, he said. 'I've asked the shop fitters to start Monday,' changing the subject. 'We're well and truly committed now.'

Helen squeezed his arm. 'I know we're doing the right thing, just know we can make a success of it.'

They saw Jack in his usual place on their return puffing aromatic blue smoke in the air. He waved his pipe in their direction.

'Just erd from a mate. Watson's goin ter live but he'll ave a squeaky voice fer ever,' chuckling.

'Do you think Mary will be safe from him?' asked Helen.

'She'll never be safe from him if she's in reach. But I don't think he'll attempt to go to Scotland looking for her,' replied Terry. They settled down to discuss their forthcoming venture leaving thoughts of Mary to one side.

Mary was happily serving shellfish to customers from her stall, Shirley chattering at her side. She had asked to be released from her job to go to Scotland on the Monday, and had been told they'd be glad to have her back whenever she needed a job. She'd been a good worker with a natural friendly way with customers. Although she hadn't asked anyone, by listening to chatter from others she'd learned that Watson was out of danger and would recover, although he would never be quite the same again!

She smiled inwardly. That was just the news she wanted to hear. She wanted him to live and be constantly reminded for life what he'd done.

Terry would give her the train ticket on Friday and she would be safe until the fuss had died down. She had slipped round the back of her digs the day after her retribution on Watson, moved the fish box back to its place and disposed of the canvas bag and contents in the bin, packed well down and covered by other debris.

On the Thursday morning, Terry and Helen were in the market asking Betty Metcalf if she could supply sufficient cakes and pies for their venture. Betty thought she could if she took on some help. They agreed to part fund the extra staff she would need. A hand shake, and the deal was done.

They stayed for lunch with her, called at the shop fitters in town and then made their way home. The next decision was thinking of a name for the café.

'A name,' said Helen. 'I hadn't even given that any thought have you?'

'Actually I have. Helen's tea room's doesn't sound classy enough, which is probably the first name that springs to mind. We want a name that gives a touch of exclusivity, and a name that locals can associate with, so how about 'The Scarborian Tea Rooms?' (Locally born people in the borough of Scarborough are known as Scarborians.)

Helen tried it on her tongue, thought about it and then said,

'Do you know, I think that sounds ideal. It's different and quite up-market sounding. Well done lover we've found a name.'

'It all seems to be coming together quite well. The fitters are starting on Monday. We'll have to let the sign writer know the chosen name. He suggested we have the exterior painted a dark green with all lettering in gold leaf. It should stand out very well against the green.' Terry sat back with a sigh of contentment.

'What a change of lifestyle in only three months. I still can't quite get my head round it.'

'Get your head round this then,' she smiled. 'After we can be sure the café is successful, when we know it's paying its way and I'm certain it will, well then, perhaps we should be arranging a wedding.'

He looked stunned, and then a feeling of sheer joy overtook him. He jumped up and threw his arms around her.

'That would make me the happiest man in the world darling. The café was a good idea, the one you've just mentioned is even better. Now that really is something to look forward to, a real incentive to make it work.'

'I'd better start dinner, don't want to starve my man.' She jumped up laughing. He grinned at her. 'Perhaps we should celebrate our new venture tonight. Have you got any tricks left in your repertoire?'

'I'll have to have a think,' she laughed. They were both on top of the world; a world that was going their way. Life was indeed good.

\*

Life was anything but good for Tom Watson lying on his back in a hospital bed, excruciating pain in his groin. An even greater pain of humiliation and anger surging through him, made worse by the whispers and giggles of nurses talking about him, thinking he couldn't hear. His mind twisted into a knotted ball of hatred. His time was spent exploring ways of torture for that slag who had castrated him. He obsessed about it. It dominated his entire thoughts. One way or another he would find her and she would regret it.

\*

The object of his hatred was also lying in bed that evening, her thoughts dominated by her increasing fantasies about Terry and Helen. She explored the most amazing scenarios in her mind ending with bringing herself to orgasm; no thought whatsoever for Watson. He'd been dealt with in a most satisfactory manner. She congratulated herself on the ingenuity of her plan which had gone to perfection. He may have thought he was abusing a simple little fisher-

269

girl. Well she'd taught him a lesson that he would take to the grave. Yes, a very satisfactory ending.

Terry and Helen were enjoying an early night in bed also. As Mary was achieving her orgasm, Terry was being introduced to the pleasures of what Helen described as a *sixty-nine*. This girl never failed to amaze. How many more ways could she devise for sexual satisfaction? He was the most willing of pupils, oh heaven!

On Friday morning, the east wind whistling off the sea gave a chilly feel to the day. It was grey and overcast, even the possibility of snow, a morning to use will power to get out of bed. Terry forced himself out. Helen as usual was still fast asleep. A morning girl she was not! He went down and got the fires roaring. Definitely a morning for a cooked breakfast. By the time Helen wandered down the air was full of the smell of frying bacon sizzling in the pan.

'God; that smells good darling; what a useful man you are.' He grinned at the sight she presented. Hair mussed, the dress just thrown on unbuttoned, it made her look quite erotic he thought.

'Slice of fried bread as well?' he queried,

'Oh, yes please.' They enjoyed the hot breakfast, so happy and settled in each-others company.

'I'm going to go up to the station this morning to get Mary's tickets. I wonder how long Watson will be in hospital.'

'Shouldn't have thought that long, she grinned. 'It's only like castrating a bull, or in his case a pig.'

'It could send him loopy you know,' he said. 'He'll get some real stick from the other men. The grape vine will've worked overtime and I'll bet everyone in the Bottom End knows about it.'

'Good, I've no sympathy for the man. I hope he rots in hell.'

'You sound really hard when you talk like that love.'

'Terry, I've told you about my past. I've no secrets from you. I've suffered in the past at the hands of men like him. Believe me; it makes a girl look on a man like that with utter contempt.'

Helen was reluctant to go out if not required; she hated cold weather so Terry set off for the station solo. As he walked up Westborough flakes of snow started fluttering down. Thank goodness for this warm coat he thought. At the station he bought the two tickets required. One from Scarborough to York, and then a ticket from York to Glasgow. He returned from the station via Makepeace and Flowers to sign the property lease details which they were handling for him, and then hurried home as it began to snow properly, big white flakes swirling in the wind. Helen had baked two large potatoes in the oven, cutting them in half and liberally applying butter and grated cheese before popping them back in the oven for five minutes. Served with slices of boiled ham they enjoyed a warming lunch.

'What time is Mary coming tonight?' he asked as they relaxed with steaming mugs of tea.

'She didn't give a time. She'll turn up when she's ready I suppose. I never thought if she would want a meal. I don't know if she'll have eaten or not before coming.'

'Well, we'll have plenty. If we prepare enough just in case then see what happens.' He sipped his tea and then looked up at Helen.

'I had thought of giving her some money for her travels. She can't have much but I'll be guided by your thoughts on the matter.'

'You mean you were going to but thought I might make a fuss, so thought you would just test the water,' she replied shrewdly. He gave her a wry smile.

'I think in a previous life you must have been a mind reader. Yes, I didn't want to do it behind your back but if you object I'll say no more.'

She laughed at the expression on his face.

'I don't object. As I've said before, you're a lovely warm hearted man Terry Sheader. I just hope it's not being warmed too much by the thought of that pretty face and figure.'

'I'd never noticed,' putting on a pretend innocent expression.

'Bollocks,' she said, both of them laughing uproariously.

They filled in the afternoon poring over the drawings of the café. Terry wrote the preferred colour details on the shop frontage plan, checking every detail, trying to make certain nothing had been overlooked.

'We're committed to spending dad's money now aren't we?'

'Are you still worrying about where it came from?'

'Not worried exactly,' he replied. 'But it niggles I must admit. I'll always keep my ears open for any information I might pick up.'

'If our business venture's a success we can put cash back in the bank, keep the level up, then it will be there just in case you decide to give it away.' She said it in a tone that made him leave the subject. Dinner that night was to be one of Betty's cod and shrimp pies, one of her specialities. Big enough to serve four hence Terry's remark about having enough if Mary hadn't eaten. A classic apple crumble to follow; with a pint of fresh cream courtesy of the milk man.

It was six-thirty that evening when a tap at the door signified Mary's arrival. She was shivering in the cold evening air, a thin coating of snow on the ground.

She was wearing the same thin blue dress covered by a waterproof cape; a scarf around her head the only concession to the snow.

Terry had already coaled the fires. Flames were shooting high, mantles on full and candles glowing on the table.

'Come in love, come and get warm.' He took the cape and scarf from her draping them over the back of a chair, turning back intending to give her a kiss of welcome when she threw her arms around him and kissed him as though Helen were not standing there.

She thrust her body against him as though about to make love leaving him gasping. She released him after gazing into his eyes in the most disturbing way. Then she turned to Helen and repeated the performance with her.

Helen was a highly physical woman. She loved sex and all that went with it. She made no excuses about it as Terry well knew. However, Mary pressing up against her in the most intimate way, kissing her once again full on the lips, in fact feeling a flicker of tongue left her gasping as much as Terry, and worryingly, feeling aroused.

Mary released her and gave them both a lingering look.

'I've been looking forward so much to coming. The two people I love most in the world.' The temperature seemed to have risen quite a few degrees. The colour had risen in Helen's cheeks noticeably. She attempted to bring things down to normal.

'Have you had anything to eat before coming out?'

'No, never thought about it. I was in too much of a rush to get here.'

'Sit down then. We've just had some of Betty's pie. It's delicious. There's a good portion left and some apple crumble to follow.

She tucked into the food with relish, enjoying being fussed over. Terry made mugs of tea for them all as Mary shifted the food as though it would disappear before she finished it. Helen caught his eye, an unfathomable look. She still had colour in her face and Terry suspected so would he if he looked in the mirror.

They invited Mary into the lounge after her meal; they'd much to talk about. Terry sat on the settee. Helen made to sit at the side of him. However, before she could sit Mary squeezed between them pulling Helen down at her side, the three of them on a two seat settee.

'That's the best way to keep warm,' Mary giggled. 'Between my two special people.'

273

For all his attempt at control Terry could feel his temperature rising, and to add to the discomfort as she said; *that's the best way to keep warm,* she placed a hand on Helen's thigh and gave a little squeeze.

Helen almost shot out of the settee. It was like an electric charge going through her leaving her feeling highly confused. Terry decided it was time to get some information out of this erotic creature before she caused any more discomfort.

'Have you written to your mum and dad to let them know you're coming?' he asked. 'No, I don't even know for certain if they are still at the same address. It's a rented place they had in the Gorbals. Its one hell of a rough district and people move around a bit, but I'll find them all right.'

'Crikey love, it sounds a bit awkward. Are you sure you'll be safe, will they be pleased to see you? No, that's a daft question; of course they'll be pleased to see you.'

'I hope so,' she said, a little woefully. 'My dad is a rough bugger. He never shows much emotion. He thinks once we're over sixteen we should be out earning a living.' She cuddled up to Terry. 'Well, I've done that haven't I?'

'How long do you intend to stop in Glasgow?' asked Helen.

'I don't know. I'll just see how I feel. If I write to you with an address will you let me know if it's safe to come back? You know, Watson...?' The last word said with deep hatred.

'Watson, yes, that's a problem isn't it?' said Helen, looking at Mary. 'Was it you?'

Mary looked at Helen with glistening eyes. 'Do you think I did it?'

'I don't know what to think love. It's one hell of a coincidence isn't it? But I admit I don't know how you could have.' Mary was stroking Helen's thigh now, perhaps unconsciously or perhaps not. Either way it was making Helen feel decidedly randy. She was the one who liked practicing new ways of sexual activity but this was something else again. Terry was looking at them both bemused, shaking his head slightly.

'Mary love, if you want to tell us anything, its safe with us. You know that. Watson deserved all that was coming to him. We would be the last to say anything to anyone.' She still didn't answer but continued stroking Helen's thigh, and then said suddenly. 'I've passed my nights thinking about you two. I can't think of anything else, you both haunt my nights. Sometimes it seems so real, it's as though you are really there.'

'What do you mean?' asked Helen in a shaky voice. She was looking highly flushed. Terry recognised the signs. Internally he was thinking I know those signs, she's starting to steam.

Mary was gazing into the distance now as though seeing things on an internal screen. 'We're all together us three, making love. It's the most erotic feeling. So much pure love just being shared between us three.'

Her hand was at the top of Helen's thigh and Helen knew she had to break this moment or burst. She grabbed Mary's hand before it went any further.

'Christ Mary, stop that. I'm only human and that's enough. We're both far too old for you in any case.'

'No, you're not, I love you both you know I do. You mean more to me than anyone anywhere. Would you like to hear what happens in my dream?'

Terry spoke before the highly flustered Helen could.

'Mary it's only a dream. You've been through such awful times your mind is looking for something or someone to take you away from bad memories; it's a way of coping with it.'

Helen suddenly sat back with a gasp. 'God almighty Mary,' removing her hand altogether from her thigh. 'Now that's enough for God's sake that's enough.' She sprang to her feet. 'Mary that's enough, it's not healthy you thinking like that. You're starting to mix dreams and reality in your mind as Terry says. Now I'll make some more tea before we all blow up.' She dashed into the kitchen leaving Terry deserted and with a mighty erection.

'Do you think I've upset her?' she whispered to him, leaning into him.

She noticed the bulge and immediately placed her hand on it.

'I haven't upset you my darling have I?' He grabbed her hand as she squeezed. 'Mary, for God's sake stop that it's all wrong.' She was quivering.

'You'd like to though Terry. Like to do what I've just described?'

'I'm a man Mary. I'd be lying if I said it didn't turn me on. You're a beautiful girl and we both think the world of you but it would be so wrong.'

'Why would it be wrong? Who says it's wrong? If we really wanted to do it, all of us, it can't be wrong can it?' He was saved by Helen coming in with three mugs on the tray. 'Split apart you two, have a cuppa. I think we all need it.'

Mary reluctantly sat up and took the proffered mug. As she took it from Helen she looked at her provocatively and ran her tongue around her lips.

'You need to think about your future. What you're going to do, running away now isn't the answer,' Terry said to her. 'I know you think you'll be in danger when Watson's up and about, and to tell the truth I think you're right. The police should be keeping an eye on him and you can always rely on us for support.'

'The police,' she spat. 'They would always be too late. No, the police won't save me from him. I know you'll be here for me,' her voice softening. 'But I need to get away. Until things die down a bit.'

'I don't think things will die down with Watson,' said Helen glumly. 'I know the type. He'll be hell bent on revenge but,' looking shrewdly at Mary. 'If you didn't do it why should you think he'd be coming for you?'

Terry squeezed her hand. 'You've just told us we're the two who mean the most to you in the world. Well if that's true then confide in us, please love. Tell us one way or the other. Neither of us could care a toss about him but if you want our support we need to know the truth.'

Tears sprang to Mary's eyes, she clutched his hand tightly.

'I hate the bastard. Yes, I did it. I wanted him to suffer as much as he made me suffer. The pain he caused me, the humiliation he put me through, the way he just destroyed my baby.' Tears were pouring down her face now. 'The mistake I made was not sticking my knife in his heart instead.'

Helen had a look of extreme compassion on her face. She could empathise totally with her and it sounded so much like her own story in places. Terry hugged her to him. 'All right love don't get upset. I said we'll help and by God we will. Thanks for taking us into your trust, now at least your nightmares should die a little.' 'How did?' started Helen, and then stopped as Terry shook his head at her.

'I haven't had any nightmares about him,' said Mary defiantly. 'I had dreams about us, nice dreams.' Terry hurriedly intervened again, we want to steer away from there he thought.

'Monday,' he said firmly. 'I have your train tickets. It will mean traveling to York and then boarding the Glasgow train in York. You depart Scarborough at eight. We'll both come up with you to the station to see you off. As soon as you find where you're staying in Glasgow, whether it's with your parents or not write and let us know your address.'

She was looking panicky now. 'I've never been on a train before.'

Helen laughed. 'Neither had I. You'll love it, it's the best way to travel, so exciting.'

'I'll be on my own in York? I have to change to another train?' The enormity of what she was going to do was starting to sink in.

'Don't worry love there are plenty of staff at York, all in uniform. Just give one of them that naughty smile and they'll fall over themselves showing you to the Glasgow train,' he grinned at her wanting to allay her panic.

'And, we have something else for you. We're giving you some money to travel with. It should be enough to get you settled and sorted without having to worry how you're going to live. Tell mum and dad it's what you've saved.'

She burst into tears hugging Terry, with Helen stroking her hair. Once again, she was a little girl needing reassurance. This really is a mixed up kid he thought. I wonder just how much damage has been done to her mind.

She left at nine thirty that night, Terry walking her home her arm through his. They got to Quay Street, and before she went in, Terry handed her a small canvas purse. 'Take this love. It should see you through for a while. We'll be down here at half past seven on Monday to walk up to the station with you. Get plenty rest over the weekend.' He gave her a hug and the usual response from her, her lips seeking his hungrily, tongue touching his, he broke away abruptly.

'Mary love, steady on. You'll give an old man a heart attack kissing like that,' trying to make light of it.

'You're not an old man. I love you so much. I know you're Helen's, but I can't help the way I feel.' She gazed up at him. 'I'll always be so grateful to you and Helen. Don't forget me will you,' a strange comment.

'You'd be very difficult to forget little lady,' he laughed. 'Go on, in with you before we both freeze.' She gave him another hug and turned and went in.

He breathed a sigh of relief, walking back with disturbed feelings about the girl. He was worried about her and concerned what the future would hold for her. Helen was waiting impatiently when he opened the door.

'I was keeping an eye on the time,' she laughed. 'If you'd been too long I would have come looking for you.'

'You might have had need to,' he said. 'I had all on stopping her sticking her tongue down my throat.'

'I suppose you'd have found that a terrible experience.'

'Not really,' he laughed. 'But seriously, that is one disturbed little lass. I worry about her.'

Helen turned to the gas ring and poured hot milk from the pan into two mugs containing cocoa and sugar to make a hot chocolate drink. She handed one of the steaming mugs to him. 'I know what you mean. She seems to be living in a bit of a fantasy world. The worst thing was I almost found her offer of the three of us tempting. Does that make me a lesbian?' 'No, it just reinforces the fact that you're a nympho,' he laughed.

'I noticed you had a bloody hard on,' she said accusingly.

'Ah! That's Bruce, he works independently of me.'

'Like hell he does.'

They sat and sipped cocoa. 'I can't help wondering how she did it,' she said after a while. 'Do you think she'll ever tell us?'

'We'll just have to see, but I'm sure as she fears, Watson will be looking for her when he's out and about.'

*

Mary, back in her room changed into her nightdress and sat on the bed. She opened the little purse that Terry had given her. Her eyes opened in astonishment, it contained thirty gold sovereigns an enormous sum. That would be more than a help it was equivalent to over four month's wages. She felt a gush of gratitude and love for him. They both thought she was a young girl with a crush. She, and only she, knew it was deep and abiding. She would do anything for them both, anything at all.

She fell asleep with the usual erotic thoughts flooding her mind. They were a wonderful comfort blanket; they and reality became increasingly difficult to separate.

279

Monday morning was bright and clear with a heavy frost; the small sprinkling of snow over the weekend was crisply preserved. They were both down at Mary's early. She was ready and waiting for them having packed her meagre belongings into a small holdall, which she had bought on Saturday using the funds Terry had provided. She took a tearful farewell of Mrs Evans who also looked quite emotional, and they then walked briskly up through town to the station. Mary with her arm linked through Helen's for a change.

The station was quite busy. Terry couldn't help noticing the number of men in uniforms, mainly Green Howards, a regiment which recruited heavily in Scarborough. The train was in, six carriages behind the hissing green loco. Mary, like Helen before her was wide eyed seeing it up close.

She stood on the platform looking lost and very small.

'That's your carriage there,' he pointed to the third one from the loco. 'Let's get you on board.' He ushered her before him carrying her little bag. It seemed pathetic she had so little and yet, he thought only recently he had about the same.

They found her seat up near the window, putting the bag on the rack overhead. 'Don't forget love ask a member of staff to help you in York; and write as soon as possible.' The doors were slamming. A tearful hug for both of them and then they hurried off the train to stand at the side of the carriage. Mary's little face was pressed up against the window.

The last doors slammed shut, the guard raising his green flag whistle to lips, a quick scan around, and then a blast from the whistle. An answering blast from the locomotive's whistle. The clank of slack being taken up in the carriage linkages and it was moving. They trotted alongside the carriage a short way before it picked up speed, waving and blowing kisses. Mary's face was pressed against the window, tears flowing freely. As the train receded into the distance they both felt a sense of loss as though waving an only child off. Helen, with tears in her eyes turned to him. 'Do you think she'll be all right? She looked like a lost child just now. I'm worried to bits about her.'

'I know what you mean. I'm like you, worried about her safety but concerned about her going to Scotland. There's some gut feeling that tells me she's still hiding something from us.'

On the train Mary fought to control her feeling of utter loss. She hadn't told them her father was a bully and wife beater, one of the reasons she'd been glad to leave home in the first place. She knew her life would be in danger staying in Scarborough, no doubt whatsoever of that but she'd made it her home town, settling in happily into the seaside environment, so different from the slums of Glasgow which she had left behind. And now, she was leaving two people who dominated her every waking thought. Who meant more to her than her own life.

It was a confused, abused, and still in many ways immature girl leaving on the train that day.

*

Terry and Helen decided to have a cup of tea in Rowntree's until nine thirty or so by which time the shop fitter's should be on site to make a start. Neither of them could wait to see a start made. The beginning of a new life, but not without risk. It was an excited but nervous couple who arrived at the shop premises. A large motor van was outside displaying the shop fitter's logo. The morning flew by, discussions about detail and colour pushing all thought of Mary from their minds.

Mary was experiencing all the excitement that Helen had on her first train trip. The speed at which they were travelling excited and terrified at the same time, watching fields and people flashing by. Wonders at sights she hadn't seen before but no one to share the experience with. Fascination as it pulled up at numerous stations on the way, watching the variety of passengers, young and old, vastly different clothing styles boarding and alighting.

This slower train than Terry and Helen had taken on their trip to York; finally pulled into the city one and a half hours later. Her train to Glasgow was not until ten thirty allowing her an hour at York. Terry had explained she could buy a drink at the station café, telling her to do so after checking which platform the Glasgow train would depart from. An obliging young man in uniform had pointed out the platform to her, looking appreciatively at the pretty girl fluttering her eyes at him, even carrying her bag to the café for her.

An emboldened Mary asked for a coffee with cream. Terry had primed her carefully beforehand giving her the first taste ever of the creamy nutty flavour.

The same helpful young man carried her bag to the platform for the Glasgow connection. Her fluttering eyes had obviously worked and he helped her into the correct carriage when the huge hissing monster pulled in.

To Mary, it seemed a bigger locomotive than the last and had eight carriages, an enormous length! She was grateful to her willing helper who guided her to the correct one, carrying her bag for her and placing it on the rack.

He gave an appreciative smile and wished her a pleasant journey. His eyes lingered for a moment on this pretty girl. She thanked him warmly with her most winning of smiles and he departed with a warm glow.

The seats were deep and comfortable. As the train started on its long journey; she was sitting contentedly chatting to an elderly lady in the seat opposite.

Back in Scarborough, the excited couple had retreated to Rowntree's for lunch after the foreman fitter had given very subtle and gentle hints they were getting under his feet and delaying progress. They had accepted the hint with good grace. All was going well and they left him to get on. Now, seated with plates of delicate sandwiches before them and the silver tea pot and China cups and saucers perfectly placed, they took stock.

'I don't think we'll be quite as welcome in here after they find out who we are,' murmured Terry. 'After they know who we are we won't need to come in here,' she grinned.

The shop fitting went at a pace. Apart from some glitches that required firm input from Terry to exact change the café was ready for opening in a fortnight.

They had discussed at length what staffing would be required. With twenty seats, at least three serving staff and one full time cook would be required. Helen would have overall control.

Advertising in the Scarborough Mercury brought many replies which they managed to whittle down to three girls who had the right personality and looks.

Terry, with some initial comment from Helen, said they needed girls who were attractive, drawing the inevitable remarks from Helen.

He disarmed her suspicions, saying,

'We want this café to succeed. Attractive girls with bubbly personalities and highly efficient at serving on will make it succeed. No one wants a plain Jane who looks as though she is just doing a job. It makes good business sense love.'

She saw the sense in that and the three girls they eventually picked fitted all criteria. Two of them had already had experience in the trade. The third was a bright girl who looked as though she would pick up the required skills rapidly. Both he and Helen stressed to the girls the need at all times to make customers feel special and wanting to come back.

They introduced a great incentive by saying they would all be paid a bonus if monthly targets were beaten.

After discussion, they both agreed a full time pot washer would also be needed. This was to cause Terry to smile inwardly when one of the girls replying to the advertisement was Jane, Mrs Kessler's scullery maid. He gave her the job immediately knowing what a good worker she was.

Even more controversial was the cook. They 'head hunted' one of the cooks from a large hotel, which brought bitter remarks from the hotel manager. But, as they offered a better wage to the man, and access to the bonus scheme it was all above board and part of what was required to succeed. Helen managed to have a sly little dig at Terry after his insistence on pretty girls for serving staff. She couldn't resist mentioning how good looking the cook was. He took it in good part, being much more used to her personality now.

A more difficult job, which he did in the first week of shop fitting, was to visit Mrs Kessler to tell her he wouldn't be returning to the gardening job. He made sure he wore the blue suit and bowler hat. It had the required effect. Mrs Kessler's eyes almost popped out of her head. He explained the situation and how he was going into business, said he was very sorry that the garden was in an unfinished state but he would help in finding a replacement gardener if she wished him to.

She gave the impression that she was genuinely upset at his departure, refusing his offer of a replacement, saying it could wait for some weeks until the weather picked up. His feeling was that she rather hoped the business venture would go belly up and he would then return to her. She wished him well in his venture without actually meaning it.

The grand opening came in the second week of March. They had placed advertising material in the Mercury and arranged for the premises to be declared officially open by the Mayor and his consort, a good publicity move.

They declared a discount of twenty per cent to all customers in the first week. The café opened every day except Sunday at nine and closed at six.

It all seemed to pay off. Trade was brisk and they were both pleased to see some of the 'upper crust' of Scarborough society among the customers.

All girls, Helen included, wore black dresses nipped in at the waist with white starched apron and hat with white banding. The dresses were cut to emphasise figure quite deliberately, and short enough to show a goodly amount of ankle.

He grinned when observing the male customers. The ploy worked well, many men having a crafty 'eye full' when they thought they were not being observed. A guarantee they would return.

The first week went better than all their expectations. They both waited to see if that pattern would carry on into the second week when the discount no longer applied. In fact it increased. Helen deliberately flirting in a very mild manner with male customers, they soon built up a regular clientele. Gambles had been taken and much money spent but it was rewarding them even more than their wildest dreams could have guessed.

*

The opening of Terry and Helen's café coincided with the first full outing of Tom Watson. His recovery had been hampered by the loss of blood and time needed to build up his strength. His repair work went well. Mary had done a good job with the filleting knife; it had been a clean efficient cut making it an easier job for the surgeon to sew.

He had been almost apoplectic when visited by the constable, who told him to withdraw his false accusation or face charges. However, on deliberation he decided to do just that. He wanted to be the one visiting retribution on the girl, not the police. He returned to living on the boat with as little fuss as possible. The only genuine sympathy shown him came from Jack Campbell, but probably because the old scot had an eye on his job. The wily old boy had kept the boat operational during Watson's convalescence, hiring a local skipper to take the boat out. For this, Watson was grateful.

The first incident signifying his return to local life took place one evening when he visited his old haunt, *The Old Steam Packet*. There were nudges and winks as he walked in quickly inflaming him. But as his drink intake increased he snapped when a local who he did not know said. 'Who's the squeaky voice over there?' in a voice designed for him to hear.

He turned in a flash, smashed his glass on the counter and raked it down the man's face. Blood spurted, and he followed it up with a mighty punch to the unfortunate man's stomach kicking him savagely as he went down.

He had to be restrained by three other seamen but the message went round in a flash. Don't make any comment about Watson's recent injury.

He next made rather unsubtle enquiries as to the whereabouts of Mary. As the only people who knew where she had gone were Mrs Evans and Shirley he hit a blank, much to his fury. The only information he did pick up was that she had 'gone away.' His fury wasn't helped by a visit from the constable who warned him he had heard about his enquiries and that he, Constable James Middleton, would be keeping an eye on him.

One bit of information he did pick up from a simple elderly seaman in the *Packet*, was that she had been cared for by Sheader and Helen Standish. The same Sheader who had opened a successful café in Westborough using his deceased father's money. It was information which inflamed him even more. Sheader he hated and Helen Standish was a Bottom End slag! And he knew where Sheader's father had got his wealth. Wealth that he should have had a share of but got nothing, not a bloody thing.

The first thing he wanted to know was, where was Sheader living now? Surprisingly, that information came from Jack Savage who was drinking in the pub at the same time as he one night. The old seaman was chatting to a chap even older than he. They were having a laugh at Jack's remarks about Terry and Helen next door keeping him awake at night. Shagging like rabbits as Jack phrased it.

Bloody typical he thought. Got my money and shagging the slag of Scarborough. His lip curled, both as bad as each other. He decided he would go up Westborough and have a look at this *caff,* fully expecting to see a working man's café. When, on enquiring he was told which café it was, when he'd seen with his own eyes the opulence of the place a rush of blood and anger came to his face. He peered in at the window and saw Helen Standish of all people in a provocative outfit serving tea to an elderly gentleman who was soaking up the attention she was giving him. 'Slag, slag,' he said aloud, making a passing woman give him an evil look.

The intensity of his gaze must have communicated itself to Helen in some way. She felt a compulsion to look up and saw him. He noticed he'd been seen, turning away abruptly and hurrying back down Westborough.

Helen dashed to the door just in time to see Watson hurrying away. She was breathing heavily, what the hell was he doing here? She had a shrewd idea it meant trouble.

I must tell Terry she thought.

She dashed into the café, scuttling through to the little office where he was sorting paper work, ignorant of the appreciative looks from her elderly customer glancing at the heaving bosom.

Terry looked up at the flustered Helen as she stormed in.

'You won't like this; I've just seen Watson staring in at the window. He saw I'd noticed him and scurried away,' she gasped. He felt a cold anger. The bloody man was starting to haunt them and he instinctively knew it was not good news. It could only mean trouble. The man was out for revenge. Perhaps he thought they were harbouring Mary.

He didn't want Helen getting upset. She had been the receiver of too much badness from the likes of Watson in the past.

'Don't let it upset you love. I'll deal with him if he makes waves. In the meantime forget the swine. There's nothing he can do to affect us.'

He didn't believe it for one minute but didn't want Helen worrying about him.

One of her regulars was an elderly chap called Mr Smith. She believed he was a local magistrate. He puzzled her because he would sit with his coffee and scone making notes in a little pocket book, always giving her a friendly wink. It was as though he knew her. We do have some characters she thought. The incident with Watson had disturbed her, the rest of the day passed with a feeling of discomfort.

Tom Watson ducked his head instinctively as he entered the tiny quarters on *Our Lass.*

He was fuming internally. All the people whom he hated and despised the most were suddenly the very people whom fate was smiling on. He was being victimised by circumstances beyond his control. That was the warped view he had on life. He never thought for a minute that his injury was an outcome of his own making, or his attitude to others created their attitude to him.

His entire waking moments were absorbed with revenge. Just like Mary fantasised about Terry and Helen, he fantasised about what he would do to her, how he would make her suffer just as she had made him suffer. And when he found where she was hiding, he was convinced she was hiding from him, and that the 'Bottom End slag' knew where that was, he would exact the most terrible revenge.

\*\*\*

# CHAPTER FIFTEEN

## Mary's return

Mary had arrived in Glasgow late that evening in a state of exhaustion. After the novelty of train travel had started to pall she nodded off for a good hour, being woken by the chattering woman opposite. Her mind was a whirl. She'd not been entirely honest with Terry and Helen when she'd told them she was no longer sure where her parents were living. She knew the exact address in the ghastly Gorbals tenement, a squalid nest of rough and desperate people.

Her father was a brewer's drayman. He was a violent man at times who terrorised her mother, especially when in drink which was often. The similarities between her background and Helen's were uncannily alike. She'd been glad to leave home when she first decided to follow the fishing fleet. It had got her away and even seemed rather glamorous at the time.

It turned out to be anything but glamorous. It was hard, filthy, smelly work, and she thought deciding to turn her back on it and stay in Scarborough was the best thing she'd ever done.

Events had driven her away temporarily but she would go back when Terry let her know it was safe. She had infinite trust in him.

In the meantime she had to hope her parents would let her stay at such short notice. As short as turning up tonight and asking for a bed!

When she arrived at the tenements eventually it was seven o'clock, and her mother, after getting over the initial shock, welcomed her in. The first sight Mary saw was the black eye her mother was sporting making her heart sink. She knew where that would have come from. There was no sign of her father.

'At the pub hen,' said her mother when she asked.

'Oh God, that almost certainly meant he would be coming home drunk!

'Will it be alright for me to stay a while mum?' Her mother looked at her shrewdly. 'Are you in trouble hen?'

'Not trouble as such mum, but there's a man intent on doing me harm back in Scarborough. Please don't start asking questions mum.'

'I won't if that's what you want and this is your home, but he,' emphasise on *he*, 'will ask and probe; you know what he's like. He'll not be pleased you're here without having found yourself a husband. One who can support you.'

Her dad was an old fashioned type. A woman should get a good man who would look after her and she should look after him and produce children. She could already feel her heart sinking. What had she been thinking about? Fleeing here, it was the only refuge she could think of at the time but now it did not seem so good an idea.

In fact her fears were well founded. Her father staggered home roaring drunk and abusive. He insisted she had run from man troubles and would bring trouble to them. He accused her of being a loose woman, only having come home because she had nowhere to run to. His tirade of furious abuse left both her and her mother in tears. What the hell had she done coming here?

She stayed only two days and then found a cheap room in a street a block away, moving into a furnished single room (so called) that made her digs in Scarborough seem palatial.

Glasgow was even more dismal and rough than she remembered. She felt depressed and alone. Sorry also that she had brought upset to her mother, putting her in an impossible position attempting to back her daughter.

Her next requirement if she was staying a while was to find a job. The money Terry had provided would soon run out without any further income. Ironically, the only job she could find after much searching was in the local market filleting fish for the fishmonger. A return to the very job she hated.

She wrote to Terry and Helen giving her address, not mentioning it wasn't her parents address, and waited anxiously for a reply.

Terry wrote her a long newsy letter describing in detail the café/tea rooms and how trade had taken off. Describing the girls who they'd taken on. How they'd *pinched* the chef from a famous hotel. He wrote in a beautiful copperplate hand, the letters long and flowing addressing it to 'our dearest Mary' and finishing with 'all our love.'

Her tears dropped onto the paper. She kissed the letter as though he were there in person. She'd never felt so desolate.

The second letter from Terry was the decider. She was going back to Scarborough! Her life here was intolerable. If there was danger from Watson well, she would jolly well face it. Terry would protect her, to hell with Watson.

The decision made she couldn't wait to let Terry and Helen know, asking them if they would enquire from Mrs Evans if her room was still available.

A huge weight had been lifted from her shoulders. Whatever the future held it would be with the two people she most wanted to be with.

It was only three weeks after her arrival in Glasgow that she was booked on a train for York. She took a tearful farewell of her mother promising to write and keep in touch. Her mother's final bit of advice. 'Keep clear of violent men hen. Look at what I've got!'

She arrived back in Scarborough in the second week of April, the train puffing in at eight o'clock. Mary felt as though she had been to the moon and back.

She looked excitedly through the carriage window as it slowed to a stop, and then her heart gave an almighty jump as she saw Terry waiting alone on the platform.

He saw her and waved like mad. As the train drew to a stop he boarded and rushed to help with her bag. Before

291

he could even reach the bag on the rack she was in his arms, smothering him with kisses to the nudges and winks from other alighting passengers. He grinned like a Cheshire cat.

'Anyone would think you're pleased to see me,' he said.

He felt the dampness of her tears against his face. 'Come on little lass, the train will be steaming out with both of us on it if we don't get off.'

He lifted the bag and took her by the hand, dropping lightly onto the platform. 'Where's Helen?' she asked.

'She's getting your bed ready in the attic. I'm afraid Mrs Evans has let your old room to another girl so we'll have to look for some new accommodation for you. In the meantime you'll be safer with us. We can keep an eye on who's hanging around,' he said meaningfully.

She was delighted and impressed when he placed her bag in a cab, helping her up into it. He gave the cabbie the address, the cabbie clicking his tongue at the horse, a beautiful grey, and away they trotted. 'Cabbie, will you pause for a moment at the new tea-rooms on Westborough, the Scarborian Tea Rooms.'

'Aye sir.' They trotted down Westborough stopping at the café.

'This is it love our new venture, what do you think?'

Mary gaped at the classy exterior. 'Oh wow, that looks really posh. Oh Terry, is that really yours and Helen's?'

'Yes and its doing well. Tomorrow you can have the guided tour.'

They were back at Overton terrace at eight thirty. The cab dropped them at Burr Bank, a two hundred yards walk to home. He paid the cabbie, took her bag in his right hand, and with her arm firmly through his left arm walked on to the terrace and up to their door. As he opened the door he turned to her and said. 'It looks as though you're back with us for a little while.' Her face shone like a beacon.

Helen looked ever so slightly wary as they entered. Mary rushed to her in her inimitable manner, threw her arms around her and gave her a full on smacker.

Terry grinned behind her back, seeing the look on Helen's face as Mary withdrew. Mary looked beseechingly at Helen. 'I can't begin to tell you how much I've missed you both. Glasgow was horrible and my dad a proper bastard. Whatever I'm going to face here it'll be better than that. I've made Scarborough my home now. I'm prepared to face whatever comes.' Helen, ever the practical one, said. 'Its good to see you love now give me that bag. I'll take it up.'

She disappeared upstairs, Mary turning to Terry.

'Tell me all about the café, everything.' He gave her the details of the enterprise so far and laughed when he said. 'And you'll meet the three 'J's.'

'Who're the three J's?'

'Well, it didn't register at first, but the three girls we've taken on to serve in the café are, Jean, Jennifer and Jane. We made small name tags for them to wear on their bibs and it was some of our regular customers who started calling them the three J's.'

'You have regular customers already?'

'Yes, its fantastic how things have taken off. And Helen had the idea to put a notice in the window saying ten percent discount for all His Majesty's soldiers and sailors. That not only proved popular with the officers in town, but the locals think we are being very patriotic. A winner all round.'

Helen came down. 'That's your room all ready. Is there anything else you need love?'

'Well, I know its getting late, but I'd really love a bath. Having travelled all day I feel filthy.' Helen turned to Terry. 'Will you bring the bath and copper up love. It won't take long to heat some water.'

'Yes, sure,' He went to the cellar head thinking, this will be interesting. Once the bath is ready I'll make myself scarce.

He brought the copper up first, connecting the gas pipe to it. And then the bath, placing it as usual in front of the fire. Helen already had the rubber pipe connected to the tap pouring water into the copper. Mary smiled sweetly at him. 'Sorry to be such a bother Terry.'

'No bother love. I'm sure you're ready for a bath and bed. You must be exhausted after such a long day.'

'I'm ready for a scrub definitely.' She nodded at the door. 'I'll just nip across the yard first.'

'Right,' as she went through the door he said to Helen. 'When the bath's ready I'll go next door for a while. We both know what she's like. It'd be better if I'm not in, she can't misbehave then. Just knock on the wall when it's safe to come back.' 'Wonderful,' muttered Helen. 'And what do I do?'

'Wash her hair for her,' he grinned. She stuck her tongue out at him, and as Mary returned he said. 'Right, I'll nip next door while you're wallowing in the bath. I don't want to be accused of being a peeping Tom.'

Mary gave him a coy look. 'You could never be that Terry.'

Helen's face was a picture, especially when Mary said. 'Would you wash my hair for me Helen?' She gave Helen an enigmatic look, Helen colouring slightly.

'I'm off then. I'm only next door. Give a knock when the coast's clear.'

He gave them both a beaming smile, a wink for Helen and left.

Helen filled the bath tub three quarters full, testing the temperature with her hand. 'That should be fine now.' Mary disrobed slowly and, Helen thought, provocatively standing before her in the nude. She couldn't help thinking Mary had a perfect figure. Long slim legs, pert little breasts with upturned nipples and a glow that belongs only to youth.

'Come on, get in,' she said abruptly. Mary gave her a sweet smile and glided over to the tub. She lifted a long leg, stepping over the side and sliding into the water like an eel. She dipped her head under to wet her hair, lifting it streaming water. 'I'm ready Helen.' Helen took the bar of soap, stood behind her and started to soap her hair rubbing it well in and running hands through the auburn locks.

She couldn't take her eyes off the firm little breasts, looking down the length of the girl as she was. Her cheeks started to burn and a familiar flutter started in her tummy. She closed her eyes for a moment. Oh God, no, no.

Next door Terry and Jack were having a good old natter. Terry bringing the old man up to date with all that had been happening at the café. He mentioned the problems that Mary had and the fact Helen had caught Watson staring into the café window.

'Aye, yon's goin ter be trouble I reckon,' he said. 'I'll let yer know if ah see im angin abaht.' Terry glanced at Jack's old Grandfather clock. Ten fifteen, whatever was keeping them next door? The worst job with the bath tub was emptying it. A bucket had to be used until enough water had been removed to make it possible to lift. Just as the thought was going through his head they both heard a sharp rap-rap on the wall.

'Ah, the royal summons,' he grinned. 'I'll get off then Jack. Thanks for the company.'

He returned next door. As soon as he stepped in alarm bells started to ring. Mary had nothing but a large bath towel wrapped around her, a deep flush on her cheeks and her eyes positively glowed. Much worse, Helen had an even deeper flush, was breathing heavily, and had a slightly wild look that he recognised immediately. The look she always had after sex!

He felt his heart jump. Helen couldn't meet his eyes.

'It can be emptied now,' she said in a tight voice. 'I'll see Mary to bed.'

Mary was looking at him enigmatically, lips slightly parted. 'Night night Terry.' She turned and followed Helen up the stairs. He sat heavily on the chair, unable even to tackle the bath emptying. Fleeting visions going through his mind. Oh shit, oh shit, oh shit.

Helen came down after about five minutes. He just looked at her waiting for her to speak. She faced him with difficulty, eyes moist, giving a little shrug of her shoulders.

'Terry, I don't know what to say. Please don't ask any questions now, not now. I couldn't cope with it.'

He didn't know what to say or do. This was the woman he loved. He had always said he wouldn't be judgemental of her. She'd been open and honest with him about her past, had admitted she had a high sex drive; in fact he loved that aspect of her in particular!

'No questions then if that's how you feel.' He turned to the tub, picked up the bucket and dipped it in.

She gave a loud gasping sob and ran to him, throwing her arms around him and laying her head against his chest. He left the bucket and put his arms around her. He held her tightly, kissing the top of her hair, waiting until the sobs and shudders stopped. 'Tell me in your own time, if you want to that is. Go and get ready for bed and I'll come up as soon as I've emptied the tub.'

She looked into his face with damp eyes, placing a hand on his cheek. 'You're such a special man,' and then turned and went upstairs.

He emptied the tub slowly allowing his mind to wander. It was disturbing and erotic all at the same time. He finished the job and went upstairs.

Helen was on her back asleep, or pretending to be. He undressed, turned the mantle off and slipped between the sheets as quietly as possible.

He lay awake for a long time, all sorts of scenarios going through his mind, finally drifting off at two am.

In the attic, Mary also lay awake for a long time savouring what had taken place. A part of her fantasy had turned into reality and it had been good. She would achieve it all eventually she was sure.

Terry woke with a thumping headache having had a disturbed night full of dreams. Helen lay on her back, an occasional light snore bubbling out.

He swung his legs out of bed and went downstairs, washed and shaved and got dressed. The time was seven forty. They were both up normally about this time ready to get up to the café by eight thirty to open up. There was still no sound of waking from upstairs and he felt a touch of deep resentment starting to bubble.

He was suffering from a mixture of emotions. Was Mary going to be a threat to their lifestyle? Was he feeling uncomfortable with the girl on girl scenario which he was convinced had taken place the night before? Was it a threat to him? He made a decision there and then. Mary had to go; she had abused his trust and hurt him badly. The quicker they could find accommodation for her the better.

He looked at the clock angrily, still no sound from upstairs. Temper building, he sprinted up to the attic opening the door without knocking and entering.

Mary was laying on her back an arm around teddy. Her eyes fluttered open at the sound of his entry. Seeing who it was a smile started, and then uncertainty as she saw the look on his face.

'Terry,' she started saying in an uncertain voice. He looked down at her with a barely controlled fury. 'You hurt me very badly last night Mary. You abused my hospitality. I want you out of here as soon as possible. I'll start looking for a room for you immediately.'

Tears sprang uncontrollably from her; she sat up with a gasp.

'Oh no, no Terry, please,' the words bubbling out in a gush. 'I didn't mean to hurt you, not you, oh God! What have I done? Terry please don't make me go. I'm sorry, so sorry, please forgive me.' Her anguish was genuine; she extended an arm to him beseechingly.

'What have I done, what have I done?' she wailed.

297

Helen was woken by the commotion upstairs. She dashed out of bed and ran up the attic stairs totally naked, bursting into the room. Mary was gasping and gulping, huge sobs coming out. Terry was standing fully dressed before her unmoving. He turned as Helen entered.

'I've just told her I want her out as quickly as possible. I'm going to go and open the café now before it looks as though we're shut for the day.'

Some of his anger spilled over on to Helen. 'I hope you can make it sometime this morning,' said to her with a touch of sarcasm. She'd never seen him like this, looking furious and implacable. As he turned for the door she said.

'I'll be up straight away,' tears glistening in her eyes.

She knew it would be impossible to reason with him in this mood, he had to simmer down first. She watched as he went downstairs followed shortly by the door banging as he went out.

'Oh God Helen,' wailed Mary. 'He's the last person in the world I'd want to hurt. What have I done, what have I done?'

'What you did was to seduce me, that's what you've done,' said Helen crossly, 'although I was a willing participant,' she added with a touch of shame.

'I'll have to get up to the café straight away. Don't want to make it any worse.'

'Can I stay here until you're back?' asked Mary in a shaky voice. She looked like a pathetic little school girl. 'Yes, you've no where else to go. I'll try talking to him but God knows what'll come of it. I suppose what we did must be the ultimate insult to a man.'

She turned away. 'I must get dressed and ready now. The longer I am getting to him the more it will fester in his mind.' She went out leaving Mary devastated.

In Mary's world of fantasy she had visualised an ultimate cosy ménage a trois as the happy ending, all three of them living together and sharing passion between them. She certainly hadn't visualised hurting the very man she would have willingly given her life for. Her world was collapsing about her. She turned her face into teddy and sobbed her heart out.

*

Terry strode up Westborough at a pace that would have been impossible before having his special shoes. He was breathing heavily, taking in the crisp air, letting it clear his mind. He was already feeling slightly guilty at causing so much obvious anguish to Mary. After all, wasn't part of this his hurt pride?

He had already acknowledged to himself that Helen was a highly physical girl, always looking for new ways of love making. That was part of her appeal was it not? It seemed Mary was from the same mould. If he'd been the object of all this attention would he have felt so angry at events?

He arrived at the café with all these thoughts swirling in his mind to find the three J's already waiting outside. John Paul, the chef was striding down the road talking animatedly to the other Jane. The ex scullery maid from the Kessler's.

'Sorry everyone,' said Terry, face inscrutable. 'Helen will be a little late coming in.'

He watched as they set the café up and made ready for opening, satisfied all was going fine he retreated to his little office. He sat behind the small desk and pretended all was well.

Helen bustled in a good half hour later, changing into her apron and dress in the back. He heard her chatting to John Paul and the other girls, waiting for her to show herself.

He steeled himself wondering what her manner would be like. Would she just start work and not speak to him?

In fact, she broke the ice by coming in after a short while with a cup of steaming coffee, closing the door behind her. She placed it on the desk and looked directly at him, her big brown eyes making his tummy flutter. Before she had chance to speak he butted in with,

'I'm sorry I blew so strongly this morning. I'd not slept well and woke with a blinding headache. Last night disturbed me more than I should've let it, but I've got to say I felt pretty humiliated this morning.'

'I know darling, and I'm so sorry that's how you felt. It was my fault. You know what I'm like, can't resist rumpy pumpy of any sort. And it was so different I suppose I was curious.' She shrugged. 'That's what I'm like, you know that.'

He gave a deep sigh. 'And how was Mary when you came out?'

'She was absolutely distraught. Soaking wet with tears and shaking uncontrollably. She's a simple lass, couldn't see how what we did might affect you. She worships you, I'm sure you realise that.' He shut his eyes and massaged his temples.

'I don't know how to handle this,' he said. 'She's at risk from Watson but while she's staying with us she's rocking the boat. I don't understand how her mind works. Is she really naïve or a little schemer? Where does she think this strange relationship with us is going? Or doesn't she think at all?'

'I've told you, I'm as much at fault as her. It was an exciting new experience.' She shrugged. 'No excuse for that I know, but she really is damaged in so many ways. She wouldn't have done anything if she'd realised it would hit you so hard.'

She was still standing before him, the coffee untouched and going cold. Terry was desperately trying to decide the best way forward.

'She's on her own in the house now?'

'Of course. There's only Jack and Sally we could trust but I had no time to say anything to them. I was desperate to get to you. I didn't want you sitting here with this hanging over us and I was afraid you'd want shut of me, the Bottom End slag.' The last said with disgust in her voice at herself.

'Oh Helen, I could never want that. Whatever's happened you're still the one for me, nothing's changed there. I'm worried about Mary now. It might be a good idea if you go back to her, make sure she's alright. The little bugger, causing all this upset.' The last said with feeling.

'Can we manage here?' she asked.

'Yes, its steady at the moment. The three J's are coping but I'll tell you one thing. If Mary stops with us she'd better not start flashing her titties at me or I might just screw her to the bed.' He grinned as he said it and put his tongue out at her in a lewd way.

She laughed. 'I'll take that as a warning then.' She came round the desk and kissed him tenderly. 'Thank you for being you,' she whispered in his ear.

She changed back into her dress, told the girls she had to go home on pressing business and set off for Overton Terrace.

Tom Watson, skulking on the other side of the road saw her come out, alone!

He watched her set off down Westborough, allowed her to get a goodly few paces in front and followed. Hat pulled down he slouched along like a wraith.

Helen walked briskly. She was more than a little concerned about Mary alone in the house, and looking so wild eyed and distraught when she left her to come up to the café.

She got back in record time, opening the door to see Mary, white as a sheet, pressing the filleting knife against her stomach.

'Mary,' she screamed at the top of her voice. 'Put that knife down now.'

Mary looked up at her seemingly in a daze, her eyes unfocussed.

Helen rushed across to her and snatched the knife from her grasp. The girl collapsed against her with an agonising wail, shaking and hysterical.

'I've ruined everything,' she cried. 'Destroyed all that matters to me. I deserve to die.'

Outside, through the still partly open door Tom Watson heard Helen's screamed 'Mary.' She's there, they've been sheltering her all along; the bitch is there. The thoughts ran through his head. Now he needed to plan, find when she went out. She would have to come out some time. He slunk away highly satisfied that he now knew where she was.

Inside, Helen hugged the hysterical girl to her. 'It's alright love, it's all right.' Stroking her hair, talking to her as she would a child.

'Is Terry going to throw me out? Is he still mad at me? He hates me now doesn't he?' The words tumbled out one after the other. 'I should finish it. I don't deserve to live.'

'Mary, we'll have no more of that talk, now stop it. How do you think he'd feel if he thought he was the person who drove you to do something like that? I had a good talk to him; he cares a lot about you. He was worried about you, sent me back here to check on you. That's not what anyone would do if they hated you.'

Helen led her into the lounge and sat on the settee pulling Mary down beside her and wrapping arms around her. Mary snuggled into her like a child sucking her left thumb. Helen was highly concerned. If she'd not returned when she did would Mary have killed herself?

She desperately wanted Terry here. When he saw the state of the girl she was sure he would relent on his insistence to re-house Mary as soon as possible. She was not only in danger from Watson, but herself. Mary settled after a while, but was still very clingy, desperately afraid of what she faced when Terry got home.

They had shut the café each night at six pm more or less and arrived home at six fifteen. As it moved closer to that time Mary kept looking at the clock, her anxiety worn clear on her sleeve. It had been impossible for Helen to get Mary to eat any lunch. In fact she almost had to prise her off to start on preparing dinner for when Terry got home.

By the time six ten arrived Mary was jumping at every sound like a cat. Her complexion was so pale she looked close to fainting. Helen kept reassuring her, but to no avail.

It was six twenty when the door opened and Terry entered.

Mary whimpered pathetically, shivering as though in fever. Tears flowed uncontrollably down her cheeks. He was horrified and immediately guilty at seeing the state she was in.

He walked over to her and she actually flinched as though about to be struck, which upset him even more.

'Come here little girl,' he said softly, pulling her to him and hugging her in his arms. He held her tight as she broke into the most heart rending sobbing he had ever heard from anyone,

Shaking with anguish. Helen was sobbing softly and he felt tears in his eyes. Whatever happened in the future he would have to support this girl or live forever with guilt.

He did the same as Helen. Led her into the lounge and sat with her, holding the shaking child/girl until her sobbing reduced to little gulps and whimpers.

'Can I stay with you please, can I stay?' she whimpered eventually, looking up with eyes like liquid green pools.

'Yes, of course you can and will, but,' and he gave her a soft smile. 'You've got to be a good girl.'

'I'll do anything you ask Terry, anything at all. I never intended to hurt you. I'm so, so, sorry.'

'Forget it, it's in the past now, let's move on.' He put a finger under her chin, lifted her head and kissed her gently. Her lips parted slightly and she responded eagerly. He held it longer than intended. What's good for the goose is good for the gander passing through his mind, meeting her probing tongue with his own and enjoying it. He broke away. 'Feel better now?'

'Yes,' huskily. 'Come on then, dinner. It'll keep your strength up.' He pulled her to her feet. 'I don't think I'm hungry,' she whispered.

'You said you'd be a good girl, so eat some dinner.' She nodded and went meekly with him into the kitchen. He gave Helen a wink; placing Mary at the table and sitting at her side.

It was like trying to encourage a child to eat but eventually she managed some, refusing any pudding altogether. They took mugs of tea into the lounge in silence. He sat on the settee drawing both girls either side of him. After drinking their tea he drew them close with an arm around each and cuddled them both. There was a very slight, or was it very slight, feeling of getting his own back and he decided he was jolly well going to enjoy a pretty head on each shoulder.

The very worldly wise Helen had an uncomfortable feeling he was enjoying just a touch of revenge but was in no position to complain.

'Do you know something I would like eventually?' he said, startling the two girls after the silence. 'A gramophone.'

'What?' said Helen, wondering where that thought had suddenly come from?

'Can you imagine sitting here in your own home? Listening to some of the greatest artists in the world singing and playing just for you. I heard the latest record from Caruso being played in a shop as I walked down, it was thrilling.'

'Caruso?' said Mary.

'Yes, the great operatic tenor. He was singing a song called 'Over There,' especially recorded for our lads in the trenches with a symphony orchestra accompanying.'

'You do surprise me at times,' said Helen.

'As much as you surprise me,' he replied. She decided silence was the answer to that; there were still some egg shells about!

'I was looking forward to seeing the café,' said Mary sadly. 'I don't suppose you want to take me now?' She had directed her comment at Terry, but Helen answered.

'Of course we'll take you, won't we?' turning to Terry.

'Yes, we'll take you tomorrow, show you round.' He yawned, 'I reckon it's bed time, too much upset for one day. I'll let you two get ready first and I'll be timing you.' He said it with a grim smile, half in jest and half, well! The two girls rose immediately and trooped into the kitchen.

I could get used to this he thought.

Mary returned in her night dress after washing. 'Night night, thank you so much.' She gave him a long lingering look.

'Go on up. I'll pop in and see you when I come up.' Her face lit up, and she turned and scuttled out. He went into the kitchen where Helen was washing herself down.

'What a day,' he said, kissing her shoulder. She turned and put her arms around him. 'Now she's gone up, I was so terrified when I came back this morning. As I opened the door she was standing by the sink with a knife to her stomach. I rushed to her and took it off her but I'm sure she was about to harm herself.'

His blood ran cold. 'Oh Christ. We'll really have to keep an eye on her. I'll go and have a chat to her when I've washed.'

'See you when you come up then.' She looked into his eyes. 'Everything is alright isn't it?' He shrugged. 'Who knows.' He turned to the sink slipping his shirt off.

She admired his muscular torso for a moment, hoping his last comment referred to Mary only, and then went up.

He stripped and had a good wash, wrapping the thick fluffy towel around his waist before going up stairs. He tapped on Mary's door.

'Can I come in?'

A tiny voice, 'Yes.'

He entered, her eyes widening as she saw his naked chest. He sat on the side of the bed and looked down into her face. 'I've just heard something that has really upset me from Helen. What were you going to do with that knife when she came in this morning?' She said nothing for a while staring up at him, eyes large and limpid, and then, licking her lips,

305

'I couldn't bear the thought of your rejection and hate. That was the worst feeling I've ever had, seeing you looking at me with such anger. I didn't want to live.'

He stroked her face with the back of his hand. 'Promise me you'll never ever do such a thing again.' She held his hand against her cheek.

'Am I forgiven Terry? Do you really forgive me?' She gave him such a beseeching look his heart melted.

'Yes, you're forgiven. Have a good night's sleep if you can.'

He bent his head and kissed her forehead. 'I'll give you the promised tour of the cafe tomorrow.'

She smiled up at him. 'My hero.'

'Silly girl,' he ruffled her hair. 'Night night,' turning and leaving her.

Helen was sitting up in bed when he entered an expectant look on her face.

'Is she all right?'

'Yes, I reassured her that all is forgiven, told her off about the knife. I said we would show her round the café tomorrow.'

'And was my friend effected this time?' she was looking hard at the towel.

He laughed. 'No, she was like a lost little girl wanting forgiveness but she worries me. She goes from little girl to sexy woman in a flash, she's a bundle of complexity. I'll bet that chap in Austria, what do they call him? Ah, yes, Freud, him. I'll bet he'd have an interesting time analysing her.'

'Never heard of him,' she sniffed. 'Now, are you coming to bed or not?'

'I'm coming,' he said as he dropped the towel.

'Not tonight you're not,' she grinned. 'It'd stop sleeping beauty in the attic from getting a good night's sleep.'

He slid into bed. 'Come here my woman, at least we can have a cuddle.'

She giggled as she cuddled up to him. After a passionate kiss they both nodded off contentedly.

Mary lay awake, just, eyes fluttering. Closed one second, and then opening again. Her relief at being forgiven her indiscretion was overwhelming. She felt as though her entire world had collapsed when Terry's burst of anger had been unleashed on her. And just now, when he had sat on the side of the bed naked to the waist stroking her face. She'd had to exercise an almost uncontrollable urge not to reach out and run her hands over him.

It was a torment the like of which she had never experienced before in her life. Her desire for him was overwhelming. It was like an ache that would never leave her, and yet, he was unobtainable, he was Helen's.

It was a highly emotional girl/woman who nodded off finally, teddy clutched in her right arm, his face pressed to hers.

***

# CHAPTER SIXTEEN

## Richard Sheader's story

The following morning they took Mary up to the café.

She was awed by the opulence of it and blushed deeply when John Paul bowed and kissed her hand.

She hit it off immediately with the three J's, being about the same age, and Terry made a special point of introducing her to Jane, the ex-scullery maid from the Kessler's. She grinned at Helen dressed in her serving maid outfit.

'I can see why you have a regular male clientele,' she said.

'Don't be cheeky young woman,' laughed Helen. 'We're thrilled with the way it's going. Better than our wildest hopes.'

They sat Mary down at a table and treated her as an honoured guest serving her a scone with jam and cream and creamy coffee.

Helen was right. They were into their third month of trading and it had taken off beyond all expectations. Terry's decision to aim at the upper crust market had paid off. Everyone who liked to be seen came for morning or afternoon coffee. It was the place for gentile gossip and meetings.

Terry confided in both Helen and Mary if the trade remained the same they would be paying out bonuses to staff in their fourth month. A fantastic performance for a new business.

Mary insisted in helping them after the luxury of her coffee and scone. The day passing pleasurably until mid-afternoon when they were in for a shock.

Terry had gone into the office to check some figures. Mary was helping and proving to be good at maths. There was a knock at the door and Jennifer, one of the three J's, popped her head round the door and said. 'There's a gentleman asking to have a word with you Mr Sheader.'

'Oh, did he say who he is or what he wants?'

'No, he said he wanted a word with you on a private matter.'

Intrigued, Terry went into the café. Jennifer pointed out the gentleman to him who was sitting at a table with a coffee. He stood as Terry approached and held out a hand. 'Hello Terry, it's a long time no see.'

As he saw the continuing lack of recognition on his face, 'I'm James Thomson, my brother and I were on *Yorkshire Lass* with your dad in 1904. Word got back to me that you've been seeking the crew from that night.'

Terry was stunned. After thinking he'd make no progress in finding out about his dad's affairs or finding any of the crew members on the boat with him in 1904, one of them had found him!

'Good God, yes, you've taken me by surprise Mr Thomson. I'd begun to think I was doomed to failure.'

'Jimmy please,' said Thomson. Terry did a quick mental assessment. He looked about the same age as his father and was smartly dressed. No one would have taken him for an ex seaman.

'I take it your dad's demise has provided this?' said Thomson, eyes flicking round the café. Terry blushed slightly. 'Yes, we couldn't have got this underway without dad's money,' he admitted.

'And you've no idea how your dad came by his money?'

'That's why I've been seeking his crew. To see if I could find out.'

'Is there somewhere we could talk?' said Thomson.

'Yes, I've a little office through the back,' he led him to the office. Mary was busy totting up some figures.

'Mary, could you leave us a while this gentleman and I need to talk in private.' He gave her the semblance of a wink. 'And would you ask Helen to join us, preferably with three coffees.'

'Yes, of course Mr Sheader.' She rose, giving him a demure look.

He gave her a *you cheeky little madam* look as she went out.

'Sit down Jimmy please. I've asked Helen to join us as she's my wife to be. She's been very active in helping me to find details about my father.'

Helen came in with a tray bearing three china cups and saucers, setting them on the desk. Terry introduced Thomson and explained who he was. Her eyebrows rose. 'That's amazing,' she said. 'We've been looking for any members of Richard's crew for a long time.'

'You knew him?' Thomson asked her in surprise.

'Yes, he saved my life,' she replied smoothly.

'Well, well, you'll have to tell me about that sometime.' She smiled at him without reply.

'I only heard you'd been enquiring when I came to Scarborough to visit my brother's grave. Sadly, he died last year; we were twins you know?'

'Yes, I knew that,' admitted Terry.

'Well, I bumped into Jack Savage. He told me you were his neighbours and had been looking for us. We had a good old natter about old times actually, he said you'd be at your café. So, here I am.'

Terry blew his cheeks out. 'Well, I've said we were looking and now you've found us. Can you help us Jimmy?'

Jimmy sat back and crossed his fingers over his stomach. 'First, let me ask what difference it would make knowing about your dad's source of money?'

'What you want to know Jimmy,' Terry said, 'is am I going to create a fuss if it turns out to be not quite legit?'

'Aye, that's about the sum of it.'

'It was Terry's turn to sit back, noting the anxious look on Helen's face.

'As you've already observed Jimmy, we've started spending it, so unless anyone was badly hurt in obtaining it then it'll make no difference, other than to put my questing mind at ease.'

'We were the buggers who were nearly hurt by the sodding Ruskies,' he said. 'But no one was hurt in the way you mean it.'

After a moment of contemplation, he said. 'Well, as they say in all good story books, I'll start at the beginning. You probably know we were crewing for Bob Pashley on his trawler *Yorkshire Lass*?' Terry nodded.

'We left Scarborough early on the 21st of October heading for the fishing grounds just off the Dogger Bank. We met up with a small fleet of other trawlers from Hull, Grimsby, and the like. We used to fish together for protection. If anyone got into trouble there were plenty boats to offer assistance.' He shuffled down in his chair to a more comfortable position. 'There was plenty of fish and all of us were doing well. We intended to set off home late that same night, but during the late evening we came under fire from warships that just appeared out of the gloom.' He sniffed. 'I can tell you it put the shits up us right. We hadn't a clue at that time who's ships they were or why they were firing at us, but Bob ordered us to slip the net and clear off smartish.'

'One of the boats, from Hull I think it was, took a direct hit. *The Crane* it was called; it was sinking as we surged away.'

He shrugged. 'It sounds a bit cowardly I know, leaving a ship sinking, but shells were dropping near us and we'd have been no use getting sunk ourselves. Bob ordered us to extinguish all lights. Some of the trawlers were flashing searchlights at the attackers. It made it worse for them.'

He took a long sip of his coffee, a far-away gaze in his eyes. 'Luckily it was quite dark by now, and a bit of North Sea mist was forming. We went at a fair lick, the old

311

paddles never worked so hard. Unfortunately, in our panic to get away we lost our bearings. It seemed only a matter of moments later when we came to a shuddering stop, we'd struck the Bank.'

He smiled at a memory. 'We had a young kid with us, Mike Watson's nephew. He went arse over tit when we struck. I've never heard such language from one so young.'

Terry and Helen exchanged glances, they knew who that was!

'Bob ordered engines stopped immediately. If the paddles hit solid ground they'd disintegrate. He said the best thing we could do was wait until light in the morning to assess the situation.' He drained the coffee.

'You do a good coffee here, where was I? Ah, stuck on the Dogger. Well, as you probably know the Dogger is a mass of constantly shifting sand. It was an exceptionally low tide as well. Any other time we might have cleared the bit we struck without even realising it was there.'

He paused again to gather his thoughts.

'Billy Jackson was our engineer. He came dashing up to say a couple of plates had sprung in the bows. Nothing that couldn't be fixed, but unusual damage for driving into sand.'

'Would you like another coffee Jimmy?' asked Helen.

'Aye, that would be very nice.' Helen stuck her head round the door to attract the attention of one of the girls, waving to one of her regulars as he caught her eye. Jimmy waited until she was seated again and then carried on with his narrative. 'Well, we settled for the night. No sign of any other boats by this time, they'd have scattered like a flock of birds. Billy and my brother spent a goodly part of the night shoring up the sprung plates with timber. We were all anxious for what the morning was going to bring. Bob was furious we'd lost an expensive trawl net. 'Don't know who those bastards were,' he said. 'But I hope they rot in hell.' It was a long night, very quiet and a still sea, and after all that excitement we eventually got some sleep.'

'As the sun came up in the morning we realised we were totally alone. Not a sight of another vessel and then Roger Graves, one of the deck hands shouted 'come and look at this.'

'We all rushed to the bows to see what he was pointing at. As we looked over on the starboard side we saw the outline of a sunken ship. The mid-cabin area was just above water and amazingly, the damage to our bows was from ramming part of the upper works of the ship.'

He paused as Jennifer came in with three more coffees, Terry thanking her as she took the empty cups away and asking if they were coping with Helen being in the office.

'Yes, Mary has volunteered to help. She's brilliant, such a lovely bubbly personality. She's hitting it off with the customers.'

Terry, looking at Helen with a grin said, 'I'll bet she is. Good for her.'

Jimmy carried on as the door closed. 'We were all interested in the wreck. Of course it's nothing to be surprised at; many a ship has come to grief on the Bank. It looked to be about the size of a schooner or similar. We were more concerned at getting off eventually.' They sipped coffee with him.

'It was Billy who said he reckoned we could get into the mid-cabin before the tide came up, see if anything of value was left.' Typical Yorkshire men thought Terry, always see if there's *owt for nowt.*

'Roger volunteered to have a go. We tied a rope around his waist and he slipped into the water. Even at that time of the year it was bloody cold. He swam over to the upper works and dived from view, coming up pretty quickly. He shouted that it looked like the captain's cabin, or pretty close if not. The cabin just showing above water had a huge strong box in the corner.'

Terry found he was holding his breath at this point. Jimmy continued. 'Well, we all know strong-boxes are made for one thing only, to hold valuables. To cut a long story short we all took turns swimming over and attempting to get ropes round it. To be fair to the nipper he was as strong a swimmer as any and did a lot to assist. It took over an hour, but eventually we secured it well enough to attempt a lift with the steam winch we used for the net.'

'It was even heavier than we realised. As it lifted the entire boat canted over to the starboard side. Bob was worried for the starboard paddle, but it stabilised and we lifted it clear.' He had another gulp of coffee.

'When we had it up in the air on the boom it was swinging like mad. We had to get more ropes on it to steady it before swinging it inboard, and then we lowered it very gently into the fish hold.' He finished his coffee with a lip smacking sound. 'We had to wait then for three hours for the tide to change to give us a chance of floating off.

He shook his head as he remembered it. 'It was bloody hairy. We thought we'd become another of the bank's statistics. The paddles were churning water like mad, but we didn't shift an inch. Eventually, everyone including Bob went as far aft as possible and jumped up and down in unison while Billy in the engine room applied full power.' He gave a deep sigh as though reliving it again.

'She suddenly came off with a huge shudder. We all cheered until Billy called up that we were taking in water in the bows.'

Terry and Helen were sitting on the edges of the chairs.

'It took a lot of caulking and more timber to stop it to a trickle and we proceeded home very slowly, arriving back in the early evening.' He straightened his legs. 'Bloody arthritis,' he said as he noticed Terry's look.

'Everyone was relieved to see us steam in. The attack by the Ruskies was the entire story by now and they must have thought we were one of the victims. We unloaded the fish as normal and then repaired to the *Old Steam Packet* for a well earned pint and natter. We stopped in the corner of the snug, talking through the best way of dealing with our *find*.

'The boat needed three new plates in the bows which meant she was in dock for four days. We planned what was the best way of dealing with the strong box, finally deciding the only way of getting into it would be by blowing off the door.'

He paused for breath.

'Mick Watson knew a local villain who was good with bangs.' Jimmy said this with a grin and wink. 'We arranged for him to go out with us on a test after the repair work was done. When we were far enough out, about three miles, the entire area around the box was padded with sacking and our bang man blew the door right off. Bob paid him thirty pounds to do the job with no questions asked.'

'We winched it up out of the hold after and dropped it in the drink. That was a job and a half I can tell you.'

He gave a huge grin. 'It was such a good bang we had to have a plate replaced in the hull. I guess you know the rest. Apart from a few items of jewellery the box was full of Dutch Kroner, all of 1877 vintage. We did a share up of them and then it was up to each man how he used them.'

Terry was fascinated.

'Did you make any effort to find what ship it was or how it had such a cargo?'

'Aye, Billy did some research. We're not sure but there was some talk, which has been denied by the Dutch government I might add, that a trial batch of coins were minted for the Dutch by an Edinburgh firm which specialised in die casting. The coins were en-route for Holland from Edinburgh when the ship came to grief on the Dogger, but he was unable to get any name for the ship. In fact it was denied any such ship was lost and we didn't ask any more,' he said with a knowing look.

Jimmy sat back. 'Well, there you have it. As far as I know there's only me and Billy still alive, so not many of us lived to see a great deal from it. Oh, and that young bugger Watson. From what I've heard he's become a boat owner himself. Don't know how he managed that but he made a real fuss for one so young about not getting a share of the find. His uncle promised to see him right but I don't know if he ever did.'

He sat back, tale told.

Terry sat back in his chair. He'd been so far on the edge he was in danger of sliding off.

'I can't thank you enough for coming here today Jimmy. The rumour going round was that you'd dredged up sunken treasure.' He laughed. 'Well, that's just about it wasn't it?'

'Aye,' said Jimmy. 'But you need to bear in mind that anything of that nature recovered from the sea has to be declared to the commissioner of wrecks. I've never known anyone do it voluntarily but it's best to keep stum.'

Jimmy took his leave of them, giving Helen a cheeky wink. He was going back to Hessle on the outskirts of Hull. He confided he'd bought a nice house and was living very comfortably. Mary couldn't wait to hear what all that had been about, the rumour mill in the café was rife.

All Terry would say was. 'All in good time.'

The afternoon was particularly busy. The café had taken off in a big way; all the girls were run off their feet. Although Terry was delighted, he couldn't help reflecting that young men, as young as he had been in the Boer War, were losing their lives in large numbers. And large numbers were coming home severely maimed while the 'haves' were carrying on in Scarborough as though no war was taking place.

They finally shut shop at seven pm. None of the staff minded as it would increase their bonus. Introducing that had been a touch of genius Terry told Helen, knowing full well the comment he was likely to receive to that!

On the walk to Overton Terrace Mary chatted animatedly. She'd found the experience of working in an up-market environment stimulating and fun. She loved the interplay with customers, being as accomplished as

316

Helen at the flirty nature with male customers, guaranteeing a return.

Jennifer had given Terry a glowing reference for Mary. He decided he would offer her a job with them if she was willing.

'You were both in the office a long time with that gentleman,' said Mary wide eyed and innocent. 'I hope it was good news.' Terry laughed.

'Is that a less than subtle way of saying what was he about?'

She pouted, and then laughed. 'Yes, I suppose so. Is it a great secret?'

He kept his face serious looking. 'Yes, it's a very great secret we can't divulge to anyone.'

'Oh,' she looked crestfallen. Helen started laughing. 'Terry, stop bloody tormenting,' giving him a playful slap.

'We'll tell you all about it when we get home love but it does need some discretion. Are you good at keeping secrets?'

'I'm not good at keeping some things secret am I?' she said, looking at Terry and Helen in turn.

'You're asking for a slapped bottom young lady,' said Helen with a sideways glance.'

'Will you, Terry, or both of you do that?' She said with a lewd look.

'You madam are getting too big for your boots. Come on, it's dinner time and I'm starving.' They arrived home with Mary's arm linked through his right and Helen's through his left.

Both Mary and Helen prepared the dinner, bustling round the kitchen while Terry narrated the story of his father's wealth to Mary. He stressed they were taking some risk telling anyone about it but he knew she could be discrete.

Mary was touched to be taken into their confidence.

'You know I could never say or do anything to harm you two, it's safe with me.'

After dinner, sitting in the lounge with coffee, yes coffee, Terry broached the idea of Mary working in the tea rooms for them.

'Jennifer said you enjoyed your experience of working in the café. She said you were a natural, do you think you'd like to come and work for us instead of at the shellfish stall?'

Mary thought for a moment. 'Yes, I did enjoy it, it was quite a buzz, but would it effect the relationship we have together. You'd both be my bosses wouldn't you? I'm grateful you've asked me, but.' And she gave a shrug.

'Would it upset you if I were bossing you about?' asked Terry grinning.

'You can boss me any time you want Terry, I've already said I'd do anything you asked,' she replied mischievously, winking at Helen.

'Well, think about it seriously. We'd both love to have you, and wipe that look off your face, I mean in the café.'

She laughed. 'You know me too well.'

They enjoyed the luxury of coffee; he couldn't help wondering at the huge changes made in a matter of a few months going from a skint disillusioned man to businessman with two, yes two, gorgeous girls both fighting for his attention.

Could anything change this life? He hoped not.

\*\*\*

# CHAPTER SEVENTEEN

## Watson's revenge attempt

Tom Watson was sinking into madness. Not that he realised it. In his opinion he was the subject of unremitting bad luck; none of it his making.

He'd been driven to fury and mounting despair by a huge brute of a seaman called Will Machon. Machon was a bully and brawler the equal of Watson. He had taken to baiting Tom every time he entered his favourite pub, *The Packet*. He'd make sly remarks about him, challenging him to a confrontation, then backing off saying. 'Oh! I'm forgetting, you haven't the balls for it.'

It drove Tom to helpless fury. Helpless because even he wouldn't get the better of the brute in a fight.

It became so bad he reluctantly started going in *The Three Mariners* instead, but it was like starting a new school. The pubs had their regulars who remained faithful to that pub for life.

He was viewed with suspicion by *The Mariners'* regulars, and even they started to snigger behind his back as word went round about his disability.

His mind was full of vengeance against the slag. She who had maimed him and that bastard Sheader who was sheltering her, freely using money that he, Tom Watson, should have had a share of.

Each time he came back from a fishing trip he would hang around the Sheader's house at a distance. He built up a picture of their daily procedure, noting that Mary went with them each day to the café and returned with them at the same time, leading him to believe she was working there.

In fact he was right. After much thought, Mary had accepted the job and was enjoying every minute of it.

He wanted to find a time when Mary was out and about unaccompanied, a rare event indeed it seemed. He wondered if Sheader was shagging them both as they were both utter slags.

His chance came one Saturday.

Mary had the day off and had decided to visit Shirley at the fish stall. She hadn't seen her for quite a while and felt guilty about it. She had lunch on her own, both Terry and Helen were at the café. Saturday was a busy day; the girls worked Saturdays one on, one off. This was her day off. It was fine and dry, a perfect day for a visit and chance to catch up on gossip.

Watson had *Our Lass* moored on the lighthouse pier today. His usual berthing place was full of ships from Grimsby.

He carried a sack containing a young seaman's clothing. Jacket, trousers and hat, and a small bottle of ether he had obtained from the chemists shop.

He'd no idea today was going to be the one. He'd usually skulk about hoping Mary would emerge alone, being prepared just in case. And low and behold here she was. Leaving the house alone and, oh gladness! Walking towards the harbour.

His heart gave a lurch of joy and excitement. How long he'd waited for this moment, a moment to be savoured. He was licking his lips as she walked the length of Overton Terrace.

Mary, oblivious to her stalker, walked happily down Burr Bank towards the sea front humming to herself.

As she started to pass the old Methodist chapel she was momentarily conscious of a figure darting behind her. It happened in a flash. An evil smelling rag was thrust into her face from behind at the same time as a strong arm encircled her waist dragging her into the alley behind the chapel.

320

She had no time to struggle as the ether soaked rag rendered her unconscious. Watson dragged her bodily into the alley, a dark and gloomy place, where he let her slide to the floor.

He ripped her dress off savagely. Taking the trousers from his sack and getting her feet into them with difficulty, he dragged them up around her waist.

The jacket was next, finally cramming her hair under the cap, pulling it down to partially cover her face. He stuffed the ripped dress into the sack, lifted her like a rag doll and threw her across his right shoulder. Her head and arms hung down his back. The sack went over the same shoulder on top of her helping the disguise.

In a strange twist of fate, Watson was going to get her back to his ship dressed as a man, the same way she had got to him when she castrated him.

He set off on the relatively short walk to the pier. 'Pissed again!' He shouted to passers bye, laughing and winking at them. It drew ribald remarks from other seamen, a sight very common to them and exciting no great interest.

He managed to get her to *Our Lass* with no obstruction dropping quickly down the steps to his cabin. He'd done it, he'd bloody done it! His elation knew no bounds. At that very moment it was almost as good as sexual release.

He dumped her unceremoniously on his bunk, grabbed a bottle of whisky and took a long swig. The look on his face was of madness. A frightening face, distorted with malice.

He dragged her trousers off roughly and then the jacket and cap. He was grinning and muttering to himself as he removed the undergarments leaving her naked on the bunk. Taking a ball of thick fishing twine he tied her wrists to the bunk head; spread eagled her legs, and tied her feet to the bunk base. Now all he had to do was wait for her to wake up.

Mary came too feeling drowsy and nauseous. The stink of ether was in her nostrils. She had no idea where she was or how she'd got there.

Her vision was hazy and unsteady. As consciousness became greater; she made out the roof of the cabin and was suddenly aware she was bound.

Her swimming vision took in a leering face hovering over her. As vision steadied she realised who it was. Nothing could have jolted her awake more than that leering face.

'Watson!' she gasped.

'Too right bitch,' he snarled. 'Too fucking right, how's it feel to be at my mercy?' He gave a cracked laugh. 'Not that I'm going to show any.'

He took another swig of whisky, giggling in a high pitched voice.

'Lovely fanny that my love.' He thrust two fingers into her savagely, laughing all the time. It took Mary so much by surprise she just managed a yelp.

'Perfect little fanny eh, just like I had two balls,' thrusting his fingers back and forth. 'Well we're going to change that my love, oh yes.'

He drew back from her turning to the cabin table.

'You're mad,' she gasped. 'Let me go you evil bastard.'

'Ahhh,' he screamed. 'I'll show you how mad I am.' He was clutching a green champagne like bottle. He turned to her. 'Is this as big as Sheader's eh? Is it? Think you could take this bitch eh?'

She screamed in terror as she saw the intent on his face.

'Don't touch me, don't touch me,' panic in her voice.

He approached the bunk, his face was contorted almost beyond recognition. He stooped and placed the bottle neck against her vagina.

'Say your prayers bitch.' He thrust with the full force of a powerful arm.

Fred Taylor, ex barman at The Grand was just coming out of the Scarborough Yacht Club premises based in the lighthouse building.

He'd worked hard during the dismantling of the light, hard and diligently, noticed by the club chairman. He'd struck up a conversation with the chairman who was surprised to find this hard working young man was bar trained.

Fred told him about his demise; or his version of it. How he had been terrified by being under fire and how the manager had dismissed him because he was terrified. Not strictly true; but close. The chairman took sympathy and gave Fred a temporary job working in the club bar. The members soon took to the fresh faced young man. He was good at his job and had a pleasant demeanour. It ended with him obtaining the job full time.

As he came out now with an empty beer crate; he heard the most awful animal like scream come from the boat tied up just down the pier.

It sent his blood cold. It couldn't be mistaken for anything but a scream of terror and pain.

He dropped the crate and ran like mad to the boat. He could hear a whimpering sound from below interspaced with sobs and groans.

What the hell? He dropped onto the deck and went down the steps from where the sound was coming.

He burst into the cabin just as Watson was pressing on the bottle and twisting it. It was horrifying to see what he was pressing the bottle into.

Watson turned as he heard Fred burst in. With a snarl, he threw himself at Fred, throwing a fist which caught Fred on the cheek. Stunned, he staggered back. Watson sprinted past him and flew up the steps.

Fred turned to the young girl spread eagled on the bunk. She was now unconscious, or fainted, the bottle projecting grotesquely. Her thighs and bunk between her legs were blood stained. He stared for a very brief moment, turned and staggered up the steps, jumped onto the pier and at the top of his voice shouted,

'Help, for God's sake somebody, help.'

*

Terry and Helen were run off their feet. The trade this Saturday was amazing the place was full. To his amazement, one of the customers who had just departed was none other than Mrs Kessler.

She'd congratulated him on their success addressing her remarks to him and not Helen, who she looked at through narrowed eyes.

She said the garden was on hold until the spring. Her eyes were for him; and him alone making him feel slightly uncomfortable. After she had gone Helen said, 'well it's clear she only has eyes for you my love, a real elderly admirer, obviously there's life after death.' She leered at him in a deliberately lewd way. He leaned in and whispered in her ear. 'Bollocks.'

She burst out laughing and it was in this moment of hilarity that Shirley, Mary's friend burst in. Looking wild and distraught she rushed across to them.

'Mary's been attacked by that Tom Watson, she's in hospital.'

Terry felt his blood run cold; Helen had her hand to her mouth.

'What's happened Shirley, how did it happen?'

'I don't know properly. He'd got her on to his boat somehow, he was torturing her,' she said with horror in her voice. 'A lad from the yacht club went to help. Watson ran away, the police are looking for him.'

'Not just the fucking police,' he said through clenched teeth.

'Helen, I've got to go can you...?' She stopped him in mid sentence. 'Go to her love, see what the situation is. Give her my love,' she whispered, tears glistening.

He grabbed his jacket and ran into the street, waved madly at a passing cabbie. 'Take me to the hospital as fast as you can.' The cab driver cracked his whip and they set off at a trot. They made the hospital in record time, Terry thrusting money into the cabbies hand before sprinting into the hospital.

He saw Constable Jameson waiting in the entrance. He recognised Terry immediately, putting a hand out to stop Terry dashing straight in.

'She's under sedation lad, nothing to be gained by charging in.' Terry was breathing heavily, his fury spilling over.

'What's the bastard done to her?' he said harshly.

'He's assaulted her in a very serious manner,' started Jameson ponderously. 'What's the bastard done?' he repeated savagely.

Jameson took a deep breath. 'He used a bottle to rape her with.'

Terry turned and staggered to the door, making it just in time as he threw up violently. A nurse had joined Jameson; he lifted his eyes at her and nodded at Terry. She went to the door and placed a hand on his shoulder. 'Are you alright love?'

He nodded weakly. 'He's just told me what happened,' he said, a nod at Jameson. 'Can I see her?' She looked at his anxious face. 'She's heavily sedated but you can have a look in, come with me.'

She led him onto the ward; Mary was lying on her back eyes closed. He sat on the chair at the side of the bed. He glanced at the nurse. 'Five minutes,' she said softly. He nodded and took Mary's hand in his. Her eyes fluttered open.

'It's me darling, I'm here. You're going to be alright.'

'Terry?' Her voice very weak.

'Yes, it's me darling.'

'He hurt me.'

'I know love.' He could hardly talk as tears flooded his eyes. 'I know love but we'll get the bastard I promise you that.'

'I love you,' she whispered.

'I love you too little girl. Get some sleep now darling you'll be fine, I promise you.' He gently stroked her head until her eyes closed, and as the nurse beckoned him, rose to his feet with a long backward look at the pale face on the pillow.' I'll get him for you darling,' he whispered in a hardly audible voice.

He joined the nurse. 'Will she be alright?'

'It's not life threatening,' she said. 'But how much damage has been done,' she left the sentence hanging with a shrug.

He saw Jameson on the way out.

'We've put word out to all our men to keep looking for Watson,' he said. 'He can't run far.'

Terry looked him in the eye. 'I hope you get him before I do then, if I get him first he's a dead man.'

Jameson had the grace to flush slightly. 'I know how you must feel lad, and in your place I'd feel the same. But you won't be doing the lass any favours if you get yourself locked up.'

Terry just nodded grimly and took his leave. On the way back to Westborough he was in a tumult of emotion. Was it possible to be in love with two women at the same time?

Because his feelings for that little girl he'd just left felt pretty close to that.

When he got back to the café Helen rushed to him as he entered the door.

He nodded grimly in the direction of the office, and she took the hint following him in. As soon as the door closed. 'How is she, what's he done to her love?'

She took in his expression. 'It's bad isn't it? He fought to control his emotion.

'The fucking bastard raped her with a bottle. God knows how much damage he's done and the bastard got away. He's on the run, of course. P C plod was there, telling me how the forces of good would find him. If I don't find him first,' he said viciously.

Helen stood looking at him in horror.

'Oh God, the poor little lass. What did they say at the hospital, will she recover?'

'She's not going to die,' he snarled. 'But who knows what internal damage has been done. They certainly don't know yet, and as for mental damage, after what she's already suffered at the hands of that bastard, well, who knows?'

A tap on the door, Jean popping her head round the door. 'The chef's having a strop in the kitchen Mr Sheader; I think you might be needed.'

He raised eyebrows at Helen. All as normal then in a busy café. John Paul was a superb chef but not lacking in temperament.

The rest of the day passed at a furious rate. They had little time to think any further about Mary as the café took all their attention. At the finish of the day Terry took time to thank them all for their dedication and hard work.

'We're a highly successful venture and it's your hard work and dedication as a team that's made it such a success. Thank you, all of you.'

He paused, looking round the little gathering.

'I'm sure you've all heard about Mary being attacked by a madman. I've visited her today in hospital. She's suffered very badly at the hands of this maniac but the nurse I spoke to thinks she will make a full recovery. I hope you all think of her in your prayers.'

There was a murmur of consent, John Paul asking if the perpetrator had been caught. 'No, he's gone on the run. The police assure me they've notified all stations to be on the lookout and his boat has been impounded, so he won't be able to return there.'

It was a sad couple who made their way back to Overton Terrace that evening. While Helen started on preparing a meal Terry went next door to let Jack and

327

Sally know what had happened. They ate in silence, both lost in contemplative thought.

After the meal; they took coffee into the lounge, sitting side by side on the settee. 'What time can we go and see her tomorrow?' asked Helen.

'Not until two,' replied Terry gloomily. 'That's the normal visiting time on a Sunday and they won't compromise for us.'

'It's going to drag until then. I just wish someone had been with her when she went out. Even Jack would have gone with her I'm sure,' she said.

'It's no good beating ourselves up over what might have been. That bastard must have been hanging about just looking for his chance.' He put his head on her shoulder, she in turn running her fingers through his hair.

'We are alright aren't we?' she whispered.

'What sort of question is that?'

'It's my female instinct kicking in again. Your reaction to what's happened. Your body language; you're in love with her aren't you?'

He sat up and took her hand. 'You know me better than I know myself. I've said that before haven't I? Yes, a part of me love's that little lass but not like I love you. You're very special darling, but Mary confuses me. I know it's flattering when she says she's in love with me, and I admit, she turns me on at times. But it's a feeling that's difficult to explain. Sometimes she makes me feel like a protective brother, other times she acts almost as a daughter. She's a highly complex girl, a child almost at times a sexy woman at others. Does all that make sense?' Helen gave a wan little smile.

'It more than makes sense. You've just described my own feelings to the girl to a tee.' She looked at him in the same way she did when first telling him boldly she enjoyed sex. In that challenging manner, her head cocked to one side, the large brown eyes glowing.

He sat up straight. 'Bloody hell love, I think it's us who're the complex ones. It sounds like confession time, don't tell me any more.'

'You've never asked me what happened that night between us have you. Apart from your touch of *paddy*, taking it out on the lass.'

'I'm ashamed of that. Yes, my imagination ran away with me and I suppose male pride was hurt. Why, are you going to tell me?'

'If you really wanted to know I would. I've told you before, I'll keep no secrets from you. Secrets destroy a relationship and ours is too precious to destroy.'

She gave a little giggle. 'Do you know what she once asked me? Do you think Terry could manage three in a bed?'

'And what did you tell her?' 'I told her I was sure you could but you weren't going to get the chance.' They both laughed at that.

He kissed her passionately.

'The randy me is itching to know the dirty details, but no, don't tell me. I love you too much to have any further boat rocking. Let's concentrate on getting that little temptress back home and well.'

'And then what?' He gave her a huge grin. 'And then we start training her for the job of being maid of honour.'

She threw her arms around him, kissing him with fervour. 'Have I told you you're a very special man?'

Sunday morning dawned with a fine drizzle. They both stayed in bed until ten, drowsy from a busy and emotionally tiring day yesterday.

They spent the day listlessly, both of them just anxious for visiting time to arrive. They were out of the house early walking to the hospital at a brisk pace, using the exercise to calm them a little. Both of them worried what they would be told at the hospital.

Terry was delighted to see the same nurse at the ward entrance. He gave her his most winning smile, introducing Helen as his wife, asking the nurse if she had any news.

'Yes, she had some stitches yesterday but no more then perhaps a difficult birth would require, which means she will not have any lasting physical damage. She's going to be very sore for some time obviously but should be allowed home in a few days.'

She smiled at Terry. She's been asking when you'd be coming, she seemed very anxious to see you.'

'It's alright to see her now then?'

'Oh yes, but if she seems to start tiring,' looking directly at him.

'If she starts looking tired or exhausted I promise we'll be off,' he said.

The nurse smiled again at him and left them, never once looking at Helen. 'Another one you've conquered,' she whispered.

He grinned at her. 'Come on, let's see our girl.'

Mary was partly sitting up in bed three thick pillows supporting her. The little face lit up when she saw them both, but it was impossible to hide how pale she looked. Helen took the initiative, kissing her gently on the lips which delighted Mary. She was doubly delighted to get the same treatment from Terry.

They drew chairs up either side of the bed, holding a hand apiece.

'Doctor saw me this morning,' she told them. 'He's very happy with me. I had some stitches yesterday afternoon,' she pulled a face at that bit of information. 'He say's I'll make a full recovery.'

'That's the best news yet,' said Terry. She looked anxious. 'Have they caught him yet?' He glanced at Helen.

'No love, not yet but the police assure us they've circulated his details to all stations, and they have a guard on his boat in case he tries to go back there.'

330

'I won't feel safe until he's caught,' she whispered. 'If you could have seen his face, it was contorted with hate. I'm sure he'd have killed me after maiming me.'

'Well, you're safe here love and when you're fit to leave hospital you're coming home to us. We'll look after you, promise.'

'Yes, that's a promise from both of us,' said Helen.

Mary's face glowed at that news. 'That's made me feel better already.' She looked at them with such love in her eyes it was almost tangible.

They both felt highly relieved when they took their leave of Mary. At least the injury was not as bad as first thought, and the visit seemed to have brightened her noticeably.

Terry said, 'the best bit of news we need now is to hear they've caught him.' They both retired that night feeling relieved.

It could only get better now couldn't it?

***

# CHAPTER EIGHTEEN

## Retribution

Tom Watson had run like a man possessed when he was disturbed by Fred. He was furious his revenge had been cut short, everyone was against him. He'd been denied his final scenario, one which had flitted like a malignant creature through his mind.

He had intended to make the bitch scream with pain before strangling her and depositing her in the sea. Cunning self survival made him run into town, slowing to a walk and mingling with the shoppers.

He'd developed the knack of skulking unnoticed to a fine art. He'd practised that when stalking the three people he hated most.

What to do now?

He'd almost certainly lost his boat. That hurt like a knife wound to the gut, twisting and turning, filling him with hate for the entire world.

He made his way to the Italian Gardens on the South Cliff, completed only the previous year. He could hide in the shrubbery easily, an entire hillside of trees and shrubs and winding paths. Oh yes, he could keep out of the way there for a while.

He planned his next move. His life would be intolerable now. The boat lost, his means of making a living denied. He was a fugitive.

Sheader! He had money, some of which should have been shared with him. He did his share of diving on that wreck and yet he'd been treated like a child. Sheader must still have some of the gold coins in his possession. They'd set him up; allow him to move away where he could start again. Oh yes, he wasn't sure yet how to do it, but his salvation lay with Sheader.

A young courting couple wandering through the Italian Gardens hand in hand, heard what sounded like a chuckle coming from the bushes above the ornate flower display in the garden. As they approached the bushes they saw a wild looking figure talking to himself. He suddenly became aware of them, cursed, and leapt out of the bush and sprinted down the hill.

The girl looked quite worried. 'Don't worry love,' said her young man. 'He's either drunk or a nutter.'

They never thought to report it. kissing and cuddling was far more important.

*

Tuesday, and Terry and Helen were as busy as ever. It was approaching the end of the month, bonus time! And how the staff had earned it!

Terry said he'd go to see Mary that afternoon. It was too busy for Helen to absent herself really, not fair on the other girls. Joint owner or not, she intended to pull her weight.

He was delighted to see the progress Mary had made. She was sitting up in bed with a cup of tea chatting happily to the girl in the bed to her left. Her cheeks had colour, the deathly pallor of the previous day having gone.

Her hair had been washed and combed the long auburn locks shining. The difference lifted his heart immeasurably.

'Wow, what a difference in you little girl,' he grinned at her. 'You look good enough to eat.'

She beamed at him, her favourite man, lifting her face expectantly. He kissed her with abandon. Her tongue touched his lips, she was definitely feeling better!

The girl in the bed she'd been chatting to watched with fascination, this looked interesting. 'I feel so much better now,' she breathed at him. 'On your own, no Helen?'

333

'It's so busy in the café she thought it'd be unfair on the girls leaving them to cope, and you lying here idling your time away,' he grinned. 'I can see without asking you're feeling better than yesterday.'

'I always feel better seeing you but I'm better than yesterday. I felt weird yesterday somehow. I'm still very sore, and it's agony going to the toilet, but I can put up with that.'

She gave him a cheeky grin. 'There's room in this bed for two. Do you want to slip in?'

'You are feeling better. Well, if I slipped in there with you I'd want to make love to you and I don't think that would be a good idea in your current state.'

As soon as the words came out he thought, what have I said here? Mary's eyes sparkled. 'Would you really like to make love to me? Just ask me when I'm back to normal and see what happens.'

'God, I shouldn't have said that love. Forget I said it, just one of those daft things I come out with.' His face was colouring. She giggled. 'Look at your face, you're going as red as a beetroot. I love it,' she hooted.

A passing nurse scowled at them, put her finger to her lips and said, 'shush.'

'Now look you little devil, you'll get me thrown out.' They giggled together like a couple of naughty school kids. She lifted his heart with her irrepressible nature. The girl in the other bed was watching wide eyed. The best entertainment in this dull place yet.

Scowling nurse walked back down the ward. 'Five minutes ladies and gentlemen,' she called, giving him a long look.

'I don't think she fancies me,' he whispered. They had another giggle at that.

'I'd be jealous if she did.'

'Mary, you're being really naughty now. Behave like a respectable girl.'

She deliberately gave him a lewd look. 'Do you know what I'd really like to do when I'm better?'

334

'That's enough you little minx it's time I was off before nurse chucks me out.'

'Will you come and see me tomorrow?'

'Yes, everyday until you're out of here.'

He stood up, her eyes following him. He stooped to kiss her. As he did so her arms encircled his neck suddenly very serious.

'You know how much I love you Terry Sheader, always remember that.'

Her lips met his, and her tongue darted in like a little animal. He enjoyed it and responded with passion. To hell with it, he was only human. He pulled away with reluctance, his heart thumping and face burning. 'I'll see you tomorrow.'

He turned away quickly, leaving without looking back. The nurse at the head of the ward watching him with pursed lips.

The girl at the side of Mary leant over. 'Wow, he's handsome. Is he your boyfriend?'

'No, he's someone else's.'

'Oh!'

Terry stood in the foyer of the hospital trying to get under control. His heart was beating ten to the dozen. God almighty, how could he allow this situation to take place? She turned him on like one of those new fangled electric switches.

Helen wanted a full report when he got back.

'She's much more like her old self, feeling better but obviously still very sore. At least her colour looked much better. I was worried yesterday seeing her look so pale.'

'Well that's a relief. Like you, I found her colour disturbing. I take it she was more than pleased to see you?'

He grinned at her. 'Yes, I think she was pleased to see me, she sends her love.'

'If she's feeling so much better I suppose she stuck her tongue in your mouth when you left.'

'Do you know I'm so fed up with people sticking their tongue in my mouth I got my own back by doing the same.'

She gave him a furious slap, looking at him through narrowed eyes. 'Yes, she's got a very active little tongue.'

'Ouch! Alright, we're even. How're things going here?'

'You need to change the subject,' she scowled. 'We're busy as ever, we could use an extra pair of hands. I've had to sort out a row between John Paul and Betty Metcalf. He said some of her famous pies were not deserving of fame.'

'Why are chef's so bloody temperamental?' he asked. 'Is it anything of real concern?'

'No, it's sorted. I poured oil on troubled waters while you were swapping spittle with her.' Phew, women!

He kept a very diplomatic silence on the subject of Mary for the rest of the day. He was starting to learn about life!

*

Brian Ventriss was an acquaintance of Tom Watson's, as in seeing each other in the pub and both of them being seamen. He was currently bobbing about on a large steam trawler off the Scottish coast in the North Sea. He was staying in the vicinity for the next month, using Aberdeen as the unloading port.

He lived in a ramshackle cottage near Scalby to the north of Scarborough. At this very moment while he was working on the trawler, his rear window was being smashed, and a dishevelled looking Watson was climbing through it.

He explored the interior. This will do, talking loudly to himself. Find some grub and this will do. Later in the day, with a change of clothes kindly supplied by the unknowing Ventriss, he stole the groceries left at the doorstep of the nearest house. The owner was at work. He helped himself to two covered jugs of milk left by Dickie

Mainprize. 'Too bloody trusting,' he sneered. He'd food and drink now he needed a plan to get at Sheader.

With two days stubble already on his face he decided to grow a full beard and moustache, a common sight among seamen. He would wear the typical seaman's clothes provided by the useful Ventriss, and with a cap pulled well down he reckoned he could avoid recognition.

He made a point of never showing any light at night; doing everything possible to give the impression the cottage was unoccupied.

During the daytime he wandered further afield, stealing food and supplies wherever the opportunity arose, becoming in fact quite blasé.

Terry and Helen were becoming increasingly concerned that Watson was still on the loose. P C Jameson said he thought he would no longer be in the district. He was sure he'd have been picked up by now if he was.

Terry didn't think that for one minute and said as much to Helen.

'He's bubbling with vengeance. He'll be hanging around somewhere nearby I'm convinced of that. We need to be on our guard.'

Mary was released from hospital just one week after being admitted. They both went to pick her up, Terry asking the cabbie to wait for them.

She was up and dressed waiting anxiously for their arrival, running to them as soon as they entered the ward. Her delight was obvious, hugging them both in turn.

She chattered like an excited little girl on the way to Overton Terrace. They were taking no chances. Terry had arranged for Sally to sit with her until they got home from the café each day. Sally made a great fuss of the girl, they left her to go back to the café; assuring Mary it wouldn't be long before they were home.

By the time the café was closed on another busy day they arrived at Overton Terrace to find a glowing Mary, with the assistance of Sally, had the dinner ready and waiting. It was a huge burden off Helen's shoulders. She greeted them both with her usual effervescence. Helen gave Sally a warm hug.

'I'm so grateful to you Sally.'

'It's no trouble dear; we've enjoyed ourselves haven't we?' addressing herself to Mary.

'Yes,' she smiled, 'I can't tell you how nice it is to be out of that hospital, and one grumpy nurse in particular. We called her pursed lips.' She laughed, looking at Terry with a knowing look.

'Talking of grumpy ones, I'll be off to feed my man,' laughed Sally. As she headed for the door, 'don't worry you two. I'll be here until Mary gets back to work.'

After dinner Terry had put the plates up on the kitchen shelf, sharing some private joke with Helen that had Mary a little peeved. They trooped into the lounge with the now customary coffee.

To the girl's surprise, he sat them both on the settee taking the solitary chair himself.

'Now you two, I'm going to share some of my latest thoughts with you.'

'Bloody hell,' said Helen, 'hold my hand Mary and brace yourself; this could be interesting.' 'Mary did just that, giving Helen an unfathomable look.

'Seriously,' he started. 'The tea rooms have taken off beyond our wildest dreams and we've hardly touched our remaining capital. I've been thinking for a while now that this house is not adequate. I'd love something a little better. A bathroom for one thing, and indoor toilet of the sort that people like the Kessler's enjoy. So I propose having a look at what's on the market.'

Helen sat stunned. 'Oh wow Terry, this is the first time you've mentioned this. How long have you been thinking of it?'

'Quite a while actually. Secondly, I think we've got the formula for the tea rooms spot on. I'm wondering if we could open one in Whitby, expand the business. And thirdly,' not giving the surprised girl's chance to chip in. 'as soon as Watson has been caught and dealt with Helen and I propose to get married. We'd both like you Mary to be maid of honour.' He sat back breathless.

Mary looked shell shocked. 'Married,' she stuttered, her eyes glistened. 'I'm glad for you; yes it's good news isn't it?' And then she burst into tears. 'But what'll happen to me? Where will I be?' She wailed.

Helen put her arms round the sobbing girl. 'Mary love, come on, what's all this about. You'll always be our special friend what are you so upset at?'

'It's going to alter everything, you two will be man and wife. I always dreamed we'd sort of be together just us three as one. It's as though I'm being pushed out, oh I don't know.' She buried her head in Helen's shoulder sobbing as though the end of the world was nigh.

In a way it was. It signified the end of her fantasy. The erotic dreams she used to comfort herself with would never become reality. Helen and Terry married, it was going to change everything. She was inconsolable. Terry looked at Helen, made a, *what do we do* gesture. She shook her head and continued hugging the girl. 'You're all confused love.

'You've been through so much trauma, we'll always be here for you come what may. Now let me help you get ready for bed. You need to get your strength up, tomorrow everything will look clearer.' Helen kissed her forehead. 'Come on.' Mary stood reluctantly looking beseechingly at Terry. 'Terry,' she said, holding her hand out.

Terry stood and took her in his arms. 'Helen's right love, in the morning it'll all seem different. As I said to you long ago now, you'll eventually meet a handsome young man who'll love you and cherish you. We'll fade away then.'

She looked into his face with tearful eyes. 'You don't understand, either of you. I can't help the way I feel. You both dominate my every waking thoughts. It's like torture sometimes. You'll never understand the longing I have. I can't find words to explain how I feel. If I'm ever separated from you life won't be worth living.'

Neither of them knew what to say. Her distress was genuine and touching, it added further to Terry's own confused feelings for this erotic girl. He released her as Helen took her hand and led her to the door.

'Bring some warm water up,' she said to Terry. He nodded and hurried into the kitchen.

He filled the large jug with warm water and hurried up to the attic.

'Warm water love,' he called from outside the door; he had no intention of going in. Helen opened the door and took it off him, meeting his eyes, rolling hers slightly, and then disappearing back in. He went down, made a cup of tea and sat heavily on the chair. Phew, how uncomplicated his life had been before meeting Helen here for the first time. It seemed an eternity away now. What a complicated situation to be in and how was it going to be resolved?

Upstairs, Helen gently helped Mary undress. She stood compliantly before her naked and unashamed, letting Helen wash her down. Helen couldn't help noticing the still fading bruising around the top of her thighs, giving her a feeling of utter revulsion for the evil bastard who had done that to her.

Mary seemed a little more composed now.

'He made a mess of me didn't he?' She suddenly said, touching her thigh.

Helen, reluctantly, allowed her eyes to travel to the little triangle of auburn hair. Either side and just above the signs of bruising were clear.

'Is it still very painful love?' she asked softly.

'Sore mainly. Internally, you know.'

Helen nodded. 'Yes, I can guess. Come on, slip your nighty on.'

Mary dutifully lifted her arms high, pulling her breasts up taut. Helen felt a slight sheen of sweat forming on her brow. Breathing deeply she pulled the nightdress over Mary's head allowing it to fall over the erotic body.

340

'Right, into bed lass,' she said. Mary didn't move, looking at Helen with bewitching deep green eyes. 'What's to happen to us Helen?'

Helen sighed. 'I really don't know love and that's the truth. Frankly, I really enjoyed what happened between us. It probably means we're both bad women. It upset Terry at the time, although his pride was hurt, and I daren't even think about a threesome as you once joked. I'd probably enjoy that too.' She gave a deep sigh. 'You and I are too much alike. We're both highly sexed. I don't think that's a crime but where we go from here God knows and that's the truth.'

Mary stroked Helen's cheek. 'Then you understand how I feel a little?'

'More than a little,' Helen replied frankly. 'Anyway, bed time, get into bed temptress.' She giggled. 'That's what Terry calls you, temptress. So get into bed before I kiss your hurt better.'

Mary laughed. 'Night night then.' She kissed Helen long and hard, and like Terry before her; Helen enjoyed returning it in kind. The two tongues intertwined like snakes.

She got back downstairs breathing heavily.

'She's in bed. Terry, how do we resolve this?'

'That's one for another day, can't get my head round it at the moment. We'll leave it until she's fully recovered.' He looked at her. 'She's got you steamed up anyway.'

\*

Watson was getting more confident. Dressed in fisherman's clothes, canvas bag thrown over his shoulder as though just coming from a ship and with a face now covered by a fair amount of beard, he shuffled through town unnoticed. He took great delight in walking closely past a policeman without any action or interest from him.

Pretending to be drunk he accosted a well dressed gentleman in Westborough, much to the man's disgust, staggering against him. Moving away with a mumbled apology, but now in possession of the man's wallet.

He hovered on the pavement opposite The Scarborian Tea Rooms. It was one pm and the place looked busy. Fury built again as he took in the opulence of the place and the number of well to do people coming and going.

He could see no sign of the slag but saw the Bottom End one serving in the café. His lip curled in contempt. Emboldened by his successful disguise he wandered across the road brazenly looking in the window, cap pulled down over his brow.

Would the slag be alone at their house? The maniacal chuckle again. He turned and started hurrying back down Westborough. He'd call at the house and check it out. He arrived at Overton Terrace like a wraith, slinking along close to walls. He disappeared round the back of the terrace checking all the time he wasn't being observed.

He sank to the ground as the back door opened and a woman he recognised as Sally Savage went across to the outside toilet. As soon as she went in and the door closed he scuttled to the still open door. He could hear what could only be the slag, humming a tune to herself.

She was there, his nemesis. Large as life the cow, humming as though happy. A surge of anger flashed through him. He slipped in to the house creeping through to the kitchen.

She was standing at the sink peeling some potatoes, unaware of the danger behind her.

Mary was as happy as she had been for a while. The kiss from Helen last night assured her she would always be a part of them. They needed her as much as she needed them; she'd convinced herself of that. She hummed the hymn, Abide with Me, her favourite.

A sixth sense suddenly sent a shiver down her spine, just as Watson darted across the kitchen grabbing her with one arm, the other clasping a filthy hand across her mouth.

He dragged her backwards throwing her off balance, causing her to fall at his feet. As she started to open her mouth to scream he hit her hard with a clenched fist. The light went out, and she sank unconscious on to the floor.

He jumped to his feet quickly, grabbed the first weapon he could see, a wooden rolling pin, and went back to the rear door. He was just in time as Sally was walking back across the yard. He stood at the side of the door, waited until Sally stepped in, and then brought the rolling pin down on the back of her head. The old lady went down like a pole-axed ox.

He closed the door and returned to the kitchen, dragging Mary into the lounge and dumping her on the settee. He searched the kitchen, returning with some string and a tea towel. He tied her hands and feet firmly, using the towel as a gag.

Now to search the house, find the coins which he was so sure would be there.

He worked his way through the house, turning contents of drawers and containers on to the floor. He created mayhem, growing increasingly furious at not finding what he was looking for. In the bedroom the photograph of Terry's mother was crumpled under his foot. He pocketed the sovereigns he found and some loose change, but it was a poor return for what he was looking for.

He spent a good hour turning the house upside down before returning to the lounge breathing heavily.

Mary's eyes were open. They widened in terror as she recognised her assailant, the wild look in his eyes even more maniacal than before.

He looked down at her.

'Hello bitch, it's me again.' He gave a high pitched giggle. 'Tell me you're pleased to see me.'

She struggled in terror, trying to say something behind the gag. He giggled again, and then went into the kitchen returning with a knife.

He played with it, making stabbing movements towards her, enjoying the terror he was instilling into the bound girl. He leaned close into her. The knife hovered in front of her face.

'Now bitch, I'm going to take that gag off. I want some information. Make a sound or shout and I'll cut you to ribbons, understand?'

When she didn't acknowledge immediately he screamed 'Do you understand me?' Spittle splattered her face.

She nodded weakly. She knew he was completely mad. She would have to humour him as long as possible. She was a stronger girl than he knew as recent events had shown.

He removed the gag roughly; unable to resist slapping her face as he did so.

She bit back a cry. She wouldn't give him the satisfaction of that.

'Now,' he said. 'You seem to be Sheader's little favourite, his little shag bag.' He giggled again, a chilling sound of utter madness. 'What I want to know slag is where they are? The gold coins, where's he hid them?'

She knew exactly what he was talking about. Terry and Helen had told her the full story as given them by Jimmy. She thought rapidly, how to stall him for time?

'Come on bitch; don't pretend you don't know what I'm talking about your time's running out, talk.'

'You mean the Dutch gold coins?' She said in a weak voice.

'Ah, you do know. Yes them, where are they?'

'Will you leave me alone if I tell you?'

'Fucking leave you alone bitch, you ask me to leave you be? Just like you left me.' Once again the high pitched giggle. 'What do you think?'

'You won't get there in time to get them,' she said, thinking desperately. 'He's going to get them after finishing in the café today. He's taking them to a dealer who's offered to buy them.'

'Where, where?' he screamed.

'He thought it'd be dangerous leaving them here in the house. They're in a big tin box, lots of them. He buried them where he thought no one would ever look.'

She was stalling for time desperately.

'Fucking tell me where,' he screamed. The knife moved dangerously near her face. She swallowed hard. 'He was working on digging a pond for Mrs Kessler on the South Cliff. It's not finished. He put the box in the middle of the excavation.'

'Where does this woman live?' he snarled.

He'd swallowed the story she thought. 'Somewhere on Belvedere Road but I don't know the number. What time is it?'

The sudden query about the time took him by surprise. He was thinking anything but logically. He rose and glanced at the clock in the kitchen. 'Half past three. Does that make a difference to you?'

She pretended to sound smug. 'You'll be too late then, he was leaving early to go up there. He's probably on his way now.'

She thought he was going to use the knife on her, his face distorted, made worse by the growth of beard. Then the kitchen door opened and she heard Jack's voice call.

'Sally, Mary, you there?'

Watson straightened up in fury, turning to the door just as Jack appeared. 'What the hell,' started Jack as he took in the scenario. Watson flew at him like a man possessed, but he didn't allow for the old seadog's experience in brawls long gone by. He flew into Jack's raised foot which sent him sprawling on his back. He got to his feet in a flash and sprinted for the back door.

Jack rushed across to Mary drawing his pocket knife as he did so. He cut her bonds with two strokes of the knife, Mary rolling off the settee on to her knees.

'Jack,' she gasped. 'See to Sally. She's by the back door.'

His blood ran cold, he ran to the door. Seeing Sally unconscious face down on the floor a huge roar of anguish coming from his lips. Mary staggered to her feet. She felt woozy and sick, her her head throbbing like mad. She had to get to Terry, had to warn him.

'I've got to let Terry know what's happened,' she gasped at Jack. 'Stay with Sally.' She didn't know if he had heard her. He was bent over Sally oblivious to all around. She ran to the door and started a steady trot towards the town centre.

She weaved like a drunk; vision hazy, but determined Watson would not blight their lives any more. Her hatred for him drove her on.

She was almost in a state of collapse when she burst through the tea room's door. There were startled looks on customer's faces at this dishevelled apparition crashing in.

It was the elderly magistrate Mr Smith who caught her as she partially collapsed, calling in an authoritative voice.

'Mr Sheader, you're needed here please.'

Terry dashed out of the office as Helen and the girls all surged forward.

Mr Smith had guided Mary into a chair where she was panting, trying to get her breath. She gasped out to Terry what had happened as he knelt besides her in concern. The entire café's customers all strained to hear the conversation.

'Look after her,' he said curtly to Helen and flew to the door.

'Terry, be careful,' she yelled after him.

Mr Smith squeezed her shoulder. 'I'll get the police my dear,' he said kindly, and headed for the door.

Terry had never felt such all-consuming anger. Watson! Would they ever be shut of that man? He sprinted in a way that would have been impossible earlier, his fury driving him on. He'd catch Watson this time and deal with him. The hurt he had caused Mary infuriated him; he was going to be a danger to all of them until stopped. As his breath started coming in gulps he slowed to a jog. He couldn't help admiring Mary who under such distress had managed to sell Watson a cock and bull story convincingly. What a feisty girl.

Not far in front, just turning into Belvedere Road, Watson loped at a fast pace. He spotted an elderly lady with a wicker basket and trotted across the road to her. 'I've been asked to deliver a letter to the Kessler's, 'he said, 'do you know which house it is?' She looked at the dishevelled figure with a strange sounding voice. Well, it takes all sorts.' 'It's that one,' she said, pointing.

He grinned in a way that she found disturbing, turned abruptly and headed for the house.

He kept close to the house side wall as he slunk around the back to the garden.

It was exactly as Terry had left it all that time ago. Nothing had been touched, his eyes wandered. Over on the left of the garden he spotted the depression that must be the pond excavation. Some of the earth had subsided back into the depression although he was not to know that.

A tool! He looked around, ah! the shed; that should have a spade. He went over to it; a simple latch was the only security which flew open at his tug.

He looked at the windows at the back of the house, could see no movement. He did a crabbed little run over to the pond site and sank the spade into the middle.

The earth was soft. He'd shifted three spade loads of soil when a deep tenor voice rasped, 'Watson.'

He knew before he turned who it was. Sheader!

Terry was advancing towards him with a grim look on his face. He grasped the spade firmly, stepped out of the depression and walked to meet him, spade held high like a weapon.

Bloody hell, thought Terry. I'm unarmed, quick thinking required. He pretended to look at someone over Watson's shoulder. 'Grab him Bill,' he shouted.

Watson spun to meet the new threat and Terry used the distraction to rush him and rugby tackle him to the floor.

They rolled in the mud, grappling and fighting for control. Watson was uttering high pitched shrieks of fury, sounding more animal like than human.

He reached for the spade again. Terry chopped his arm with a rigid edge of hand and Watson howled with pain.

Mrs Kessler, having woken from a nap by the commotion in her garden couldn't believe her eyes. Two men rolling around in the mud in her garden! Acting as though they were at a wrestling match. She watched fascinated.

One of them broke away and got to his feet. As he did so she recognised him. It was *her* Terry Sheader. He dashed to the hut, probably looking for a weapon to counter Watson's spade. Watson sprang to his feet and gave Terry a mighty kick to his left leg. The injured one!

Terry felt a blinding pain in his knee which almost made him sick. His leg folded and he collapsed to the ground unable to shift, lying there immobile.

Surprisingly, Watson left him, dashing to pick up the spade again and driving it into the soil in the pond.

He thrust it into the ground with a maniac's strength, again and again. There was a metallic clang as the spade struck metal. He gave a shrieked. 'Yes,' that was inhuman to hear and drove the spade in again.

The *Derfflinger's* twelve inch shell which had ploughed into the soil inert during the attack didn't like being struck with a spade. It did what it should have done on the 15th December.

Once again, Scarborough's South Cliff reverberated to a mighty blast. A huge fountain of soil and debris was thrown into the air. Every window for a hundred yards around was smashed.

Tom Watson was pulverised into a red mash and dispersed over a wide area, and Mrs Kessler slid slowly to the floor, a look of utter surprise on her face. A large shard of glass projected from her chest like a dagger.

\*

Terry opened his eyes slowly; his vision was hazy and swimming. He could make out lights above him. His ears buzzed constantly. He felt his fingers, they seemed to move alright. He put his hand onto his chest which felt strange, and felt bandages.

Where the hell was he? He heard a voice that sounded muzzy and far away as though heard through a layer of cloth.

'He's awake, oh thank God, he's awake.' Was that Mary's voice?

He moved his head a little towards the sound of the voice and the room tilted and his vision swam. He blinked, tried to focus. Yes, it was Mary leaning over him. 'Terry darling, oh Terry.' Was she crying? Another hand grasped his from the other side. The realisation that he was lying in bed came slowly. He turned his head the other way, Helen! Holding his hand and stroking his head.

A little voice inside said, 'this is all rather nice.' The next thing he saw was a man in a white coat bending over him and peering into his eyes. He was wearing spectacles which made his eyes look distorted. It was very strange all of this.

He closed his eyes again and drifted off to sleep.

The doctor stood. 'If you would like to come with me ladies.'

Helen took a long lingering look at the now sleeping Terry, and then followed the doctor into a little cubicle.

'He's been a very lucky man,' he started without preamble. 'The fact he was prostrate on his back when the shell exploded undoubtedly saved his life. He has multiple minor cuts and bruises to his chest and legs, but nothing serious.'

He blew his nose on a large handkerchief. 'His hearing should return to normal over time. All he needs is a period of rest.'

The girls left the hospital with an immense feeling of gratitude. The police had arrived just after the blast. In fact, if they had been seconds earlier they would have been caught in the blast.

The Scarborough Mercury carried it on its headlines the following day, *'DELAYED SHELL EXPLOSION. WIFE OF PROMINENT STEEL MAGNATE KILLED IN BLAST!'*

No mention whatsoever of the circumstances of the explosion. Indeed, the only independent eye witness was dead. The other one was still woozy in hospital, and so far he hadn't said a word. The police spent a great deal of time attempting to piece together the circumstances. They had brief statements from the girls and Jack about events just prior to Terry setting off after Watson.

Sally must have been a tough old bird. She had a lump the size of an egg on the back of her head and a thumping headache, but no obvious lasting effects.

She was making the most of it, enjoying being molly-coddled by Jack.

The girls were very grateful to Mr Smith who gave the police a very detailed account of Mary's arrival at the tea rooms; almost word for word. Obviously someone who was used to recording and listening to detail.

The police had a pretty good idea of events leading up to the blast. All the information given showed the fugitive, Watson, had believed a cock and bull story given by Miss Duncan. Bravely given it was added, under great stress for which Miss Duncan was to be commended, that some sort of buried treasure existed in the Kessler's garden.

Watson had made his way there after Jack had prevented him committing murder at Overton Terrace. Mr Sheader had chased after him, unwisely in their opinion, and a confrontation had taken place in the Kessler's garden.

They were unable to explain how a shell from the December bombardment had chosen that time to explode. That remained a mystery, but tiny fragments of flesh and clothing seemed to indicate Watson had been a direct victim of the blast. Strangely, the blade of a spade with a shattered shaft was found embedded in a tree trunk some three gardens away.

The incident made the national press, mainly because of the death of Mrs Rosemary Kessler, her husband being a prominent man.

Mr Kessler had been so distraught he had retired temporarily to his home in the village of Dore on the outskirts of Sheffield; being comforted by his young mistress!

It was some three days later before Terry was fully *with it*. He had no recollection of the blast. He could only remember fighting with Watson, and he thought he could remember falling down with intense pain in his leg. The rest was a blank. The police had found him flat on his back, unconscious, almost buried under soil and stones. Of the shed there was no sign. It had been obliterated in the blast.

To the two girl's relief, he started acting like the Terry of old but complained of a constant ringing in his left ear. The doctor thought that would recede with time. Apart from that he could be discharged to home.

To the wonderment of neighbours and passers bye, he was delivered to Burr Bank in a new Daimler motor ambulance, being carried from there to the door.

It wasn't strictly necessary but he enjoyed the fuss.

Sally volunteered to administer to his needs while the girl's were at 'work.' That was the way Helen now described it. The tough old lass quite enjoyed looking after him. The bandages were off, but the cuts were very sore and he was a mass of bruises on his chest area. The hospital had given instructions to keep them clean and covered lightly. Sally quite enjoyed wiping the muscular chest down. She thought I can see the attraction.

351

The evenings were the best when he had the undivided attention of both girls. He had more kisses and surreptitious strokes of his body than ever and he thoroughly enjoyed it.

Helen whispered. 'I hope Bruce wasn't damaged,' to which he replied. 'You'd better have a look.' She did! He was waiting for Mary to say the same, but disappointingly it didn't happen.

It was a good two weeks before the ringing in his ear finally went and his cuts had healed to a few scabs. Thank God he was a good healer! He was more concerned with his leg which, once he was up and about gave considerable pain.

He resumed his roll at the tea rooms everyone making a fuss of him on his first day back. And he confided to the girls he would arrange a trip to Whitby shortly.

Strangely, as though the near death experience had changed them, the two girls no longer bickered over him. Either of them attended to him when he was confined to bed and Helen seemed very placid about it.

It was about this time that an excited Helen brought a copy of the Mercury to his attention. The property for sale copy, and she pointed to a house for sale.

It was a superb Edwardian villa situated on the South Cliff on Esplanade road. It had all they required, bathroom, three bedrooms, well-furnished kitchen, lounge and dining room. And only a stone's throw from the Esplanade proper with its magnificent views of the bay.

He immediately contacted the estate agent. He told them that they were serious buyers but would require a Sunday viewing as that was the only day free to them. That created a furore until Terry mentioned it would be a cash sale if it suited their requirements. The viewing was duly arranged. He wanted the opinion of both girls. It was now accepted that Mary was a permanent part of the family. They were both delighted with it, more than delighted, ecstatic.

The bathroom in particular entranced the girls. There was a large bath with hot and cold running water, a water closet, courtesy of Mr Shanks and a large wash basin also with hot and cold water supply. And wonder of wonders, electric lights throughout the house. Terry immediately said yes and instructed the agent to start sale proceedings. He was happy to give the seller the full asking price, and asked the agent to handle the sale of Overton Terrace.

They arrived back at Overton Terrace breathless and excited.

'I can't believe we've bought a house just like that,' said Helen, snapping her fingers. 'It's a palace. Tell me we're not dreaming Terry. Tell me it's actually just happened.'

He grinned at them both. 'I've shocked myself. It was as though I was outside of myself and someone else was making the decision with me as a bystander.'

'Jack and Sally will be upset,' said Mary.

'Yes, I suppose so,' said Terry thoughtfully. 'They've been really good friends, more than good, more like family. We'll have to throw a really good party for everyone. Well, almost everyone. I can think of a few we'll not invite.'

The girls excitedly discussed what and who to have for the party. Terry got the impression far more people would be there than he realised if the girls got their way, which he thought ruefully they would.

'The luxury of a proper bath,' said Helen dreamily. 'No fetching and carrying from the cellar. No heating water and then all the hassle of emptying the tub, oh wow.'

'And no traipsing across the yard on a cold night to the toilet,' giggled Mary.' 'Who said you're included in all this,' said Terry slyly to Mary.

An instant look of panic shot across her face. Before she could say anything he grinned and said. 'I'm only winding you up little girl. I can't imagine life without you now.'

'You sod,' she cried, and jumped on him pretending to fight. They were laughing and giggling and ended up rolling onto the floor Mary on top. Helen joined in, a huge release of the tension of recent days.

They rolled about larking like kids until Terry groaned. 'Oh that's enough; my flaming leg's killing me.' The girl's were immediately concerned. He'd told them how much it hurt more since the savage kick from Watson. He scrambled back up into the chair breathing heavily. 'Wow, that's really painful.'

'Do you think you should have a word with the doctor?' asked Helen anxiously. 'Can't see him telling me anything I don't already know. It'll probably take a while for it to settle down again.'

Mary shot into the kitchen. She certainly pulled her weight, returning after a while with three steaming hot mugs of cocoa made in the navy style, thick and sugary. The three of them retired to bed that night happy and contented. Mary happy that Terry had said she was one of the family. Helen dreaming of luxurious hot baths and flush toilets!

\*\*\*

# CHAPTER NINETEEN

## Turmoil

The following morning they were up early ready for work. None of them actually mentioned yesterday, but there was a feeling among them that a decision had been made concerning the future of them all.

'I'll go round to Jack and Sally's tonight and tell them about our decision to move,' said Terry with a mouthful of toast. Helen nodded, likewise chewing toast. Mary just stared at him with big green eyes.

The day was busy again. Monday was the least busy day when they first opened the tea rooms but trade seemed to have levelled to a week-long constant.

It had been very satisfying for both Terry and Helen to pay the first bonus at the end of the last month, the staff now taking on the feel of a large family. Jane, the ex-scullery maid couldn't believe her luck. The change in her fortunes had been immense.

Terry shot off to the estate agent's at lunch time to finalise details for the sale of Overton Terrace and the purchase of their new house. It seemed the sellers of the new house wanted a quick sale. Perfect as far as he was concerned. Mary was working in the café with a new spring in her step, bubbly and effervescent which communicated itself to the customers. Terry thought she was showing her feeling of greater security.

He reflected on what had taken place the day before. His sudden commitment to Mary's future had been instantaneous and Helen had raised no objection but he wondered what the future held for all of them relationship wise.

He decided when next visiting the estate agent he would sound them out about a possible property in

Whitby for a tea room on the same style as this one. He was convinced they had a successful formula. Any town which attracted visitors would be a good possibility. The war had reduced visitor numbers, but after the conflict the holiday makers should be coming back in droves.

He was also deeply satisfied Watson had been removed, literally, although he was unable to remember any of the final fight which had led to the explosion. He was at as much of a loss as the police as to why the shell exploded when it did. The police had visited them a couple of days ago for final statements. Helen dictated hers to a constable, a little ashamed at telling him the reason why.

It had amused them all watching the constable writing laboriously in pencil, his tongue sticking out of the corner of his mouth. Mary proved an expert little liar. Her face was guileless and smiling at the policeman who flushed deeply. She said she hadn't a clue what the treasure was that Watson babbled on about. To her, it simply proved his madness. But when he kept asking where Terry had hid this treasure, she gave a little shrug and twiddled her finger at her temple at this point; she said Terry had told her about working at the Kessler's in another life. And then she had told the made-up story to Watson hoping to gain time, which luckily had worked when Jack arrived. She gave the policeman another charming smile which had him squirming in the chair.

'Very brave and very commendable miss,' he said.

A reporter from the Mercury had also called and interviewed her. An article appeared in the paper entitled, *HEROIC GIRL FENDS OFF MANIAC AND INSTRUMENTAL IN HIS DOWNFALL.*

Mary loved it, cutting it out to keep. It included a photograph of her looking sweet and demure. A photograph which had startled her when the Mercury photographer had taken it, she wasn't prepared for the bright flash and puff of smoke from his magnesium flare. Terry had said to Helen. 'We've a heroine living with us now,' and giving Mary a lewd look.

'Is there nothing this girl can't do?'

Mary stuck her tongue out at him. 'Just wait and see.' She met Helen's eyes and they both burst into fits of giggles. He shook his head and read the paper out loud, specifically for Helen's benefit. Both he and Mary said they would start giving Helen reading lessons.

'I think it's time for a trip to York again,' announced Terry suddenly. 'We need to get rid of incriminating evidence, those coins. The quicker we get shut the better.'

'You mean that crook Steiner?' asked Helen indignantly. 'He'll give you far less than they're worth.'

'I know he will,' said Terry patiently. 'But that's the price we'll have to pay for discretion as dad was obviously aware. We're not in a position to argue.'

She pursed her lips. 'I suppose you're right,' doubt in her voice.

'There' no suppose about it,' replied Terry. 'We have to get rid of them. Better a smaller amount without advertising what we're doing than getting caught trying to sell them on the open market and questions being asked about their provenance.'

'What's that word mean,' asked Mary.

'Proof of our ownership and where we got them from,' he replied.

'Ah, I see,' said Mary.

'Well we can't all go, we'd leave the tea rooms dangerously short staffed,' said Helen. 'You'll have to go on your own Terry.'

'I'd love to see York,' said Mary wistfully. 'I've never been.'

'Neither had I until Terry and I went to see that crooked jeweller when we were trying to find out what Terry's dad had sold to him,' said Helen. 'But we couldn't let you go with Terry. As I've said, we'd leave the café short and I'm not sure what you two would get up to on your own,' she added darkly.

Mary gave a coy little look, hand behind her neck, head in the air, posed like a film star, 'Helen, really.'

'Exactly,' scowled Helen.

'Right, I'll go alone,' he laughed. 'Probably on a Monday when it's least busy.'

*

He took the trip to York a fortnight later. Forty six coins in a tough leather brief case which he had bought specifically for the job, thinking it would be useful afterwards to carry paper work from the café back home as required.

Steiner was as unpleasant as last time. The man had an air of greed and slime about him but, as he had told the girls, they were in no position to argue. He came away finally with a price that he was prepared to accept, £150. He told Steiner, to Steiner's delight that he did not want a receipt.

The journey back was uneventful although he had a strong feeling of needing to wash his hands. It had been an uncomfortable experience for him.

Three weeks after that the keys to the house on Esplanade Road were received, a time of great excitement for them all. It was actually happening. Until this moment it had seemed slightly surreal as though it were all a dream that they would wake up from to find it had disappeared into the ether.

They went up to the house for the first time after receiving the keys one evening after the café closed. It seemed like magic to the girls as they entered the door for that first time. At the touch of a polished brass switch the hall was bathed in light. Terry showed them both how a press down on the switch put the lights on; and flipping the same switch upwards turned them off. They wandered in a daze from room to room. With the house now being empty of furniture it seemed enormous. Even bigger than the first time they had seen it.

'What are we going to do about furniture?' asked Helen suddenly. 'The few bits we've got are going to be lost here.'

'I was waiting to here you say that,' he grinned. 'Ask me what I've done.'

'You do like your games of mystery don't you?' laughed Mary. She met Helen's eye, 'Should we actually ask him, or wait for the master to speak?'

He slapped her bottom playfully. 'Cheeky madam. Well if I'm not going to have the satisfaction of hearing you beg me to tell you, here it is. I've opened an account with Rowntree's store'

'Pheeeew,' whistled Helen through her teeth. 'Can we afford that?'

'I've already paid £150 into the account from the sale of the coins so that makes a good start. If we pick frugally to get the house furnished, and add items as we go along we should be alright.'

They explored all the rooms in detail. Terry suggested the large front bedroom be theirs, the one furthest from theirs to be Mary's.

Mary's voice was neutral. 'Why that one?' with raised eyebrows.

'Because you know how noisy this one can be,' nodding at Helen with a grin. 'We don't want your sleep disturbing at night do we?' He realised he'd touched on a delicate subject. The look on Mary's face was inexplicable, a sudden glistening in her eyes. Helen was silent, biting her lip. He looked in turn at the pair of them shrugging.

'Come on girls we have to be realistic, don't we. This is real life, if there's a problem, tell me now.'

Mary looked close to tears. 'I know you're right, it's just the thought of you and Helen making love a couple of doors away and, well, oh I don't know.' He put his arm around the girl's shoulder. 'Helen and I are going to get married; you know that. I love her to bits and I'm not a monk. Of course we'll make love, often I hope. Now if this is going to cause you real heartache perhaps the idea of living with us is not the right one.'

The flood gates burst. She sobbed as though her world had collapsed, utterly distraught, clinging to him while Helen looked on with pain in her face.

He caught Helen's eye as he held the sobbing girl, lifting his eyes, questing. Helen looked almost as distraught as Mary. No help coming from that direction then!

'Think things through love,' he said, holding her away and looking deep into the tearful face. 'You don't have to make any decisions now. Let's leave it until you feel calmer.'

The return to Overton Terrace was traumatic. He had to flag a cabbie down as Mary looked close to collapse; her face a deathly pale, looking from one to the other with big haunted eyes.

When they got back Helen said she would get the girl to bed. She was in such a state, almost having to be carried up the stairs.

Mary allowed Helen to undress her giving no help at all, standing like a doll. Helen decided to get her into bed without even attempting to wash her before she fainted. She pulled the covers up around the girl, Mary looking up with big wet eyes. 'I'd be better dead,' she whispered. 'I'd be no trouble to you then.'

'Don't you dare say that,' Helen said angrily. 'You silly girl you, don't even think like that.' She stroked the girl's hair.

'If you wanted to break our hearts, that would.' She kissed her gently on her forehead. 'I'll send Terry up to talk to you.'

She went downstairs in turmoil. 'Terry, go up to her, talk to her, I've just played hell with her for saying she'd be better dead.'

He went upstairs with a heavy heart. Like Helen, Mary pulled at his heart strings on so many levels. She was childish and mature in equal portions. Undoubtedly highly attractive as a woman but emotionally disturbed. She'd endured so much it would be difficult for any young woman to come out of it unscathed.

He tapped on her door and went straight in.

'Hello love, it's that terrible man.'

She lay on her back, face as pale as the sheet around it but looking a little more composed. 'No, it's the man I love more than life itself. I've put you in an impossible situation haven't I?' He didn't know what to say to her. This was the mature Mary, the one to whom he never knew what to say.

'It's not going to work is it, me living with you. I'd be consumed with jealousy and desire to the detriment of us all, it'd destroy us. I said I loved you enough to let you go and that's what I have to do.' She stared up at him. 'If you get the tea rooms at Whitby, could I work there? That would be better wouldn't it? I'll need a job won't I? You see, I'm being very practical aren't I?'

He could also see she was struggling to keep control. He felt totally useless, unable to say anything against her proposal but devastated it had come to this.

'Oh God Mary. I can't believe it's come to this but common sense tells me you're right. Will you be alright love?' He laid his face against hers. She covered his face and hair with wet kisses.

'Go down and tell Helen what I've decided, tell her I won't do anything silly.' He stroked her cheek, swallowed hard and went down to Helen. She was sitting upright on one of the kitchen chairs, hands between her knees, looking pensive. He told her what Mary had said, how she had seemed very positive. Even the suggestion she had made about Whitby. She nodded,

'It has to be, doesn't it? She was right, it would destroy us. Even though it's my man she's in love with, I can sympathise with her feelings. We weren't living in the real world were we, when we planned for her to live with us?'

361

He gave a helpless shrug. 'No, perhaps not. Hindsight is wonderful isn't it? But we have to make sure she's alright. I'd like her to stay here until we move, I'm serious about Whitby. If we could find premises with accommodation above perhaps?'

They went to bed with heavy hearts. It felt to Terry as though a new chapter in his life was about to start. Let's see what tomorrow brings, he thought.

***

# CHAPTER TWENTY

## All change

The following weeks were hectic after the traumatic episode. Mary stayed with them. She had no where else to go but the atmosphere had undergone a change. The laughter and banter they used to enjoy was missing. Mary seemed withdrawn and morose. Helen had asked her to go with them to choose furniture from Rowntree's but she declined, adding to their increasing feelings of despair for the girl. The new house was requiring a lot of time, and a message from the estate agent saying they'd identified a possible suitable property in Whitby added to the pressure. With an eye to the future, Terry took on another girl for the café, a bubbly girl called Vera Hemsley, previously employed in the Town Hall restaurant. She had catering experience and fitted his requirements exactly. She was a great help as the house needed attention during the move in and both he and Helen needed to be there when furniture etc was being delivered. Mary steadfastly refused to go near the place again, which upset them both immensely. The move was finally accomplished in the second week of June, and as Overton Terrace was still not sold, they told Mary she could stay there until such time as a sale was achieved.

They threw a moving-in party on the Saturday evening. A lavish spread of sandwiches and cakes had been supplied by Betty Metcalf, and they invited all the staff from the tea rooms and Jack and Sally, of course. It was only the second time Mary had come to the house. She knew she had to make the effort for the benefit of everyone else. She didn't want the rest of the staff thinking a rift existed between them, but she sat pretty morosely nibbling a sandwich, not joining in with the cheerful chatter around. Terry watched her with concern. Even her old flirty self would have been better than this. It distressed him greatly seeing her like this. He had a fondness almost bordering on love for this girl he finally admitted to himself.

Helen was also observing Mary. She felt pretty much as Terry. It was like seeing an alien being; not the pretty alluring Mary of old.

The party didn't break up until ten-thirty. Terry insisted on walking with Mary back to Overton Terrace, a long walk at night. He tucked her arm firmly in his. 'I hate seeing you like this love it distresses both of us. I wish I had a magic wand that would make everyone happy ever after but that's just in pantomime isn't it?'

'I don't like you being unhappy either, you of all people,' she said, 'but life doesn't always work out as we'd want it to.'

They walked in silence mainly, both lost in their own thoughts. As they approached Overton Terrace Mary felt bereft at the thought of Terry leaving her there. 'Do you want to come in for a moment?' she whispered.

He shook his head sadly. 'No love, my willpower is already at breaking point and we both know what would happen if I did. Go to bed my little angel.'

He kissed her gently, pulling back as she attempted to turn it into one of her long passionate affairs. 'Good night darling, lock the door.'

She went in locking the door behind her. She sank onto the solitary remaining kitchen chair, burying her head in her folded arms on the table and sobbing uncontrollably.

It was turned midnight when he got back to Helen. She was sitting up waiting for him in the lounge, newly furnished with a pretty floral three piece suit.

'She's back safe then,' she started lamely. 'Did anything, you know...,' shrugging her shoulders.

'No love, nothing like that happened. But it's about to! Come on, let's christen that bed. I know it's not a new one but it's in a new room.'

He held out his hand, and she allowed him to pull her up. 'Its time to make an old man happy.' She giggled. 'Which old man would that be then?'

They went to bed for their first night, or, more accurately, early morning, in their new home, Helen happy and relieved.

In Overton Terrace Mary lay curled up in a ball clutching teddy Terry, wishing it were him. Alone and in the depths of despair.

They all met up again on the Monday morning at the tea rooms. Terry and Helen were unable to miss the pale and wan looking Mary. It was when he was working on some figures mid-morning in the office that a tap on the door came.

'Come in,' he called. It was Jennifer. 'There's a lady outside asking for you Mr Sheader. She won't come in. Doesn't look like one of our sort if you know what I mean,' she said with a lifting of the eyebrows.

'Outside, as on the pavement?' he asked.

'Yes, hovering outside the door.' He went out onto the café floor, nodding at regulars and made his way to the door. 'Just popping out for a moment,' he called to Helen who observed him. She made a gesture which he interpreted as *where to* but ignored it. For the first time in his life he had a strange premonition. He went out of the door, and standing just to the left was a woman. As he turned to her he knew instinctively who it was the likeness was striking. 'Mr Sheader,' she started hesitantly.

'It's Mrs Standish isn't it?' he said softly. 'You're Helen's mother.'

Her eyes widened in surprise. 'Yes, how did you know?'

'It's like looking at an older version of Helen,' he smiled. He slipped his hand through her arm. 'Come on, let me take you for a coffee, we'll startle the opposition,' he said, nodding across the road at Rowntree's café.

He led her unresisting across the road into the café. She looked around in wonderment as he led her to a table. As they sat he could hear the buzz of conversation. The staff here knew who he was. They vied for attention at his table, the unspoken question; what's he doing in here?

He ordered two milky coffees, Helen's mother looking wide eyed as they came. He knew, like her daughter before her, she would never have tasted coffee before. 'Put a spoonful of brown sugar in and see what you think,' he whispered to her.

She did as told and took a tentative sip. 'Oh, that's lovely,' she murmured.

'Now, you wanted to see me,' he leaned forward. She flushed a deep red.

'I didn't know how to tell her, Helen that is. She wouldn't have seen me and I don't blame her,' she said bitterly. 'But someone needs to tell her that her dad is dead.'

He reached across the table and took her hand. 'You won't believe this but I had a premonition. When I was told a lady outside wanted to see me I somehow knew it was you and I had a pretty shrewd idea what about.'

'Perhaps you have gypsy blood,' she smiled, 'I can see Helen's found herself a very handsome man. She's a lucky girl. Do you love her?'

'Yes, very much. In fact we plan to marry in the near future but that can wait. What happened to your husband?'

'Heart attack,' she said bluntly. 'Probably brought on by too much drink and too much blood pressure when he was mad, which was most of the time,' she said with bitterness. 'It may sound as though I'm a callus woman but I'm glad he's gone. I won't have to worry about being a punch bag again before going to bed.'

He squeezed her hand. 'Helen told me you know, about why she left home. But she probably didn't realise how bad it was for you either.' She had tears in her eyes. 'I should have protected her. Stood up to him, but I'd had all the stuffing knocked out of me long ago. I just couldn't face another beating.'

'When's the funeral?' He asked.

'It was two days ago,' she said savagely. 'The bastard's in the ground.'

'Are you still living in the same cottage?' he asked.

'Yes, but not for long. I'll be out by next week, can't pay the rent now you see. There's no pension or anything.' He was horrified. 'How much is the rent?' 'Three pounds a week,' she said sadly. I do some work sewing for the men, sailcloth and the like. I can eat but can't afford much more.'

'Leave it with me,' he said. 'I'll break the news to Helen and get back to you. Meet me here outside Rowntree's at twelve tomorrow. I'll do what I can, I promise you that.'

She swallowed hard. 'I can see what a good man my daughter's found. That means the world to me, thank you Mr Sheader.' She stood up and he walked with her to the door. Outside he gave her a hug. 'Bugger the Mr Sheader,' he grinned. 'It's Terry, or perhaps, soon, son,' he laughed. Tears flowed down her face. 'That's the first time anyone's hugged me for a long time without it feeling threatening,' she gulped. He had a lump in his throat as she hurried away.

When he went back across the road Helen was the first person to ask where he'd been. 'Can't tell you here. I'll give you full details tonight at home.'

They shared a sandwich together in the office for lunch at midday. She started asking him again but he asked her to trust him until later. He wanted to take his time, time to deal with the inevitable explosion of temperament and emotion he was sure would follow.

'It's nothing to do with Mary is it?' she asked anxiously.

'No, it's nothing to do with Mary,' he said exasperatedly. 'Leave it now until later.' She pursed her lips to show disapproval but accepted his request.

He'd only been back on the bookwork half an hour when the door opened again. Jane this time. 'Mr Atkinson's here, he asks if you can spare a moment?'

'Yes, show him in.' Atkinson was the estate agent's business property clerk. He bustled in taking his bowler off as he did so.

'Good afternoon Mr Sheader. I'm sorry to call on you unannounced but a most desirable property has been brought to our attention in Whitby. It meets all of your requirements but we've been informed another party is also interested. We rather think speed is required to view.'

'How soon can you arrange that?' asked Terry practically.

'We've already looked into it,' replied Atkinson. 'Would you be able to manage Wednesday lunch-time?' Terry made an instant decision. 'Yes, I'll be at Whitby railway station by eleven thirty, if you could meet me there?' They shook hands and Atkinson shot off. He called Helen into the office and explained what Atkinson had to offer.

'I think I should take Mary with me. She needs to see the accommodation above, her decision will be vital.' Helen thought for a moment.' Yes, right. That makes sense, behave yourself.'

He laughed, 'I knew you'd say that.' She stuck her tongue out at him and went back into the café.

Mary came in on a tap on the door. 'Helen says you want to see me.'

'Come and sit down love.' She looked at him with a touch of wary panic.

'Don't look like that. The estate agent has just seen me. They think they've found the perfect property for us in Whitby but you'll need to see the accommodation above. It will be your decision. If you don't like it then that's that. He wants us to view it Wednesday lunch time. It seems someone else is also interested so we have to get a move on.' He sat back waiting for her reaction.

'If that's what you want me to do then I'll do it,' she said listlessly. 'It'll put a good distance between us won't it?'

'Mary, I need your cooperation on this love. If you have doubts then say so. I need someone I can rely on. That's essential.'

'Don't you dare question my loyalty to you,' she said hotly, a spark of the old Mary surfacing. 'You know I'll do anything you want, anything.'

'I wasn't questioning your loyalty love, that's not fair but I don't want you saying yes, just because it's what I want. It has to be what you want too.'

'What you want is all that matters to me,' she said sadly. 'If you wanted a slave I'd be that slave, but I'll promise to look carefully at this property and tell you truthfully what I think.' He had to leave it at that. Once again she'd touched him deeply. 'Alright love, we'll leave from here Wednesday. I'm not sure, but I think the Whitby train is ten o'clock.'

He felt mentally exhausted by the time they had finished that Monday night. The stroll up to Esplanade Road on a fine evening did him good. Helen was chaffing at the bit to know who he'd seen that morning. What a day!

'I don't feel like eating yet,' she said as soon as they got in. 'Can you just put me out of my misery and talk to me?' He hung his hat and coat on the stand in the hall.

'Make a couple of coffees and come into the lounge then.'

He settled into the comfy sofa pulling the coffee table up. Helen appeared in record time with the coffees, putting them on the table, and then sitting at the side of him.

'Go on then my master.'

He made a face at her. 'Right, this morning Jennifer popped her head round the door to tell me a lady outside wanted a word with me.'

'Outside?' said Helen.

'Yes, outside, she wouldn't come in to the café. So I went outside to see what it was about. Strangely, I had a sort of premonition about who it was and I was right.'

'Bloody hell, spooky eh,' she said.

'It was your mother love,' said very quietly. She gasped and sat back all banter gone. 'She was frightened of your reaction if you saw her. She was in a bit of a state. She'd come to let you know your dad has died.'

She sat stunned for a moment.

'So the fucking bastard's dead at last. Well bloody good riddance.'

He pulled her head onto his shoulder waiting for the flood of venom to drain from her, stroking her hair gently.

'I took her across to Rowntree's for a coffee and a chat. She was like you, never had a coffee before, never been in a place like that before either I dare say. She said she was so ashamed at not standing up for you when you needed her most. But the sad thing she said was she just couldn't stand another beating from him. She said he'd knocked all the stuffing from her.' Helen was snuffling softly, a pathetic sound which tugged his heart strings.

'She told me he was buried two days ago and she was glad he was in the ground. I said I'd tell you, and do you know what touched me? I gave her a hug outside when we parted. She burst into tears and said that was the first time she had ever had a hug that didn't feel threatening.'

She buried her face against his chest shoulders heaving. He held her tightly letting it work through her system, running his fingers through her hair.

He waited until she eventually lifted her head. 'You're such a lovely man, such a good man. I love you so much.'

'I love you too darling. There's something else.' She said your father had left her destitute. She couldn't afford to pay the rent and she would be homeless in a week.' Helen closed her eyes as though unable to take any more.

'And, she asked me if I loved you. Of course I told her I did and that we would be getting married in the not too distant future.'

She gave a deep sigh. 'Oh Terry, what do I do?'

'Well, I for one won't let her become homeless. It's only three pounds a week so that can be sorted. Secondly, its time for you two to make up. I know it'll be difficult and awkward but she's your mother. I never knew mine and that's a deep regret. Don't let what's happened in the past fester any longer. I know you well enough now. You can put it behind you and make a new start with your mum. I'll pick her up and bring her here and stop around to offer support if needed, but its something that needs doing.'

'My wise man,' she smiled up into his face. 'I owe you so much my darling.'

He grinned, a very wicked grin. 'Well, you have to pay a forfeit for all that advice that's only fair.'

'I do? What might that be then?'

He placed her hand on his crotch. 'My friend is feeling left out of all this talk.'

'Are you not ready for dinner yet?'

'No, that can wait.' Her deft fingers undid his buttons and released his friend. Her head dropped to his lap, lips parted. In no time he was in the throes of ecstasy. Roll on the next crisis!

*

Mary had eaten a meagre meal, no interest in cooking for herself. She spent most of the time now in her little attic room. The rest of the house seemed an empty shell without Terry and Helen. Her heart ached for them. Would it have been better living with them and putting up with the sound of them making love? At least she would have had their company at all other times. Had her decision been made in haste?

The questions and indecisions flew around her head until she thought she would go mad. She lay on the bed, her only company teddy and the hissing gas mantle, misery flowing over her like a blanket. This house was now a prison with only memories of the two people she longed for. Whitby would be better; at least there were no ghosts there.

Tuesday was as busy as ever in the tea rooms. Terry and Helen both remarked on how Mary seemed to look a little more gaunt each day. They were desperately worried about her but had no remedy. Even regular customers were asking if *the little lass* was alright as they thought she looked ill. She worked furiously to pass the time wanting Wednesday to come. At least she would have Terry for a good chunk of the day to herself. Just the thought of being with him, in his company cheered her a little.

Terry disappeared again before lunch time. 'See you later,' he whispered to Helen. She was consumed with doubts and uncertainty. He was going to her mother's to invite her to their house Wednesday evening. He thought it better to go straight to her instead of waiting for her to meet him at Rowntree's.

She had said alright when he insisted, but now he was actually going to do it well, pheeew!

He walked quickly down to the old town, found the cottage and knocked on the grimy door. Helen's mother opened the door and took a step back startled when she saw who it was.

'Has she said she won't see me?' she gasped. 'I suppose it was a lot to ask, I'll bet.' He put a finger to her lips and said, 'Shush, I know where your daughter gets her impetuosity from now,' giving her a cheeky grin.

'Oh, I'm sorry; I was off at a rush wasn't I?' She smiled back at him. 'Come in, err, Terry,' blushing slightly.

'Your daughter blushes like that,' he laughed. She laughed with him, taking a surreptitious look. My God he's handsome. If I were Helen's age! She startled herself with the thought that passed in her mind.

'I had a good talk with Helen last night. As you can imagine we had some tears but she and I want you to come up to our house tomorrow evening. Lets see if we can make bygones be bygones.'

'She really wants me to?' she asked, tears in her eyes.

'We both do. I told her I never knew my mother and have always regretted it. It was in her power to make amends all round, so will you come?'

'Yes, yes I will, of course I will.' And then with a touch of panic. 'But I've nothing nice to wear.'

He laughed heartily. 'Only a woman could say that, how much like her you are. I'll be here at seven to pick you up then,' and with another chuckle, 'Mother.'

He put his arms round her and gave her a squeeze. For a moment she laid her head against his chest. 'Thank you so much Terry. You don't know how happy you've made me, oh, and it's Rebecca if you like, sounds better than Mrs Standish.' He took his leave giving her a naughty wink. He left behind another devoted Sheader fan.

He reported back to Helen happily. 'All on track my love. You can take that alarmed look off your face it's going to be alright.'

Mary saw the conversation flowing between them. I would have been included in that before I made such a fuss she thought. Terry and Helen were unaware of her looking at them, tied up with the current thoughts of Helen's mother.

*

Wednesday morning came eventually; it seemed an age for Mary who had waited impatiently for the day. Well now it was here.

It was a beautiful warm June day. If only her feelings were as bright also.

She had made an effort, wearing a summery flowered dress with a pretty straw hat, a matching ribbon around it. Terry had on a smart suit, the picture of the successful business man. He said to her at half past nine. 'Are you ready?'

Her heart jumped as she looked at those bright blue eyes. 'Yes, ready as I'll ever be,' putting on her bravest face.

Helen wished them luck, her face inscrutable. As they walked up Westborough Terry took in her dress and hat. 'You look lovely Mary, as pretty as a picture.'

She didn't let him see the effect his comment had on her. Fobbing it off with a light hearted, 'thank you kind sir.'

He purchased two return tickets at the booking office and they went out on to the platform where a rather grimy engine with two coaches waited. They boarded it and settled side by side facing forward. She didn't know if her recent decision to distant herself from him was to blame, but his nearness was overpowering. She wanted to just grab hold of him and never let go.

He turned to her. 'Don't forget love, take time when we get there to think things through. Don't let any feelings about the business influence you, it has to be what's right for you.'

'Yes I will,' she murmured. What is right for her? What could ever be right for her now? If he only knew the turmoil inside her. If he only knew the sheer agony she went through alone at night. Pouring all her love onto a teddy bear because he had bought it for her. Oh God, if he could only feel what she felt.

He thought he heard her give a little whimper. He'd been watching the guard with raised flag. 'Did you say something love?'

'No,' she attempted a little laugh. 'You must have heard my thoughts.'

'A penny for them eh?'

'No, if you really wanted them you could have them for free.'

She gazed up at him, the green limpid eyes like lights. He felt a shiver go down his spine.

'Don't look at me like that, it churns me up inside.'

The moment was broken as the guard gave a blast on his whistle. An answering blast came from the locomotive's whistle and there was a jerk as they moved off. He sat back in his seat. This girl got to him in a way he was unable to shrug off, think of the business Sheader. You're letting your thoughts wander.

The run to Whitby was a scenic delight passing along the length of the coast. They passed through the pretty little station at Cloughton and puffed up the steady incline to the summit at Ravenscar. The magnificent view from there took in the sweep of bay looking down on the picture perfect village of Robin Hoods Bay.

It was a romantic train trip; beautiful views of one of Britain's most scenic coast lines. Romantic thought Mary, oh how romantic this could be.

The final run into Whitby gave a splendid view of the harbour as they steamed across the Larpool Viaduct. It was a magnificent red brick structure. In the harbour vessels of all types in view, even a couple of armed trawlers, the sun sparkling on the sea.

*

If it weren't for the two armed trawlers in the harbour one could be forgiven for thinking all was well with the world. No muddy trenches in France, men dying in their hundreds each day. As they steamed into the station at West Cliff Terry could see Atkinson waiting on the platform.

The train came to a halt with a squeal of brakes and Terry held Mary's hand as she stepped from the carriage. Atkinson rushed up to them, raising his hat to Mary his eyes taking in the pretty girl appreciatively. Terry

375

introduced her as the young lady who would be living in the premises if suitable and running the Whitby business.

Her eyes opened in surprise; that was the first she'd heard of that.

He deliberately avoided her look, following Atkinson from the station.

At the roadside was a large Renault motor car. Atkinson grinned at them as they walked over to it. 'Borrowed this from my brother,' he announced. 'He runs a motor garage in Ruswarp you know.' He opened the back door. The hood was down, the seats a beautiful red leather.

'Hop in,' he said grandly. Terry gallantly handed Mary up into the seat climbing in after her and sitting up close. It was the first time either of them had ridden in a motor car. Atkinson disappeared around the front and bent down. He took a firm grasp of the starting handle giving it a good swing. The engine rattled into life with a puff of smoke from the rear.

Mary grabbed Terry's arm nervously as Atkinson climbed into the driver's seat. 'I'll take you the scenic route,' he shouted over the noise of the engine.

He fiddled with a lever on the steering wheel stalk and then released the big outside parking brake. They lurched off, Mary looking terrified.

Atkinson took them via the Royal Crescent onto North Terrace with its broad view of the sea, past the famous Royal Hotel and down the steep winding road known as Khyber Pass to the harbour front. As they went down the steep incline, not a single horse was to be seen in front! Mary clutched Terry's thigh in panic.

'Can it stop alright?' she breathed.

Atkinson, oblivious of any concern in the back seat called cheerfully, 'I'll take you on the harbour side. We're heading for Baxtergate where our property is. It's a good site in a busy shopping area.'

He drove slowly along Pier Road alongside the harbour wall, Terry taking in the intense activity in this busy fishing port. As they reached the swing bridge leading into the old town Atkinson swung right into Baxtergate. He squeezed the bulb on the horn to warn pedestrians of their approach.

He drove half way along stopping at a shop frontage on the right. A large 'To Let' sign on the double window.

'This is it,' he announced yanking the parking brake on. The engine spluttered to silence and he hopped out and gallantly opened the rear door for the couple. He obviously enjoyed offering a helping hand to Mary as she stepped down. The ribbon on her hat fluttered in the breeze, pretty as a picture.

He produced a key from his jacket pocket and unlocked the door stepping aside to allow them to precede him into the shop. Terry spotted the potential immediately. The shop went well back. It was much deeper than it would seem from the outside, the floor space would certainly allow room for eighteen or so seats.

They wandered through to the back. Terry particularly wanted sufficient room to install kitchens; that was essential. The current small kitchen was just that, small! Not adequate for what they would need but if it was extended forward slightly it could be made adequate. So far so good, now for the accommodation. This was to be crucial. If Mary didn't like it or it was not adequate then he was prepared to scrap the idea so important was it that Mary should be happy.

The *flat*, Atkinson's description of the upstairs was not very impressive.

A largish room which could be used as a sitting room/lounge. A bedroom of medium proportions and a small room that contained a wash hand basin with cold water tap; that was it. The toilet was across the yard downstairs just like Overton Terrace. As soon as they saw it Terry saw Mary's face drop, and he didn't blame her. It was not adequate at all.

She turned to him a look of dismay on her face, 'Terry, I...' He stopped her before she went any further. 'I know love; this is no good at all.' Atkinson seeing a let disappearing down the pan, said.

'I know what you said re the accommodation Mr Sheader but I think a lot could be done with this,' he waved his arms at the room. 'This room is rather large. If a small amount was taken off it, with a false wall there would be room to install a bathroom and toilet. I'm sure it could be done very cost effectively.'

Mary looked at Atkinson. 'Do you think that could be done Mr Atkinson? I know Mr Sheader wants to open a tea room here in Whitby. It would be a shame if the accommodation prevented the progress of that.'

Terry gave her an appreciative look. 'You're right, we want to open tea rooms here but this aspect is vital,' he turned to Atkinson.

'If you could draw up a design that Miss Duncan approves then the deal is done. But it does hinge on Miss Duncan. She's the one who will be living here,' he said. 'I'll get cracking on that immediately,' said Atkinson. 'Can I liaise with you in Scarborough?'

'Yes indeed and I'll need to get our people onto the interior design.'

He shook hands with Atkinson, refusing an offer of a lift back to the station. 'I'm going to take Miss Duncan for lunch first, although, on reflection, perhaps you could drop us at The Royal?'

'Certainly, it would be a pleasure.' He gave Mary a beaming smile leading them both out to the motor car and again offering his hand to Mary as she climbed onto the back seat. He went through the ritual of fiddling with the lever on the steering wheel stalk and then jumped down to swing the handle.

He retraced the route up Khyber Pass swinging to the right at the top and stopping at the front of The Royal Hotel. After handing Mary down he bid them goodbye, doffing his hat to Mary with a bow and drove off.

Terry grinned at her. 'I think you've made a conquest madam. Would you do an elderly man the pleasure of taking lunch with him?'

She gave him a wan smile. 'Is the elderly man prepared to get tongues wagging taking a young woman to lunch?'

'Ouch, do you think I really am an elderly man?' The green eyes burned into his. 'You know what I think on that score. Now, are you taking me to lunch or just teasing me?'

'No more teasing. I'm taking a beautiful woman to lunch. Come on.'

He held his arm for her to slip hers through and they entered the grand portals. They went into the dining room and ordered sandwiches and a cake to follow complemented by a pot of Darjeeling tea for two.

'You never mentioned me being in charge here; that came out of the blue. Do you think I'm up to it?'

'Yes, I do. You've had plenty of experience in the café now. You know how it works, have the right personality. I think you'd be perfect, and living here you'll have your finger on the pulse. We'll need to advertise for suitable staff and a good cook plus a supplier for cakes etc but it can be done.' He sat back. 'I'm sure we can make the flat suitable. You can pick décor and furniture; I want that to be right for you. What do you think?'

'I made the decision to come here didn't I? This will probably be as good as it gets.' He reached across and took her hand. 'If you have doubts love, say so. The last thing I want to do is make you think you're under pressure. If you're having second thoughts so be it, you can still live with us if you want.'

She squeezed his hand. 'You know why that won't work. You see I'm madly in love with this elderly gentleman. He may think it's a teenage crush. I know different, that's life isn't it? Nothing's straight forward is it? I'll make the best of it here; see how it pans out and thank you for your trust in me. I'll do everything in my power to make a success of it.' She gave him one of those bewitching gazes. 'You see the effect you have on me. I do whatever you ask of me, whatever you ask at all.'

He gave a deep sigh. 'I wish you wouldn't look at me like that! It turns my heart inside out. I think the world of you Mary, more than I really care to acknowledge to myself, what does that make me? An immoral man some would say. Is it possible to be in love with two women? I feel so torn. I love Helen deeply but I would be telling lies if I looked you in the face and said I have no feelings for you. I felt bereft when you said you'd decided not to live with us. I think Helen did too.'

Her look said it all. 'Oh Terry, if anyone is immoral it's me. You were already Helen's when she first introduced me to you down on the pier an eternity ago. I knew in that first glance, felt a pull the like of which I've never experienced before.' She was interrupted by the arrival of a waiter with their food.

Terry thanked him as he set the plates before them. A silver pot of tea and delicate china cups and saucers.

'I love Helen too,' she continued as the waiter left them. 'She's so special; you're a lucky man Terry Sheader.'

'I know,' he acknowledged. 'Is this going to work for you love? Have you made the right decision?'

'Only time will tell but I have to give it my all. If the flat can be made more comfortable then my answer is yes. Let me try to make a success of it. None of us can read the future. We'll just see what happens.'

She wasn't to know how prophetic that comment was.

***

Terry's busy day was to continue on return to Scarborough. He had a meal with Helen after the tea rooms closed and then set off to collect Helen's mum.

She was awaiting his arrival with nervousness. It was clear she'd made a huge attempt to present herself at her best wearing a pretty but faded floral dress, her hair brushed and shining. Just like her daughter's.

'You look lovely,' he said gallantly giving her a warm hug which made her eyes glow.

'Is Helen really alright with this? Does she really want to see me?'

'Yes, she does. Don't worry it'll be fine.'

He helped her on with a coat that had seen better days and then handed her up into the waiting cab. He nodded at the cabbie who already knew the destination and they set off, the hooves clopping loudly on the cobbles.

As they pulled up outside the house on Esplanade Road she was shivering, probably from nerves as it was a warm evening. Terry gave the cabbie a half crown; jumped out and helped her down onto the pavement.

'Here we are, home sweet home,' giving her a broad reassuring smile. She gave a nervous little smile in return. He tucked her arm in his and walked up to the front door reaching out to the knob and thrusting it open.

Helen came into the hall as she heard the door open, standing there with a look of indecisiveness on her face as she saw her mother. The two women stood immobile for a while and then her mother gave a great sob saying,

'Helen, oh Helen love, can you ever forgive me?'

It broke the ice. Helen rushed to her mother and threw her arms around her, one word escaping, "*Mummy*", in an agonising little girl's voice.

Terry diplomatically guided the two into the lounge, taking her mum's coat and then busying himself in the kitchen making coffee as the two hugged and cried together. He waited until the sounds of tears subsided to be replaced by urgent chatter. And best of all, a few giggles, before taking coffee into them.

'I like the sound of that,' he said.

'What?' asked Helen in surprise.

'The sound of you too giggling. That has to be a good sign.'

He turned to her mum. 'If Helen agrees, we have loads of room here. Tell your landlord to get stuffed, come and live with us.' Her eyes widened with surprise and a touch of longing. 'Oh, I don't know,' looking at Helen. 'Would you really want me after, well you know, all that's happened in the past? And I couldn't contribute much to my keep.'

Before Helen had time to reply he butted in. 'We've had enough of broken families and upsets. Now's the time to put it all behind us. God knows, I bitterly regret not making it up with my dad before it was too late. You too have much in common and you've both suffered at the hands of the same man. Bury it now and move on.'

Helen gave him a longing look. 'I've said it before, you're such a good man my darling. You're right. It is time to move on,' turning to her mum. 'You're welcome here mum. Terry has said it's alright so that's good enough for me.'

Terry took hold of her mum's hand. 'And as far as being useful, we're both often shattered when we get home, neither feeling like preparing a meal so if you ran the house for us it would be such a help. Will you say yes?'

She looked at this wonderful handsome man. She could see what her daughter had fallen for without any doubt. 'Yes I'm so touched,' she said tearfully. 'I've dreamt of making things up with my daughter for so long. I can't begin to say what this means to me.' Terry thought she looked so much like an older version of Helen, the same brown eyes and beauty of looks. Still a handsome woman. That augured well for Helen in future years. He grinned cheekily at her.

'But I must tell you it can get noisy at night. This daughter of yours is unable to keep quiet. You'll just have to ignore that.' Helen flushed a deep red, her mum roaring with laughter.

'Like mother like daughter, 'she laughed. 'We gypsy stock have always been passionate.' Her eyes flashed just like Helen's. As she looked at Terry she couldn't help thinking my daughter's a lucky girl.

They helped her settle in two days later letting her have the bedroom that had originally been designated for Mary. The help with housekeeping and food preparation was going to be a great assistance to them allowing them both to concentrate on the business. It had been part of the healing process for Helen and a bonus in the house. All in all he thought things had worked out very well.

*

The next few weeks were hectic. The lease of the Whitby property was obtained, and Terry decided to use the same shop fitters who had done such a good job in Scarborough. It wasn't that fitters were not available in Whitby they were, but the Scarborough people knew what he wanted and his formula. Plus, they were offering a very good price to retain his trade.

He and Helen wanted the same corporate identity as the Scarborough tea rooms which had worked so well. The plush interior, dark green paintwork outside with gold lettering; an air of class to it. They had already decided to set on an extra member of staff for the Scarborough café in readiness for Mary's departure.

In a departure from the previous staff requirements of an all female one Terry interviewed and employed a handsome young man from one of the local Italian ice cream families, well know in the area.

The Manfredi family had moved to the area in the late eighteen hundred's, setting up a very successful ice cream making business. Young Roberto had no wish to follow his grandfather in the business hence he had applied for an interview with Terry.

Terry was immediately impressed by his enthusiasm and personality. He also had tanned good looks and flashing white teeth which, as he said to Helen, 'Will be good for our regular female clientele.'

Helen gave him a saucy look and said. 'He could practice on me any time.'

'With all those good looks on show it's almost too good to be true,' he replied laughing. 'There's forced to be a catch. He'll probably not have much below the belt.'

'Shall I check? Just as part of the job requirements of course.' She said, giving him a leer.

He shook his head in mock exasperation. Roberto proved a great attraction, settling in with alacrity and as Helen said with a wink, very popular with the three J's.

The work on the Whitby premises went at a pace. The flat conversion turned out better than expectation. Helen had a day off to accompany Mary on wallpaper shopping the two girls laughing and giggling like sisters.

Terry insisted she pick furniture from Rowntree's well stocked store. The quality was assured, and as an account holder of some standing now he was able to negotiate good prices. The job of interviewing staff started, both Terry and Helen travelling to Whitby.

To accommodate the sort of opulence they required, the tea room being slightly smaller than the Scarborough one, seating for fifteen was the maximum. The floor space had been reduced by making space for an extended kitchen. It was an essential requirement. And once again rather naughtily they had poached a chef from The Royal. They decided two girls and a 'pot washer' would be adequate along with Mary acting as hands on manager.

The finding of a baker able to supply the shop was more problematic. They wanted outstanding quality - not just average. Although they eventually found one who would bake to their standards, it was not ideal. It was an area that Terry thought might be a future business venture.

The grand opening was scheduled for the first Tuesday in August.

They had taken extensive advertising coverage in the Whitby Gazette, arranging for the mayor to do the opening ceremony. All the preparation paid off. Just like the Scarborough premises it took good money from day one.

Helen had expressed doubts about calling it 'The Scarborian Tea Rooms,' thinking it might upset Whitby sensibilities. However, Terry wanted the name to become a corporate identity in its own right; it certainly didn't stop people from flooding in.

Mary seemed to blossom with her new responsibility. It gave her a sense of purpose stopping her dwelling on matters of the heart. She was delighted to give Terry a tour of her finished flat when he came over to check on progress. Helen had already had input into it helping Mary choose décor and furniture.

The input of two girls was clear to see... It was very feminine, lots of pink and flowers, the bathroom being a great success. A gas boiler had been installed to provide hot water both to the flat and the kitchen downstairs.

She took him coyly into the bedroom. Light pink floral wallpaper, matching covers on the bed, teddy sitting up on the pillow. He raised his eyebrows in surprise at the fact it was a double bed.

'Who knows,' she said, looking at him with those luminescent eyes. 'I might get lucky.'

He wisely let that slip by uncommented on. The bonus scheme had been retained; being an immediate hit with staff. It was a brilliant idea, giving staff an incentive to go that bit further.

The year passed, an unqualified success for both establishments. They seemed to have a winning formula - which was more than could be said for the British army in France. The early finish to conflict that so many had originally predicted, Terry included, seemed far away. Terry was becoming increasingly vocal about the steady trickle of maimed and injured soldiers and sailors coming home and being left to fend for themselves.

'Just like it was for us when we came home from Africa.' he would tell anyone who listened. It was indeed a disturbing sight especially for those whose families were unable to support a non-worker in the family. As always, the poorest suffered the most. Any qualms Terry had about the source of his father's wealth, and the fact it had not been declared to the appropriate authority, faded away. He determined to do something to help rectify the injustice.

His chance came in the New Year of 1916. He'd had his eye on a large disused house, one of an Edwardian terrace on Whitby's Belle Vue Terrace high on the west Cliff. It had been allowed to fall into disrepair and the owner had died without leaving a will. He made enquiries of the council, explaining he was looking for a property to convert into a home for disabled ex service-men. He had the backing of an influential councillor who felt as strongly as he on the subject. With the aid of the council they managed to track the person in line to inherit the house, a man in Bradford who was happy to sell his windfall at a suitable price.

Terry and the councillor started an intensive fund raising campaign to get the house up and running. They raised sufficient cash to start the conversion in April of that year. It was completed by July with accommodation for ten men, run and staffed by enthusiastic volunteers. It was a project which gave both Terry and Helen immense satisfaction.

At this time it looked as though the Sheader business venture was unstoppable. After much discussion they had bought a rundown bakery in Scarborough. They set about making it into a small factory to supply their own premises and supply other caterers and cafes.

They found time in June of 1916 to finally tie the knot getting married at South Cliff Methodist church. The same one in which his parents had married.

This caused Mary the greatest heart ache. She agreed with good grace to be maid of honour but internally she was distraught. Jack was the best man and a select few of their friends were present including Bob Tanner his old buddy from gardening days. The Scarborough tea rooms were closed for the day which allowed them to have their reception there. It also allowed all the staff from there to attend the wedding.

It was decided to put off a honeymoon until later. They had so many plans to bring to fruition. Eventually they retired to their house on Esplanade Road where they could party into the early hours. They'd invited Mary back, asking her to stay in the spare room until morning. She certainly couldn't get back to Whitby that night. The party broke up about one am leaving the newly married couple and Helen's mother and Mary. The three of them collapsed in the lounge with hot cocoa. Helen's mother had met Mary for the first time although Helen had told her a great deal about the relationship they'd had in the past.

Mary had made a great effort for the wedding. She wore a beautiful cream dress with blue piping and a collar that emphasised her figure; it was simple but eye catching. She had blushed deeply when Terry had told her she looked stunning. Helen hugged her in delight. At the point in the service when Helen had looked into Terry's bright blue eyes and said. 'I do,' she could have collapsed. Tears rolled down her face uncontrollably. Everyone thought she was overcome with happiness for the couple. She had an intense fight to keep her feelings hidden.

Now, as the four of them sat sipping cocoa she wanted more than anything to get away. She would be in the bedroom next to the couple and dreaded what her reactions would be. Helen's mother observed her. She noticed the way she looked at Terry when she thought he was not looking, and strangely, the way she looked at her daughter.

'I think it's bed time,' said Helen as she drained her cocoa. 'To be truthful I'm shattered.' She got up and gave her mother a kiss. 'Night, night mum, thanks for all your support.'

Her mother hugged her warmly and stood up as both Terry and Mary got up. Helen turned to Mary. 'Mary, special Mary. I'm so glad you were here today love.' She said it very softly. 'Thanks for being with us,' kissing her unashamedly on the lips, lingering just a second too long.

Terry blew a kiss at Mary and Rebecca. He didn't dare kiss Mary; it wouldn't be fair on either of them. 'Night night you two,' and left the room holding Helen's hand. Mary sank shakily back onto the sofa. Her legs suddenly feeling wobbly, her reserve of control fast running out.

Rebecca was looking at her intensely; she came and sat at the side of her.

'Has that been very difficult today my love?'

'Difficult?' she stammered. 'In what way?'

'Seeing the man you're in love with marry my daughter.'

'Is it that obvious?' sobbed Mary all semblance of control evaporating.

The older woman put her arms around her hugging her tightly. 'It is to a psychic old gypsy like me,' she murmured. 'He's a man any red blooded woman could fall in love with very easily, even an old one like me. I don't know what to say to ease your pain my dear. I'm so sorry you're in this position.'

Mary curled into her as though it were her own mother. She felt a huge need to get it off her chest telling her full story haltingly and between gulps to this sympathetic mother figure. She even mentioned her attraction to Helen and the night it had gone a little too far. The older woman was a good listener stroking her hair gently as though she were a child. It helped her relieve herself of the frustrations and disappointments of the last two years.

It was turned two thirty am when the exhausted girl was led upstairs to bed by her new found mother, falling into bed and sleeping the sleep of exhaustion. Her new mother kissing her gently on the head and tucking teddy in at her side.

She had no intention of stopping anywhere overnight without teddy Terry, Especially tonight! Luckily, no sounds of exertion from the next room disturbed her. The couple were as exhausted as her and were fast asleep before Mary and her *mum* came to bed.

Two days later after Mary was back in Whitby, Helen and her mother were chatting after the evening meal while Terry worked on some figures in the little study. Rebecca mentioned the long chat she'd had with Mary on the night of the wedding and her state of distress.

'I know mum it's a long story, although it sounds as though Mary has told you a lot of it. Both Terry and I think the world of her. Truth be told we're probably both in love with her to some degree. You know what we gypsies are like! Hot blooded and passionate. At one time it almost looked as though we would become a threesome. Are you shocked?'

Her mother chuckled. 'Me? Shocked? I could tell you things that would have your hair standing on end. You young people think you've invented sex; you take after me my girl. Even at my age I could eat that man of yours.' They both laughed, mother and daughter now completely at ease with one another.

'Did she tell you we were planning for her to live here originally?' asked Helen. 'Yes, and she told me why she turned it down. It's very difficult for the girl and I'm not going to offer words of wisdom because I've no idea what the right thing is in this case.'

They left it at that. No one could see how the situation would be resolved.

*

By the end of 1916 two very successful tea rooms were running with a rapidly expanding bakery employing ten staff. The bakery was actually taking more revenue than the tea rooms as they increased the number of hotels and other catering businesses they supplied. A new development which was to assist in the running of the business was the installing of a telephone at each property including the house. It was late September when they were working madly at all premises that Terry was sounded out about becoming a Justice of the Peace.

He was taken by surprise, especially as the person who had put his name forward was one of the managers at Rowntree's restaurant.

He went for an interview at Scarborough magistrate's court. His application was forwarded to the Lord Chancellor for consideration and he promptly forgot about it.

They had a grand party on New Years day 1917. All the tea rooms were closed and staff from both tea rooms and the bakery in Whitby were invited to the party held in the Grand Hotel Scarborough. Terry hired a motor charabanc so the staff from Whitby could attend.

He announced at the party that he was in the process of opening another Scarborian Tea Rooms in the wealthy town of Harrogate to the cheers of all.

It was a joyous occasion for all. Especially for staff as it was being funded by the business. 1917 looked like being another year of success and profit for them, but an event which occurred was to cause a huge change.

It was mid-January. Terry went to Whitby for a routine visit. It had just started to snow and as the train puffed into West Cliff station a thick covering had settled. By the time he got down to the tea rooms his feet were wet and he was wishing he had some stout boots on.

Mary greeted him warmly as always. She was delighted to see him, her eyes shining like torches at his arrival. He concluded his inspection of the operation, chatting to the staff and congratulating them on the continued quality of service they offered. He believed in giving praise where due. It kept the family feeling of the business going all of them thinking they made a difference, which of course they did.

It was mid-afternoon when he was intending to depart that he was informed the train service was suspended because of heavy snow fall between Ravenscar and

Scarborough. He reluctantly had to accept he was stuck in Whitby until at least the morning. Mary immediately offered him the use of the flat. At the look on his face she said. 'You can sleep on the sofa.'

'Thanks love,' he said sheepishly. I'm well and truthfully stuck here, but would it be better if I booked into the Royal?'

'If you'd prefer that then so be it, it would be more comfortable wouldn't it?' She said, an inscrutable expression on her face.

'That sounds churlish of me doesn't it?' He said softly. 'If I stay with you can I trust myself to stay on the sofa?'

'Only you can answer that Terry.'

He nodded. 'I hope you're not offended love. I'll book into the Royal.' She said nothing, just stared into his eyes until he was the first to look away.

'Right then, I'll get up there before they say they're full up.' Still she did not reply. He gave a wry shrug, turned away and trudged through the snow towards the Royal Hotel.

Mary turned away as he left, her heart thumping as though to burst, tears pricked her eyes. He'd gone!... Well what did you expect she thought? What could you have hoped for? She went up to her flat in a mood of utter dejection.

Terry entered the entrance of the Royal. The trudge up Khyber Pass in the snow had tired him. His leg ached like mad; he signed in at the reception desk explaining who he was and his predicament.

After getting the key to a single room he asked if he may use the telephone. He needed to let Helen know where he was and why he was staying in Whitby tonight. He got the exchange girl to put him through to his home number, waiting impatiently for Helen to answer.

She answered after what seemed an age. He explained where he was and why, hoping the rail service would be restored tomorrow. Helen was silent for a moment.

'You're at the Royal?' she repeated in a flat voice.

'Yes, it's the only hotel I could think of. I'm wet and tired. I'll get a meal here and have an early night.'

'Have they a number I could call you on if anything crops up?' He knew why she was asking.

'Just a moment darling,' he turned to the receptionist. 'Would you give my wife your number please,' handing the phone to her.

She looked startled, why couldn't he do that? They did get some eccentric customers. She took the proffered instrument.

'Hello Mrs Sheader. Your husband has asked me to pass the hotel telephone details. Its quite simple, just call the switchboard and ask them to call Whitby 537, that connects directly here at reception.' She passed the telephone back to him. He held the receiver against his ear. 'Did you get that love?'

Helen's voice floated out of the earpiece sounding much happier. 'Yes, got that darling. I'm missing you, hope it will be alright for you to get back tomorrow.' 'So do I. Far too much to do than waste time here. I'll call and let you know what's happening in the morning, good night love.'

'Good night darling, love you.'

He went wearily into the restaurant and ordered a meal, not very hungry but he needed something. The look on Mary's face as he had left haunted him. He couldn't get the image out of his mind. He chewed his food listlessly when it came.

Back at the flat, Mary decided to do an easy omelette. She didn't fancy much, eating it with a slice of bread and butter and washing it down with a cup of tea.

She changed into her nightdress at eight o'clock sitting under a little electric reading lamp reading Bronte's Wuthering Heights. After half an hour her eyes started feeling heavy. She shook herself and went to look out of the window.

Fine particles of snow were still drifting down the road outside covered with a film of white. As she was about to turn from the window she saw a familiar figure approaching the tea rooms.

He was wearing the same light jacket as before, totally unsuitable for the weather and as he got nearer she saw the look of desperation on his face.

Her heart did a somersault as he looked up and saw her at the window.

He stopped, just standing in the snow looking up at her, giving a helpless little shrug after a while.

She dashed down to the door totally unconscious of only wearing her nightdress, opened it and taking him by the hand led him through the tea room to the stairs up to her flat not a word passing between them.

She almost pushed him into the flat shutting the door behind her and turning to face him with her back to the door, her chest rising and falling breathlessly.

He looked at her helplessly. 'I just had to come. I don't know what or why, I just...' He stopped with an expression of bewilderment, looking at her with arms spread. She went across to him, slipping the straps of her nightdress off and allowing it to drop to the floor. She stood before him naked.

He made a little agonised sound and then was covering her with hot kisses. Her lips, neck, breasts, stopping only to whip his coat off followed by shirt and shoes and socks. He hopped on one foot crazily. Mary grabbed at his trousers and pulled them down. He was soon as naked as her, his erection huge. Mary grasping it firmly. At last, after more than two and a half years she was actually clutching that which she had dreamed of on so many nights.

She led him into the bedroom putting a finger against his lips as he attempted to speak. Pushing him almost roughly onto the bed she fell on him like a starving tigress kissing him passionately. She ran her lips down his chest to the nest of curly hair, taking him in her mouth, her head bobbing up and down energetically. After almost being driven to ejaculation he lifted her head gently, drawing the wild girl onto the bed and rolling her onto her back. He returned the hot kisses with abandon, lowering his head to the erect nipples and sucking greedily.

She was gasping and squealing. She muttered his name over and over as he parted her legs and eased into her. He was determined to use all the technique he'd been taught to make it as good for her as possible.

His long steady strokes were sending her into ecstasy. He judged it carefully, increasing rhythm and speed as her orgasm approached, slowing slightly at the crucial point to allow it to build. Her orgasm when it arrived was like an explosion of the release of years of frustration. She gave vent to a mighty scream and shuddered like a young thoroughbred horse. Her legs were tight around him, hands clutching his buttocks. She held him tight against her.

He had no idea how long they laid like that gasping and recovering breath. Her arms were around his neck now covering him with kisses. Her eyes were wet and gleaming. 'Oh my darling, my lovely lovely man. God, how much I love you.'

Feelings of guilt swept over him. Had not Helen told him she loved him as he put the phone down on her? How had he allowed himself to be drawn into this?

His logical mind called him all the fools under the sun but logic had nothing to do with it. He knew he loved this girl in the same way he loved Helen. He had no doubt in his mind however bizarre it seemed, he was in love with two girls.

*

In Scarborough Helen lay in bed alone. A feeling of premonition swept over her. As much as she attempted to thrust the thought from her mind she was certain Terry and Mary were together. The feeling was so strong it was as though she had received a call telling her so.

*

It was eleven-thirty that night when a night porter admitted Terry back into the Royal Hotel. He'd reluctantly refused to stay the night with Mary as it would be impossible to explain his presence to staff arriving in the morning without the jungle drums going frantic. Mary had implored him to stay but even she understood the reason for him not doing so. As he was being let into the hotel she was curled up in bed with the warmest of warm glows. Her head snuggled up to teddy, she finally nodded off with a deep smile on her face.

The rail line was cleared at eleven the next morning. Two locomotives coupled together with a snow plough on the front clearing the stretch below Ravenscar. He was on the way back to Scarborough by twelve o'clock.

He'd telephoned Helen to tell her he would make his way directly to the house for a bath and change of clothes when he arrived back. Rebecca greeted him on return to the house, fussing over him and running the bath.

She giggled. 'Give me a call if you need your back washing,' said in such a way it sounded like Helen all over again.

He laughed. 'Well if I find I'm struggling I'll give you a shout.' She gave him a saucy wink. 'Fresh towels placed ready, have a good splash.'

He lowered himself into the hot water, feeling the warmth seep through his bones; he'd got thoroughly chilled on the train. Sliding down into the bath, letting the water come up to his chin he luxuriated in the warm water before applying soap. He'd just started soaping himself when the door flew open to reveal Helen, standing there breathing heavily.

'Hello love,' he said in surprise. 'I thought you'd be at the tea rooms until teatime. Nothing wrong is there?'

'You tell me that,' she replied in a savage voice. 'I suppose you're about to tell me you spent last night at the hotel bar just filling time in until bed time.'

'Well...' he started.

'Well,' she sneered. 'When I telephoned last night the receptionist said you'd just gone out, or as she said,' *putting on a posh voice.* 'Mr Sheader has just left the premises.' He wasn't a natural liar, in fact didn't think he could lie to her under any circumstances, his face gave him away every time.

Before he had chance to say a thing she continued. 'Well I knew where you'd be. I felt it last night, I just knew.' She came fully into the bathroom and knelt at the side of the bath. 'You fucked her didn't you? Went to Mary and gave her a good fucking?' This was vintage Helen. When in distress or upset she would come out with the coarse language.

'Well, didn't you? You're not going to deny it are you?'

He looked at her angry face. 'No,' he said softly, 'no I'm not going to deny it.'

'You bastard.' She slapped his face, a resounding slap that knocked his head backwards against the tap. He felt blood spurt staining the bath water, his head spinning briefly.

Helen looked in horror at what she'd done, gasping at the amount of blood seemingly changing the water red.

'Mother,' she shrieked.

Rebecca came running into the bathroom, saw the blood stained water, turned and ran out. She rushed back in shortly with the first aid kit from the kitchen.

'Sit up,' she said crisply to Terry. 'Help him,' to her daughter who seemed to have frozen. Helen reached in, putting her arms round him and helping to pull him upright. As she did so her mum pressed a wad of gauze against the wound to stem the flow of blood.

'What have I done?' moaned Helen.

'Can you stand love?' Rebecca said to him, 'let's try and get you out.' He stood up shakily. Doing so made his head swim and he tottered for a moment. Rebecca put an arm around his waist as he lifted a leg over the bath side.

'Get him into the bedroom,' she said. 'Lying down on his tummy.'

They took an arm either side as he staggered into the bedroom flopping onto the bed. Rebecca pressed the gauze against the wound again.

'Go and get a towel for God's sake Helen, cover his bottom before I smack it.' She jumped up giving her mum an evil look, mumbling to herself. 'Everyone wants to fuck him, even my own mother.'

She returned with the big fluffy towel laying it over his back. She watched as her mother removed the gauze to look at the wound, assessing how bad it was.

It wasn't that bad. A scalp cut that bled profusely. She cleaned around it with a wad of cotton wool soaked in surgical spirits and then pressed a pad of gauze on, securing it with strips of adhesive plaster.

'Get the flannel soaked in warm water,' she commanded her daughter, who did as told with a scowl. She brought it back and handed it to her mother who then cleaned his back and shoulders with great tenderness, wiping it dry with the towel.

'You enjoying that?' grumbled Helen.

'I offered to wash his back,' grinned her mum. 'This is the closest I'll get to it.'

'Can I get up?' said a weak voice from the bed.

'Yes, sit up slowly and you should be alright. I'll leave you two to get on with damaging each other. Don't turn over until I've gone, 'laughed Rebecca. 'I'm likely to get too excited.' He sat up and wrapped the towel around himself. He had a large red weal on his right cheek; he rested his back against the bed head.

'I deserved that; I'm so sorry Helen, more than I can say.'

She looked stunned not knowing what to do. Her emotion running high, tears started to flow down her cheeks.

'Are you going to leave me for her?'

'Leave you? God, of course not, not unless you want me out.'

'Want you out! No, no, no. I want you, want you for me,' she wailed.

She threw herself on him face pressed into his chest. 'I didn't mean to hurt you but at the same time I could kill you. I just knew the temptation would be too much. Stopping in Whitby, I suppose she forced herself on you?'

'No love, she didn't it just happened. We both know what effect she has on both of us, it just happened.'

'Has it happened before?' she asked dully.

'No, it hasn't this was the first and last. Don't blame Mary. It sounds vain but she's been in love with me for a long time. She's been frustrated for three years. She didn't make it hard for me but I was a willing participant. I'm to blame.' 'That's you, loyal to the end,' she said bitterly. She lifted her tear stained face to his. 'Was it good, better than I provide for you?'

'Oh Helen! Did I enjoy it, yes. I'd be lying if I said otherwise. But you and I have something special. No it wasn't better, just different. You know damn well you never have any trouble turning me on. We said long ago when I got all steamed up about you leaving me. We said we would always be honest with each other. Well I'm being honest now. I'd never leave you nor would I ever want to.'

He stroked her hair. 'You also said, very crudely, that a standing cock has no conscience. It's true.'

She gave a deep sigh. 'I've no need to talk have I? The Bottom End slag daring to expect you to behave impeccably when I've done things that I'm ashamed of. And yet you've never asked.'

'That's in the past love. Look at what we've achieved since we met. I was without hope and totally demoralised. You were the one who gave me hope, made me think that a relationship could actually happen. If you can forgive me for this, and I accept it's difficult, we can move on. Do you think you can?'

'I'm in no position to say no. It's not just the sex, I can forgive that. It was the fear that you would leave me. That I couldn't handle.'

He lifted her face and kissed her. 'That will never occur darling, never in a million years.'

A knock at the door, Rebecca's voice. 'Are you two alright in there?'

'Yes, we're fine mum; a couple of coffees wouldn't go amiss.'

'Good as done,' she called disappearing to the kitchen.

'I'll not go down to the tea rooms today, I feel a bit bashed up,' he said, a wry smile on his face.

'Serves you right for upsetting a passionate gypsy. Stop in bed and get a rest.'

She went down to her mum in the kitchen.

'I got the gist of all that,' said Rebecca. 'Mary spilled her heart out to me as you know. You can't blame her for jumping at the chance to get him in bed. Nothing worse than unrequited love and he's a red blooded man. They never say no when it's under they're noses, that's the way they're made. But I know one thing. He loves you passionately and I don't have to be psychic to see that.'

'I know he does mum. I'm jealous like any woman would be. It makes it harder because it's Mary. I don't want her hurt either. Does that sound bizarre?'

'Life can be bizarre at times love. Man makes rules but nature ignores them, carry on as before. Don't let it destroy what you have. But if he goes to Whitby again find an excuse to go with him.'

With those pearls of wisdom delivered she put three coffee mugs onto a tray and said. 'Come on,' mounting the stairs to the bedroom.

He was sitting up in bed, bare chested, head back on the head board.

Rebecca walked over to the bed. 'Here we are hunk; a coffee. You need your mother with you.' Helen sat on the side of the bed, sipping her coffee looking at him.

He grimaced at Rebecca. 'I don't suppose we've any aspirin have we?'

'I'm sure we have, I'll go and see. If you get away with nothing more than a headache today you'll have done rather well.'

'Yes mum,' he grinned, with a touch of humour.

She returned with a couple of aspirin which he quickly swallowed with a gulp of coffee. 'I'll get back to the tea rooms,' said Helen as she finished her coffee.

'Do you have to?'

'Yes, I need to be busy to unwind a bit. And I hope that headache turns into a stinker; it'll serve you right.' She grinned and stuck her tongue out at him as he made a wry face. 'See you at teatime.' She left him sitting up in bed to think things through.

Rebecca popped her head round the door as Helen departed. 'You alright Terry?'

'As right as I deserve Rebecca. What a day and all my own bloody fault.'

She smiled at him. 'Let me have a look at that head.' She came over to him and examined the back of his head. 'I think I'll change this pad, blood's seeping through. It's only a scalp wound but they can bleed a lot.' She went for the first aid box returning with scissors and a roll of adhesive plaster. She very gently removed the pad of gauze, placed a new one on that she had carefully cut to size taping it in place with plaster. 'You'll have a job explaining this tomorrow,' she chuckled. 'And if you look behind you you'll see you need a new headboard.' He twisted his head to look. 'Oh bugger.' It was smeared with blood. As it had a silk fabric covering it meant it was totally ruined. 'Does this thick head need a stitch Rebecca?'

'No love, it'll be fine. Just keep it covered until it scabs. If there's nothing you want urgently I'll go and clean the bath.' As she turned to go he said softly. 'Rebecca, do you think I'm a right bastard?' She stopped, turned and looked at him in an uncanny Helen like way. 'No love, you're just a man. They're all flawed you know,' she said with a chuckle. 'But seriously you need to sort this relationship out. Mary had a very frank talk with me on the night of the wedding. She's madly in love with you as well you know. Can't blame the lass, you'd be a fine catch for any girl. But it needs sorting to the satisfaction of all.

And if one of you is hurt in the process that's the price that has to be paid.'

Having delivered that homily she went to clean the bath leaving him with a sore head, sore conscience, and a splitting headache.

\*

The relationship between him and Helen was not destroyed. On the contrary, when she arrived home on that day she didn't even mention the incident surprisingly just asking him how his head was. He had to make up a story the following day for the benefit of staff. An attempted mugging was the best he could think of. Helen just raised her eyebrows and shook her head. It was clear he wasn't going to get too much sympathy from that quarter.

Two nights later she exhausted him with the most erotic performance in the bedroom yet. As though to say this is what you have at home, can the girl in Whitby do any better?

The next three months went like wildfire. He had to travel to Harrogate a number of times to settle negotiations on the site there, once again using the Scarborough shop fitters to do the job of conversion to a suitable standard. This one was bigger that either the Scarborough or Whitby tea rooms and he had interviews with potential staff to conduct. It was on one of the trips to Harrogate, a full day outing for him with a late return, that Helen got a telephone call from Mary.

It was only eight thirty but Mary as manager of the Whitby branch had been informed of his trip to Harrogate and progress to date. She would have known he was away early. Rebecca took the call, listened for a moment and then turned to Helen who had walked into the hall where the phone was situated.

'It's Mary, she wants to speak to you,' handing the receiver piece to her.

She picked up the phone in her right hand placing the receiver against her left ear. She was still uncomfortable with the instrument, never feeling fully confident with it.

'Hello Mary,' said cautiously. She hadn't spoken to Mary since Terry's return from Whitby on that dreadful day. Mary's voice floated into her ear faintly sounding far away. 'Helen I know Terry's in Harrogate today. Could you get over to see me here in Whitby, its important or I wouldn't ask.'

'What! Today? Now you mean?' asked Helen, startled. 'Is it an emergency?'

'Yes, yes I suppose it is, please Helen. I know you hate me now but this is important.'

Helen was silent for a while, silent for so long Mary, panic in her voice,

'Helen, are you still there?'

'Yes, I'm still here and no, I don't hate you silly girl. I just hate the situation we're in. I'll get Mr Edwards to drive me over It'll be quicker that way. I'll see you in about two hours.' She replaced the receiver on the hook and in answer to her mother's questing look. 'I'm going over to Whitby. According to Mary it's pretty urgent. If Terry phones mum, make an excuse for me please. I've a feeling this is something just between the two of us. Can you phone the tea rooms and explain I won't be in today because of business reasons?'

Rebecca phoned Mr Edwards while Helen was changing and getting ready. Edwards had set up a motor taxi business which was doing well offering a speedier ride to destinations than a horse cab.

He was pulling up to the house front in his big Daimler half an hour later.

The ride to Whitby was uneventful. They arrived at the tea rooms at ten o'clock, Helen telling Mr Edwards she

402

had no idea how long she would be. If he was prepared to wait until one o'clock and come back she would pay his time charge.

That agreed she entered the tea rooms.

Mary, in her tea maid dress and apron saw her immediately. She had a word with one of the girls and then beckoned Helen to follow her upstairs.

They mounted the stairs in silence. Mary opened the door to the flat, going in followed by Helen. As Helen closed the door behind her Mary stood in the middle of the room staring at her.

They faced each other like a couple of prize fighters for a second, and then Mary rushed across to her and threw her arms around her.

'Helen I'm so glad you've come. I thought you'd tell me to go to hell.'

Helen returned her hug. Mary led her to the sofa and they both sat together.

'I suppose Terry told you what happened?' asked Mary, her cheeks reddening. 'Yes, he did. At least when I challenged him. He was in the bath at the time. I smacked him so hard his head snapped back on the tap. I've never seen so much blood.'

Mary looked aghast. 'You hit him, split his head open? Oh no.' She put her hand to her mouth in horror.

'Don't worry it was only a cut. He's lucky I didn't cut his cock off.'

Helen again, speaking to shock, watching keenly to see what the effect on Mary would be. Mary had tears in her eyes now.

'Are you two alright now? I mean, it's not...?' Helen stopped her.

'No, we're alright. I'm the last person in the world to climb on a high moral horse but I don't know where we go from here.'

She smiled wanly at Mary. 'Anyway, what's this terribly urgent problem you want to share with me?' Mary took a deep breath, gulped, and said,

'I started being sick in the mornings a couple of weeks ago.' She paused and looked directly into Helen's eyes. She could see the realisation was already dawning on her. 'Yes, I know you've guessed. I'm pregnant.'

Helen closed her eyes her face drained of colour. For a moment Mary thought she was about to faint. She recovered and sat up straight.

'And it's definite?'

'Oh yes, I've never had a relationship with anyone else, or more to the point, sex. There was only ever one person who I wanted to have sex with. You know that Helen. The only man anyway,' she said, giving Helen a look that sent a shiver down her spine. 'What am I to do? I'll do whatever you think is right for you two. That's the least I can do to make amends.'

It was just starting to sink in with Helen. 'Oh Mary, the very thing I've never been able to give him, a child. The one thing I'd love with him, and you shag him once and you're bloody pregnant, just like that.' The last said with a touch of subdued fury.

Tears big and wet were flowing from Mary now.

'I knew you'd hate me and I don't blame you. I hate myself.'

Helen sniffed. 'A bit of Terry inside you. It's not fair is it? God, oh God, it hurts.' Mary almost threw herself on her. 'Helen, you're the last person I'd want to hurt. I'll have an abortion, anything to make it right.'

That comment really hit Helen.

'Oh no, kill Terry's baby, no Mary, we can't do that. Let me think.' She drew Mary to her. 'Is that what you want? To get rid of Terry's baby. His flesh and blood.'

'No, no,' wailed Mary. 'I don't, but I will if you wanted it. I'll do whatever you think is best Helen.'

Helen pulled Mary's head on to her shoulder.

'Let's think this through love. You can forget abortions and the like. You have to have this baby, but being in Whitby as a single mother is impossible. I think you should come back to us, have our baby at home. The

404

home you should have had with us. We can replace you here, come and live with us. Terry would want that. And he would definitely want the baby. It can be ours, all three of us.'

'Do you really mean that,' asked Mary hopefully. 'What about the objections we had before. Will it still be a problem?'

'I don't know,' sighed Helen. 'But it's the best I can think of at the moment. I'll have to break this to the master.' She grinned at Mary like of old when she said that.

'I think we can mould him into our requirements. I'll sit him down tonight and break the news.'

She looked at the expectant face of Mary, hope showing. She bent her head and kissed her tenderly. 'Perhaps this has happened for a reason. It will provide our shared love with an heir.'

Helen returned to Scarborough uplifted. The more she thought about it the more she thought it would provide Terry with the one thing she could not supply him with, and they could all share the joy of the child. Perhaps this indeed was fate and meant to be.

\*\*\*

# CHAPTER TWENTY ONE

## R.A.F. Driffield 1938

Flying officer Terence Richard Sheader shivered in the early morning dew laden air, a fine crisp day but oh so bloody cold. It was eight am and 77 Squadron was getting prepared for its open day. A day when parents and relations of serving members could see what their offspring actually did.

He was a tall handsome man with a head of thick auburn hair and keen blue eyes who had just had his twenty first birthday. He was looking forward to his father and mother, accompanied as always by Aunt Mary, visiting him on this auspicious day. The squadron would be displaying its new mount the Armstrong Whitworth Whitley bomber which they had just converted to.

It seemed a huge machine after the single engined Vickers Wellersley he'd flown at RAF Finningley.

His machine, only two months old, was standing outside the hanger with fitters and mechanics swarming over it. They were preparing the machine for later when three of them would fly in formation for the benefit of the expected spectators.

He took a deep breath of the cold air. He loved seeing the airfield come to life; flying was his passion. It had been ever since his father Sir Terrence Sheader JP had treated him to a flight with Sir Alan Cobham on one of his barnstorming tours of Britain.

He allowed his mind to wander, thinking of how lucky he was in having parents who were so modern in their outlook. It was true his father was disappointed when he declared he really wanted to join the Royal Air Force. He almost as a right expected him to follow into the family business. His father had created a catering empire in the north of England and been knighted in 1924 for his continuing work supporting disabled servicemen.

Three Helen Sheader Homes for the disabled now existed, named after his feisty mother who ran them hands on. Aunty Mary who had lived with them all his life was almost like a second mother. In fact at times he was almost tempted to call her mum. She fussed over his every need to the point of embarrassment and was worried sick when he first asked his father if he could take flying lessons. Fortunately his father was a very modern man in outlook who believed no one should have their future pre-mapped. He told Tets, as everyone referred to him from school onwards, that although he would love him one day to take over the family business, it was his choice in life that mattered.

He had enormous respect and admiration for his father who had told him he had made the great mistake of falling out with his own father, only realising his mistake when it was too late. Thus he bent over backwards in his relationship with his own son.

He'd been filled with pride when he obtained his private flying licence at the age of eighteen. His father drove him to Sherburn-in-Elmet every Saturday in the big Rolls Royce for his lessons. They were usually accompanied by his mother and Aunty Mary. He couldn't recollect ever being anywhere, on holiday or whatever when Aunty Mary was not there. They would have picnics on the grass and waved as he took off in the Tiger Moth.

The day he took off solo was a moment he would recall for ever. Zooming down the grass strip and kicking the rudder to keep the machine straight, and then soaring into the sky. Just him and the burble of the Gypsy engine; he and only he in control.

After returning to earth highly elated he'd been mobbed by his delighted parents. Aunty Mary had hugged him and kissed him with abandon, her eyes wet with tears of joy. He'd found it a little disturbing. Like most young men of that age girls and the thought of girls occupied a lot of his time. Aunty Mary was a good twenty years younger than mum and dad at least, or so she seemed. And she was slim with auburn hair that had still to see a grey strand.

As older women went she was quite attractive. Her enthusiastic hugging and kissing left him a little hot under the collar. Mum and dad of course looked as all mums and dads should, old!

His thoughts were interrupted by the coughing bark of the port Tiger engine of his machine starting. A puff of blue smoke followed by a steady beat as the fitter checked oil pressure and mag drop. It was followed by the starboard engine starting, and then a bellow as both engines were run up to maximum revs, the sound reverberating from the hanger walls.

The entire machine quivered as though alive. He never failed to thrill at the sight. This big powerful aeroplane was his, allocated to him and his crew, with two powerful engines, not one as all aircraft he'd flown previously had. This was the height of modernity.

The entire station personnel had contributed to today's events. The ground staff had worked unceasingly to make stalls to display items for sale, all proceedings being donated to the RAF Benevolent Fund.

Terry and his crew and the crew of three other bombers would conduct a group take off, flying in formation overhead to let spectators on the ground obtain a good view of the RAF's latest bomber. Chosen members of the public and visiting VIP's would then be allowed a tour of the machines.

He'd joined the RAF only eight months after obtaining his private flying licence, starting his initial training at RAF Finningley in South Yorkshire, a newly created station.

Like most young men his initial wish was to be a fighter pilot, but he realised his real fascination was with large aircraft. The larger the better, and he applied for attachment to a bomber squadron.

He was successful and joined 215 Squadron; learning the technique of flying a twin engined machine on the ubiquitous Avro Anson the RAF's maid of all work. He also spent some time flying the Vickers Wellesley. It was a rather dated bomber with a single Bristol Pegasus radial engine and an enormous wing span of 74 feet. It was a pleasant enough aeroplane to fly but the performance left a lot to be desired.

215 Squadron was eventually broken up into two. 77 Squadron being one of the new squadron's formed from it, hence his posting now at Driffield.

His father had phoned yesterday from Scarborough to say they would be arriving at approximately lunch time. The flying display was scheduled for two pm. This was his chance to show his parents how he could handle the big Whitley bomber. He wandered over to his aeroplane as the engines coughed and spluttered to a stop. Flight sergeant Rowlings; the man in charge of maintenance was just climbing out of the machine. A grizzled veteran who was close to retirement he was never the less a superb fitter. His knowledge of his flock was second to none. He threw a salute at Terry as he approached.

'All systems OK flight?'

'As right as they'll ever be sir.' The old veteran gave him a cheeky grin. 'Hope you don't break it sir.'

Terry laughed. 'I'll try not to Flight; my parents will be here this afternoon. Don't want them to see me put up a black eh?'

He left the ground crew to get on with their jobs walking over to the briefing room to find the rest of his four crew mates. They were already a closely knit team.

At the age of twenty one he was the oldest member. His bomb aimer was the next in age at twenty; navigator and radio operator were both nineteen and the rear gunner eighteen and a half.

Briefing was scheduled for ten so he mooched into the canteen for a cuppa first, getting instant respect from his crew when he stood the cost.

He was particularly looking forward to seeing his parents. The last visit he'd made home was two months ago. He still found the new house on Filey Road alien. His father had bought it in 1937 after he had entered RAF service. The old house on Esplanade Road to him was home, this new one although being much bigger just didn't feel like home yet.

Strangely, although it had six bedrooms Aunty Mary still had the one next to his parents. As indeed she had done in the old house. It even had a connecting door which he thought rather bizarre but dad had always said she suffered with her nerves at times and they needed to be close to her.

The sun had finally come out burning the earlier chill off.

As eleven thirty approached he felt elated seeing the familiar black and yellow Rolls Royce turn into the designated parking area. He strolled across the grass to meet them, his father being the first to alight. He leaned on the stick in his left hand, the left leg giving some problems these days.

He was still a handsome man. Hair now pure silver but retaining his fine physique, partly by playing golf as much as possible.

His mother gave him a cheery wave, her black hair now sprinkled with silver. Approaching her fifty eighth year she still had a trim figure and fine features. She rushed over to him. 'Hello darling, you look so handsome in that uniform. How are you?'

'Fine thanks mum. It's good to see you,' as she gave him a warm hug.

His father grinned and held out his hand.

'Good to see you lad. I'm looking forward to this, that's one heck of a mean looking machine of yours.'

'Yes, it's a tough bird dad. I'm looking forward to showing you around after the display.' He turned to the third figure who had alighted from the car, his Aunty

Mary. 'Hello my boy,' she said eyes shining. 'You cut a very handsome figure.'

She gave him a warm hug.

'You look as pretty as a picture aunt,' he replied. 'We could be brother and sister, we share the same hair,' he laughed. He caught a glance that passed momentarily between her and his father which was puzzling.

'There are three of you in the display then?' His father asked quickly.

'Yes, myself, Paddy Thomas and Smudger Smith.' He laughed at the expression on his father's face. 'As you see we've all got nicknames. I'm afraid I'm Tets Sheader.'

'Ah, here's the adjutant Flight Lieutenant Robinson,' as Robinson approached them. 'May I introduce my parent's sir, Sir Terrence and Lady Sheader.'

Robinson shook hands with them both.

'Pleased to meet you Sir Terrence, Lady Sheader,' he turned to Mary. 'And this is my aunt Miss Duncan.'

Robinson took in the attractive woman before him. 'I'm very pleased to meet you Miss Duncan.'

An enigmatic smile hovered on his father's face.

Terry led his parents and Mary to the officer's mess. He'd arranged in advance for them to have lunch there. It was pretty full of excited chatter from the airmen; the other VIP's already being there including the Driffield mayor and his wife.

His father was soon engaged by an officer, questions and answers flowing freely. His mother was chatting to a large lady on her right with some sort of badge of office around her neck. Mary sat close to him, a little too close he thought.

'Have you heard all this talk about Germany,' she asked, looking at him in a disturbing way. 'Mr Churchill keeps banging on about it in the press saying we need to re-arm quickly. Is that what your new aeroplanes are about?'

'Oh old Churchill's been stirring for ages he's a bit of a warmonger. No, these new machines are just the latest type that's all. The RAF is always trying to improve our aircraft just to keep up with the rest of the world.'

'I'd hate to think you could ever be in danger in one of those things,' she said huskily. 'Promise me you'll never do anything rash; look after yourself.'

He felt quite touched; the way she was looking at him sent a little shiver down his spine. 'Of course I will. It's rather good fun you know being paid to do what you love; its big toys for big boys aunt.'

'You're not a boy now though are you? You're a handsome young man. You look so much like your father did at your age; you have his good looks.'

He looked around desperately for salvation; this was getting a bit too heavy.

'Ah Smudger, come and meet my aunty.' 'Aunty this is Smudger Smith. He'll be flying that clapped out old crate alongside me in the demonstration.'

'Hey steady on old boy, that old crate is my pride and joy.' He turned to Mary. 'Hello Sheader's aunty.' He shook hands with her. 'This cad never told me he had a very pretty aunt tucked away. Does he keep you all to himself?'

Mary laughed at this ridiculously young looking airman with a smattering of freckles across his nose. 'You're very gallant Smudger; I'm pleased to meet you. I'm looking forward to seeing you all in the air.'

Any further flirting from the cheeky young man was halted by the station commander Alan Lees standing up and announcing, 'Ladies and Gentlemen. After lunch our station adjutant will escort you to the viewing area. I offer a warm welcome to you all and hope you find the visit interesting. Of course, because any monies raised are in aid of the RAF benevolent fund I urge you to spend spend spend at the various stalls.' Laughter all round. 'Enjoy your lunch and I will see you all at the viewing area.'

They did indeed enjoy the lunch, an affable affair which passed quickly. They were soon trooping out to the viewing area thankful the British weather on this occasion was being kind.

I'll see you all after the flight,' he said to Mary and his parents, trotting off to his waiting machine.

As they were only flying a short overhead display there was no need for the gunners. His wireless operator, Grumpy Grunfield and navigator, Wally Walpole only would be accompanying him.

He climbed up into the pilot's seat on the left of the cockpit; the fitters had the battery trolley plugged in. At a wave of his hand to let them know he was starting the engines he pressed the button for the port engine. The propeller turned jerkily a couple of revolutions before the engine roared into life, a gust of blue smoke blowing back in the slipstream.

He repeated the procedure with the starboard engine letting both engine's warm up and settle to a steady rumble.

Ahead of him Squadron Leader Barnoldswick had his machine ticking over, and behind, Smudger was starting his. They would take off in line astern, form up into a vic and conduct three passes of the airfield.

The radio receiver in his ear crackled as the control tower gave permission to taxi. As Barnoldswick's machine started to move he gave the sign to the ground crew to whip the chocks away, advanced his throttles and followed the machine in front.

It was a rather clumsy aircraft to manoeuvre on the ground. He was highly conscious of the forty foot of wing either side of his cockpit although the view forward was decent.

Barny up in front had turned onto the runway and lined his machine up. The big propellers were whipping a dust storm back at him. A green flare shot up in the air and Barny's machine started to accelerate away. Terry turned onto the runway, aligned his machine and then opened the throttles wide.

The big machine surged forward, Terry kicking on the rudder bar to counteract the swing to port as they accelerated down the runway.

A slight forward touch on the stick to get the tail in the air and then with a minor touch in the opposite direction they were lifting off, the sudden loss of wheel rumble very noticeable.

Sitting in the viewing area Mary clenched her hands anxiously as Terry's bomber lifted off, watching its progress avidly.

The time from her little baby boy growing up to this handsome young man, showing such competence as an airman seemed so short. She could remember every milestone in his development as though it were yesterday.

Helen, like Mary, breathed out slowly as the bombers climbed away. She only realised now that she'd been holding her breath as they flew down the runway.

Terry senior watched them dwindle to three spots in the distance pride swelling his breast. He remembered the day vividly when Helen had returned home with the news from Whitby.

He certainly hadn't expected the proposition Helen had laid before him. He was expecting histrionics from her when she broke the news of Mary's pregnancy.

Instead she was excited about a baby in the family. Her family as she saw it.

The pregnancy joined them as one in her eyes. She'd been horrified when Mary had mentioned an abortion and deeply moved when she said she was prepared to take that action if it was best for Helen and him.

In the event, Terry had agreed with alacrity to the idea of Mary moving in with them. He knew what the status of an unmarried mother was. They made plans immediately to officially adopt Mary's unborn child as their own with Mary having full shared care of the child.

Roberto Manfredi, who was doing so well in the tea rooms, was promoted to the manager of the Whitby business, getting the flat as part of his contract.

It worked remarkably smoothly. Mary's desire for a ménage a trois had moved closer to reality!

There was no doubt that the birth of a baby boy brought them all closer together. The little chap came upon the scene on the 16th of August 1917.

It was the desire of both Helen and Mary to call him after his father and Terry suggested adding Richard in memory of his father.

He was christened in South Cliff Methodist Church on the 3rd of October, Mary taking on the role of god mother.

Rebecca was equally delighted. She loved helping with nursing care when the two women were involved in the business, taking the baby and pram for strolls on the Esplanade in fine weather. She turned a very broad minded eye when Mary moved to the bedroom adjoining her daughter and her husband. She had a shrewd idea how the relationship was developing between the three bearing in mind what both Helen and Mary had confided in her before.

When Terry employed a builder to fit an adjoining door between the rooms it clinched what she thought.

It was their business, nothing to do with her and the bloom that had returned to Mary's cheeks seemed to point to that particular young woman being very happy with her lot.

Helen also seemed contented and happy. Her relationship with the younger woman had taken on a new dimension. Rebecca would often catch the two exchanging glances and grins that suggested deeper meaning than the look itself signified.

Terry was appointed to the Scarborough Magistrates bench in 1918 just three months before the end of the war. He became heavily involved in his role being a great believer in the rule of law applying it firmly and fairly.

He delegated more work to his appointed managers as the catering side of the business grew, spending happy hours with his new son and his son's two mothers.

It was a moment of family unity when Terry junior started school in 1922, another milestone passed.

Helen was spending more time with the homes they'd established for disabled servicemen. Like her husband, she'd developed a passion for the plight of the men who had received life changing injuries but were then left to fend for themselves.

Not only did they open three homes eventually but put a lot of effort into fund-raising for charities connected with ex-servicemen, culminating in Terry's knighthood in 1927.

All three of them travelled to London, another first, for the investiture, spending three nights in the capitol sightseeing after his appointment with the King.

Terry junior went to Queen Ethelburga's college near Boroughbridge at the age of eleven. A private boarding school with an outstanding record of excellence.

The young man thrived growing up into the well rounded adult that was today flying the RAF's latest bomber.

Mary, who'd been allowing reminiscences to float through her mind, was brought back to the present with a jolt as the three aeroplanes flew back over the airfield in a low pass, flying in a vee formation with her son on the left side.

The roar of six powerful engines thrilled the crowd as they flew past in close formation, pulling up at the end of the runway to gain height.

They came back at medium height flying slowly with the bomb doors open allowing the crowd a view of what they were designed for.

By the time they came in to land the spectators were chattering excitedly the display having been hugely successful.

All three machines taxied back to the hard standing in front of the hangers, the propellers jerking to a halt as the engines were switched off.

Terry junior walked over to the three as he alighted from the machine. He looked dashing in flying overalls his leather helmet swinging nonchalantly.

Mary could feel tears pricking her eyes. He looked so much like his father at the same age. The same muscular build and rugged good looks, the blue eyes bewitching.

'Would you like to come and look at my bus?' he called as he approached them.

His father jumped at the chance walking back to the aeroplane proudly with his son. The two women followed taking delight in seeing the closeness of the two in front. A small pair of wooden steps had been placed at the door on the rear left of the fuselage. Tets didn't mention it but he'd had them made especially for this visit. He was conscious of his father's leg but didn't want to embarrass him by it being difficult for him to climb into the machine.

Terry was like an excited child being given the chance to scramble, with some difficulty, up the narrow fuselage to the cockpit and sitting in the pilot's seat.

He waved with a huge grin on his face to the two women looking up. They, in turn, waving excitedly back.

Tets pointed out the various controls and allowed his dad to push and pull the control column which he did with great enthusiasm.

The two women were given the same conducted tour after his father. Mary found it more than a little claustrophobic. It seemed much smaller inside than it looked from the outside.

The day passed highly successfully both for the proud young airman, his parents, and the RAF benevolent fund which raised a worthwhile sum.

Tets assured his parents that he had a four day leave at Christmas starting Christmas Eve and he would be coming home for the holiday.

The intervening months were spent getting the squadron up to efficiency on the new aircraft. They practised bomb aiming over the North Lincolnshire coast and mastered the intricacies of navigation. Particularly the salient points in Europe as they were all aware now of the rising tensions on the continent.

Christmas Eve came remarkably quickly. The flying and training after the open day was intensive. Tets was more than ready for the break.

His father picked him up from the railway station at lunch time the big Rolls Royce causing some interest in the station forecourt.

It was an uncomfortable feeling for Terry waiting on the platform seeing the train disgorge so many men in uniform. He had a not again sense of it all being a repeat of the earlier conflict. Would mankind never learn from history?

The tall figure of his son jumping down from the carriage lifted his heart. He looked incredibly fit and strong, kit-bag slung over his shoulder waving to his dad.

It was difficult for the casual observer to decide which of the two men was the most excited. Laughter and questions flowed between them in a torrent of words as Terry led his son out to the car.

It was an excited pair who arrived at the big house on Filey Road, watched as they turned into the drive by two mums and a remarkably fit looking grandmother.

Mary and Helen were out of the house before the car rolled to a stop, throwing themselves at Tets like an unstoppable tidal wave. He was smothered with kisses from both sides, his gran standing in the doorway awaiting her turn.

He wallowed in the display of affection. He'd always been grateful for the love he'd received as an only child. The feeling of being so loved could at times be a little overbearing but it made him a compassionate and well rounded adult.

His seventy five year old gran allowed the excitement to die a little before giving him a warm hug. She reminded him so much of an older version of his mother, a person he could always confide in when he needed a bit of advice that may have been embarrassing asking a parent. She was incredibly wise and non judgemental; and very good at keeping a confidence.

It was his gran who insisted in relieving him of his kit-bag, taking it up to his room. His mum bustled him into the lounge for a light lunch and hot 'cuppa.'

He spent most of the afternoon regaling them all with stories of the squadron progress, what he thought of the situation in Germany and mentioning they were to receive an improved version of the Whitley shortly.

His father was amazed at that bit of information. 'A new version? 1ou've only just taken delivery of the ones you have now.'

'They're not new in aircraft terms dad. They were ordered straight off the drawing board and put into production. The development is always ongoing especially in the light of feedback from squadrons. There's nothing like using a piece of equipment to highlight any changes needed.'

'That's enough of shop talk,' said his mother. 'Have you found a girlfriend yet?'

He laughed, 'trust you mum. 'Do you want to see me married off?'

'Well,' she said. 'It's not normal for a healthy young man not to have someone in the pipe line. Are you still...?' Terry stopped her in full flow.

'I hope you weren't about to ask the lad if he'd had you know what, yet? Really Helen!'

Mary was sitting forward on her seat listening intently.

'You were about to ask if I was still a virgin mum I take it?'

'Sorry love,' she said grinning. 'You know what I'm like. Didn't mean to embarrass you pet.'

'Well you can rest easy mum. I'm perfectly normal thank you.'

'Oh, does that mean you have, oh God! You have haven't you, hell, do we know her?'

'Helen, that's enough. He's twenty one for goodness sake. You don't start telling your mother about intimate details at that age.'

His mother subsided into the chair; I want to know written all over her face but maintaining her silence. His gran bless her, gave him a broad wink and smile. She knew but would keep his secret.

They chattered happily around a blazing fire. The three women had made the room sparkle with a tall Christmas tree dominating the room. Glass baubles twinkled as they caught the light, coloured paper streamers festooning the ceiling. It brought a smile of delight and a flood of memories of Christmas's past to see the clockwork Santa on the hearth. It had been bought when he was only three. A large key projected from the back and when wound the Santa would nod his head and the bag on his shoulder would jiggle up and down.

As a child he'd spent hours playing with it. It was amazing that it still remained in working order.

His father snapped him out of his reverie. 'Did you get a single ticket at the station as I asked?'

'Yes, I did dad but it's an easy trip you know. I don't like putting you to the trouble of driving to Driffield.'

'No trouble lad. I've got special transport arranged for your return.' He gave him a wink. 'A Christmas surprise.'

'I hope it's gorgeous dancing girls pulling a sled then', he laughed. 'That would suit mum.' His mother stuck her tongue out at him cheekily, Mary giggling at the remark. He caught his gran's eye again, a glance passing between them.

When he'd been in the last year of boarding school he'd had a crush on a girl called Sylvia who was the daughter of the school caretaker. The interest had been reciprocated, and for a while they had illicit meetings which added to the excitement, although the school was out of bounds to members of the opposite sex. At the age of seventeen he'd spent most of these get togethers with an almighty erection which she was more than happy to relieve by masturbation.

It was during term time spent at home that his wise gran picked up on the love lorn symptoms, and after a while he confided in her his love for Sylvia.

She knew all that would be likely to follow at that age away from home and knew it would resolve itself one way or another. But on the day he was due back at college the worldly old girl slipped him two packets of Durex, telling him to take all precautions. She gave him a kiss goodbye with a broad wink.

It was good sound advice. Both young people had their first full sexual encounter that final term but with safety. The contents of the packets caused much mirth. Sylvia insisted on the fitting of the little rubber items, sheer eroticism in itself!

The romance didn't survive after he left college, but he'd had his first sexual encounter and gran was well aware of it!

He often wondered after that episode in his life how gran had purchased the useful items without embarrassing herself. He really would have to ask one day.

Dinner that night was a wonderful family affair. The lights sparkled in the big chandelier, a roaring log fire, followed afterwards by glasses of sherry.

Oh how sherry had played its part in this family! His father settled in *his* chair at the side of the fire. Rebecca and Helen sat side by side on the two seat settee. Mary joined him on the other settee.

Tets had no idea how many times his glass had been replenished, but his head had that slightly swimming sensation that went with a drop too much.

They'd settled into comfortable chat covering all the subjects under the sun.

Tets turned to Mary. 'I'm surprised you've never married aunt. Have you never had a boy friend?' He would never have been so personal if not for the sherry!

421

Mary started at his direct question looking just a little uncomfortable. She didn't answer at first, just looking up at him with mesmerising green eyes.

After an uncomfortable pause she said. 'Do you think your aunt is a dried up old prune?' He blushed. 'I'm sorry aunt that was a real black wasn't it? Must be the sherry talking. No, you're certainly no prune. More like a juicy plum.'

Ha gave her his most winning smile hoping to retrieve the situation, not realising the chatter around had ceased and they were all listening avidly.

'Well, you've asked the question so I'll tell you. I have a secret boyfriend.'

His eyebrows shot up in surprise. 'Oh wow! Do mum and dad know him?'

He heard his dad splutter into his sherry glass.

'Your dad's known him for ever. He's called Bruce but for our own reasons we prefer to keep the relationship as it is.'

'You mean he's never been here? Never visited?'

'Oh he's slipped in the back door once or twice.'

There was the sound of breaking glass as his father dropped his glass on the hearth. 'Oh bugger,' he exclaimed. 'Exactly,' said his mother.

The room was starting to sway slightly; he knew the signs. Hard drinking in the mess always producing this feeling. 'Oh, I say. I think I should head for a landing before crashing.' He stood grabbing the settee arm as he staggered. 'Sorry about this. Flying a little left wing low.'

Mary laughed relieving the situation. 'Come on big boy let's get you to bed. I'm feeling just a little tiddly myself. You're going to have a thick head in the morning.' 'Oh I never suffer from hang over's aunt, quite immune to those,' he giggled. 'Night mum and dad, got to go into hanger.'

There was a chorus of goodnights from them as he left the room Mary hanging onto his arm and steering him in the right direction.

He mounted the stairs in a zigzag giggling all the way, Mary guiding him into his room.

He flopped onto the bed. 'Well, you are a dark horse aunt. Crikey, all this time with a secret lover. I am impressed.' She laughed at him; her own face had a great deal of colour. 'I'm glad you don't think I'm an old prune. Night night, see you at breakfast. That's if you can make it.'

'My darling aunt that's a date.'

He crashed back onto the bed and felt his eyes fluttering. The last thing he remembered before sleep overtook him was the sound of uproarious laughter from downstairs.

He woke up at two am desperately needing to go to the toilet. He tiptoed to the bathroom feeling more than a bit unsteady. Passing his aunt's room he noticed the door was ajar. Purely on impulse he peeped round the door. The bed could just be made out in the gloom. It seemed to be empty!

Had she gone downstairs for a drink? Was she an insomniac?

It seemed very strange; however the toilet need was calling. He completed his business and walked slightly unsteadily back to his room.

He didn't surface after that until ten in the morning, waking with a raging thirst, but as he had told his aunt with a clear head.

The sound of voices downstairs indicated he was probably the last up. Completing his wash and shave in record time he wandered down to the source of the chatter which was in the dining room.

He poked his head round the door to a chorus of merry Christmas's. Mary said chortling. 'The drunkard is up. How's your head darling?'

'Its fine thanks. I wasn't drunk - just a little woozy.' A chorus of laughter greeted that. 'Did you sleep alright?' asked his father.

'Yes, absolutely fine, more so than you aunt. I looked in during the early hours seeing your door open. Couldn't you sleep?'

'Oh I often go down and make a drink, not such a good sleeper.'

'As long as you weren't going down to let this secret lover in,' he laughed.

She gave him a coy look. 'You're being very naughty young man. I wouldn't tell you in any case, but I can assure you for your peace of mind that he didn't get in last night.'

His gran came in at that point and asked him if he would like a cooked breakfast.

'Oh super gran; that sounds just the ticket.'

'A drop of sherry hasn't put you off your food then?' That comment from his mother.

'Never, it would take something pretty dire to do that.' He followed gran into the kitchen missing the grin that went from his father to the two women.

He sat at the kitchen table for a good old fashioned fry up, his gran sitting at the opposite side chatting happily to him.

'Have you seen this secret boyfriend of Aunt Mary's then gran?' He asked.

'No, I haven't dear but I'd quite like to see him. Just to vet him you understand.'

Her tone of voice made him look up. It was almost as though she was trying to hold a chuckle back.

'Gran,' he said quite annoyed. 'I get a feeling that everyone is having some sort of joke with me. Is there something going on that I'm not aware of or not privy too?' 'Darling boy, you ask far too many questions.

let's enjoy Christmas. Get that food down. We can't start opening presents until you're ready.'

'Oh crikey is everyone waiting for me?'

'Well who else? Lazing in bed half the day while your poor old gran slaves in the kitchen.' She ruffled his hair fondly. He had a huge fondness for her; she had always been available when growing up. Someone whom he could confide in when it would have been embarrassing to talk to parents.

He'd steadfastly refused any financial help from his father when he joined the Royal Air Force saying it would be good to learn to stand on his own two feet.

His father respected him for that, but it did mean he had few funds for buying presents although he had little opportunity for shopping in any case.

He had the squadron's motto beautifully coloured and mounted on a plaque for his father. A super job which had been lovingly crafted by his ground crew to his eternal gratitude. He had found a row of pearls in an antique shop in Driffield which he knew his gran would love. A pearl encrusted handbag for mum and something which he thought Aunt Mary would love.

He wandered into the lounge after shooting back upstairs to retrieve the presents from his kit-bag.

'That feels better, a good fry up is always the answer to a night of drinking,' he announced with a grin. 'Merry Christmas everyone. At least I'm not merry now.'

'Pleased to hear it my boy. Come and join us for the opening of presents. I'm not sure who's the most excited, me or these two.' Bubbly laughter all round. How lucky he was to have family like this. He gazed at them all fondly; he'd heard awful accounts from some of his colleagues about family rifts and feuds. Nothing like that had ever blighted his life.

He gave his presents out. Dad, as he expected was delighted with his squadron shield. It went immediately on the mantelpiece. Mum and gran were both delighted with theirs. It was the reaction from Aunty Mary which took him by surprise.

He'd found a gorgeous teddy bear in Driffield. It took his eye straight away and when he got it back to the airfield he had one of the canteen ladies make a leather jacket and flying helmet for him. It was completed by a pair of goggles, made once again by resourceful ground staff.

'I rather thought this was just right for you aunty,' he said, presenting it to her.

Mary took the paper wrapped soft bundle from him with a questing look. When she opened it her face registered a multitude of emotions.

'Oh!' She gasped. 'Oh darling, it's lovely it's such a gorgeous bear.' Her eyes were brimming with tears. 'It reminds me so much of another bear which was bought by someone special. Now I've got two that both mean so much. Oh thank you darling.' She threw her arms around him giving him a crushing hug, kissing his cheek and leaving wetness behind.

Once again he caught a look exchanged between his father and mother. He was beginning to believe there were family secrets of some sort that he was not privy to.

His aunt's reaction to his present seemed a little extreme, and she mentioned another bear of which he had no inkling. He'd never heard her mention a bear during all the time he'd known her.

'Am I missing something here? You've all been exchanging glances surreptitiously. If it's a secret that I'm not privy to please say so, but it's getting rather annoying being excluded from whatever it is.'

'I'm sorry darling,' said his aunt. 'We forget you're not our little boy anymore. Yes, you're right; there is a family event you have no knowledge of. Sit down and I'll explain.'

His father butted in with concern in his voice. 'If this is going to be painful to you I'm sure Terry will understand if you keep it.' Mary stopped him with a hand on his arm. 'No, he's old enough to know now.' She turned to Tets who had seated himself at the side of gran.

'When I was very young darling, seventeen in fact I suffered a horrendous attack from a fisherman I knew. You'll be horrified to know I had in fact had a fling with him, what you nowadays would call a one night stand.'

426

She gave him a wan smile. 'So you see I haven't always been a prune.'

'Unfortunately at a later date he attacked me and forced himself on me in a vile way. He even assaulted me physically after that which caused me much pain.'

'You don't have to,' started Tets.

'No, it's alright dear its time you knew. Well, after this attack I was in a bad way. Your mum and dad were the ones who took me in and looked after me. One of the things that lifted me up when I was at my lowest was your mum and dad buying me a teddy to cheer me up. I still have him; he sleeps with me most nights. You buying me a teddy is almost like a repeat of the past and touched me immeasurably. Thank you again darling he'll be great company for teddy Terry.'

'Teddy Terry?'

She laughed. 'Yes I called him after your father as he bought him for me. He's been a constant companion through the years.'

Tets sat back in his chair. 'Oh wow aunty, I didn't mean to put you through all that,' and then as the thought hit him.

'Did they get this swine who attacked you?'

'It's a very long story darling. In the end he was blown to smithereens by an unexploded shell from the attack on Scarborough in 1914. It almost killed your father too but we'll tell you that story some other time. Its time for your Christmas present.'

He looked at his aunt in a different light now. Obviously there was a lot more he didn't know, and after what she'd said about being saved by his parents what actual relation was she to the family? He'd simply accepted her as Aunty Mary all his life never for one moment asking who she was related to.'

His mother broke into his confused thoughts. 'Come on my lad. We decided to get you a joint present from all of us so if you'd like to follow your dad he'll show you what we've got.' He stood up, lots of questions floating round in his head now but deciding to leave it to later.

Mary took his hand as they followed his father, giving it a quick squeeze and giving him one of her green eyed looks. His father walked out of the house making Tets wonder what was in store. They followed him as he took them down the side drive to the big double garage, inserting a key into the door and throwing them wide.

Tets eyes widened in surprise. At the side of his father's Rolls was a two seat sports car beautifully finished in British racing green.

'There you are my lad,' said his father proudly. 'We thought it time you had some transport of your own. A car with a bit of performance. It's a Frazer Nash TT Replica. Six cylinder model with four speed gear box.'

His mouth dropped open. 'Good God, that's magnificent dad what a machine. I don't know what to say to you all. Thank you sounds a little feeble, oh what a beauty.' His aunt was still holding his hand. 'I take it you like it darling?' She looked up at him eyes shining.

'Like it! Its absolutely wizard. I'll be the envy of all the chaps on the station. Thanks again all of you. Dad you must have spent a fortune.'

'It was well worth while lad,' said his father giving his son a lingering look. 'I can't begin to tell you how incredibly proud of you we all are. Happy Christmas son.'

'I bag's the first ride,' said gran with a huge grin that created laughter all round. 'You can be the first gran. I promise you that,' he laughed.

'No time like the present,' said his father producing the key from his waistcoat pocket. He gave it to Tets. 'Go and start her up lad.'

He sat in it gingerly familiarising himself with the controls. Just as he would with a new type of aeroplane, spending some time doing so. When satisfied he knew where everything was, he pulled the choke knob out three quarters of the way, switched the ignition on and pressed the starter button.

The six cylinder Blackburne engine roared into life with a throaty crackle, sounding every inch the sports machine it was. He inched it out of the garage onto the drive, stopping and engaging the hand brake. 'Come on gran. Hop in.'

The game old lady did just that to the laughter and encouragement of all waving gaily as they headed out of the drive and onto the open road.

He turned left into Filey Road and headed towards Cayton Bay, the road which went all the way to Bridlington. The car accelerated rapidly. The feel of all that 'oomph' and wind in the hair was highly exhilarating.

He got the feel of it very quickly. The polished wood rim of the steering wheel slid through his hands as though he'd handled it for ages.

'Yippee,' yelled gran causing him to laugh at her spirit. What a star she was.

He drove all the way to the Bay turning back to come through the villages of Cayton and Osgodby on his way back to the house.

The journey was repeated twice with his father and mother before getting Aunty Mary into the passenger seat.

He set off to repeat the same tour, her face glowing in the cold air. 'I hope I didn't cause too much anguish for you aunty asking all those questions. I'm afraid I can be a bit impulsive at times.'

'No darling. I'm sure there are many questions you want to ask. I could see it in your eyes; you have a right to know. When we get a chance to be alone I'll tell you as much as possible. I just hope you will be as non-judgemental as your father.'

'Non-judgemental, that sounds as though you're suggesting we have skeletons in the cupboard.'

'Life can be very awkward at times. It throws up all sorts of different challenges. How we meet them is down to us all as individuals. I've nothing I'm ashamed of but I certainly did things that the purists might frown on.

However, the outcome suited us all and that's all that matters.'

'When you say us all, are you referring to mum dad and you?'

'Yes, the way we've lived together since. And your gran as well of course. There's so much you don't know about darling. You'll just have to be patient.'

They were heading back towards home. So much he wanted to ask. Why had it taken him so long to suddenly start wondering about his family and his roots?

'Will I ever get to meet this Bruce aunty?'

'No darling you won't. Don't ask again. That's my business and mine alone.'

'Oh I'm intruding again. I'm sorry aunt its just all so confusing. It must be the age I'm at. A sudden desire to know about my family and my roots that you never think of when younger. Am I explaining myself or making things worse?'

'I understand darling. I promise I'll tell you more when the opportunity arises, ah! Here we are.'

They were approaching the house putting paid to any further probing. If anything he was more confused than before. He had a feeling he'd started to open a can of worms.

The opportunity to probe any further never happened prior to his return to Driffield. The rest of his leave was full of good cheer food and family chatter, but no chance to corner his aunt on her own and he was convinced she was the one to tell him more.

Driving back to Driffield was exhilarating in the car, almost as much fun as flying. The car had a good turn of speed and handled well, the wind blowing through his hair as though in an open cockpit. He did the journey in record speed.

He would get no home leave now for three months. New Year would be spent on the base. A huge amount of training needed to be accomplished on the new machines both for flying crew and ground staff.

The Whitley they were flying was the mark three but rumour was rife that an improved version with Rolls Royce engines was about to replace it. As usual, if you needed to know anything the ground crew were the first to know. The officers reckoned to know nothing about an improved model.

The training was just as intensive as prior to the pre-Christmas break. Bomb aiming was proving to be difficult. Targets aimed at on the Lincolnshire coast were rarely hit accurately, practise bombs falling sometimes a good four hundred yards away and that was when flying low.

The machine also struggled to reach a height of twenty thousand feet with a full load of petrol and bombs. Not ideal if they would ever operate over Europe and the increasing tension there made the possibility less rare than initially thought.

Back in Scarborough Terry listened avidly to the BBC news on the radio. The thought of a further conflict arising horrified him after seeing the devastation from the last war.

The three homes for disabled servicemen were still all fully occupied from that war. He and Helen spent enormous amounts of time helping with the running and finance of them on top of time spent on their business.

He would also spend three or four days each month carrying out his duties as a magistrate in the local court.

Tets next spell of leave came in April one month later than originally thought; and it was only for three days. Whatever the politicians were saying the station was now gearing up onto a war footing. The station commander had been told they should be fully operational by the end of December.

Tets enjoyed the drive over to Scarborough immensely, the invigorating drive acting as a release of tension. The car had been the envy of his colleagues. A few of the officers had cars but they were a fairly rare sight. He was generous in providing lifts to his mates, especially when they'd been on a pub crawl.

The Monday of his leave he'd set off early to arrive in Scarborough well before lunch. He intended to have as much time with the family as possible. He strongly suspected that the next spell of leave would not be for a while.

It wasn't the only reason. He'd spoken to his father on the phone prior to leaving. His father had told him that his mother and he would be tied up in the business until tea time regrettably, but would have the Tuesday off to spend time with him.

That meant Aunt Mary and his gran only would be in when he arrived. It might just be his chance to quiz aunty some more.

He arrived at the house at ten thirty. The car had flown like the thoroughbred machine it was, the sound of the exhaust crackling like an aero engine.

His gran had been looking out of the window for his arrival. She was out before he'd climbed from the car hugging him tightly.

He grabbed his bag from the passenger seat and accompanied her into the house.

'He's here,' she called excitedly as they went in. Aunty Mary was standing in the hall waiting for him her face lighting up at his entrance. 'Hello darling boy, just the tonic an old lady needs.

Did you have a good drive over?'

'Fine thanks aunt perfect weather for it too. You look as stunningly beautiful as ever.' She laughed at that. 'That sounds so much like a Sheader male,' she said. 'But thank you darling it's much appreciated.'

'Well, as dad is the only other Sheader male are you saying he tells you you're stunningly beautiful as well?'

'Ah, I see its question time again, is that why you're here early today? Yes, you don't need to answer that I can read you like a book.'

'Am I so transparent?' 'Yes my darling like your father before you. He could no more lie or be anything but truthful if he wanted, you're so much like him.'

432

'Coffee or tea?' Shouted gran from the kitchen breaking the moment.

'Coffee please gran, same for you aunty?' 'Yes same for me,' she called.

She went into the kitchen calling over her shoulder. 'Take your kit upstairs and then come into the lounge. We can have a chat in there.'

In the kitchen she said. 'I'll take the coffee into the lounge. He's determined to ask me questions. Will you give us some time?'

'Can you cope with it? He's a bit of an innocent love, do step carefully.'

She nodded. 'I know Rebecca. I'll just have to see how it goes. God knows I'm the last person to want to upset him.'

She took the coffee into the lounge putting it on the coffee table and sitting on the settee. Tets joined her at almost the same time, sitting at her side which she thought would make it less easy for her.

'Gran knows you want to have a chat darling so she's stopping in the kitchen for a while. I said I'll tell you as much as possible when we had some time together didn't I? So fire away, just treat me gently.'

'Do you need treating gently aunt?'

'Yes, I've had my share of the horrors of life as you found out at Christmas. I don't want to be hurt again.'

'The last thing in the world I'd want to do is hurt you aunty. If I ask anything that's going to cause you pain tell me to stop.'

'Alright, we're sitting comfortably fire away.'

'Well, this sounds silly after knowing you all my life but I've never even thought of it before as relevant. What blood relation are you to the family, are you on mum's side or dad's?'

She took a deep breath. 'Neither darling. I'm not a blood relation at all.'

He looked stunned. 'Oh wow, I don't know what to say to that, what, err, what?'

She put her hand on his arm. 'I'll try to explain, but where to start?'

She felt quite deeply in the mire. How much to say without him being horrified? Or was it best to just tell the truth as it was? What a dilemma.

'I told you about that horrible attack and how your mum and dad rescued me. Well your mum first met me when I was a scruffy fisher girl working on the pier here in Scarborough.'

'I can't visualise you as ever being scruffy aunt.'

'Flatterer, well your mum introduced me to your dad one day. I'd settled in Scarborough instead of chasing the fishing fleet. I was tired of that and wanted to settle here.' She gazed up at him. 'Has your mum told you how she and your dad met?'

'She said they met after my granddad died, but thinking about it dad was always a little hazy on detail.'

'I didn't know how much you knew. That's difficult; it wouldn't be fair of me to tell you anything he hasn't. It was a complicated affair but it was the making of your dad. He'd always thought that his leg injury would prevent him ever finding a wife or girlfriend but your mum taught him different. They both fell madly in love and they still are to this day.'

'That sounds very romantic doesn't it aunty, nothing bad there.'

'No, it's the stuff dreams are made of isn't it? The problem that came along was a very young fisher girl who also fell madly in love with him. It was thought at the time it just a teenage crush but it never diminished and it still hasn't.'

She had a bright red flush now as she turned those mesmerising eyes on him, waiting for what she had just said to sink in.

He sat at her side looking stunned. 'Are you telling me that you're that girl?'

'Yes darling I'm afraid that's exactly what I'm saying. I'm that girl who fell in love twenty four years ago; with

434

both of them would you believe? I went through agony feeling frustrated and distraught at the situation. It was resolved eventually to the satisfaction of all three of us and here we are twenty four years later living under the same roof happily.'

'I don't know what to say,' he stuttered. 'What can I say? But if what you've just told me is true then who the hell is Bruce?'

'I can't tell you that, it would be breaking too much of a confidence. I told you there are some things I couldn't divulge. Perhaps if you can have a similar chat with your mum or dad, see how much they're prepared to let you know.'

'I think a drop of whisky's called for,' he said faintly.

Mary rose and went to the drinks cabinet pouring him a stiff double. 'Would you like some water with it?'

'Err, no, just as it is please.'

He swallowed it in two gulps. 'So should I ask what sort of relationship you all have now or is that two much to ask?'

'You're right darling. Its two much to ask.'

'You're saying that you're in love with my dad even though he's what? Some fifteen years older than you. And mum knows that and still has you living here?'

'I did say both of them.' She said it very quietly her eyes boring into him.

'Well I'm sure dad's very happy. Bloody hell aunty, is he, well you know, looking after both mum and you?'

She smiled at him without answering just looking with that disturbing look.

'Well the old bugger. The bloody old bugger.'

'Darling, I know all this is a shock, but as I said it's not a perfect world. We make of it what we can. Your father has been and is a father in a million. You know that, but he's also a man and a lovely one. Don't judge him or your mother or me unless you get to know all the facts. I've been brutally honest with you, please don't be too judgemental.'

435

He returned her gaze. He could easily see what his father must have seen. Even now she was a highly attractive woman. He was mentally in turmoil. How to figure out what he'd just been told? If what she had told him was correct then it would seem they were living some sort of menage a trois. Bloody hell! His parents. Old folk, or in his eyes they were. And she still said she had a secret lover called Bruce. Where did he figure in all this? He was brought back to earth by her.

'Is it all too much to take in just now darling? It must seem bizarre to you. I'm sorry you've been put through all this but you did want to know. You're at an age where you were questing and the truth is always best.'

'Yes it's a bit of a stunner what you've told me aunty. There was I virtually calling you an old maid and now you're dispelling all that in the most shocking way.'

'I'm sorry it's hit you like that darling you mean so much to me. I'd be very upset if you thought the worst of me after knowing you and cherishing you all your life.'

'I couldn't think badly of you aunty, you've always been my second mum. I think the world of you but its difficult thinking of you as a bit of a raver. It makes me see you in a totally different light.'

She laughed. 'Well, I haven't been called a raver before is that some new jargon? I hope it's not too derogatory, it sounds quite modern.'

She squeezed his hand. 'It's never a comfortable thought thinking your parents might have a sex life. Mums and dads don't have sex do they? It just doesn't feel right does it? That's one of the truths though that you have to face when you're old enough to understand the birds and the bees. No one can control falling in love. It's beyond control it just happens. It doesn't follow any sort of logic. At least man made logic, you have all this to come my darling. I hope when you do fall in love it's a straight forward affair and the girl you fall for is available for you and you alone.'

'Christ aunty; and I thought flying an aeroplane was difficult. It makes that sound tame in comparison.'

He spent his break pleasurably for the next two days but things would never be seen in the same light again. He and Mary didn't mention their talk to his parents when they came home; it was a tacit agreement between them. But he knew a little of his parents life style now which was disturbing to say the least. He returned to the airfield with much to think about.

Life back at the airfield intensified. Deliveries were made of munitions and war materials; it was frightening to listen to the radio and hearing politicians talking about peace when those same politicians were ordering the country to a state of readiness.

The pace of training and working the squadron up left little time to think of family matters. All thought of family relationships were pushed from his mind on the 3rd of September at eleven in the morning.

They had been informed the Prime Minister was to make an important broadcast on the radio. They clustered round the crackly set in the Officers' mess to listen to it.

The sound of Big Ben chiming heralded the hour, and it was followed by the Prime Minister. There were gasps of dismay and a feeling of inevitability when they heard his chilling words.

'This morning the British Ambassador in Berlin handed to the German Government a final Note stating that, unless we heard from them by 11 o'clock that they were prepared at once to withdraw from Poland, a state of war would exist between us. I have to tell you now that no such undertaking has been received, and that consequently this country is at war with Germany.'

There was a stunned silence for a brief millisecond, then a multitude of voices all talking at once.

'That's it then lads, the shit's hit the fan. All that training is to be put to use for real.' The adjutant's comment summed it up for them all. Tomorrow was going to be a very different day!

In Scarborough, Terry, Helen and Rebecca were also grouped around the *Pilot* radio waiting for the set to warm up in time for the widely advertised broadcast.

Like Tets, the content of the broadcast left them stunned.

'Oh Christ, not again, the bloody Germans again,' groaned Terry.

'And our lad will be flying into danger,' said Mary softly.

They sat in silence, each one of them wondering what the future now held.

Only time would tell.

****

# AUTHOR'S NOTES

THUNDER FROM THE SEA is, of course, a work of fiction, but it is mainly set during the bombardment of Scarborough during the First World War.

Very few people outside the town are even aware nowadays that Scarborough was attacked during the early stages of World War One. It attracted country wide condemnation at the time and 2014 will see the centenary of that event.

For the most authoritative account of the bombardment of Scarborough Whitby and Hartlepool, I highly recommend Mark Marsay's meticulously researched book,

*'Bombardment, the day the East Coast Bled'* which is without doubt the definitive historical document on these events of 1914.

The book is published by *Great Northern Publishing.*

Overton Terrace does exist in Scarborough. A large proportion of the terrace remains, although sadly the houses are used as mainly seasonal holiday lets today.

For any of you who seek them out, the views from there are spectacular.

I have made no attempt to emulate the style of speech which would have been used in 1914. To the modern ear it would be almost unintelligible.

Of the three German ships which caused such damage in the attack, their fate is as follows: The *Derfflinger* survived the war. It was in action in the battles of Dogger Bank and Jutland.

Its reputation as a pugnacious fighter earned it the nickname *Iron Dog* from British sailors. In the Jutland battle she was jointly responsible in sinking *HMS Queen Mary* and *HMS Indefatigable*, although receiving considerable damage in the process. She was interned after the war at Scapa Flow and along with the other interned German fleet was scuttled on the 21st July 1927. She was raised for scrap in 1939 but the Second World War intervened and she was not finally broken up until 1948.

*Von Der Tann* also survived the war. She was in action at Jutland helping *Derfflinger* sink *HMS Indefatigable*. She was interned with the rest of the German fleet, being scuttled in 1927. She was raised on the 7th December 1930 and broken up for scrap between the years 1931-1934.

The light cruiser *Kolburg* was involved at Dogger Bank but missed Jutland as she was under maintenance at that time. Like the above two she survived the war and was transferred ultimately to the French Navy who re-christened her *Colmar*. She was broken for scrap in 1927.

As you will have seen, I have ended the novel at the start of the Second World War. Hopefully a follow-on book will be written. This one has taken a huge amount of time to research and write and was an attempt to get a plot which had formed in my head on to paper, a plot which I've thought about for some considerable time.

This is my first attempt at writing a novel.

I thank my wife profusely. She was denied access to the computer for hours on end, but she supported me whole-heartedly throughout.

To you dear reader, I hope you found the novel enjoyable and I send you my very best wishes.


Malcolm Bruce,
Scarborough 2012